BONDED
Chronicles of Calan: Book II

Written by Nikki Moore
Illustrations by Ryann Armstrong

FIRST EDITION
ISBN 978-0-9982380-3-6 (print)

For Jonnelle, who left us much too soon

The Realm of Nowles

(more commonly known as the Old Kingdoms)

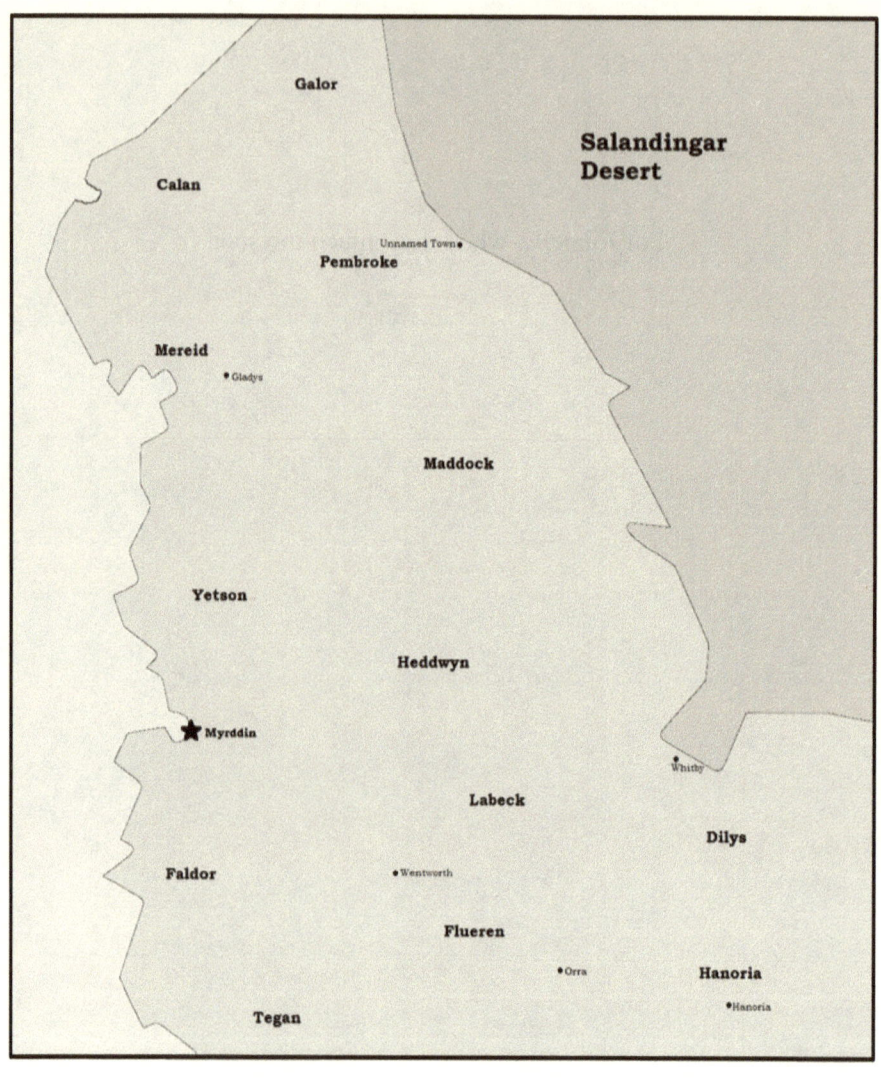

PART I

Chapter 1

Pale moonlight trickled through the shadowed canopy of branches overhead. The silence of the surrounding forest swelled palpably. All the nocturnal animals remained quiet, or, more likely, had vacated this place. The hunted paused, listening for the hunter. Settled in the bushes, her senses stretched, detecting her pursuer. Heart pounding loud in her chest, she knew it would not be long before her hiding place would be discovered. Nibbling at her bottom lip, she contemplated moving, but instinctively knew she had paused too long, had hesitated once too often. Now trapped, she could only wait for the inevitable. Barely breathing, Kyreen focused on the dark figure slipping through the woods on silent feet. Then the hunter turned away from Kyreen's spot amongst the bushes, moving away, disappearing into the shadows. Kyreen breathed a silent sigh of relief.

"Oy! You are dead!" A quiet voice remarked, a hand descending upon Kyreen's shoulder from behind her, away from where Kyreen had been looking.

Kyreen silently groaned, but did not speak. The voice in her ear laughed warmly, tinged, not with malice, but amusement. Unseen hands lifted Kyreen to her feet by the elbows.

"Do not fret," Synnove said, her voice quiet, patting Kyreen's shoulder. "You were not the first."

Kyreen did not take solace in the young woman's words as she began the trek back to camp and Synnove disappeared into the shadows, presumably to seek out her next target. Exiting the tree line, however, Kyreen's spirits lifted seeing not one, but three figures gathered around the fire. One would be Magnar, the Training Camp's Hunt Master, but the other two would be trainees just like her. Walking towards the firelight, she tightened the cloak around her body against the winds which were much more biting without the cover of the forest.

"Hallo, Kyreen," Magnar greeted Kyreen. "Who?"

"Synnove."

The Hunt Master nodded. The two other trainees exchanged a glance without speaking, but neither look happy. Ignoring them both, Kyreen settled down on a log before the fire.

For weeks, she had been enduring these nighttime training exercises, and for weeks she had been the first trainee returned to camp, every single night, sometimes the first by as much as an hour. There were no teams, only individuals, and the concept of these sessions was straight forward—be the last person undiscovered. This meant either being proactive as Synnove and hunting your contemporaries or remaining hidden. Kyreen, so deficient in her tracking skills, had selected the latter method by finding a hiding spot in the woods. Considering how much trouble she had negotiating the dark, both the geography and stealth, along with her trouble concealing emotions, Kyreen knew she would never be able to evade detection while actively searching. Being so passive night after night not only embarrassed Kyreen but also frayed her nerves.

Tonight had been the first night Kyreen had settled into her hiding spot relatively confident her movements had been stealthy and her spot undetected. She had also, for the first time, sensed one of the other trainees moving through the trees, searching, but not specifically for her. Unfortunately for Kyreen, the presence upon whom she had been concentrating on had been several yards away, heading in a direction opposite to Kyreen's location. Thus, Kyreen had not even heard or felt Synnove's approach.

The group assembled about the fire remained silent as more figures slipped from the woods. After another hour, all the trainees had been found save two—Synnove and Yngve, the eldest child of Kyreen's cousin Aren. Kyreen, though she had no formal claim towards Yngve, felt pride at his achievements, and she knew the youth's father, Aren's mate Viggo, one of the best trackers, if not the best, in all Calan, would also be proud of his eldest child's accomplishments.

Another hour of silence passed with no movement from the trees. Finally, Magnar stood, placing his hands to his mouth to issue the all-clear signal, an audible hooting imitation of a night owl. Within a minute, two shadows emerged from the forest, ambling towards their fellow trainees. The two victorious youth grinned at each other, then at their peers.

"Good work," Magnar said. "Dismissed for the eve."

Without any talking, the trainees dispersed, heading towards the tents, glowing white in the pale moonlight. As the last ones left, Magnar turned toward Kyreen, still standing by the fire.

"You are improving," he commented, his tone and gaze encouraging, before heading towards his own tent.

Alone in the circle of firelight, Kyreen sat back down. Improving, but not excelling, she silently chastised herself. These young Calanians, years younger than Kyreen, were years more advanced than she in tracking. In sword combat, Kyreen managed to hold her own, splitting matches evenly with Ebbe, son of the camp's weapon master. As for hand-to-hand combat, Kyreen always triumphed. While she held her own in horsemanship and archery, she chafed how these tracking sessions highlighted her deficiencies.

"Kyreen?" Synnove said, returning to the fire ring for her tentmate. "We all are heading to the pools. Will you join us?"

Kyreen shook her head, torn at the invitation. "Not tonight, Synnove."

Synnove sighed, lingering a moment before turning away. Not two steps away, the young woman paused to turn back. "Why not, Kyreen? You never join us after exercises. You never have fun. Are we not your friends?"

Now it was Kyreen's turn to sigh. How could she explain to the young woman standing across the fire when she did not completely understand herself? How could Kyreen point out that she was so much older than they without sounding dismissive, or worse, condescending? Simply stated Kyreen did not belong to their world. The time for her to indulge in frivolity and adolescent pleasures had passed her by while she had been in Hanoria caring for her sick foster mother, tending the farm, taking on the day-to-day duties of someone older. These youth, though very skilled and outshining Kyreen in their training here, were painful reminders that Kyreen's youth had passed her by and now any attempts to reclaim it felt hollow.

"Synnove, it is complicated," Kyreen said reluctantly. "I feel old, out of place, when I try... when I am with..." Her voice trailed off, unable to complete the thought out loud.

Synnove apprised Kyreen a moment before nodding. "You are wrong," she stated bluntly, crossing back to squat in front of her friend. "'Tis not complicated. You are not old. You are beautiful. You are desirable. Anyone in this camp would tell you the same, if only you would allow them the opportunity to get close to you."

Blood rushed to Kyreen's face. Even after months of living with Synnove, the young girl's bluntness still shocked her. When Kyreen opened her mouth to protest, Synnove raised a hand. "Do not deny it. Just know we welcome your presence should you change your mind."

Kyreen chuckled, giving up the argument. "Fine, Synnove. Thank you."

"Good eve, then. Do not wait up for me," Synnove stood to move towards the cliffs, calling back softly over one shoulder, her tone light and teasing. "Anyone, Kyreen, anyone."

Kyreen shook her head, watching her tentmate disappear into the shadows. The young girl's exuberance and confidence, though misdirected, warmed Kyreen's heart. Maybe there were a few of the youngsters who would enjoy spending an evening with Kyreen, but she knew of one person in camp who would be most unwilling.

Her stomach churned as Kyreen's thoughts involuntarily wandered towards Lang, Aren's second-in-command, or rather former second-in-command, who last summer had so fiercely rejected, vetoed, and denied anything remotely connected to Kyreen. When Kyreen had agreed to Aren's invitation to join the youth at Training Camp after harvest, one highlight had been leaving Lang behind at the Council Camp. Her relief had been short lived, however, as the grim-faced Calanian had shown up after less than a fortnight to take over the hand-to-hand combat training.

Rumors had flown around the camp regarding his presence here. Some said Lang had resigned his position on the Council, feeling remorse at his lead planning the castle attack last summer. Others claimed that Lang had been forced out and demoted to the Training Camp. Still others had mentioned a nervous breakdown. Kyreen had to admit Lang looked paler and more gaunt than usual when he arrived at camp. Synnove had relayed gossip to Kyreen that the tall bearded Calanian had been severely injured during the battle and concerns still continued over his infection.

Lang had not been the only Calanian to suffer from last summer's failed attempt to retake their castle from the Galorians. Aren's mate Viggo's injury had very nearly cost him a limb. Whenever Kyreen saw the man, she still worried for his sanity. Though the healers had managed to save his arm, they had not been able to reverse the muscle damage. Thus, Viggo had not fully recovered use of the appendage. Although he had never said anything to her, had never complained, Kyreen could see the loss had hit her cousin's mate hard, especially since he could no longer wield his favored weapon, his bow. Despite his physical appearance not changing, Kyreen felt he seemed more diminished with each of her visits, as though he were slipping away one tiny piece at a time.

Shaking off thoughts of her cousin's mate, Kyreen returned her mind to the problem at hand. Whatever the reason, Lang's presence in camp unsettled Kyreen. Fortunately, the area Lang supervised just happened to be the one in which she had the most proficiency. So far Lang's injury had prevented him from participating fully in the spars, or doing any grappling demonstrations, so Kyreen had not had to face off with her adversary. Simply being in the same space with Lang during practice had been punishment enough.

"Not joining the other trainees tonight?" a voice asked from the shadows.

Kyreen suppressed another groan. She had been so distracted with thoughts of Lang she had not heard Atle's approach. The weapons master and camp chief stepped into the light. His voice had been neutral, absent of judgement. As he took a seat beside Kyreen, not too close, yet close enough for conversation, she inadvertently felt something in his mood, a feeling she was unable to pinpoint precisely.

"I... it is complicated," she finally replied.

"As you told Synnove," he said.

"You were here?" Kyreen's face blushed anew. How could she have not sensed the Camp Master's presence? Why could she not grasp this simple fundamental Calanian skill? So busy silently berating herself, Kyreen almost missed Atle's response.

"Nay. I did, however, startle Synnove on the trail," Atle paused, his gaze locked on the dying fire, assuring the significance of his words sunk in.

Knowing the answer, but also knowing Atle would remain silent all night if necessary, until Kyreen asked the question, "How were you able to surprise her?"

"You," came the expected answer. "Synnove is concerned for your well-being."

Kyreen cringed again, opening her mouth to respond.

Atle raised a hand, staying Kyreen's protests unspoken. "I came here to tend the flame, child, not to lecture."

They sat in silence for several moments before Atle spoke once more, "Tending the home fires is similar to tending memories. Tis the task of elders, those who have already lived life to the fullest. These are hard time for our people. We ask much of our youth, Kyreen. The opportunity for fun and fellowship must be made available and the young adults must be allowed to participate. To squander such time is to squander life and that is the greatest transgression of all," Atle paused and chuckled. "I said I was not here to lecture yet the teacher in me cannot help it. My apologies."

Kyreen took the opening presented and stood. "Thank you for your words, Atle. By your leave, I shall retire."

"Good eve, Kyreen, and safe travels in the morn," Atle replied, referencing Kyreen's impending trip to Myrddin.

As Kyreen turned to leave, he continued, "Please consider this final statement. The youth do not see you through your eyes. The instructors here do not see you through your eyes. You are a part of this camp. Only you make yourself uncomfortable or unwelcome."

Kyreen inclined her head towards Atle before turning away. Once in the dark, however, she paused, torn. Though no sounds carried from the cliffs, she could sense the joy and amusement of the participants. At long last she turned and headed towards the sleeping area. Tomorrow's ride would be a long one. As she ducked into her tent, Kyreen paused to glance around, but saw nothing in the shadows. Once the tent flap had settled into place, Lang slowly slipped out from behind a nearby tree and headed towards his own tent.

The following morning, before dawn, before the camp woke, Kyreen headed out towards Myrddin. As always, she felt a jolt of excitement to be on the move. She loved being on horseback in the woods, watching the light seep into the morning. Inhaling the crisp air tinged with the smells of pine and sea, she kept a tight rein on the gelding.

"Once we are pass the lookout, you can run," she promised, not willing to risk running into a stray Galorian patrol by allowing the gelding loose, even though the likelihood of a patrol this close to the cliff-side camp was quite slim.

Once the gelding realized he would not be able to run and settled into his easy jog, Kyreen relaxed in the saddle. Though she kept alert for anything amiss, she allowed her mind to wander especially when her path to the border took her by the Silver Lake, which stirred up memories from last summer, when she had ridden to Myrddin before the summer's battle, to rescue Engla and to confront the Faldorian mercenary.

After her task in the city had been completed, after killing the mercenary, after finishing the deed she knew had to be done, Kyreen had expected to feel not pleasure but relief, closure, comfort, something positive.

Instead a feeling of foreboding had descended upon her with each of the gelding's strides, building up within her so that she nearly ran into a patrol on the outskirts of the tiny village of Gladys. Luckily the two soldiers had been groggy or drunk, or perhaps both, and she avoided discovery, waiting impatiently in the shadows until they had disappeared around the bend.

Still, once the small village fell behind her, Kyreen had pushed the gelding hard, willing to risk an encounter in order to make her journey quicker. When she had finally relented to resting the fatigued animal just before dawn, she found herself, though thoroughly weary as well, too keyed up for sleep. Pacing the clearing, listening for patrols, she had waited while the sun made its slow journey across the sky. Back on the road, it had taken all of Kyreen's self-control not to urge the horse into gallop, relying instead on a more sedate pace.

Approaching the pass, Kyreen had felt, without trying, the grief emanating from the two sentinels waiting there, two extremely young, inexperienced soldiers. Gazing upon their faces, Kyreen had known without asking that Aren had been unable to delay the attack; had known the battle had been lost; had known too many had perished. Once she had received Aren's location at Silver Lake, Kyreen had abandoned caution, and pushed the gelding as hard as he would go. Only when she had approached camp with the setting of the sun and the initial wave of grief had flowed over her, had Kyreen pulled up her horse, both of them road weary and dusty.

The soft breeze had spread gray mist across the clearing, tendrils clinging to everything. The fog had magnified the mournful mood of the camp inhabitants and the emotions had assaulted Kyreen, settling wearily into her bones with an inaudible sigh

Once dismounted, she stood unnoticed in the dusk, watching people, her people, vague forms milling in the mist, headed into the woods. Nobody spoke. Even the surrounding forest had fallen silent. Torn between caring for her worn-out animal and joining the group, dreading what she would find when she followed the path to the lake beyond the forest, Kyreen had finally compromised with a speedy unsaddling and a quick swipe to remove the sweat from the beast's hide. Unable to wait any longer, she had set the gelding loose, not bothering to hobble him.

Steeling herself, she had started through the woods. The last of the people had entered while she cared for her horse, but even if the path had not been there she would have been able to find the beach, just by following the tremendous grief flowing from the shores of the lake.

Though the summer sun had disappeared behind the mountains, plenty of evening light remained. The slow-moving current of the lake reflected a murky gray, then Kyreen had turned to look down the shoreline. The sight before her had torn at Kyreen's heart and she longed to turn away, go back to camp, to ride away, to be anywhere but here on this beach. Bodies had been lain out, side-by-side, stretching out farther than Kyreen could bear to look.

"Please tell me Falk is dead." The voice behind Kyreen barely reached her ears, as though the act of speaking took more energy than the speaker had to offer.

Kyreen had turned, surprised to see Aren standing behind her on the path, her face gaunt with dark circles under her grief-stricken eyes. When Kyreen had looked back at the row of the fallen, the memory of her fight with the Faldorian mercenary had felt so faded, so far away, so long ago, yet not.

"Yes," she had replied, not trusting her voice to much more than that one word.

Family and friends had begun to gather and hoist the bodies of their loved ones onto funeral rafts. As she watched, a question formed in Kyreen's muddled thoughts. She had glanced back at Aren, eyes widening.

"Where is…?" her voice trailed off, unable to complete the thought as she glanced back down the row, searching for a familiar face among the bodies.

"No," Aren had replied, her voice brittle, but not loud. "Viggo is not here. He is at the Family Camp, with the other injured. So are the children."

Kyreen had experienced a brief momentary flash of relief. Then a mourner caught her eye. Ebbe, the husky youth with whom she had grappled with in her first spar, stood beside a burly man, who dwarfed the large youth and possessed Ebbe's face in fifteen, twenty years. The two bent down together to raise a body between them onto the funeral pyre. Kyreen had suppressed a gasp upon recognizing the body of Olina, the steely-eyed council woman, one of Kyreen's few open supporters on the Council.

"I must tend to my duties," Aren said. "You are welcome to walk with me."

Without waiting for Kyreen's answer, Aren had walked to the first gathering of mourners in the long line. Following at a distance, Kyreen hung back as Aren embraced a woman, her young face slick with tears, a curly headed toddler asleep in her arms. Kyreen's heart had ached with each embrace, each hushed conversation, each family in mourning. Some families had consigned more than one deceased. For the first time Kyreen had begun to understand the weight of leading a country, especially these displaced people.

After Aren finished speaking with Ebbe and his father Atle, Kyreen had caught the young man's eye, bowing her head in condolence. Ebbe had returned the gesture, face solemn. Following Aren to the next group Kyreen wondered when the young man would be able to smile again. Not very soon and even then, she doubted he would ever sport the blithe grin he had flashed her after their initial sparring match.

Down the row Aren had continued, offering a hug, a touch on the arm, and words of comfort. The number of familiar faces—both those grieving and those departed — distressed Kyreen, but not as much as the unfamiliar. For every person she recognized there were five, six, seven she did not. Aren knew every person by name, even the youngest child received the leader's notice. Kyreen did not know how long the ceremony took but night had fully fallen by the time Aren spoke with the last family.

Kyreen glanced down the line, surprised to see several pyres with their kindling on fire, floating away from the beach.

"The current is steady here," Aren had explained, having said her farewells and moved to stand beside her cousin. "The dead will be carried out to the middle of the lake, then down the river to the bay. By the time the ashes reach the ocean, the smoke will have carried our fallen to the Fifth Hall, where they shall rejoice with our ancestors." Aren's voice had been wooden and tired, the words a rote recitation, a memorized fragment told to children.

The two women stood side-by-side as families concluded their farewells and sent their loved ones on their final journey. Kyreen had forced herself to remain as motionless as Aren, then she spied the pyre of Signe. She had been such a bright young woman, just a trainee as Kyreen was now, barely more than a child. There was Niel, who had worked kitchen duty at Council Camp, always serving meals with a twinkle in his green eyes and a joke to share, and then another familiar face from the Council. Everything had blurred and

Kyreen had blinked away the tears. On the shore, many of the families had begun to disperse as their deceased floated out of sight. Aren had shown no sign of leaving so Kyreen continued to remain still, her tears flowing freely now.

As the last pyre had glided away, Kyreen could not remain still any longer. Wrapping her arms about her body, she had turned away, running into the comforting embrace of the woods. Dropping to her knees, she had doubled over, retching. Her last meal had been long before midday so her stomach had nothing to offer except the sour taste of bile. Once the spasms ceased, Kyreen had returned to her feet, wiping her mouth with the back of her hand.

Aren had followed her cousin into the trees and now stepped forward, proffering a water skin "My apologies, Kyreen," she said quietly.

Kyreen had taken a long drink, trying to wash away the bitter taste, not only of bile but frustration of yet another failure.

"What now, Aren?" she had snapped, her voice husky from the rawness of her throat.

"It was insensitive of me not to remember this is your first Internment. You are not as intimately acquainted with death as us."

Kyreen had covered her face with a hand, knowing Aren spoke the truth. Though death had surrounded Kyreen and affected her life she had always been removed from it. Even Falk's death in Myrddin the other night felt surreal by comparison. These were people with whom she had talked, and laughed, and interacted. Now they were gone, not just absent. Gone. The essence of each person's life had disappeared from this world.

"I need to return to the camp," Aren said. "Would you like to accompany me? There is much work and recovery to be done but for today we venerate life and mourn our deceased."

With a nod, Kyreen had fallen in step with her cousin. The beach had been deserted when they emerge from the woods, the lake dotted with burning pyres, the shadowy dark tendrils of smoke curling up into the starry sky.

Now, pulling her thoughts back to the present, Kyreen dragged her free hand over her face. The day had brightened into a sunny, if chilly, winter morning. She was headed to the city. This was not the time for woolgathering or skulking in the past. Though the city still overwhelmed her, Kyreen could not deny she enjoyed it in small doses, and especially looked forward to seeing Engla. With that thought in mind, Kyreen pushed away thoughts of last summer and concentrated on the road ahead.

Chapter 2

"Ye are looking thinner," Engla proclaimed, her voice tinged with love and worry. "Do they not feed you in that place you call home?"

Kyreen smiled at her best friend over the rim of her mug, taking a tentative sip of the sweetened tea. Finding the liquid still too hot, she set it down. Across the table, Engla sat on a stool, a pile of chopped vegetables growing under the steady knife. At the fireplace, Glain assembled the base for her fish chowder. Engla continued talking, now filling Kyreen in on all the news from Hanoria.

As her friend spoke, Kyreen's eyes moved around the kitchen. This was her first visit back to Glain's house--technically Collin's since he inherited it from his brother. As she gazed across the room at the unused fireplace, Kyreen briefly wondered if Engla knew of the hidden passageway out to the back alley. She also recalled, and quickly banished, the memory of Collin's hand in hers as they made their escape in the early morning hours. Curled up by the back door, the black and white cat napped, now all grown up, much larger than the tiny kitten Kyreen had cradled in her lap in Collin's room, bringing to mind the late afternoon sun pouring through the diamond-pane windows illuminating Collin's hazel eyes. Kyreen's gaze shifted again, eager to avoid that memory as well, but her eyes rested upon the metal tub hanging on the wall, the one in which Glain had prepared a bath for Kyreen, and unbidden she recalled the sweet taste of apple on Collin's tongue as they shared their first kiss in this kitchen.

"Kyreen, are ye listening?" Engla's teasing voice broke into the memories.

The Calanian wrapped her hands around the mug, shaking away the cobwebs. "Sorry. Long day."

"How did the sale go?" Glain asked, glancing at Kyreen over her shoulder. From the expression in the other woman's brown eyes, Kyreen figured Glain had guessed what, or who, had caused her distraction. Though fairly certain Engla remained blessedly ignorant, Kyreen could not be sure how much Glain knew about the relationship that had been between Collin and Kyreen.

Thankful for the distraction, Kyreen replied, "It went well. The guild contacts were successful in securing buyers for all the yearlings. I feel a little bad that I slipped away and left Amund to buy the needed supplies."

"Please," Engla protested, sliding off the stool, "no business talk."

"Here, let me," Kyreen hurried around the table, her hands extended to take the plate of chopped vegetables.

"Do nay be daft, Kyreen!" Engla said, slapping her friend's hand away. "I am pregnant, not incapacitated!"

Kyreen relented, stepping back to allow Engla passage. Except for the thickening of her small torso, Engla did appear the picture of health. The babe within, though, worried Kyreen. He should more active, projecting more life force. That she had not felt his presence until Engla had hugged her earlier weighed heavy upon Kyreen's mind. Now her brow pursed as she watched her friend walk across the floor to dump the vegetables into Glain's prepared cauldron. When Engla turned, catching the expression on Kyreen's face, she misinterpreted the frown as concentration, not concern.

"Will ye tell me?" she asked eagerly. "What be the sex of the bairn?"

"What is this? Witchcraft?" Glain questioned, raising an inquiring brow.

"No, no," Engla replied, grabbing both of Kyreen's hands to place them upon her burgeoning stomach. With the contact, Kyreen realized she had underestimated how far along Engla's pregnancy had been. "Kyreen has a knack. Stian told me. She always knew whether a mare bore a filly or colt long before the birthing. He said she could do it with all pregnancies."

Glain stirred up the chowder, setting the cover in place before walking over to Engla and Kyreen. She wiped her hands on her apron, eyeing the tall dark-haired woman doubtfully. "Very interesting," she mumbled. Kyreen easily felt the other woman's doubts, misconceptions, and worries.

Engla looked up at her dearest friend, crystal blue eyes wide. "Please, Kyreen?"

With a sigh, Kyreen nodded. Though she had already perceived the babe's gender, she knew Engla wanted a show. So, Kyreen closed her eyes and pressed both hands against the girl's abdomen. This was Engla's baby, she silently told herself, trying desperately to ignore the fact that it was also Collin's baby. Clearing her mind, she concentrated on the unborn child. A boy. She already knew that. Unbidden Collin's face flashed into her mind.

Curly brown hair. Twinkling hazel eyes. Lopsided, lazy grin. Kyreen jerked her hands away, eyes opening.

"A boy," she announced before the startled Engla could speak.

"I knew it!" Engla squealed, clapping her hands together with excitement. "I told Collin the women in my family always have a boy first! I kinnae wait until he gets home!"

Glain stepped up, placing a hand on the mother-to-be's shoulder.

"Engla, would ye be a dear and set the table? We have five boarders tonight," she glanced as Kyreen. "I thought we women could eat in here."

After Engla scurried off, Glain leveled a steely gaze at Kyreen. "Ye need tae work on hiding your emotions, love."

"Emotions? For Collin? You misunderstood, Glain. I worry about the…"

"Do nay try to deny it." Glain interrupted, holding up a hand. "I have been a part of this family long enough to know Collin, the good and the bad. Though I know not what happened out there in the wilderness, ye were smitten with Collin the day ye arrived here and he with you. Then he comes home with this girl as his wife. Engla is a sweetheart, but she only sees what she desires to see, and she does not desire to see that her best friend is in love with her husband. He has made his choice and ye lost. Deal with your emotions how ye may, Kyreen, but do nay hurt Engla."

Kyreen opened her mouth to protest, but hearing Engla's steps she held her tongue. Of course, Glain would think Kyreen's dismay would be over the loss of Collin. She could not understand Kyreen's concern for the babe.

"Will ye be staying the night then?" Glain asked as Engla walked back into the kitchen, acting as though the previous conversation had not happened. "The room upstairs that ye stayed in last time is available."

Kyreen shook her head. "No. As soon as Amund is done with the purchases, she wants to leave."

"Kyreen, tis nay fair!" Engla protested, her face dropping. "I missed ye the last two times ye visited Myrddin because of my trip to Hanoria. Now ye only stay an afternoon?"

For an instant, Kyreen felt a tug at lying to her best friend, then she caught the disapproving look in Glain's eye. "My apologies, Engla. Tis business."

"Ye are here now, though," Engla relented with a forced smile. "Let us enjoy the visit."

She grabbed Kyreen's hand and headed for the back door. "Let me show ye the garden Glain has. Tis amazing she can grow anything here in this city."

Kyreen followed her friend, trying to ignore the disapproving looks from Glain as they exited into the small yard.

Much later, after dinner, Kyreen exited the same doorway to the alley, now shrouded in shadows. Giving her best friend a final hug, she attempted to suppress the guilt rising within her breast.

"I will be back when the babe is born," she whispered into Engla's ear.

"I shall count on it. I am sorry Collin missed dinner. He has been spending more time at the guild hall. Lots of work to do I suppose. Safe travels," Engla replied, blinking back tears. Over the pregnant woman's shoulder Glain shot a final disapproving glare in Kyreen's direction.

As the door closed, Kyreen paused to allow her eyes a moment to adjust to the twilight. Maneuvering through the close quarters, she exited into a major thoroughfare. This time of night, with fairly light foot traffic, she made good time, weaving through the streets, winding away from the house towards the market district. The closer she moved towards the docks, the more the air became tinged with salt and the more people she encountered on the streets. Hugging the shadows, Kyreen slipped into an alley which wound around the back of a large building. Stopping before a solid door, she pulled a chain out from under her tunic and turned the key in the lock. This particular door opened into a hallway in a cylindrical tower between the first and second levels of the Brodyr Llafur hall. From the left downward hall wafted the sounds of voices, some already slurred. Evening meal had concluded and many guild members were well on their way to drunkenness.

Kyreen headed up the hallway to the right, ascending three floors, to the fifth level. Here she walked down the deserted hallway, around a corner and up the staircase, winding up two more levels. She met no one on her travels, one of the reasons this particular route had been chosen. The fewer people who saw or knew of her visit, the better.

Throughout her ascent, Kyreen's pace quickened until she almost ran the last stretch of deserted hallway. Her breathing accelerated, from anticipation not exertion, her pale features flushed and her eyes sparkled with excitement. Reaching out a hand to the doorknob, Kyreen paused, Engla's face rising unbidden in her mind. Reminding herself that lying to her friend had been a necessity, Kyreen suppressed the guilt, glancing over her shoulder before slipping through the doorway. Had anyone been present in the hallway, they would have seen Kyreen move into the embrace of the man waiting on the other side of the door, eagerly pulling his face to hers, his hands wrapping around her waist, pulling her close, their lips meeting as the door drifted shut.

Much later Kyreen stretched out, luxuriating in the crisp linens. One thing she missed most and greatly relished during her trips into civilization was fresh laundered sheets. Her companion rolled over, standing to walk across the room. A brief rustling of clothing and the sound of a door opening, then closing again. Hearing hushed voices from the outer room, she wondered if her own clothes were still strewn along that floor. When the door opened again, she rolled over to eye the man entering with a bundle of clothing—hers—in his arms.

With a grin, he dumped the load into a side chair. "I thought about sending them out to be cleaned, but figured there was not enough time. I did order food," he chuckled at Kyreen's expression. "It is good to be the boss."

"I suppose," Kyreen answered, lobbing a pillow at Rhun, who promptly tossed it back before turning to the sidebar. She sat upright, positioning pillows behind her back, watching him as he poured two glasses of amber mead.

Clad only in his trousers, barefooted and bare-chested, Rhun made quite the enjoyable vision to gaze upon. A big man with wide shoulders, his training with guild mates kept his body firmly muscled, but not overly bulky. A full head taller than Kyreen, he made her feel petite. The light reflecting off his ebony skin fanned her desire anew, making her hands ache to run along his body.

Rhun paused when he turned around, catching Kyreen's expression. "The livestock sale is over, my dear," he commented lightly.

"Just admiring the view," Kyreen responded, taking the proffered glass. Lamplight reflected off the tiny crystal vessel, just big enough for two, three swallows. She tilted back her head, draining the glass. The honey wine exploded sweetly upon her tongue and a comforting warmth spread from her stomach to her extremities. Placing the empty glass on a side table, Kyreen slid back down into the sheets, stretching and rolling over onto her stomach with a soft purr.

Rhun took a seat on the edge of the mattress, watching her over the rim of his glass. With his other hand, he ran his fingers through the mop of ebon curls, then traced the colorful tattoo on her right shoulder blade—a red rose entwined about the blade of a short sword—the vibrant colors even more so against the alabaster of her skin. He enjoyed the contrast of her pale skin against the dark of his own. Discarding his empty glass, he leaned over, lifting her hair so as to kiss the nape of her neck.

"Your hair is getting longer," he murmured, trailing kisses down her shoulder.

Kyreen rolled onto her back, sighing softly. "Almost ready for a braid, but not quite."

Sitting back up, Rhun brushed an errant curl from her cheek.

"Twill be a shame," he commented, winding a curl around his index finger. "I love your hair loose like this."

Kyreen chuckled, running her nails lightly along his bare chest. "Maybe I will take it down for you…sometimes," she joked.

Rhun smiled, gazing down upon Kyreen. This was his favorite version of Kyreen, playful, uninhibited, desirous, just the two of them, no one and nothing else tugging at either one's attention. Tracing his finger along her jawline and down her neck, Rhun leaned in to kiss Kyreen's lips. His light touch continued down, grazing the swell of a pale breast to the ridges of her ribcage, finally lingering on a spot of puckered pink skin.

"All healed up," he whispered pulling back to gaze at her bare torso. His finger loitered another instant, remembering the night last summer when he stitched the wound after Kyreen's battle with the mercenary. Rhun wondered if Kyreen knew how close Falk's strike had come to being the final blow of the fight.

"These," he added, moving to brush across the network of bruises in vary shades of purples and greens, "are new."

Kyreen groaned. "Souvenirs of Lang," she commented, the man's name on her lips turning her stomach sour. "Since his arrival at camp, the spars are getting harder. I do not know if his presence is distracting me or if the youth are improving under his tutelage. Mayhap a tad of both."

Rhun watched her with an amused glint in his eye. Lang was a subject they had covered in length during previous visits, mainly Rhun listening while Kyreen railed about the man who continued to be a thorn in her side.

Idly he traced patterns over and between the marks while she continued to speak.

After a moment, she paused. "Oh, dear goddess! My apologies, Rhun! I should not waste our time together, especially with the likes of that man."

Rhun leaned in again, brushing his lips to hers. "However ye wish to pass the time, my dear, is fine with me. Mayhap I can distract your mind, eh?"

Kyreen chuckled, running her fingers over his closely shorn hair, pulling him in for another kiss, this one deeper and longer. When the food arrived a few minutes later, neither paid attention to the outer door's opening.

"The tea is cold, but the food is still edible." Rhun offered Kyreen a piece of meat encased in bread. Leaning around him, Kyreen instead snagged a handful of dried figs, dipped in honey then rolled in powdered sugar, before moving over to settle down on a velvet side chair. Rhun grinned. Having noticed Kyreen's propensity for sweets on previous meetings, he now ensured the guild kitchen prepared an assortment of the latest confectioners' treats whenever she visited.

"These are luscious," she murmured, savoring the sweet textures.

As Rhun continued to build himself a plate of meat, cheese, bread and fruit, her eyes move around the room, his private parlor here in the guild hall. The first time she had entered his sanctuary she had been amazed, not only by the luxurious furnishing but the sheer number of books lining the walls in floor-to-ceiling bookcases.

"The only claim I hold here are the books," Rhun had said that first evening. "When I first moved in here there was nary a book present. The guild carpenter built the shelves for my collection."

"Your predecessor was not a big reader," Kyreen had teased.

"Most of my guild mates do nay read, except the occasional manifest or bill of lading," Rhun had answered.

Kyreen had walked around the room, fingers trailing over the leather-bound books. Some titles familiar, but most not. A few even written in other languages.

"There are so many," she had commented, visibly awed. "Have you read them all?"

Rhun had shrugged and Kyreen had smiled at his obvious embarrassment over a side of his persona the guild master wished to keep private. She had paused and turned to face him, waiting for his answer.

"Yes," he finally relented. "I have read most of them. A few I could not finish, but several have been read more than once. Unlike my guild mates I have no family, nor a desire to throw away my wages on gambling, women, or ale. I usually spend my evenings alone with my books."

Crossing over to him, Kyreen had slipped her arms around his waist, leaning up for a kiss. "Your secret is safe with me, if…" she paused, eyes twinkling. "…you agree to loan me a book or two? Please?"

"Agreed," Rhun had chuckled.

Now, enveloped in one of Rhun's linen tunics, licking sugar from her fingers, Kyreen eyed the closed tome on the side table, the title written in a foreign language. This man continued to surprise her every time she saw him. When she first met Rhun last summer, Kyreen could not have guessed at the man's very diverse layers. Yes, he had proven a welcomed ally and, after the fight with the mercenary, an accomplished medic. As soon as Kyreen had left Myrddin, however, so too had Rhun left her thoughts.

When Aren had asked Kyreen to head the contingency travelling to Myrddin to negotiate a trade agreement with Guild Brodyr Llafur at fall solstice, Kyreen's concern had been visiting Engla and avoiding Collin. Seeing Rhun across the table, however, had been a pleasant surprise. Under his guidance, the contract had been quickly and easily negotiated with fiscal benefits on both sides. Subsequently, their business concluded, Rhun had invited Kyreen to join him for the evening meal, after which they had lingered in the dining hall, talking about innumerable topics. Kyreen, so engrossed in the conversation, had been quite surprised when an apologetic kitchen maid had interrupted them in order to set the table for breakfast, early morning sunlight streaming pink through the eastern windows.

On their next meeting, this time in the small village of Gladys, Kyreen had travelled alone for the final signing of the contract. Though she had not given much thought to who may be meeting her from the guild, she had been delighted to spy Rhun sitting in the village's lone inn and tavern. Again, the two had lingered after evening meal, only this time the sleepy innkeeper had shooed the pair out of the dining room and up the stairs. On the landing, lingering over their farewells, Rhun had taken a chance, kissing Kyreen there in the hall before asking her to spend the night with him. To both of their surprise, she had acquiesced. Tonight marked their sixth covert meeting.

Following the debacle which had been Kyreen's involvement with Collin, she had requested discretion from Rhun regarding their relationship. Not even Aren knew of their connection. The hesitation had nothing to do with Rhun, for whom Kyreen held the greatest esteem and respect. If forced to admit it, Kyreen would have to confess Collin still affected her, but not in the manner Glain may have imagined. No, whenever Kyreen thought about her time with Collin she felt intense embarrassment. Even now, just thinking about him, made her cheeks burn and the sweet treats she had ingested sour in her stomach.

Seeking distraction, Kyreen looked to Rhun, voicing the question that had been on her mind, "Where did you learn to read?"

"Me mum," he answered after setting his plate down on a small round table beside the couch and taking a bite of food. Kyreen smiled at the warmth of emotions he exuded. "Her da was a barrister who preferred his books to his clients. Hence, he struggled to make a living and, unfortunately died in pauper's prison, but he did instill a love of reading in both his son and daughter. Mum did her best after her father's death, but life is tough for an intellectual woman without family connections."

Rhun paused. Though his gaze rested upon Kyreen, she knew he did not see her, being lost in his memories, deciding how much to reveal. At long last, he continued, "I know not how she met me da. I do know she loved him and she tried to make it work. Twas he who finally left, when she became ill. Two years later she died."

"How old were you?" Kyreen asked softly, her heart aching with his sorrow.

"Seven. My brother and sister were but toddlers. The city orphanage took us in."

"What about family? Your mother had a brother?"

"After his father's death and no family inheritance, my uncle took to the seas, not a wise profession for someone more predisposed for scholarly endeavors. He…" Rhun paused again, and Kyreen sensed his struggle to search for the words. "Let me say, his journeys were rough and, when Mum passed, the guilt over failing his baby sister consumed him. Fortunately, he had enough money to purchase a small cottage on the beach, but he was in no shape to care for me nor my siblings. Seren and Colwyn did not survive that first winter after our mum's death. With my siblings gone I had no reason to stay at the orphanage, so I left."

The two sat in a somber yet companionable silence, each immersed in their own thoughts about lost siblings. Kyreen snuggled against Rhun, drawing his arm around her body, her head upon his shoulder. After a few long moments, she glanced over at him, surprised to see his dark eyes upon her. She smiled and he dropped his lips to hers for a tender kiss.

"Enough lingering in the past," he murmured. "I do not wish to waste any of our time together."

"I agree," Kyreen whispered, rolling so she straddled his lap. Cradling his face between her hands, she kissed him deeply, relishing the feel of his hands slipping under the linen tunic to caress her body. Soon all thoughts of past, present, and future had faded away.

Chapter 3

The circle of tents cast long shadows when Kyreen returned to the Training Camp. Aside from a few individuals beginning preparations for evening meal, the campsite appeared deserted. Deciding to take advantage of the quiet, Kyreen treated her gelding to an extra thorough grooming and before long his sorrel coat gleamed golden. In the lull of the unseasonably warm spring afternoon, coupled with her lack of sleep, the task completely engrossed Kyreen until a familiar tension snuck in, knotting her stomach. Dropping her head against the tall gelding's shoulder, she took a deep, calming breath before turning around.

"Good afternoon, Lang," she said to the bearded man standing there, his arms crossed, his expression-as always when dealing with Kyreen-sinister and irate.

"Did you enjoy your little holiday?"

"The trip was profitable for our people," she responded cautiously, attempting to keep her tone neutral.

"This camp may feel safe to you, but we are at war. You put us all in danger."

"I am grooming my horse. How can that possibly put the camp in danger?"

"You did not hear my approach," Lang raised a hand when Kyreen opened her mouth to protest. "Do not embarrass yourself further by lying."

His thinly veiled accusation cracked the fragile hold Kyreen had on her emotions. Abandoning care, she crossed the distance between them, ignoring her discomfort at his close proximity.

"Tread careful, Lang," she hissed, taking pleasure at his flinch when hearing her speak his name. "I do not take lightly the charge of duplicity. If you wish a challenge, then declare one. Quit quibbling."

"You are the one who should tread lightly," Lang responded. "You may be Aren's darling and a favorite of the other instructors here, but I am not so easily swayed. And remember, you need my approval to be declared battle worthy."

"Is that why you are here? In this camp? To prevent me from joining the battle?"

"You abandoned my people last summer. What is to prevent you from doing that again?"

"Is that truly what you think?" Kyreen asked, taking a step back. As fast as her temper had flared, the anger drained away just as quick.

For a moment, something flickered in the man's cold green eyes. Was it misgiving? Shame? Regret? In Lang's silence, another voice spoke. "I think Kyreen needs to finish her chore before the others return."

Both Lang and Kyreen turned in surprise. Atle had approached undetected during their exchange. Fleetingly Kyreen considered teasing Lang, but the man's discomfort washed over her, staying her tongue.

Lang cast Kyreen one final dark glance before stalking away without comment. Atle stepped up beside Kyreen and together they watched Lang walk away. Embarrassed, Kyreen fiddled with the brush in her hand, teeth nervously nibbling her bottom lip. It took all her will power to hold her tongue, to not apologize, to remain silent. Instead she concentrated on calming her emotions, quieting her rapidly beating heart.

After Lang was out of sight, Atle turned his gaze to the young woman standing beside him, refusing to raise her eyes to him. Once again, he found himself at a loss for words with this trainee. The raw talent in this young woman continually impressed him. Were it not for her lack of self-confidence and the depth of her constant self-criticism, Kyreen would stand alone at the top of the class, much like her mother Tyra, his classmate, had. Atle ran a hand over his face, sighing softly before speaking.

"You and Lang have a dilemma, Kyreen. One which must be resolved sooner, rather than later. For if it remains unsettled I fear Lang may be correct and the two of you together will put your allies in danger when in battle."

Kyreen nodded, blinking back the tears pricking the back of her eyelids. Her jaw muscle clenched, but otherwise she remained completely still, waiting for the head master's next comments.

Atle placed a soft hand upon her arm. "Look at me," he commanded, pausing until she raised her eyes to his. "The others will be back soon, but you have no duties until tonight's exercises after supper. Why not head to the springs? Take some time to swim, clear your mind so you can perform the track this eve."

"Thank you," she responded, swallowing the lump in her throat. Leading her gelding to be set out with the rest of the camp's horses, Kyreen felt Atle's gaze heavy upon her back. Since arriving at the Training Camp last fall, Kyreen had successfully avoided heading to the springs, desperate to hide yet another failure. She knew not how to swim. Yet she dared not defy the Camp Master's direct order.

After a quick stop at her tent, Kyreen headed towards the ocean cliffs, where a set of heated mineral springs, a favorite recreation spot of the trainees, sat nestled amongst the cool shadows of the tall granite cliffs. Shedding her clothes and slipping tentatively into the pool, Kyreen allowed the mineral-laden water's embrace to cradle her, clinging tenuously to the edge. Ever mindful of her lack of swimming skills, she dunked her head under the water, allowing her tensions to float way. When she finally resurfaced for breath, she laid her head back, allowing the edge of the pool to support her body, tears spilling out to mix with the spring water on her face.

Try as she might, she could not calm her mind, her thoughts continually twisting back around to Lang. The strength of his animosity bewildered her. Though they had had their conflicts last summer over the battle, the man's hostilities towards her had begun the moment Kyreen had first entered the Calanian camp. Kyreen could not figure out a reason for the strength of his emotions. While Atle had been very clear that the two needed to work on the tension between them, the idea of speaking with Lang riled Kyreen. Lang had the issue, not Kyreen. At every opportunity, he snuck up on her, initiated these confrontations. Kyreen's life was easier when he ignored her. It had been even better when he had been absent from the camp. Still mulling over the issue, Kyreen dunked her head once more, immediately sensing another presence when she emerged.

"Greetings, Kyreen," Synnove hailed. "I saw your gear in the tent. I hope you do not mind my company."

Though Kyreen had come to the springs for solitude and worried Synnove might discover her secret, she found herself delighted at the younger woman's presence. She smiled up at Synnove. "Not at all. Plenty of room."

Synnove's glee evident, she immediately began disrobing. Kyreen turned away, carefully edging around the side of the pool. Even after months sharing a tent with the other woman and camp with the other Calanian youth, Kyreen found their lack of modesty disconcerting. These people, her people, were not inhibited in the least.

Kyreen waited to turn back around until after ripples across the water's smooth surface indicated Synnove had slipped into the pool. To Kyreen's surprise and great embarrassment, the younger woman stood in the pool, walking, albeit on tiptoe, to settle in a spot opposite from Kyreen. Ducking under the water to hide her blush, Kyreen straightened her legs, humiliated anew when her feet hit the granite bottom.

"Tell me all about your journey to the city?" the younger woman asked, settling her head back against the pool's edge, legs floating out in front of her body, her blue eyes twinkling merrily through the shadows of the weakening light.

Unbidden the image of Rhun flashed through Kyreen's mind. She quickly suppressed it with a spark of guilt, hoping her tentmate did not sense the emotion, though Synnove's widening smile indicated the opposite. Still, Kyreen attempted to act nonchalant.

"Nothing too exciting," she replied. "An unexciting auction, from which we secured enough funds to purchase supplies for the remaining winter, then dinner with Engla."

"Kyreen, please," Synnove snorted softly, the teasing tone of her voice removing any sting from her words. "Maybe you could fool those outsiders with whom you were raised, but now... Now you are back amongst your kin. Such foolery does not work on me. Besides you wear your sentiments about your shoulders like a cloak."

Kyreen's cheeks flushed red as uneasiness flooded through her anew. For a long moment, Kyreen struggled to suppress the emotions.

Synnove watched in silence, aware of the surge of emotions, but she could not comprehend the underlying reasons for the emotions that so often flowed through her tentmate. Even after sharing such close quarters with the older woman for months, Kyreen confused and fascinated Synnove to no end. Self-doubt and anxiety were foreign emotions to the younger woman. Escaping the relative quietness and, to Synnove's mind, dullness of Family Camp had been the younger woman's dream as long as she could remember. Training Camp had been her chance to escape, to see some more of the land, to escape the watchful eye over her parents and other adults. To be free like Kyreen, to have the opportunity to travel outside the mundane forests of Calan, to see a village, a town, much less a city like Myrddin, would be the absolute pinnacle of freedom in her young mind. Synnove could not begin to imagine living in one place or even in a permanent house for the entirety of one's life.

"Kyreen, I mean no foul," Synnove said, breaking the uneasy silence after many long moments. She continued, her tone still affable, "I just…wish I could see the world outside these woods. You have such freedom I envy you… all your travels, your adventures, your life."

Kyreen settled back against the rough stone, eyes widening in surprise. Envy? Synnove envious of her? All these months Kyreen had envied her tentmate… Synnove's ease with the other trainees, her proficiency in the drills, her carefree exuberant headlong crash into new experiences and life in general.

"So, will you tell me or must I use my imagination?" Synnove teased, her eyes sparkling mischievously.

"Synnove, there is nothing to tell. Just a quick trip to sell last year's foals followed by dinner with my oldest friend," Kyreen chuckled despite her discomfort, hoping that if she kept repeating it the younger woman would believe her.

"Better. Much better. Still not the whole truth, but better," Synnove nodded.

Suppressing a groan of frustration, Kyreen opened her mouth to protest, but before she could speak Synnove raised a hand.

"Stop. I will not press," the young Calanian conceded. "Tell me of your friend. Engla is her name, yes? She is the one who came to the camp last growing season, looking for you?"

"Aye, she is," Kyreen nodded, surprised. "How did you know? We were at Council Camp. Were you there?"

"My sister, Signe. I believe we have discussed that she was a trainee on council rotation when you arrived, up until the battle."

Of course! Kyreen silently chided herself. How could she have forgotten? How callous. Images of Signe's face flashed through Kyreen's mind. Aloud, she murmured, "Synnove, my apologies. I did not mean to… I am sorry."

"For what?" Synnove's forehead wrinkled.

"For bringing up your sister."

"Signe? Why would you apologize for that?"

"Because…," Kyreen hesitated, "you must miss her."

Now it was Synnove's turn to pause thoughtfully, ruminating on Kyreen's words before answering, "Yes. Yes, I do. Every day. But you sound as if to say her name, to speak of her memory is… wrong?"

Confusion flared again in Kyreen. Belatedly she realized her reluctance to discuss Synnove's sister had to do with the Hanorian ways she learned as a child. Kyreen's foster parents, Jorn and Ildri, had done their best to instill their belief system into their adopted daughter. Although Kyreen could never be mistaken for a deferential Hanorian woman, that culture still guided Kyreen's thoughts and actions more than she cared to admit, and it made her feel a misfit in Calan.

"I must apologize once more. This time for the misunderstanding. Where I was raised. one did not discuss a loved one who had crossed over…passed thru…" she paused. "Died."

"But why?" Synnove questioned. "How does that honor the deceased? If you never speak of the departed, how will their memories carry on? If no voice speaks on the gifts of the departed's life, how can she gain honor and make her way to the Great Hall? It is the job of the living to plead the case of our departed, to ensure their journey across is paved with their good acts and deeds from this realm."

Synnove pushed off the pool wall, quietly gliding through the water to settle on the ledge upon which Kyreen perched. With their shoulders just touching, Kyreen repressed her discomfort, barely containing the urge to shift away. Synnove leaned her head back on the edge, eyes raised to the stars just beginning to emerge.

"My sister, Signe, came into this world with the same thoughtfulness and respect with which she lived her entire life," Synnove spoke quietly, her emotions radiating strong, full of love and admiration. "Our mother always said that of all four of her children, Signe was the most considerate. Signe arrived exactly on time, waiting until after supper. The birthing pains started just as our brother, just a year old himself, fell asleep. Labor lasted but a short while and when Signe arrived, her wails were strong but not loud. She fed immediately, falling asleep in our mother's arms directly afterward, and always continued to be easy. My mother never lost a night's sleep with her."

Synnove paused, chuckling, "Which is why Signe has always been the family favorite."

She glanced at Kyreen. "How can a memory such as that be harmful? With its telling I honor my sister's memory, I renew the love I feel for her, and I share her with another person."

"Thank you," Kyreen murmured. "I, too, remember your sister. She was at the meeting hall the first night I arrived. She displayed much composure and was the first to cast a vote to grant me respite."

"I saw Signe shortly afterward. She felt very honored to have been a part of your return," Synnove paused, glancing over at Kyreen. "Is it true? That you knew not of the mark upon your shoulder?"

"Aye," Kyreen replied, her cheeks flushed anew.

Feeling the other woman's confusion, Kyreen tried to explain. "The tattoo.... My brother and I... we were very young... so many years had passed that I had forgotten most of..."

Synnove placed a soft hand on Kyreen's arm. "I apologize. Please forgive my curiosity. If the memory hurts..."

"No," Kyreen shook her head. "It has been too long since I truly thought upon those events. The whole castle was preparing for the Spring Festival while I was more concerned about our birthday. I remember my back itched but I was not to scratch."

Kyreen chuckled. "I was also concerned that my tattoo was not as pretty as that of Quillan's."

"Your brother?"

"My twin," Kyreen nodded slowly, her attention on the memories rising in her mind.

"Oh," Synnove leaned back, her eyes again lifted to the sky above. "Signe and I were very close. I felt so empty when she left for Training Camp. I could not imagine had she been my twin."

"I still miss him," Kyreen confessed, her voice very quiet. "Every day."

"Yet you never speak of him, or your mother."

"My foster parents... it was not their custom to speak of those who were absent, especially those who had crossed over. Their people feared that to talk of the dead would distract them from their journey, even call their spirits back from where they needed to go," Kyreen replied. "Also, I did not wish to disrespect my foster parents by discussing my family. They might have thought I was ungrateful."

"You are no longer in that land, no longer with your foster parents," Synnove stated not unkindly, her tone soft.

Synnove's words hung between the two women, the invitation resting there unspoken. For many minutes, the women sat in companionable silence. Each lost in thoughts of her departed sibling. Except, Kyreen reminded herself, Quillan had not died, somewhere out in the world he still lived. She could not imagine why he had not returned to their people. Could life with Arvis, among the elves, maybe be more preferable to living here? Though she knew very little about the elven people, Kyreen had heard stories, stories of untold riches, palaces for all, magic everywhere. Elves were rumored to be magical creatures and, when magic had been outlawed by humans, they had retreated across the Salandingar Desert, fading from human life to become legends and myths of terrible evil creatures that went bump in the night. Kyreen stemmed her dark thoughts, remembering these tales had come to her via Hanorian superstition and fear. Instead she remembered the tall pale elf with the violet eyes, the one who always had time to answer a precocious toddler's questions, the one who told enthralling bedtime stories, the one who played hide-and-seek in the castle, a true game hide-and-seek as the elf's presence, a blank spot to Calanian empathy, could not be sensed.

"My apologies," Synnove said, bringing Kyreen's thoughts out of the past. "I did not mean to stir up unhappy memories."

"No," responded Kyreen with a smile, "you are correct. I am no longer with my foster parents. I need to be reminded of that at times."

"I can do that," Synnove quipped, winking at her tentmate. Then she looked at the growing darkness. "We probably should head back for supper."

As they walked towards camp, Synnove's arm slipped through her own, Kyreen reflected on the recent conversation. Synnove had been right. Kyreen no longer lived among the Hanorians. She needed to shift her behaviors accordingly.

She leaned into Synnove, her voice quiet. "After tonight's training exercise," Kyreen said, "I would like to tell you about my brother."

"I would like that," Synnove responded with a grin.

Chapter 4

Over the next few days, Kyreen settled back into the rhythm of training—morning's physical training, afternoon's tactical lessons, and evening's tracking. Despite her recent revelations, Kyreen still had difficulty opening up to her tentmate, which had less to do with culture and more with the evening training sessions that continued to leave Kyreen frustrated and desiring solitude. Synnove wisely left her moody tentmate to her seclusion, though Kyreen recognized reproach in the younger woman's silence.

One morning, a warm sunny dawn with the promise of spring in the sun's rays, a courier arrived. The bag hanging from his saddle contained letters from families, and even one for Kyreen. So accustomed to not receiving mail Kyreen had barely paid attention, very nearly missing her name being called by Atle.

Still Kyreen could not deny the surge of excitement fluttering within as she held the parchment scroll between her fingertips. For once she did not feel left out, the only one of the trainees to not receive communication from family scattered between the camps. This time when Atle postponed the first training session until mid-morning, Kyreen did not have to wonder or worry how to best occupy her free time. Lang, she noticed, received multiple letters. The sound of his name being called grating down her spine.

Synnove clutched her packet of four scrolls, always the same number— a letter each from her father, her mother, and her two remaining siblings, an older brother and a younger sister. Cheeks flushed red, blue eyes sparkling, Synnove linked an arm through Kyreen's as they moved away from the campfire.

"Shall we head to the tent, my friend, or remain outside in this glorious morning?" The younger woman's laughter was infectious and Kyreen joined her.

"Outside, I believe," Kyreen answered, raising her face to the rising sun, whose light, though weak, already felt warm upon her skin.

Synnove nodded, adjusting their path accordingly. The pair walked in silence towards a rocky grouping of boulders on the outer edge of camp. Kyreen relished her friend's touch upon her arm, the intimacy of their shoulders touching, for once comforting, and a general mantle of contentment settled upon her being. Synnove's naturally decisive nature propelled them to their destination before the other trainees decided to enjoy the weather as well. Thus, the two were the first to arrive. Synnove guided Kyreen to a rather flat rock, elevated above the rest, clambering up before turning to offer a hand to Kyreen. Suppressing a skeptical look, Kyreen accepted the superfluous help. They settled upon the rock, back to back, thus creating support for one another. Additionally, and more importantly Kyreen realized, her eyes scanning the area, offering a 360- degree view of around them. Even without speaking, the pair had settled into a defensive position, ever diligent for danger, ever aware of the perils surrounding them. Kyreen's gaze followed the movements below as more trainees arrived, always in groups of two or three, never alone. She, it appeared, was the only trainee still prone to wandering solo. If not for Synnove's persistence to include Kyreen in all activities, Kyreen would always be alone, never a part of the group.

"Who has written you?" Synnove's voice broke through Kyreen's musings.

Kyreen looked down at the scroll and her name written in black ink. The writing is legible, precise, unadorned.

"I do not know," she finally replied. "I have not opened it."

"What are you waiting for? Another winter storm to drive us back to the tents?" Synnove teased but Kyreen heard the distraction in her friend's voice as the pages in Synnove's hands rustled.

Grinning Kyreen slid a finger against the seam, breaking the wax seal. Without registering the words, she quickly moved her gaze to the bottom of the page.

"Aren," she said softly. "Aren has written me."

Synnove mumbled an incoherent acknowledgment as Kyreen lifted her gaze from the page once more to scan the area. Everyone appeared to have arrived and settled into reading the words written by loved ones, feasting on the news from family and friends. Kyreen's brow wrinkled, suddenly hesitant to read the words on the page. What reason would Aren have for writing? Though they are related, Aren had never written to Kyreen before. What could have happened? Aren had Yngve, her son, here to write to and she had the Council to supervise. So why now? Kyreen's movements between the camps were planned ahead of time in regular intervals. The next supply run to Myrddin would not occur for another fortnight.

What had happened? What was so time sensitive to compel Aren to send a letter? Was it Quillan? Maybe he had returned, or worse maybe word had been received of his death. Kyreen shook her head. No, her twin could not be dead. Somehow, she knew with certainty that she would feel it if he had died. If not Quillan, then who? Vidar? The elderly close friend of Kyreen's grandfather, god-father to her mother. His health could have faded quickly, especially in the bitter heart of winter up in the mountains. The Training Camp experienced a much milder, more temperate season here on the coast.

A soft chuckle from Synnove brought Kyreen out of her musings. She looked at the parchment in her hand one more long moment before focusing on the words written upon the page. Aren was as succinct and efficient with her words as her handwriting:

> *Kyreen*
>
> *Your presence is requested at Council. Proceed in the morn to the camp location from last summer when you and I visited the castle. Atle has been notified.*
>
> *Your cousin, Aren*

A summons? In that brief moment, before the relief flooded into her being, disappointment flared, a ball in her stomach burning, a deep hot flash that she quickly suppressed.

Synnove, however, always the empath, sensed Kyreen's discontentment. "Not bad news I pray," she whispered.

Kyreen felt rather than saw Synnove pause, lifting her eyes from the page turning her head slightly, leaning an ear towards the older woman.

"Not exactly," Kyreen muttered. "A summons. I must leave for the Council Camp in the morning."

Synnove twisted around completely. "Not really bad news? Oh, to be in your boots, Kyreen!" she exclaimed quietly. "You travel and move about with such freedom. I am envious. Never once in all my seasons have I ever been farther than a shout away from an elder. This bluff is the most exotic place I have ever visited. To go to Myrddin, a dream. To travel as you have, unfathomable!"

The young woman's eyes dropped to the folded parchment in Kyreen's grasp. "Does it say how long you will be gone?"

Kyreen shook her head, glancing up at the other groups now slowly dispersing. "Nay. Tis time to head out. What news have you of your kin?"

Synnove began to recount her letters' contents as the two women joined their classmates. Kyreen listened with half an ear, her mind trying to decipher the summons from Aren. Why so formal? Was Kyreen's paranoia unwarranted? If so, why did she have such a terrible feeling about her impending trip?

The next morning in the gray predawn mist, Kyreen's trepidation materialized anew as she exited her tent. Even before she could see the details of his face, Kyreen recognized Lang waiting for her by the gelding she had hobbled outside the tent overnight so as to quicken her departure. Her stomach sank when she saw the saddled sorrel mare standing beside her horse.

Without a word, Kyreen bent down to remove the gelding's hobble. As she began to pull the bridle onto the horse's head, her eyes briefly met Lang's, floating away before either acknowledged the other person. Resolutely, she bit her tongue, mechanically moving through the task of preparing her gelding for the day's journey, refusing to break the silence. What did they have to discuss? Kyreen would not open herself up to Lang's scorn for asking the obvious question. By his presence and that of his horse, he quite plainly had received the same summons as she. Not only did Kyreen have no right to inquire his business, she did not wish to give Lang the impression she had any curiosity about him.

With the gelding saddled, Kyreen returned to the tent for her knapsack. Synnove mumbled a farewell before rolling over and drifting back to sleep. Still chuckling, Kyreen stepped back outside. Again, without consciously meaning to her eyes locked with Lang's and the sound choked in the back of her throat, blood freezing in her veins. Swallowing the lump now crowding her throat, Kyreen mentally squared her shoulders and strode over to her mount. She had at least one full day on the trail with this man. She was strong. She could do this she told herself as she swung up into the saddle.

As the motion of Lang caught the corner of her gaze, however, Kyreen's resolve crashed. Doubt dripped from her head down to her toes as though someone hit splashed a bucket of ice cold water over her head. How could she do this? How could she concentrate on the hazards of traveling through hostile territory when one of her greatest dangers rode alongside her? How in the goddess's name would she ever close her eyes and sleep knowing this man lay just a few meters away? She thought no way could she survive. There had to be something she...

"Would you control yourself already?" Lang's voice, though he whispered, rang out sharply through the fog. "A toddler could read the animosity you project. "

Anger flooded through Kyreen, an improvement over the anxiety. Animosity? Her? Then she took a deep, centering breath, concentrated, and did as Lang had requested. In her mind, she pushed down her feelings, imagining a bag into which she could store her feelings, drawing close the mouth of the bag. As she basked in the quiet aftermath of the inner turmoil she had sequestered, Kyreen realized Lang projected no feelings what so ever. The man had shut down his own essence so much she barely registered his existence, despite their close proximity.

"My apologies," Kyreen mumbled.

Fog clung to the valley, the trees, and even the two riders and their horses long after dawn. The sun, a mere dot of faded yellow, barely visible, traversed slowly across the dense grayness. While quiet suffocated the woods, the horses' hoof beats echoed loudly, the sound oddly amplified. Lang's presence, the eerie weather, the unknown waiting for her at the Council Camp, each by itself enough to set Kyreen on edge, now combined to drive an icy blade of apprehension deep into her core. Something felt off here, unnatural.

Even as the thought the rose in her mind, Lang pulled up is mount, his hand shooting out towards Kyreen, silently urging her to hold as well. Once the echo of hoof beats had faded, the silence descended heavily. Kyreen's ears rang as she strained to hear something, anything. Her eyes offered no aid, even Lang's form as close as he was, shifted in shadows.

Still without speaking, Lang dismounted. Kyreen followed his lead. Though the tension still hung between them as they stood side by side, shoulders almost touching, their attention focused elsewhere, on a common target. Faintly Kyreen heard men's voices, muffled and indistinct. Just beneath this came the sound of wheels and leather creaking.

Kyreen glanced inquiringly at Lang, who whispered the word 'wagon,' his voice so low it barely carried to her ears.

A wagon? Why here? So far from the castle, from the roads leading to Galor or the harbor or even Myrddin. Kyreen's confusion must have been clear and, as she opened her mouth to question, two things happen simultaneously. Lang's free hand, the one not occupied with his reins, shot out pressing over Kyreen's mouth staying her question, and somewhere behind the pair, an ax blade struck a tree trunk. The sound echoed loud, startling both of the Calanians. Even as Lang's touch sent electric shock waves through Kyreen's body, icy tendrils of fear flooded as well. Not only did the ax strike loud, it struck close by, much too close.

Lang dropped his reins and twisted around to close the already narrow space between their bodies. His now unoccupied arm snaked around Kyreen's shoulders and he drew her close, his cheek to her, his other hand still firm over her mouth, his breath warm against her ear. It was all Kyreen could do to not jerk back, to wrest away from his embrace. She struggled to contain herself mentally and physically. Tears welled up in her eyes, every muscle in her being rigid, acutely aware of the warmth flooding from the length of his body pressed against hers. Even through her own struggles, she realized she could now sense Lang's own high emotions.

She could also feel the shaking of his body, the trembling of his breath, his rage barely in check as he whispered through gritted teeth, "Do. Not. Move."

Taking a deep breath, difficult with his hand pressed over her mouth, she attempted to quell her panic. Lang's body continued to press warmly against hers, even though she sensed his attention to be focused solely on the nearby Galorians, not her. With mortification, she felt her body begin to respond to his contact. Reaching her arms back, she clutched at the tree behind her, fingers digging into the rough bark as she attempted to pull away from the intimacy of his embrace, but she had nowhere to go. Her cheeks flushed as arousal spread through her like wildfire. Suddenly the danger of their situation rested no longer in the Galorians, but the Calanian before her. She had to get away from him.

Closing her eyes, she forced her body to go limp. Before the surprised man could react, she slipped to the ground, out of his grasp. Silently she twisted around, rising back up to her feet, so she could press against the side of the tree, opposite Lang, safely out of his reach. Keeping her eyes closed, Kyreen pressed her cheek against the rough bark, allowing the pain to chase away the desire coursing through her veins. Certain Lang must have felt her traitorous body's lust, Kyreen concentrated on centering, on calming, silently reciting her meditations. After what felt like an eternity, but only took the span of a few ax strikes, Kyreen felt composed enough to open her eyes. Nothing looked different. The fog still washed the forest in eerie gray shadows.

Suddenly Lang's hand closed over Kyreen's wrist, causing her heartbeat to spike anew. He tugged her gently away from the tree, his eyes never leaving the spot in the shadows from where the sound of the ax generated. At some point, he had gathered up the reins of both their horses. Without a sound, he led her and their mounts back through the forest in the direction from whence they had arrived.

After they had moved a sufficient distance, he released her wrist and wordlessly handed Kyreen the reins to her gelding. By the time he had glanced in her direction, she had dropped her gaze. Keeping her eyes averted, Kyreen followed the bearded Calanian's lead, swinging up into the saddle. She felt his eyes upon her but, coward that she was, she refused to lift her gaze to meet his. At last he turned his mare away and resumed their journey. After a heartbeat, Kyreen nudged her gelding to follow. Soon all sounds of the Galorians faded away, but the two travelers remained alert for more work crews and patrols, the silence between them growing with every step. Several times Kyreen felt Lang turn in his saddle to look upon her, but she kept her gaze resolutely fixed on his mount's hooves.

When the Council Camp loomed through the late afternoon fog, Lang pulled his mare to a halt, turning once again in his saddle to look at her.

"Kyreen," he said quietly, his voice gravelly.

The sound of her name upon his lips sent a jolt of electricity coursing through Kyreen's body, freshly igniting her fear. Like a jackrabbit startled by the fox, she spurred her mount into a lope, riding away from her companion and into camp. Blinking back hot tears of frustration, she determined she never wanted to discuss what had transpired in the woods, resolving to push those memories away into a dark corner of her mind.

"Kyreen!" Gunda, Aren's youngest child, exclaimed when she spotted Kyreen entering the equine area.

Relief coursing through her body, Kyreen dismounted and warmly embraced her young cousin. If Gunda sensed anything amiss, she did not outwardly react. Chattering, the girl began assisting Kyreen with the gelding's care. When Lang rode in just moments later, Kyreen had already begun wiping down her horse's sorrel coat.

"Hail, Lang," Gunda greeted the man cheerily. "Mama asked for you to report to the Council Tent right away. With your permission, I can care for your mare."

"Thank you," Lang responded, handing his reins to the young woman.

Though she refused to look around, Kyreen felt his eyes on her back. After a long moment, Lang turned and walked away. Kyreen released her pent-up breath, resting her forehead against the gelding's withers.

Once Lang had move out of hearing, Gunda patted her cousin's shoulder. "I know how you feel," the young woman whispered. "That man is too handsome for words. He makes me nervous, too. My heart races and I get all tongue-tied. Can you imagine me tongue-tied?"

Kyreen's face blushed, but fortunately her young cousin took no notice, having started unsaddling Lang's mare and resuming her chatter about the camp news. As Kyreen continued to rub her gelding's coat, she thought on Gunda's comment about Lang's looks. While Kyreen avoided looking at the man on most occasions, she had always found him achingly good looking, which could account for her reaction to him in the woods earlier. If not for the animosity they held for each other, Kyreen imagined she might just be as infatuated with Lang as her young cousin. The thought made her shudder and she worked to push the man out of her thoughts, concentrating instead on making her gelding's coat gleam red gold. Just as Kyreen finished stowing her tack, a page from the Council approached.

"Your presence is requested," the young girl, about nine summers old, said, her voice so quiet Kyreen had to lean forward to hear her.

Chapter 5

"After some long and in-depth deliberations, the Council would like to launch another attack upon the castle this summer," Aren said, as soon as Kyreen had settled into a high-back chair at the oval table in the Council Tent. "We would respectfully request your assistance with the campaign."

Kyreen nodded warily. She glanced around the table at the various council members. Some she recognized from last summer, but three had been added last fall after the failed attempt at retaking the castle, replacing those who had lost their lives in the skirmish. She read some anxiety from the council members, as though they worried what her answer might be. As usual, Lang's face showed no emotion and she dared not allow her gaze to linger too long upon him. Finally, Kyreen returned her gaze to Aren, saying, "I gave you my vow last summer. Whatever assistance I can provide, you know I am your servant, cousin."

Something—gratitude, relief, humor—flashed in Aren's eyes and Kyreen knew her formal response had been the correct path. She cast another look around the table, wondering about the politics that happened in here. Then Aren began speaking again and Kyreen focused on her cousin.

"Before committing any of our people to a battle, the Council needs to be assured our plans to infiltrate through the tunnel system will be viable."

Kyreen began to realize where Aren headed as the Calanian leader said, "We would like for you to journey to the castle to interact with the creature that occupies the tunnels."

"Vaktare," Kyreen murmured without thought.

"What?" Aren asked, her eyes narrowing.

Until she had uttered the name, Kyreen had not known the gargoyle who protected the castle tunnels had a name. It had simply appeared upon her lips without conscious thought.

"Vaktare," Kyreen repeated. "That is the gargoyle's name."

Another look rippled across Aren's face, this time one of triumph, before her customary mask of neutrality slipped back into place. Kyreen wondered who on the Council had been challenging Aren's theory that Kyreen had a bond with the gargoyle.

"You may choose a team to accompany you to the castle to assist," Aren continued.

Something in her cousin's tone pricked at Kyreen's mind. A team to assist her in meeting the gargoyle? Why would she need assistance? Realization dawned, causing Kyreen to sit a little stiffer in her chair, her jaw clenching slightly.

"I believe the word you meant to say is witness," Kyreen said. The quick flash in Aren's eyes informed Kyreen that she had guessed correctly and that her cousin was not pleased with the Council's directive.

Kyreen inhaled quietly, leaning back in her seat, attempting to appear calm while her brain raced. She had already stated she would be cooperative so she could not now renege. How could she force the Council to back down? She tilted her head inquiringly at Aren. "A team? Of my own choosing?"

"That is correct," Aren nodded. "The camp moved here, closer to the castle, so you and those you select will be able to walk in, meet with the creature, and be back here in the shortest period of time."

"Very well," Kyreen responded. "I choose Synnove, Yngve, and Ebbe."

A few of the council members looked perplexed, but most knew at least two of the names, knew that Kyreen had named trainees. Aren did not visibly react except for the tightening of her lips. Having Kyreen name her son had evidently not been part of the leader's plan.

"Unacceptable," a husky man interjected, licking his lips nervously. Kyreen recognized him from last summer. Geir, an ally of Lang's, had continuously blocked any actions involving Kyreen or her assistance. She figured he could possibly be the one challenging Aren now. "Those are unqualified prospects, unprepared for a mission of such importance. We cannot permit it."

"Are you questioning the training of our youth?" a woman seated near Kyreen asked. Her position on the Council was new, she had only come on after another member perished in last summer's battle. From her unlined face, she appeared as though she might have been a trainee herself quite recently. Though Kyreen did not know the young woman, she admired her direct approach which gave Kyreen basis for her argument.

Before Geir could respond, Kyreen spoke. "While it is true my comrades at Training Camp are young and untested in the field, you are wrong about them being untrained. These three youth are top in this year's class. I have been working with them for months. They... we work well together, but most importantly I trust them. Anyone else who would accompany me would be a distraction, would not trust me any more than I would trust them."

She paused to glance around the table. "If the Council has a problem with my choice, then you may send someone else to the castle without me."

Geir looked as if he wanted to say something, but after a quick glance at Lang, he settled back in his chair without speaking. None of the other council members appeared ready to talk either.

"Are we in agreement of Kyreen's choice, then?" Aren asked. Everyone around the table nodded. "Any objections?"

As no one spoke up, Aren dispatched a page to fetch a courier. Within a few minutes the messages to Atle and Kyreen's friends had been drafted and sent on their way.

"Your team members should arrive by the morning after tomorrow," Aren told Kyreen after the courier had exited the tent. "Once they arrive, we shall have a briefing, until then you are dismissed with our gratitude."

Kyreen inclined her head to her cousin. Standing, she swept her gaze around the table as various council members murmured their farewells. Quite by accident, Kyreen's gaze caught Lang looking at her, causing her heart to almost explode in her chest. It took all of Kyreen's self-control to continue exiting the tent without hurrying or trembling. Once outside, Kyreen paused to catch her breath and allow her racing heart to slow back down. Taking a deep, centering breath, she also attempted to drive away the image of his glittering emerald eyes boring into her with such raw fierceness.

Kyreen passed the rest of the afternoon assisting her youngest cousin with the herd. If pressed, however, Kyreen might have admitted her sole motive had been to avoid any further contact with Lang. In truth, she need not have worried. With the news of the Galorians' lumber expedition, the Council remained in session after her exit, taking swift action by dispatching two sentries to reconnoiter the Galorian activity.

At dinner, Aren expressed concern about sending Kyreen and the other trainees to the castle since the Galorians were indeed being so bold once again. Viggo had waved Kyreen over to join them in a spot removed from the rest of the diners. Even Gunda and her brother Reidar dined with friends instead of their parents. Belatedly Kyreen wondered if this had been on purpose, especially with Aren's next words.

"The Council wants to send a guide, someone who knows the area, has experience," Aren explained.

Kyreen's temper flared. "A nanny to watch the toddlers would be more the truth," she snapped, resisting her urge to throw down her dinner and storm away. Aren had chided her before about backing down, for not expressing her opinions. This time, Kyreen decided she would take a stand. "Tell me, Aren, how much of this directive is truly coming from the Council? I could see possibly Lang or Geir objecting, but mayhap it is just you in an attempt to protect your son?"

From the shocked look on her cousin's face, Kyreen wondered if she had judged Aren too harshly and her blood ran cold. Before Kyreen could apologize and as Aren's mouth opened to respond, Viggo placed a hand upon his mate's arm.

"Kyreen has a point, my love," he stated quietly. "Yngve knows these lands completely. Between he and Synnove, no patrol could easily surprise them. If need be, Ebbe could easily dispatch a threat as could Kyreen from what I witnessed with last year's spars. Though they may be young and untested, your cousin has assembled a talented team."

As the man's words faded away, the two women stared at each other in silence. Finally, Aren sighed, dropping her gaze to her plate. Setting her meal to the side, Aren ran both hands along her face, shoulders sagging.

"You are both correct," she admitted quietly. "I just wished... I had hoped this conflict would end before... before my children, my son, my baby would be sent into the fray."

Viggo wrapped his arms around Aren as her tears began to flow freely. Embarrassed by the intrusion of an intimate moment, of seeing Aren so vulnerable, Kyreen stared glumly at her own meal, her appetite turned to dust. Not for the first time, Kyreen felt the weight of her mission and the mantle of her responsibility. Yes, she meant everything she had told the Council of trusting these trainees, of her confidence in their abilities, of the cohesive team they made, but, too, they were her friends. What would happen if they were ambushed? How could she live with herself if something were to happen to any of them, especially if Kyreen's shortfalls as a leader were the cause? What if she had to leave one of them behind, or worse deliberately send one of them to their death? Kyreen exhaled sharply as the full realization of this upcoming venture swathed her.

"I… if you both will excuse me, I could use a walk," Kyreen said quietly rising to her feet.

Viggo met her glance with a small supportive smile and a nod, Aren's face still buried against his shoulder. "Be well, Kyreen," he offered quietly.

After depositing her dishes, Kyreen strolled slowly around the perimeter of the camp through the mild twilight, hugging her cloak around her body against the wind. Though the forest called to her soul, she resisted. Guards had already started evening patrols and did not need the distraction of her wanderings. As Aren had mentioned earlier in the day, the camp had been moved in as close to the castle as the Council dare in anticipation of this, of her upcoming mission. Proximity coupled with the new knowledge of Galorians expeditions caused tensions to run high, and the already subdued camp to operate in absolute silence. A thought Kyreen kept in mind when she spoke to the presence trailing her in the shadows.

"I know you are there, Lang," she said quietly, turning to face him. "What I do not know is why you feel it necessary to follow me."

Lang stepped forward, his silhouette looming large, yet his features still obscured by the still-moonless night. Despite the distance between them, Kyreen distinctly felt the turmoil of emotions rolling off the man. Instinctively and without conscious thought she took a small step back. Having spent so much of her life amongst others with skills so inferior to her own, Kyreen had rarely felt intimidate or truly feared for her safety. At this moment, however, she understood the fight or flight conflict of a trapped animal. Lang stood a full head taller than her, plus substantially outweighed her. His skills went without question, although Kyreen thought herself to probably be quicker and might could use his recent injury against the man should he attack her. All this flew through Kyreen's mind and her body automatically assumed a defensive staff, tensing in anticipation, all in the quick instant before Lang responded to her words.

"Kyreen," he said, voice cracking as though he had not had water for days. "I…I cannot say why… I simply…"

"You simply decided to intimidate me? You think you can bully me? Keep me from this mission?" Kyreen's temper flared again, but she managed to keep her voice low. "Let me make this extremely clear for you, Lang. This is my home. This is where I belong. Nothing you say, nothing you do, especially a clumsy ambush in the dark, will ever make me leave, unless of course you plan to murder me."

Now Lang took a step back. "You think I mean you harm?"

Her blood pounding furiously, Kyreen's anger overrode common sense. She closed the distance between them, standing so close she could feel the heat from his body. "You can try. Others have and failed," she hissed, staring up at him. "Now get out of my way."

Without thinking through her actions, Kyreen pressed her palms into Lang's chest intending to shove the man away. Instead his hands locked around her wrists, preventing her from pulling back. While Lang did not clamp down or cause pain, when his bare hands connected with the bare skin of her wrists, a jolt coursed through Kyreen's body, freezing her in place, stealing the breath from her lungs. For a moment, a terribly long moment, unable to move, unable to breath, Kyreen stood rooted in place, now thankful for the dark obscuring their faces. Once again, she felt her body responding to his proximity.

"I..." Lang started to speak without success. "Kyreen..."

The sound of her name upon his lips broke the spell. Kyreen wrested her hands from his grip.

"Do not ever touch me again," she growled softy before spinning away and hurrying back to the safety of camp.

The following morning as Kyreen finished up her morning meal, she spied Vidar heading towards the equine area. He held onto a young woman, her face and body beginning to round out in pregnancy. Kyreen put away her dirty dishes and hurried to catch up with the blacksmith, an old friend of her grandfather's. When he heard her footsteps approaching, the blind man patted his companion's arm softly before turning around.

"Hail, Vidar," Kyreen greeted him quietly.

"Ah, Kyreen, my dear!" Vidar responded, a wide smile breaking out across his wizened face. "I had heard you arrived in camp yesterday. Do you have time to visit with an old man?"

"Yes. I am waiting for my comrades to arrive. I have all day," Kyreen nodded before remembering he could not see her. She took the hands he held out to her, taking care for fear of hurting him. She had not seen him since the Harvest season and felt concerned at how much he had aged over the winter.

"Britt, try to get some food to settle on your stomach and get some rest," Vidar said to his companion. "Kyreen can take me to the herd this morning."

The woman flashed Kyreen a smile of gratitude, the dark circles under eyes and unhealthy tint of her alabaster skin a confession to her recent attacks of morning sickness. A boy, Kyreen thought with a glance to the barely noticeable bulge under the other woman's tunic, though she kept the thought to herself. Britt kissed Vidar's cheek and walked back towards camp.

Vidar held out his arm, which Kyreen took. As they resumed walking, he inquired about Kyreen's training at the cliffs camp. As always, being in Vidar's presence soothed Kyreen's nerves. Something about him smoothed out the rough edges of anxiety running through her.

When they reached the herd, Vidar spent several minutes speaking with the head hostler, inquiring about a few horses needing work done on their hooves. Kyreen watched the herd, only partially listening to the conversation. The horses, a glorious mix of chestnuts and sorrels, wore their winter coats, scruffy and warm. She spied her gelding nibbling at the dry grass, just a little bit apart from the herd, not exactly outside, but not particularly inside. Just like her with her people, Kyreen thought.

"Very well, my dear," Vidar said, drawing Kyreen away from her thoughts with a soft pat to her arm. "Shall we head back? My old bones could use some time by the fire. You can tell me more about your life."

Once settled by the main fire in the center of camp, the area practically deserted as everyone went about their daily chores, Kyreen continued to relate to Vidar all that she had been up to over the winter. To her ear, it all sounded so mundane, but the elderly man seemed riveted.

At one point Vidar reached over to gently squeeze Kyreen's knee. "I sense an undercurrent of tension, unspoken, and not just from the tracking exercises."

"Yes," Kyreen admitted reluctantly. "I am at odds with one of my instructors."

Vidar nodded, encouraging her to continue speaking.

"He said something to me a while ago," she remarked. "Something I cannot shake."

"Go on."

"He said I had abandoned our people last summer before the castle attack," she said quietly. "Now I keep wondering if his opinion is shared by others."

"Oh, my dear," Vidar responded. "You remind me of my dear sister, always concerned about others. What does it matter how others perceive you? You know the truth. The Council knows the truth. Those who know you, know the truth. You did not abandon your people. You dealt justice upon our enemy, the man who led the Battle, who killed your mother."

Kyreen silently reflected on Vidar's words. His tone had grown fiercer as he had talked until he had ended with almost a growl in his voice. In addition to his conviction, his words themselves made sense in her head, but in her heart, she still wondered and worried.

"Have you asked this instructor why he feels you abandoned your people?" Vidar asked, bringing Kyreen out of her pondering.

Guiltily Kyreen admitted she had not. She did not wish to admit out loud how unnerved speaking with Lang made her feel.

"Mayhap you should," Vidar remarked. "The direct approach is always a good technique. It keeps one's adversaries on their toes."

Kyreen chuckled, feeling a little better. As they stood to queue for midday meal, she resolved to do just that the next time Lang confronted her.

When Kyreen's friends arrived the next morning, they made their plans to set out for the castle that same evening. With the camp's proximity so much closer, the four traveled on foot, heading out just after sunset. Only Yngve had family at this camp to see them off on their journey. Many from the Council, however, Lang included, came to bid farewell, though he hung back at the edge of the crowd.

Kyreen watched with a mix of emotions as Gunda, then Reidar and Viggo, and finally Aren embraced Yngve. She envied her cousin's family but mainly she worried about her capabilities to lead and keep these young Calanians safe. Now in the woods, with Yngve leading and Synnove at the tail, Kyreen pushed this fresh crop of doubts away to better concentrate on the trail. Though they traveled in silence, Kyreen could feel the youthful exuberance spilling over from her three friends, raising her own spirits. A sliver of moon graced the clear skies above shedding enough light to make the woods visible but not so much as to make Kyreen feel exposed whenever the group crossed a stream or entered into a meadow.

Just as the horizon turned a purple bruise in anticipation of the new dawn, Yngve paused at the top of a hill and waved his companions forward. Still shadowed within the trees, the four gazed down on the dark spill of the castle. Unlike last year when Aren had brought Kyreen to the best vista point to view, not approach, the castle, Yngve had guided them to the tunnel side of the castle. As the sun began to rise, Kyreen stared at the now faded road, that final memory of her home rushing back.

"Kyreen, alright there?" Synnove asked in a hushed voice.

"Vaktare stood at the mouth, unable to leave," Kyreen whispered. "I waved goodbye to him."

"Do you believe it still lives down there?" Ebbe asked.

"I do," Kyreen replied. "The Galorians do not use the tunnels. Vaktare must still be there."

"How does it survive? In the dark? Without food or water?" Yngve inquired, shifting his gaze from the castle to Kyreen.

"The tunnels were originally a cave system. I do not know if the creature needs nourishment, but there are plenty of small wild life, mice and such to hunt, and a spring feeds fresh water to the tunnels. Quillan and I always wanted to wade in it but Mama forbade it," Kyreen commented with a chuckle. All three of her friends stared at her.

"What?" Kyreen asked, worried that she had missed a sound or issue.

"Kyreen," Synnove responded softly. "We grew up on tales of this place, so shrouded in myth and mystery that most youth our age do not believe them. You... you lived here. You have memories, details I have never considered. You just made this castle, this mission, this war..." Her voice faded as she returned her gaze to the castle.

"This is no longer training," Ebbe finished for Synnove. "It is real."

Yngve tensed a split second before Synnove. "Back," he hissed and the four as one slipped back into the grey shadows of the forest.

A moment later the morning patrol appeared through the front gate, but based on the relaxed postures and jaunty discourse of the soldiers, the little band of Calanians had no need to worry.

"Come," Synnove said, once the patrol had moved on. "Let us make camp. Rest until dusk. I will take first watch."

Kyreen had been sure she could never sleep during the day this close to her childhood home, but she easily drifted into a restful slumber until Synnove woke her at noon for her shift. Kyreen rose quietly so as not to disturb Yngve and Ebbe, Synnove following her out of the shadowed grove. Kyreen paused at the edge of the trees, eyes on the castle. The early afternoon sunshine flooded down, illuminating the white stone walls, a stark contrast to the green grass. The muffled sounds of the Galorians inside, doing whatever it was invading armies did, maintenance work, drills, floated to her ears. A few soldiers loitered about the base of the outside wall, near the open gates, while another group patrolled the battlements. Even though from this distance Kyreen could not feel their emotions, boredom and inattentiveness could be seen in their posture. Her mind drifted back to the last day she had spent within those walls, the festive air, the people relaxed and jubilant, her three-year old naivety.

"Banners had been hung on the merlons," she commented quietly. "Everything looked so bright and colorful for the Festival. I was thrilled I would be riding my very own horse, all by myself in the parade, not a training pony. The kitchen staff had spent days preparing sweet rolls, cakes, pastries, so many confectionaries. That last night, after supper, while Mama and Arvis talked with other grownups, Quillan and I snuck away to the kitchen. One of the cooks who always spoilt us, I cannot recall her name now, gave us each a little treat. All I remember of the sweet is that it was covered in powdered sugar. Quillan had it all over his face," she chuckled, low and sorrowful. "Looking back, I am sure I must have as well."

She sighed, glancing over at Synnove. "My apologies. It seems this mission has stirred up a cloud of memories."

Synnove shook her head. "Do not apologize, Kyreen. Your memories are precious and not just to you. Every time you reminisce, I learn more about the life that should have been. I learn for what it is which we are fighting," she paused, her sapphire gaze fixed on the castle below them. "Your memories help me make sense of the deaths our people continue to suffer."

Something in her friend's voice alerted Kyreen. "Synnove, what is the matter?"

Now it Synnove sighed. "Tell me about the tunnels," she finally asked, her gaze never leaving the castle.

"What is there to tell?" Kyreen shrugged. "Several lines, like the entrance here, were created by nature. Many generations back, when the castle was under construction, our people expanded some areas out, places to connect the whole system."

At Synnove's silence, Kyreen's brow furrowed. "What troubles you?"

"I…" Synnove struggled with her words. The younger woman licked her lips, outwardly exhibiting more nervousness than Kyreen had ever witnessed. "I have never… been inside."

"No, of course not," Kyreen responded. "No one has since…"

"No, that is not what I mean," Synnove interrupted, her voice quiet, yet uncharacteristically agitated. "I have never been inside anything other than a tent. My heart races when I think about… about the walls… closing in… being trapped… the ceiling falling down…"

As Synnove's voice trailed, the two women stood several moments, silently staring down at the tunnel opening. The dark opening, which beckoned Kyreen home, silently mocked Synnove.

"You need not worry about the size of the tunnels," Kyreen finally responded. "They are wide and tall, designed to accommodate wagons and horse traffic. I cannot say after this many years if, or with what, the tunnels will be illuminated. I brought a few torches and the lanterns may still operate."

"Always so logical," Synnove chuckled, sounding a little more like herself. "I must rest now."

She turned to hug the other woman. "Thank you for not teasing. Please do not mention my fears to the others?"

"Of course not," Kyreen replied, returning the hug.

Once Synnove had faded into the shadows, Kyreen settled down, her back against a tree trunk to keep watch, along with her faded memories.

Chapter 6

Shortly after sunset, under the cover of dark, the four Calanians made their way, one at a time, across the wide-open expanse to the mouth of the tunnel. Having sprinted across first, Kyreen struggled to see Synnove's form in the shadows when she felt, not heard, the gargoyle's arrival.

Heart pounding, afraid to breathe, Kyreen turned to face the dark of the tunnel. The gargoyle's massive body created a darker, inky shadow amidst the shadows, and Kyreen's mind filled in the details. Yellow glowing eyes absent pupils. Erect cropped ears, folded close against the skull. Compact, whiskerless muzzle. Its dense, muscular body a mottle of browns, tans, golds, designed for camouflage against the tunnel walls.

Without conscious thought, Kyreen closed the distance between her and the creature, realizing, just as her hand lay upon the creature's massive head, that she had never touched the gargoyle. Its smooth, hairless skin felt cold almost like granite in the winter. The woman had been expecting coarse hair much like a horse's hide, maybe because the gargoyle stood tall on four legs, reminding her of a large pony or small horse.

The gargoyle tensed beneath her hand, alerting Kyreen to Synnove's silent arrival.

"All is well," Kyreen murmured quietly. Not knowing for sure if the creature understood her spoken words or her tone, or if the gargoyle communicated telepathically, she continued speaking aloud. "Synnove is friend. She is with me, Vaktare."

"Kyreen, alright there?" Synnove asked quietly, uncertainty in her voice.

Through the dark, knowing her friend could not see the motion, Kyreen still nodded. She had confidence Synnove could feel Kyreen's calm.

Shortly Yngve and Ebbe joined the two women and the gargoyle at the tunnel entrance. Kyreen's hand remained atop the gargoyle's head, both of them receiving a level of comfort in the physical contact. While Kyreen attempted to remain alert to the exterior environment, the gargoyle occupied most of her attention.

Yngve, the last to arrive, his grin echoed in his tone, commented, "Well done there, my cousin. It remembers you. Now what?"

Kyreen hesitated, unwilling to leave so quickly after arriving. She nibbled at her bottom lip, contemplating.

"We should check on the condition of the tunnel," she finally replied, grinning at the waves of excitement immediately exuded by the trio watching her expectantly.

"Hand me one of your torches," Synnove said, holding out a hand towards Kyreen.

Once the torch was in hand, the younger woman ignited it with a spark from a flint she wore about her neck.

"Handy," Kyreen remarked, having noticed the pendant before, but never having comprehended its utility.

"A gift from my brother. He enjoys the irony," Synnove winked impishly, tucking the necklace back under her tunic.

Before Kyreen could question the cryptic remark, Synnove raised the torch up, motioning for Kyreen to take the lead. With the gargoyle walking alongside, Kyreen led the group farther into the tunnel. One of her hands absently rested easily atop the creature's broad back. After a few steps, the loose dust of the entrance gave way to hard ground, dirt firmly packed from centuries of use. Barrels lined the corridor, coated in dust, adding to the tunnel's atmosphere of abandonment. Fresh air circulated from the age-old ventilation system, but still Kyreen detected the underlying musty smell of disuse. Setting upon a barrel, she found a dirt-encrusted lantern. After a quick clean-up, the lantern produced a better illumination of the tunnel than the torch, which was doused and returned to Kyreen's pack. She had been tempted to leave it upon the barrel the lantern had set on, but the engrained training made her reconsider leaving any evidence of their presence.

Because of Synnove's comment earlier in the day, Kyreen remained cognizant of her companions' awe when the tunnel widened into the first chamber. She paused to permit them all a moment of adjustment to soak in this new, novel environment. Old memories for Kyreen reemerged with every glance, smell or sound.

"This is where the horses were stabled," Kyreen explained unnecessarily. Dozens of stall doors stood gaping open, ancient bales of hay and straw crumbled along the walls, abandoned tack hung along the wall. Kyreen struggled for control as adrenaline coursed through her body, her mind replaying memories from decades ago.

"Kyreen, alright there?" Synnove asked once more, placing a gentle hand upon her friend's arm.

At the contact, the gargoyle tensed, swiveling his massive head to peer at Synnove. Though his gaze remained neutral and he uttered no sound, the message came through clear. After decades of dormancy, the guardian was back on duty.

"Just gathering memories," Kyreen replied quietly, nodding.

Synnove drifted away from Kyreen to one of the open stalls. Ebbe went to a barrel, lifting the top to gaze inside.

"All this feed. Wasted," he commented dejectedly.

While her companions roamed about the massive space, Kyreen continued to gaze silently.

Making her way to the far side of the chamber, Synnove glanced back to Kyreen, her eyes inquisitive, clearly asking the question on all three of the young people's faces.

Once again, Kyreen hesitated, her fingers absently running down the gargoyle's back and once again curiosity countermanded good judgment. From her pack she withdrew a scroll, a map surreptitiously handed to her by Viggo as they had bid each other farewell at Council Camp.

"I know well the temptation of exploration. I only give it to you to keep my son safe," her cousin's mate had whispered in Kyreen's ear. "Aren cannot know you received it from me."

Striding to a table, Kyreen spread out the oil cloth page on a dusty tabletop. All three of her companions moved over to join her in gazing down at the map.

"Where did you get this?" Ebbe asked the question on everyone's mind.

Synnove reached out a hand, her fingers lightly tracing the lines outlining the design of the cavernous tunnel system. Each line, every compartment meticulously documented by people no longer in this realm.

"Does it matter, Ebbe?" she asked. "The better question is where do we go?"

"We can go anywhere," Yngve said, his eyes tracing their current position down the single entrance/exit from the stable.

"Here," he added, his finger landing on a small antechamber several passageways into the tunnels.

Kyreen tilted her head to read the label. "The armory?" she asked.

"Yes!" Yngve replied, his quiet voice filled with emotion. "If there are any functioning weapons remaining, we can take them back to camp with us."

"What about the pantry?" Ebbe asked, his index finger pointing to a chamber down a separate tunnel system. "Weapons we have. Food is always scarce."

All three looked to their leader, who gazed down at the map. Her own eyes had been drawn to the main entrance farther into the tunnels. The entrance she, with her mother and brother, had descended so many years before called to her heartstrings.

After a long moment, she nodded, lifting her gaze to her companions. "Very well. You both make good points and we have little time. Ebbe and Synnove take that lantern over there and head to the food stores. See if there is anything salvageable. Yngve, you and I will go to the armory."

Whether from nerves or her overactive imagining of all that could go awry, Kyreen's heart pounded as they made their way up the corridor, away from the stables, away from the exit, away from safety. After a short distance, the corridor widened into an even larger space. Ebbe and Synnove silently moved into the left tunnel while Kyreen and Yngve bore right. The passage here widened so that the lantern in Yngve's hand did not reach the craggy walls beside them. The naturally occurring nooks and crannies danced in shadows. Kyreen glanced back as she entered the tunnel, the light from the others' lantern barely visible. Doubt rushed over her anew and her feet quit moving. Unaware, Yngve continued farther into the tunnel and around the first bend, leaving Kyreen and the gargoyle in total darkness.

"Kyreen?" Yngve's voice rang through the dark. Although he barely spoke above a whisper the sound reverberated against the walls, echoing down the deserted passages.

Mentally shaking the cobwebs, Kyreen hurried around the corner to catch up with Yngve at the mouth the next cavernous chamber, a man-made one with artificial symmetry, ballooning out into a cylindrical shape. Though the lamplight did not reach that far, Kyreen knew the chamber would curve at the opposite end, a large column with several finger-shaped off-shoots before narrowing down to a passage way that inevitably led to the stairway leading up to the war room. One of those narrow off-shoots would be the room Viggo's father and Vidar had sealed off so many years ago.

Upon Kyreen's arrival, Yngve turned to her, his shoulders sagging. "Everything is gone. Nothing useful remains."

Kyreen glanced around. Dusty spear racks stood empty, cupboard doors stood ajar, their shelves bare. Even had they not known the story, this space had unmistakably been hastily ransacked and abandoned.

"Efficient and speedy," Kyreen muttered under her breath before raising her voice to address Yngve. "Not surprising. With the evacuations, weapons were most likely issued to everyone for defense. Many of the civilians present for the Festival may not have brought a weapon."

Her gaze drifted to the shadows obscuring the far end of the chamber, feeling a pull on her to continue.

"Shall we continue?" Yngve asked, making no attempt to conceal the eagerness in his voice.

"Just to Vidar's workshop," she answered, the desire to see the sealed room pulling her.

The tug, however, only grew stronger once the pair stood before the rubble that had been a doorway. She gazed down the darkened tunnel, where another blockage of stone rest, all her sense straining. Then she realized the gargoyle by her side had disappeared. Kyreen glanced around, finally resting her gaze upon Yngve. "Did you see Vaktare leave?"

Confusion flashed across her young cousin's features. "The creature? No. It was just there, standing by your side. I looked over at the doorway for a moment and when I looked back it was gone."

Both froze at the sound of voices from the tunnel. Instinctively the two moved as one away from the blasted room to take refuge behind the massive columns. Yngve lowered the lantern flame until the two could barely see the other. For what felt like an eternity they waited behind the column. The voices all male, at least three the Kyreen could decipher, although she could not make out the conversation. From the sound of it the group moved something heavy. Kyreen imagined they tackled the rubble further up the tunnel that needed clearing.

Yngve tapped Kyreen's shoulder, to get her attention, then pointed across the chamber to the tunnel they had originally entered. He wagged two fingers, mimicking walking. Kyreen nodded. She started away from the safety of the column, heart racing, mindful of stealth. A glance over her shoulder confirmed Yngve followed with the lantern in hand, his body shielding the light from shining in their wake. The hard-packed dirt floor absorbed their footfalls as the pair made their way back to the tunnel split where they had left their friends. Kyreen fervently hoped Ebbe and Synnove had returned but remained unsurprised to find the passage empty. She and Yngve paused. Kyreen heard nothing from any direction. She glanced at Yngve in the dim lantern light. He pointed in the direction they had just come with a negative shake of his head and again in the direction of their initial entrance. Then, pointing towards the tunnel down which Synnove and Ebbe had taken, he shrugged and held up four fingers, followed by a fifth digit before flatting his palm to wobble the universal sign of uncertainty.

Kyreen's head swiveled and she stared down the occupied tunnel, nibbling her bottom lip. She took a tentative step towards the dark tunnel. Muffled voices travelled down the passageway anew. Yngve grabbed Kyreen's elbow, tugging her down the tunnel from whence the Calanians had entered the tunnel. After several yards, he stepped into a niche stacked with crates. He pulled her down to hide, pressing a finger to his lips. Moment later the muffled voices faded away, presumably heading down the passage towards the armory. Kyreen again felt the pull to follow. Only Yngve's hand on her arm kept her from standing. After what felt like an eternity, but, in reality, only took a moment, Yngve stood.

"We should leave, go to our camp," he whispered into Kyreen's ear, his grip tight against her arm, as though he intuited her compulsion to go back into the tunnels.

Kyreen hesitated, torn and reluctant to leave her friends.

"Now," Yngve insisted.

Heart heavy, Kyreen relented, following her cousin down the deserted tunnel. At the mouth, they paused briefly before sprinting across the darkened meadow. At the forest's edge, Kyreen stopped, glancing back at the castle's shadows veiling the tunnel entrance.

"I need to go back," she asserted quietly.

"No," Yngve shook his head. "That just increases the risk. Ebbe and Synnove can handle it. We stick to the plan."

Reluctantly Kyreen turned away, knowing Yngve to be right. Still she felt the tunnel tugging at her core and it took all her strength to follow Yngve to their camp. She did not wish to confess to her cousin that the pull was not for their friends' safety, but something else, something she could not quite name. A split second before stepping into the small clearing, Kyreen felt their friends' presences. Synnove and Ebbe had exited ahead of her and Yngve. In her relief, Kyreen hugged them all, first Synnove, then Ebbe, and even Yngve.

Afterwards, she took a deep centering breath to calm the blood pounding in her ears. "My apologies," she said quietly, barely able to see their faces in the weak moonlight shed by the crescent moon almost risen to the peak of its axis. "Yngve stayed true and had faith. I did not."

Now Synnove reached out to give Kyreen a hug. "Tis alright, Ky. I, too, would have hesitated in your position."

Kyreen seriously doubted her tentmate's words, but not her sincerity. So, she returned Synnove's hug without words.

"I do not believe we should linger," Ebbe commented, glancing in the direction of the castle, invisible thru the trees.

"I agree," Yngve replied. "The Council should know the Galorians have access to the tunnel."

"How?" was the first word Aren asked as the four related their story. Though Aren controlled her emotions and features, Kyreen could sense her cousin's rage.

The four had returned at dawn and the Council had hastily assembled. Road-worn and exhausted, Kyreen had relayed only the brief highlights of their expedition, of meeting the gargoyle and of the presence of men in the tunnels.

"Who?" another council member inquired.

"I know not how," Kyreen replied, her gaze fixed on Aren. "One moment Vaktare stood at my side. The next the gargoyle had disappeared, presumably to the entrance from whence the Galorians entered the tunnels."

She swiveled her head to look at the inquiring council member, thankful it had not been Lang's question. "None of us saw the soldiers, but the voices were male and the Galorians occupy the castle, therefore…"

"Therefore, you failed your mission," interrupted Geir, Lang's closest ally on the Council. "Why did you not investigate, discover if these people in the tunnel were friend or foe? Why did you flee before you had the information we need?"

"Geir! Do not be disrespectful!" Aren scolded, her voice quiet yet hard. Then she returned her gaze to the four standing before the Council. Kyreen saw that Aren wanted to say more, question further, but instead she merely said, "Thank you, all, for your service. I am certain you are tired from the journey. Eat, sleep, and relax. If we have more questions, we will call for you after evening meal. Otherwise, you four and Lang can head back to the Training Camp after sunset."

As the four turned to leave, the other council members murmured their gratitude for the trainees' service. Kyreen furtively snuck a look at Lang, but his gaze rested firmly on the table in front of him, his lips set in a severe line.

"Cheer up," Synnove said, linking her arm through Kyreen's once they had exited the tent. "Let us grab some food, then sleep. I feel I may drop in into my porridge like a toddler."

"Do not say it!" Synnove continued, laughing and pointing a finger at Ebbe, who had opened his mouth to respond to her toddler comment.

Kyreen allowed herself to be propelled towards the breakfast line. Her companions laughed and joked amicably through the meal, while she ate silently. She did not feel lonely or isolated. She could have participated had she felt so inclined, but she did not feel excluded by her silence either. For the moment, she just *was*. She did not angst over the mission, what she should or should not have done. She did not fret over the future conversations that may or may not be had with at least two of the people currently sitting at the council table. Instead she ate her porridge within the circle of friendship of these three young Calanians, which existed within the circle of this camp full of her people. Kyreen felt the peace of connection and of just *being*. As they finished their meal and headed towards the trees for sleep, Kyreen felt more complete than she had before, ready to face whatever waited when they awoke. They had all returned unscathed from a dangerous mission, brushing perilously close to their enemies without injury or detection. She had not blundered too poorly. She had made contact and connection with the gargoyle. But…but why had the gargoyle disappeared? What, or who, had drawn the creature from her side? These were Kyreen's final thoughts as she drifted off to sleep.

At mid-afternoon, when Aren and the others departed from the Council Tent, Kyreen, refreshed from her nap, waited for their exit. Lang's gaze briefly met hers before they each quickly looked away, both visibly uncomfortable. Aren moved away, avoiding Kyreen, who hurried after her.

"Kyreen, please," Aren said quietly. "I am not in the mood."

"Too bad. I am," Kyreen replied, surprising them both with her assertiveness.

Aren managed a wry smile, saying with a glance around the camp, "Fine. Let us take a walk. Find some privacy."

The pair headed away, into the woods, walking in silence until they found a small clearing, ample distance away from camp. Aware of their rather close proximity of the camp to the castle, ever mindful of random patrols, Kyreen kept her voice low.

"Aren, I apologize for taking Yngve and the others into the tunnels," she said. "I know my orders were to make contact with the gargoyle, nothing more. I had no right endangering…"

"Stop, Kyreen," Aren commanded quietly, holding up a hand. "I will admit I was livid this morning, upon hearing your report. But after you left, after the Council's discussions, after some contemplation, I realize you did exactly as I might have done, as any other Calanian probably would have done, as your mother most definitely would have done in your place. So, I realized my anger had nothing to do with you as the mission leader and everything to do with my emotions, with Yngve. The reality is that the four of you have infiltrated the castle farther than anyone else has in decades. Plus, you returned undetected. It was wrong of me to greet your report with anger. Therefore, please, accept my apologies."

Surprised, Kyreen nodded, mumbling, "Of course, Aren. I do not know what to say. I am unsure of how to respond."

"You can thank your friend Lang for opening my mind," Aren chuckled quietly.

"Friend? He most definitely is not…"

Aren halted Kyreen's words with her hand, smile widening. "I jest. Tis no secret the animosity you hold for Lang."

"The animosity that I…? Tis he who is hostile," Kyreen defended herself.

"Of course, it is, cousin," Aren placated Kyreen with a smile. "Of course, it is."

She placed an arm about Kyreen's should, turning them towards camp. "Come now. Let us return to camp so I may spend some time with my first-born before you lot leave."

A few hours later as twilight descended, Kyreen and her group headed out. With the castle mission complete, the rest of the camp also prepared to move away from this location at dawn. The Council Tent had been lowered and people had begun packing away the kitchen area. Tomorrow's breakfast would be cold rations on the trail.

Aren bade Kyreen farewell with a long hug, whispering in her ear, "You did well in the tunnel, cousin. Now you need to resolve your issues with Lang."

Kyreen pulled away, ready to protest.

"No," Aren said, her hands firmly gripping Kyreen's shoulders. "I am serious. Before the Spring Festival, this must be settled."

Aren's gaze held Kyreen's until the younger woman complied. With a shrug of her shoulders, Kyreen mumbled, "Fine. It will be done."

"By your word? By Spring Festival?"

Kyreen nodded as Aren pulled her in for a final hug, saying, "Safe journeys."

With farewells complete, the group of five headed out. Letting Yngve, Lang, and Ebbe move out front, Kyreen held her gelding back, partly to ride near Synnove, but mostly to avoid Lang and any confrontations. Not until they returned to the Training Camp without incident did she relax her defenses.

Chapter 7

For the first few days after returning from the mission, life settled into a comfortable routine of training and avoiding Lang. The latter activity Kyreen found more and more difficult as time went by. It seemed she could sense his presence everywhere she went. As a safety precaution, Kyreen avoided being alone, seeking out Synnove's companionship during any free time. In the mornings, instead of heading into the woods for solitary morning exercises as she had become accustomed to doing, Kyreen remained in her tent, reading. She took all her meals within her small circle of friends—Synnove, Yngve, and Ebbe. After evening exercises, Kyreen even attended the trainees' expeditions to the cliffs, avoiding the pools, but passing time at the nightly bonfire on the beach. Synnove, of course, took great joy at this transition in her tentmate. Although Kyreen suspected that Synnove had deduced the true reason behind Kyreen's new social behavior, the gregarious young Calanian took great pleasure at her tentmate's transition and seized every opportunity to set Kyreen up with a lover. Finally, almost a fortnight after their return, Kyreen decided she must speak with Synnove to stop this behavior.

"Synnove," she said, one evening after tracking exercises, as the pair were in their tent, preparing to head to the cliffs, "I must request you cease attempting to match me up with anyone."

"So, you have decided on someone then," Synnove looked innocent and sincere, but Kyreen could sense otherwise.

"No," Kyreen shook her head. "It is not like that. I do not need or want anyone right now."

Synnove regarded her tentmate silently for a long time, then finally she nodded. "Very well. I will cease my matchmaking. In return, I simply ask that you do not go back to your reclusive ways. Promise me you will accompany me to the cliffs in the evenings."

"Not every evening," Kyreen countered. "Every second night? As long as the weather is not foul."

"I agree to your terms," Synnove grinned, tugging on Kyreen's hand. "Now, I am claiming tonight as a cliff night, since you head to the city in the morning."

Laughing, Kyreen allowed Synnove to pull her out of the tent. As the two walked arm-in-arm across the clearing, neither took notice of the dark shadow lingering along the tree line.

The following morning, Kyreen found herself once more on the road to Myrddin, enjoying the warm weather, an early promise of summer. For the first leg of her trek, she relished the peace or more specifically the lack of tension, relief at being away from Lang. Strangely, though, the farther away the gelding carried her, the stronger the pull became, tugging her back towards camp. By the time the massive front gates of the capital city rose to greet her, Kyreen already felt ready to turn around, to return home. Home. With a jolt, she realized Calan had indeed become her home over these last several months, more a home than Hanoria ever had been.

Guilt about Jorn and Ildri immediately flooded the young woman's mind. Her foster parents had done their best to make the young orphan a home and the elderly pair had been caring surrogate parents. Hanorian parents, Kyreen thought, pulling the gelding into the queue to enter Myrddin. As a Calanian child, she had needed Calanian parents. A flash of understanding, now so many years later, lifted the heaviness from her soul that Kyreen had not been aware of, and now her memories of her Hanorian family settled back into place, unburdened by the guilt.

With a smile upon her lips, Kyreen entered the city, still bustling with activity on a market day, but less crowded due to the late winter's chill, for the pleasant spring of the Calanian coast had not followed Kyreen to Myrddin. Here the damp salt air hung in heavy fog and chilled Kyreen to her bones as the gelding maneuvered the streets to the stable. The stablemaster Ifor, the same man who had assisted Collin just last year, though it felt so much longer ago, took the gelding's reins from Kyreen.

"How long?" he inquired curtly. Knowing him to be gruff by nature, Kyreen had learned not to take offense at the stable master's brusque mannerisms.

Kyreen hesitated. The camp did not expect her back for a sennight or more, but she had no desire to linger in the city.

"Three days," she finally replied, adding, "Maybe less. I will send word if I intend to leave sooner."

The stablemaster nodded and turned to lead the gelding into the shadowy stables. As always, Kyreen's heart tightened anxiously watching her horse walk away. Swallowing the lump in her throat, she strode away towards her first destination.

"Kyreen!" Engla squealed upon seeing her best friend enter the room behind Glain. The petite woman sat in bed, her loosed hair billowing in a golden cloud around her, a tiny blanketed bundle in her arms. "Ye are just in time. The babe has just finished nursing."

"Ye were correct," Glain commented, a hint of animosity tinging her voice, just enough for Kyreen to hear and feel, but not so much that Engla noticed. "Twas a boy."

Kyreen saved herself from answering by scooping the proffered babe from Engla's arms. She smiled down at the cherub with a milk-sated expression, drooping gray-blue eyes, rosebud mouth still smacking quietly.

"He is beautiful," she pronounced to the anxiously waiting mother.

Sensing Engla was about to burst with pride and with Glain still hovering like a disapproving mother hen, Kyreen asked, just to get her friend talking, "How was the birth?"

As Engla launched into her tale, Glain stoked the fire then excused herself to the kitchen to continue the supper preparations that Kyreen's arrival had interrupted. Kyreen moved over to settle into the rocking chair in the corner, a piece of furniture she recognized from Engla's home in Hanoria. Softly rocking and snuggling the babe, she listened absently to her friend.

Engla beamed watching her newborn babe in the arms of her best friend. Sitting in the large bed, propped up with bunches of pillows, she looked so tiny, reminding Kyreen of the young girl she had met so many years ago. Watching the firelight glint off Engla's beautiful golden hair, Kyreen realized she could not recall ever having seen her friend's hair unbound. It had always been braided when they were children and, once Engla had reached adulthood, the braids had been coiled up around her head. Though Engla's blue eyes sparkled, Kyreen detected a weariness within her friend's countenance that matched the pallor of her friend's fair skin. Engla's fatigue went beyond the quick and routine birth she had described in great detail to Kyreen. Something else bothered Kyreen's friend.

Kyreen gazed down at the now sleeping babe, still listening with half-an-ear.

"Glain has been an angel. I do not know what I would have done without her assistance and counsel these last several days since the baby's arrival."

"What about your family?" Kyreen gestured to the rocking chair upon which she sat, keeping her voice low so as not to wake the newborn. "Did they bring this when they visited?"

"Mama and Poppa will be visiting shortly," Engla replied. "They wanted to wait until the birth before making the trip. We brought the chair back with us after our visit to Hanoria, me and... Collin."

Kyreen noted the hesitation and sadness when Engla mentioned her husband for the first time. So that is it, she thought. Aloud, she asked, "And Stian? Will he be joining your parents on their trip?"

"Tis doubtful," Engla answered with a shake of her head. "The farmstead keeps him busy these days. Between the herd and the wheat, he will not be able to get away."

Of course, Kyreen thought, but did not say anything aloud. Birthing season was just beginning. Depending on how well the herd had bred last summer, Stian could expect up to a dozen or more foals. Coupled with his desire to farm, it would take all his youthful ambition and strong friends to get the long barren fields planted. Recalling their many discussions, Kyreen remembered that wheat had always been Stian's ambition.

Glain's return announced the evening meal ready, interrupting the friends' reminiscing. Kyreen placed the swaddled baby, still sound asleep, in the waiting cradle before moving to assist Engla from the bed.

Once standing Engla slid her arms around Kyreen for a proper hug, alarming the Calanian at her friend's leanness. Though never a large person and short in stature, Engla had always been curvaceous with the ample bosom and birthing hips typical of Hanorian women. Now, under the voluminous nightgown, Engla felt like skin and bone. Kyreen pulled back from the hug to gaze down into her friend's face, noticing for the first time the gauntness of the young woman's features. When she had first arrived, given the shadows of the dim room, Kyreen had failed to notice, but now up close within the fire's full light, the hollows of Engla's cheeks and sharp bones of her clavicle could clearly be seen.

"Engla?" Kyreen asked quietly startled. "Have you been ill? You made the birth sound uneventful."

Engla avoided Kyreen's gaze, turning away to pick up the dressing gown lying at the foot of her bed. Pulling on the garment, she cinched it tight about her waist and pushed her feet into the waiting slippers before answering.

"Ye have always been so observant, Kyreen. I do not know why I thought I could hide from ye after all these years," she remarked, adding, "but I do not wish to discuss the matter except to say I had hoped my son would meet his father before he met my best friend."

Engla started for the door, teetering off-balance, so precariously close to falling that Kyreen had to leap forward to steady her friend. Arm in arm, the pair silently made their way out of the room, towards the kitchen. Kyreen's thoughts spiraled at Engla's revelation. The baby's birth had happened almost a sennight hence, yet Collin had not been home? No wonder Engla had not conducted a proper introduction upon Kyreen's arrival as Hanorian convention dictated. For tradition held that the father would reveal a son's name. Without Collin's presence, it could be Engla did not know what the babe's name would be. Kyreen could not imagine Rhun sending the prospective father out to sea or even out of the city so close to Engla's due date, but evidently Collin had taken to staying at the guild hall. That Kyreen could understand, but to not come to his home, to support his wife, to see his son? That she could not forgive.

Supper was a quiet event taken in the kitchen with just the three women. Glain explained that she currently had no long-term boarders and had stopped taking any new ones just until Engla recovered. As Kyreen ate, she watched her best friend pick at the food upon her plate. After the effort of getting out of bed and walking to the kitchen, simply sitting at the table appeared to sap all of Engla's remaining energies. She did not attempt at all to keep up pretenses or engage in the limited conversation. Never had Kyreen witnessed her usually loquacious friend so quiet, lacking sparkle, so apathetic. Engla had always been vibrant, always busy with some task, and always vocal.

After Glain and Kyreen had finished eating and their plates cleared, Engla excused herself.

"The babe will be waking soon, ready for another nursing," she said, pushing away from the table, using the momentum to propel her body towards the bedroom.

After watching her friend safely make the short trek, Kyreen picked up the abandoned plate, still full, nary a morsel eaten. She carried it to Glain, working to clean their dinner dishes.

"Ye tell that lad he best come home," Glain hissed at Kyreen, her voice quiet yet venomous. She vigorously scrubbed a pot, avoiding eye contact with the taller woman.

"Me?" Kyreen asked.

"Aye," Glain replied, shooting an acidic glance up at the Calanian. "When ye get to the hall for your meeting."

This last word Glain spat, as though she had a bad taste in her mouth. She continued, keeping her voice down so as not to alert Engla, "I know ye have been going to the hall when ye leave here. Tis disgraceful! That poor girl in there has enough troubles with Collin and now with a new bairn, all without a traitorous, so called friend mucking about."

Taken aback, Kyreen's brow furrowed. "Yes, I do visit the guild hall. My people have a contract…"

"I do not give one care to hear ye stories," Glain interrupted. "All I care about is that bairn and his mother. She has the birthing sadness, has it hard. And, Collin, the father of her child, her *husband*? He needs to be here, not frolicking about with some green-eyed strumpet."

"Fine," Kyreen responded, her face flush with the accusation, but knowing she would not convince Glain otherwise. "I shall seek Collin out and speak with him."

Glain nodded brusquely before turning way, dismissing Kyreen, who walked to the bedroom. The baby had awakened, but still lay in the cradle, softly squirming and making quiet gurgling noises. Back in bed, Engla had burrowed into the linens, her back to the door, only the top of her golden blonde head showing. Kyreen paused at the cradle, placing a hand upon the child's swaddled form, gazing down at him thoughtfully. The child stilled, his unfocused eyes gazing dimly back up at her. She stroked a light finger down his cheek before placing a soft hand upon his head, covered in dark down, then issued up a silent prayer to any deity that may be listening, Hanorian's Ten Lords of Hayrik, her own Calanian goddess, the stoic omnipotent martyr of the Myrddins. She prayed for blessings upon this innocent soul, that his journey through life might be full of light and love, and that he might be spared the pain of loss for many years. Though deep in her heart, Kyreen felt her prayer to be in vain, she still thought the words and sealed them with a gentle kiss to the babe's forehead.

Next Kyreen moved to the bed, sitting gingerly upon the edge. She placed a hand upon the crown of Engla's head, much like she had just done with the newborn, but this time, instead of praying Kyreen opened her awareness, dropping the mental barriers she now kept in place around her own people. Kyreen allowed Engla's emotions to wash over her. The despair. The loneliness. The fear. This all hit Kyreen hard. Such anguish had never been a part of Engla.

"Oh, my friend," she whispered, her eyes filling with tears. "I am so very sorry."

Standing, Kyreen took a deep, centering breath. Breaking contact relieved the intensity of Engla's despondency, but the residual emotions lingered, a sourness in the back of her throat. The second deep, cleansing breath ignited Kyreen's anger, which burned hot, quickly snuffing out the sadness.

Kyreen strode out of the room and into the kitchen, startling Glain who turned around in surprise, thinking something was amiss with Engla or the babe. Kyreen collected her knapsack and sword from where they rested by the decoy fireplace.

"Tell Engla I shall return tomorrow or the following day, most likely midday, after my meetings are concluded, but before I head back to Calan," Kyreen paused from fastening the sword harness to glance at Glain. "I know you do not believe me, Glain, but that woman in there is very precious to me, as is her child. I would never knowingly do anything to harm her, especially something as dreadful as bedding her husband. I plan to do whatever I can to make this better. I may not be able to cure her, but I can drag Collin back here by his boots if that is necessary."

Without waiting for Glain to respond, Kyreen turned, fastening the last binding on the sword harness as she exited the house.

Chapter 8

The flames of Kyreen's anger stoked with every step. Her boots rang out on the cobblestones a quick, harsh staccato. Heart pounding, she hurried through the dusk lit streets, thankful for the thinning crowds given the hour. By the time Kyreen reached the guild hall's street, she practically sprinted. Hesitating at the corner, she stared at the stone steps leading to the main entrance. Since her appointment to discuss the trade contracts was not scheduled until the next morning, she doubted the sentries would grant her entry. Even as the thought crossed her mind, her hand drifted to her chest, feeling for the small metal key hidden under her shirt, resting against her skin.

With a final glance, up and down the street, Kyreen made an impulsive decision and headed into the alley way. At the side door, once again ensuring there were no observers, she turn the key in the lock and slipped inside the building. Unlike her previous visits, this time Kyreen headed left, away from the upper levels, down the hall winding to the main floor, towards the noisy refectory.

At this time of day, the fairly full dining hall inhabitants could be divided into three groups—men just finishing up their evening meal and ready to depart; men just newly arriving for an evening of drinking; and the last group, the one Collin most likely fell into, men finished or finishing their meal who were already well into that night's drinking.

Kyreen paused, initially unnoticed, at the entrance, peered around the doorframe, her eyes scanning the massive hall. The room's air was cloudy, not from the lanterns, their flame turned low, suspended about the space, but from the cheroots and cigarillos favored by the handful of men indulging in a heavier liquor than a tankard of ale. The musky scent of men, a mix of stale sweat and old beer hung heavy in the room, assaulting the Calanian's senses.

Then Kyreen spotted him at a table across the room, closer to the far wall, surrounded by several guild mates. As she suspected, the group appeared well into their nightly drunk. An empty tankard rested on the table before Collin, who held another in his hand. A lively conversation flew amongst the men, commencing in a roar of laughter as they all lifted their tankards high to toast before swiftly downing the contents.

Kyreen unsuccessfully attempted to quell the memories rising to the surface. The last time she had seen Collin had been in this very building, that dark night the previous summer when Falk had been stopped for good, when Kyreen had taken the Faldorian mercenary's life. Kyreen recalled Engla, and how she had looked that evening. Not bound and gagged, but after the fight, rescued from her kidnappers. Standing in the training hall that resided somewhere beneath Kyreen's feet, between Stian and Collin, her golden hair glittering in the torchlight, her bright blue eyes glistening with love for the two men, looking so youthful, so beautiful, so vibrant, so alive. The anger, which had receded within Kyreen, flared anew.

Without taking her eyes from Collin, Kyreen began weaving her way through the jumble of tables. At first the men she passed paid the woman no heed as Kyreen dressed in trousers, her curls no longer than some of the men present. Slowly, however, one or two took notice, then several. By the time Kyreen had almost reached Collin's table, many conversations around the room had ceased, a hush falling in her wake. Collin and his companions, engrossed in their own circle, were slow to recognize the change in atmosphere. As Kyreen paused at their table, however, Collin turned his face her way. The tankard froze, poised halfway between his lips and the table, the man promptly forgetting which way he had been taking it.

Even without the Calanian's empathic abilities, Collin knew Kyreen's appearance here at his table, in the mess hall, in his guild hall, would not be a social call. His heart simultaneously skipped a beat and jumped into his throat. He coughed softly to clear said throat and set down the tankard. Collin stalled, licking his suddenly dry lips, his mind racing for what to say. He had forgotten the intensity of her direct gaze, and freshly experienced the wonderment at her exotic beauty, the dazzling emerald eyes, a cloud of ebony curls much longer than the last time he had seen her, the alabaster skin taut against granite features, which only reminded him how soft her body could be. A part of Collin longed to wrap his arms around Kyreen, slide his fingers through those silky curls, and press his lips to hers. The rest of him, however, the survivalist part, recognizing the anger in those glittering eyes and merciless press of her lips, reacted quite differently.

Collin scrambled ungracefully off the bench from between his two comrades, awkwardly finding his feet to shuffle backwards, towards the wall behind the table, away from Kyreen.

Without speaking, Kyreen followed him, wanting Collin to move away from the table, away from his support group, but she could see time had run out. Collin's tablemates had ceased talking and were staring at the stranger glaring at their pal. Like a ripple on a lake, other tables, other men, even the handful of women serving alcohol, stilled and turned their full attention to the pair, Collin clumsily making his way through the tables ever backwards and Kyreen gracefully sliding in his wake, her eyes never leaving her prey.

Just as he reached the outer ring of tables, Collin tripped. He had been looking over his shoulder and, whether from his inebriated state or his panic, had misjudged the final obstacle, an empty chair. As Collin went sprawling into the hallway, onto the hard marble floor, Kyreen swiftly closed the distance between them stopping directly over the fallen man. When Collin rolled to his back and stared drunkenly up at her, Kyreen paused, dreading some residual flicker of her former emotions. She had always worried what her reaction would be the first time confronted with him. To her great relief, meeting his hazel eyes merely stoked the anger in her blood. No lust, no love, not even pity. Rage roaring anew, she bent down, prepared to haul the man to his feet. Unseen hands from behind, however, pulled her away, multiple men having surged forward to restrain her.

Bolstered by the support of his guild mates, Collin rose shakily to his feet, his muddled brain racing. Leaning back against the wall to mask his dizziness, he stared at Kyreen a long moment before speaking.

"What are ye thinking, ye crazed doxy? Coming for me like this? In my home? I told ye last summer. We are through. Let it be, woman!"

Unsure laughter rippled through the onlooking crowd. Kyreen quirked an eyebrow at the man, too angry to be shocked or embarrassed by his statement. After a long moment, she relaxed, shrugging.

"Fine. If this is the way you wish to play at this, Collin," she replied, spatting out his name as though it brought a bad taste to her mouth. "Have these men release me so they all can witness my amorous intentions."

She glanced over each of her shoulders at the men grasping her arms. Beyond them, the entire hall's attention focused on the scene. Several men had risen to their feet, a hand upon their weapons. She brought her gaze back to Collin, continuing her verbal taunt, "Unless, of course, realizing my true intentions you are afraid of me."

As she finished speaking, Kyreen relaxed her body, going limp so as to slip to her knees and out of the grip of those restraining her. Rolling forward, she crossed the distance between her and Collin before anyone could react. Popping back to her feet, she grabbed Collin's shirt front, drawing his face close to hers.

"I am here for Engla, your wife, your *ill* wife, who is laying abed, after birthing *your* child, a healthy little bairn, a son. Right now, I do not care your excuse for abandoning them, nor do I care to be in your presence, but my friend wants her husband home, so I intend to deliver you to her, willingly or unwillingly."

Collin's eyes widened and he struggled against Kyreen's hold. When she pulled back a hand, fully intending to slap him across the face, a dark hand wrapped around her wrist, staying the strike.

"That is enough," Rhun stated quietly, stepping in between the two.

He faced Kyreen, his angry dark gaze staring into her glittering emerald eyes for a long moment, before glancing towards the group of Collin's friends.

"Tremain, Owen, you two please escort Collin to his home. The lady is correct. It is past time for Collin to meet his son," Rhun commanded, before glancing over his shoulder at Collin. "I do not want to see you in this hall for at least three days. Do you understand?"

"But she... I have..." Colling stammered.

"Do. You. Understand?" Rhun repeated, his tone and his expression making it clear he did not wish to repeat the phrase again.

"Yes," Colling muttered sullenly.

Rhun returned his gaze to Kyreen.

"You come with me," he said, tightening his grip around her wrist, swiftly leading her out of the dining hall.

Kyreen, consciously aware of every eye trained on her, followed him meekly. Although Rhun outwardly appeared calm, waves of anger rolled off of him. Once in the hallway, Kyreen opened her mouth to speak, but Rhun merely tugged at her arm, quickening his pace.

"Not. Here," he snapped quietly, between gritted teeth.

Instead of heading up towards his private quarters, Rhun took Kyreen through a hidden passageway. The tight twisting corridor, dimly lit with flameless orbs, wound around a few times with a number of branches and doorways, before terminating at a closed door. Rhun clicked the latch and the pair emerged into the guild master's public office, via a hidden panel behind the desk. Rhun released Kyreen's arm to raise the flames of the lanterns scattered about the room. Judging from his mood, she determined that this would not be the time to ask him why he did not use the strange lighted orbs in here instead of the flames. Instead she took a step into the room, glancing about the office. Though she had been to the guild hall many times, this was her first visit to Rhun's official office.

Unlike his personal quarters upstairs, this room did not reflect the guild master's personality at all. A rich tapestry of reds, blues and golds covered the marble flooring. In the center of the room, monopolizing the space, stood a big mahogany desk, looking more like a statement piece than a comfortable piece of furniture. The chair behind the desk, however, looked inviting with rich burgundy leather, as did the matching pair of leather guest chairs. Tucked unobtrusively against a wall sat a leather couch, flanked by a number of wooden straight-backed chairs. Kyreen judged the seating available could handle a dozen people. Decorations were limited to a handful of oil paintings, all depicting seafaring vessels, hung upon the paneled walls.

Completing his lighting task, Rhun moved to stand behind the massive desk. Placing his hands flat on the surface, he leaned on it, head bowed, eyes closed. Kyreen stood with her back to the hidden panel through which they had entered, watching the man centering himself without speaking, something a Calanian would do, or maybe he counted to ten silently, something she had witnessed her Hanorian foster father Jorn do, in an attempt to calm the anger that continued to radiate off of him. She nibbled at her bottom lip, but wisely held her tongue. Her own anger, so hot against Collin, had dissipated. Now she stood perplexed while the large man before her struggled to regain his composure.

After what felt to Kyreen to be an eternity but was merely a few moments, Rhun sighed quietly and raised his dark eyes to stare at Kyreen. When he spoke, his voice remained quiet, though tinged with a fury Kyreen had never experienced from this man before.

"I do not know what to say, Kyreen, except that your actions have deeply wounded me."

"My actions wounded you?" Kyreen said. Taken aback she stepped towards the desk. "I have done nothing to you, Rhun. I merely called out that louse for shirking his duty. How could that…"

She paused when Rhun lifted a hand, shaking his head.

"Those were your words, Kyreen," he replied.

"I do not deny Collin needed confronting but," he continued, pausing to stand up straight, his fierce gaze boring into her anew, "everything you did up to then, gaining access to the building, using a key *I* gave you, publicly accosting one of my men, someone I as guild master am sworn to protect. All this you did against me, breaking my trust, snubbing my authority."

Rhun paused, taking a deep breath. "Truth be told, I am more disappointed and angry with myself than I am with you."

Kyreen quirked a brow, silently questioning, not yet trusting herself to speak calmly.

"By giving you that key, I broke one of the most sacred assurances of our guild. This building is meant to be a haven where my men can relax and be safe. Now I must go before my men tomorrow morning to admit my transgression."

"Rhun," Kyreen said quietly, her hand drifted to the key freshly hidden beneath her tunic to draw it out and over her head, extending it to him. "I am sorry. I did not think…"

"No, you did not!" Rhun snapped, his voice, though tight with anger, remained eerily calm. "You did not consider why you had that key. You did not think about the trust I placed in you with its gift. In short you did not think of me at all."

Rhun sighed again, settling down into the big wingback desk chair.

Chastised, Kyreen stood in silence, her face burning with shame. What Rhun had said was true. So focused had she been in her fury, acting out in a rage so blind that not only had she not considered the rashness of her actions, but the possibility that they might affect this man had never entered her thoughts.

"Rhun, I am truly sorry," she said again, her voice and posture both expressing the sincerity of her apology this time. She placed the key upon the desk between them, turning to leave.

Rhun's voice stopped her before she reached the door.

"You do not have to go," he paused, adding, "unless you so desire."

Kyreen turned around, standing with her back pressing against the door. "I do not wish to leave," she confessed.

Rhun wearily waved her to one of the chairs flanking his desk. "I was just about to have my dinner when… you arrived," he said. "Are you hungry?"

"Not for food," Kyreen admitted, a twinkle in her eyes which drifted towards the panel hiding the secret passage. "Does that perhaps lead upstairs?"

"Yes, it does," Rhun chuckled, shaking his head, "but we will not be going upstairs this evening."

"No?" Kyreen inquired, arching one eyebrow suggestively.

"No," he replied, his tone amiable and a playful smile upon his lips. "I cannot risk taking you up to my quarters right now."

Kyreen bit at the inside of her cheek, torn between the two extreme emotions of playfully teasing or bursting into anger. With great effort, she quelled both to neutrally ask, "Risk?"

"Kyreen, you improperly gained entry into this building," Rhun explained patiently. "You then very publicly verbally assaulted a well-known and well-liked member of the guild, an officer no less. God in heaven only knows what physical damage you might have done to the man had you been permitted to continue. All this you did before no less than 200 members of my guild, my men, my responsibility. No doubt news of this altercation has already travelled to anyone not present except those few currently at sea, but you can be certain of that lot hearing of it as soon as they make dock."

Rhun stood up and moved around to stand before Kyreen. He gazed down at her a long moment before continuing, "I will not deny I had been very much looking forward to this evening, but you will be gone once the contact agreements are finalized. These men are not only my responsibility, but they are also my only family. This place, this hall, it is my home. This is where I live." He raised a hand to silence Kyreen who had opened her mouth to speak. "Allow me to finish, please."

She closed her mouth, nodding.

"I have greatly relished our times together, but we both know these few quick trysts are just that. Our lives are too different, and that is fine with me. I expect no commitment and ask nothing from you except your company. That said, after tonight's debacle, you are welcome to stay in my office, but that is as far as you can go."

"Is it?" she asked, arching an eyebrow at the guild master.

When he returned the look with a grin of his own, she drew her shirt over her head. Stepping up to press her body to his, her other hand slipped around his neck, pulling his face down to hers for a kiss.

A while later, Kyreen reclined upon the leather sofa, wrapped in a woolen blanket, her forgotten clothes strewn about the office floor. From the hallway, she could hear Rhun speaking with someone, but she could not make out the words. Just as she rose to a sitting position, the blanket wrapped about her shoulders, and reached for the first of her garments, Rhun entered, closing the door behind him. Kyreen was unsure if he had purposefully blocked the doorway to shield her from seeing out or to prevent the person outside from gazing in. Probably both, she decided, silently watching him place the covered plate and two tankards down on the desk. Strolling over to Kyreen, Rhun gathered up her clothing, placing it in a pile on her lap.

"Time to dress," he stated, then turned back to the plate of food.

"Am I going somewhere?" she inquired. "I thought you said I was welcome to stay here in your office."

"It occurred to me that you may be more comfortable spending the evening in a bed," Rhun explained, bringing the plate of food to the settee and settling down beside her. He placed a soft kiss upon the exposed shoulder closest to him, adding, "As delightful as this couch has been, you so rarely have the opportunity for linens and a bed and such. Therefore, I have made arrangements for you to lodge at a nearby pub."

Before Kyreen could respond, he kissed her lips, saying, "Dress while I eat. Someone very inconsiderately interrupted my evening meal and, for some reason, I am particularly famished right now."

Kyreen chuckled, unable to feel offended and began drawing on her clothes. Rhun, his eyes following her movements, set to work on his recently delivered replacement dinner.

Just as Kyreen pulled on her second boot, there came another knock at the door. Rhun quickly stood, placing his almost empty plate upon the desk, and moved to the door. As he stepped into the hall, once again blocking the doorway from view, Kyreen stood and drifted over to the desk to gaze upon the half-empty platter. Seeing nothing to her liking, she sniffed at the tankards. Ale. Her nose wrinkled in distaste. Rhun stepped back into the office, catching her leaned over the tankards.

He chuckled, motioning with his chin to the heretofore unnoticed side table. "Mead is over there if you are wanting liquid. Here," he said, placing a small wrapped package on the desk beside his place, "are some treats I had wrapped up for you."

"You are too good to me, Rhun. Thank you!" Eagerly Kyreen tugged at the string around the small box, but her glance at the other item in the guild master's hand stilled her hand.

"This?" Rhun asked, seeing her questioning gaze. He held up the contraption that looked similar to a bow but yet was not. "This is called a crossbow. A new design from across the Great Sea. A shipment arrived from the New Territories a week ago."

"It is a remarkable contraption," he continued, his dark eyes sparkling. "Once the string is drawn, it is locked in place here, so the shooter does not have to exert any strength to keep it drawn whilst knocking the bolt in place and aiming."

To demonstrate his point, Rhun transferred the loaded weapon to one hand and picked up a tankard with the other for a sip. He then slipped the bolt from its perch and unlocked the string, saying, "Quite a remarkable weapon."

Kyreen set the unopened box of sweets on the desk and reached for the crossbow. "May I?"

Rhun nodded, handing her the crossbow. He sipped at his ale, watching her heft the weapon, testing its weight and balance. She found the weapon to be surprisingly balanced, not nearly as bulky and unwieldy as it had appeared. She made this comment to Rhun who nodded.

"Aye, it surprised me as well," Rhun answered, picking up a cross bolt to show her. "These, however, are not light or ineffective. The damage they inflict is just as deadly if not more so as a normal bow."

"I would like to send this back to Calan with you," he said, adding, "for Viggo."

"The draw can be operated with one hand," Kyreen remarked, at once realizing what this could mean for her cousin's mate, as she pulled the string back into the latch. It was not easy and would take some practice to feel natural, but it was a viable weapon for Viggo, something to replace his bow. "This is remarkable, Rhun! Thank you so much for…. everything."

She released the string then threw her arms around Rhun. The big man's thoughtfulness and generosity never ceased to amaze her. Though he had never met Viggo, Rhun had remembered their discussions about Kyreen's concerns for her cousin's mate over his injuries from last summer, the damage to his shoulder, the shredded muscles, his inability to hold the draw on his bow, and his mental well-being.

Now Kyreen pulled back to gaze up at Rhun. "I cannot express how very grateful I am, nor can I ever repay you," she said. "You are the most generous person I have ever known."

"I have received plenty of compensation," he replied, leaning down to kiss her thoroughly.

When they parted, Kyreen asked, "So is this bed at the inn big enough for the both of us?"

"Most definitely," he murmured, trailing soft kisses along her jaw line to nibble at her neck. "But only if that is what you desire, my dear."

Kyreen placed a finger beneath the man's chin to tip his face back up to hers.

"Oh, yes." she whispered. "I do desire."

Chapter 9

Three days later Kyreen rode into the Council Camp. The contract agreement had been easily negotiated and, while she enjoyed her time with Rhun, she had been anxious to return. When Gunda ran out excitedly to greet her older cousin, Kyreen chuckled at the young Calanian's enthusiasm. Inwardly, however, she admitted it felt good to be met by a family member at the edge of camp, to have someone notice her arrival, to not be invisible.

"How is Engla?" Gunda inquired after Kyreen had dismounted and the two had embraced.

"She is recovering," Kyreen answered, having decided to avoid the topic of Engla's melancholy, of Collin's behavior, and that she had only seen Engla the one time upon her arrival in the city.

As the contract negotiation meeting had been drawing to an end, Kyreen had sent word to Engla that she would be stopping by before leaving the city. Instead of receiving a routine response, however, Glain had shown up at the guild hall, requesting to see Kyreen.

"Ye need not bother the lass, "Glain had stated directly, not beating around the bush or even pausing for social niceties such as greeting Kyreen when she walked up.

Rhun, who had accompanied Kyreen to the guild hall foyer, quirked a brow. "Good afternoon, Mistress Glain," he remarked quietly.

Glain had started at the big man's presence. So intent had she been on Kyreen, she had not noticed his entrance. Immediately, Glain curtsied and responded with her belated salutation. Kyreen had realized this had been the first time she had interacted with Glain outside of the boarding house. The woman appeared flustered, nervous, her hands wringing at the bag she held. As she watched the other woman genuflect to the guild leader, Kyreen wondered the source of Glain's anxiety. Was she truly intimidated by the guild hall and the presence of the guild master? Was she nervous outside her personal domain? Or perhaps it had nothing to do with the environment and everything to do with the message she conveyed?

"Are those Engla's words?" Kyreen had inquired, not bothering to respond with her own salutations. Keeping her gaze fixed on Glain, Kyreen suppressed a smile as she felt rather than saw Rhun's resignation at Kyreen's own rudeness.

'He can play diplomat,' she thought. 'I shall be the crude lummox.'

Glain shifted nervously, her gaze swinging from Kyreen to Rhun. "Aye," she replied unconvincingly. "The lass does nay wish tae see ye."

Kyreen inhaled, prepared to unleash a torrent of angry questions, but Rhun stopped her with a light hand upon her shoulder.

Seeing Rhun restrain Kyreen bolstered Glain's confidence. The woman straightened up, lifting her chin to glare up at the taller woman.

"Engla does nay wish tae see ye," she had repeated. "We heard how ye attacked Collin last night..."

Kyreen started at these words and opened her mouth to interrupt. Rhun, however, increased the pressure upon her shoulder, lightly squeezing, just enough to stay Kyreen's question as Glain continued unchecked, her words rapidly building up speed.

"...Kyreen, lass, ye must know that ye have lost. Collin does nay wish tae be with ye. He is wed to Engla. Ye need to move on, accept it, girl. Quit mooning over him. Ye have to stop coming around, sniffing after him like..."

"Enough," Rhun had commanded quietly. He stepped to Glain, taking her elbow and spinning the woman around so as to escort her toward the exit. "You have delivered your message. Thank you."

With that Rhun had shepherded Glain out, quickly returning to a fuming Kyreen. Seeing the flush of her cheeks, Rhun had suggested that they retire to his office for mid-day meal before Kyreen headed back to Calan.

Kyreen had nodded, holding her tongue until the door had closed behind them.

"How could she... who does Glain think she is? Warning me? Off of...Collin?" Kyreen had spun around focusing her frustration toward Rhun. "And you? Why did you stop me? That woman had no right... She was clearly lying. Engla would never, send a message... like... like that..."

Kyreen had paused for a breath, Rhun's expression spoiling some of her anger. "What is so amusing?"

Rhun had pushed away from the door to slide his arms around Kyreen, lightly kissing her lips before replying, "You are. So animated. Such emotion."

Kyreen had pulled back slightly, still enclosed within his light embrace, "I am glad you find me amusing. But that woman is lying and delivering false message. And worse she thinks I am sabotaging my best friend's marriage!"

"What does it matter?" Rhun had responded, gazing down at Kyreen. "You know the truth. What would come from you confronting Glain? Another public quarrel? What good could come from that? Glain would never believe you. Any argument or protestations from you would merely reinforce Glain's suspicions; just convince her more that you are still in love with Collin."

"That man," Kyreen had muttered, grimacing, the acerbic taste of bile rising in her mouth.

"Now we get to the root of the issue," Rhun had grinned.

"I just wish I could forget the whole thing with Collin," Kyreen had admitted. "Every time I think about it, about him and me, about our time together, I feel such the fool. Goddess knows I wish I never met the man, let alone…" She let her voice trail off, sighing.

Rhun had pulled Kyreen to him for a tight embrace, murmuring into her hair, "I, for one, am ecstatic you met him. As for what transpired between you two, that is history. We mere mortals do not have the luxury of re-writing our past."

Kyreen had slid her arms around Rhun, settling into his warm embrace. "You are right, as usual," she said. "Thank you for saving me from myself and another embarrassment."

"Besides I still have to go before my men at this afternoons meeting to clean up last night's mess. I do not need another public assault to explain away," Rhun had chuckled feeling Kyreen tense "Relax. I am joking."

"And the babe?" Gunda's question jarred Kyreen back to the present.

"Healthy. Beautiful," Kyreen replied with a genuine smile.

"These," Kyreen said, reaching into her sack and pulling out a small white box tied with twine, "are for you."

Gunda squealed her delight, taking the proffered box and hugging Kyreen, all without releasing the gelding's reins.

Kyreen watched Gunda work her way into the box containing an assortment of sweet confections, leftovers from the pile Rhun kept on hand.

Since discovering she and Gunda shared a fondness for sweets, Kyreen made sure to bring treats for the youngster

"You spoil her," Viggo commented, having walked up.

"Do not be too hasty in your judgment of me," Kyreen replied as the two embraced, "for I come bearing a gift for you as well."

"Me?" Viggo looked perplexed, his gaze moving to the bulky package in the woman's hands.

Kyreen dropped to her knees, placing the package on the ground. Deftly she untied the twine and pulled the canvas covering away to reveal the crossbow and bolt case.

"A gift from Rhun in truth," she said, picking up the weapon to hold it out for him. "It is a…"

"Crossbow," Viggo interrupted quietly.

He took the weapon in his hands, his expression unreadable.

Kyreen nibbled at her bottom lip, as she watched her cousin's mate. Had she offended the man? Was it the gift? Was it about his injury? What had seemed like such a grand idea in Myrddin suddenly felt awkward. She rose to her feet, dusting the dirt from her trousers.

"Viggo, I apologize if…"

"No, Kyreen. Nothing for which to apologize," he interrupted a second time, a smile on his face. "This is truly wonderful. Thank you."

Kyreen relaxed, a smile breaking out on her face. "I worried I yet again messed up."

"No, no!" Viggo laughed, shifting the crossbow to one hand so as to draw his other arm around Kyreen's shoulder and hug her to him. "I was merely lost in my thoughts. I have not seen one of these since I was but a lad."

He leaned over to pick up the bolt case. "Brynja could probably fashion up more bolts," Viggo commented, referring to the camp's weapons smith. "Do you mind if I take my leave to find her? When do you head back to training?"

Kyreen shook her head. "Of course. I need to report in anyway. We can talk over dinner. I look forward to hearing how the crossbow works. Depending on the Council, I should be heading back in the morning."

After an evening in the Council Camp, which included a lengthy visit with Aren, Viggo and their two youngest children, Reidar and Gunda,

Kyreen headed back to the Training Camp first thing the following morning. As they hugged farewell, Aren reminded Kyreen about her vow to resolve her issues with Lang. This conundrum occupied Kyreen's thoughts on her ride back to the cliffside camp. Without any encounters of patrols, Kyreen made very good time, and afternoon training sessions were in session when she rode into camp. After caring for her mount and grabbing some food for midday meal, she found her fellow trainees assembled along the saltgrass meadow near the cliffs overlooking the beach.

The day had dawned clear and warm, an early promise of summer heat beating down upon the entire group. As she approached Kyreen saw the trainees standing in a circle around two people engaged in hand-to-hand combat. One of the participants in the spar was Ebbe, and the other, much to Kyreen's surprise was Lang. Never before had the instructor participated in sparring. Evidently his wounds which had been preventing him from sparring had finally healed sufficiently to allow him to once again train.

Kyreen stepped up to the circle behind Synnove, who smiled briefly over her shoulder at her tentmate before returning her attentions back to the match. Under the warmth of the day both competitors had removed their shirts, and Kyreen could not help but compare the two men. Amidst a people given to tallness, both Ebbe and Lang stood amongst the tallest. Aside from their similar height, with Lang just a bit taller, their bodies could not have been more different. Where Ebbe reminded Kyreen of a bear with his wide shoulders, heavily muscled limbs and broad face, she thought of Lang as a mountain lion, lean and lithe. Relieved of his tunic, Kyreen could see the wiry muscles, but also the sharp angles of his body, ribs and clavicle. She wondered if he had lost weight over the winter season due to his injury from last summer's skirmish. She took this rare opportunity to gaze openly upon Lang's face, and noticed his features, always chiseled and beautiful, now looked more severe, bordering on gaunt, with shadows in the hollows of his cheeks that his beard could not disguise. Even so, she felt her body respond to the sight of his body, so dropped her eyes to the angry pink slash along his toned abdomen, the scar stark against his pale skin. It had been a wide gash, a jagged laceration that spanned almost hip bone to hip bone. She doubted she could touch the ends of the scar with a single hand span. Kyreen shook off thoughts about Lang's injury to refocus her attention on the match.

The two combatants circled each other, watching, wary. From experience Kyreen knew Ebbe to be a more than competent opponent. The first time she had faced the youth in a spar she had barely beaten him, and that had been before he had received any training. Now, after months of experience, Ebbe's sparring skills had vastly improved and he stood second only to Kyreen in this year's trainee class.

Lang's skills and fighting technique, however, remained unknown. Kyreen found herself wavering between the desire to evaluate her nemesis and her discomfort observing Lang. She knew the eventual possibility existed that she would find herself where Ebbe now stood, across from Lang. She only hoped it would be in a practice circle, not somewhere isolated and alone with the man who seemed to hate her very existence. Sensibility prevailing, Kyreen pushed back all conscious thoughts about Lang to concentrate on his stance, how he held his hands, how he positioned his feet, where his eyes went. As if sensing Kyreen's gaze, Lang's emerald eyes snapped in her direction, causing the tall bearded Calanian to lose focus just for a heartbeat. That split instant of distraction provided all the opening Ebbe needed. He shot forward with a speed surprising for someone of his bulk, grappling Lang into a strangle hold. A ripple of shock coursed through the silent circle of trainees. For a long suspenseful moment, the two sparrers appeared frozen, only the tensing of their torsos revealing the strain as they struggled against each other. Then, in less than the span of an eye blink, Lang's body maneuvered, sliding away and around in one fluid movement, and Ebbe found himself flat on the ground, completely immobilized, his cheek pressing into the dirt, arms stretched behind him, the weight of Lang heavy upon his back.

Lang released the youth after a couple of heartbeats, springing to his feet to address the stunned onlookers.

"That," the spar instructor said, "is how quickly an advantage can be gained and lost."

He turned to offer a hand of assistance to Ebbe, who popped up with his customary congenial grin.

"Well done," Lang consoled the youth. He looked around the circle, his gaze avoiding any contact with Kyreen's gaze. "Now split up into practice groups of 3 or 4. Those not actively sparring are to work on creating a distraction for those combating."

As he finished speaking, Lang finally rested his gaze upon Kyreen. She braced for a snide comment, but before Lang could speak, Synnove grabbed Kyreen's arm, pulling her into an embrace.

"Welcome back," the younger woman gushed. "Come. Let us work with Yngve and Ebbe."

Kyreen allowed herself to be pulled away, fighting the urge to glance back over her shoulder to lock eyes with Lang.

As had become their habit since returning from the castle mission, the four friends worked together on the training assignment. Though insecurity still filled Kyreen at times, she did enjoy that feeling of belonging. Standing with her back to Lang, she concentrated her attention on Yngve and Synnove as they prepared to spar. Ebbe stepped up to stand beside her, his gaze also on their two friends.

"So, Kyreen," he said quietly, "how best to distract these two?"

Kyreen thought a moment before an idea struck her.

"I could tell you about my trip to Myrddin," she replied, her voice loud enough for the fighters to overhear.

"Boring contract negotiations?" Synnove snorted, her voice teasing, not missing a step as she avoided a lunge by Yngve. "Are you even trying?"

"Baby news then?" Kyreen asked.

"Humph," grunted Yngve, barely missing a grapple hold as Synnove danced out of reach.

"They are definitely much too focused," Kyreen remarked, her voice full of a seriousness that her twinkling eyes contradicted. "But I am sure you, Ebbe, would be interested in hearing all about the crossbow my lover gave me to bring back to Viggo."

Kyreen's words had the desired effect on the sparring duo. Both immediately dropped their stance to turn and stare at Kyreen, speaking simultaneously.

"Crossbow?" asked Yngve.

"Lover?" gasped Synnove.

After a split second of silence the four friends burst into laughter.

"Your faces!" chortled Ebbe.

"A little less chatter over there," Lang's voice admonished the group.

With all her strength, Kyreen managed to suppress a grimace, all humor fleeing. Her friends, however, simply shrugged it off and brought their attention back to the practice. Synnove waved Kyreen forward to face off with Yngve who groaned.

"No fair, Synnove," he complained. "Kyreen will never get distracted."

"He is right," Ebbe agreed. "Besides Kyreen does not need the practice. Let me have a go at Yngve."

Kyreen stepped aside, sweeping an arm, saying with humor, "Be my guest."

Not too long ago such a banter would have disconcerted Kyreen, but now she took their words for the compliments they were. The youth were not trying to tear her down or belittle her. Kyreen inhaled deeply, relishing the smell of the ocean mingled with the heady fragrance of the pine trees. As she exhaled, a tension within her, one she had not consciously perceived, released.

"It is good to have you back, my friend," Synnove commented, leaning her body towards Kyreen so that their shoulders touched. Both women's eyes were trained on their two grappling friends.

"It is good to be back," Kyreen murmured, enjoying the peaceful feeling for the short moment. Then her stomach clenched and she gritted her teeth.

Feeling Kyreen's tension, Synnove glanced over her shoulder to see that Lang had approached their group.

"Spar Master," she greeted him, turning to face Lang.

Kyreen sighed quietly, also turning around, saying, "Spar Master."

"You two do not appear to be working too hard to distract Yngve and Ebbe," Lang commented, his steely gaze fixed on the two young men wrestling. "This is not to be a practice in sparring. It is a concentration exercise."

Before either woman could respond, Lang turned and strode off towards another group of trainees.

"I am sorry, Synnove," Kyreen apologized, her temper barely held in check. "That was him taking a jab at me. Do not think for a moment that it had anything to do with you."

"No worries," her friend replied, a merry twinkle in her eyes. "Besides Lang gave us the distraction on his own."

Kyreen glanced over her shoulder to see Yngve and Ebbe standing behind her, their spar forgotten. Synnove laughed gaily and the others joined in. A moment later the gong sounded, announcing the end of training. The class began wandering back towards camp to begin pre-dinner chores. As the four friends started walking, Synnove slipped an arm through Kyreen's.

"Do not fool yourself," Synnove teased, leaning in close to Kyreen's ear so no one else could hear her words. "I have not forgotten your mention of a lover. Tonight, you will answer my questions."

Kyreen chuckled anew. She had known the consequences when she spoke the words earlier that, somehow, she would have to pay. She thought on Rhun and their time together, a warm flush creeping into her cheeks. Then a now familiar tension crept into Kyreen and she glanced over her to see Lang watching her, his expression undecipherable. Under his gaze all thoughts of Myrddin and the guild master fled. Kyreen resolved to address this tension with Lang tonight after evening exercises. Now that his animosity had begun affecting her friends, it was past time.

Chapter 10

"How shall we spend our evening getting ready for the tournament?" Ebbe's question once the four friends were seated with their plates took Kyreen by surprise.

"What is this tournament?" she inquired. "Are there no training exercises tonight?"

"That is right! You were not here when the Camp Master made the announcement," Synnove responded, her sapphire eyes lighting up. "It is time for the Tournament!"

"Finally!" Yngve pitched in, his face reflecting the excitement in his voice.

"Still confused," Kyreen commented, her gaze swinging between her three friends.

"A fortnight before the Spring Festival begins the trainees partake in a competition to determine the top trainee for the year," Yngve explained. "A contest of five skills—horsemanship, archery, tracking, sword play and grappling."

"It is bound to be one of us," Synnove added, her tone very matter-of-fact, without any arrogance. "We all are top in the five areas."

"I could care less for the title. It is the top prize which I covet," Ebbe commented. "I will not hold back on any of you. There is no friendship on the field of competition."

Synnove and Yngve both nodded their agreement.

"What is the reward?" Kyreen asked, her forehead furrowing. She could not think what would be so desired by her friends. A horse? A weapon? Armor?

Synnove leaned close to Kyreen, her voice dropping low. "No chores for the rest of the year! The top trainee gets exempted from all chores. Meal preparation, clean up, horse duty, sanitation, patrol, everything!"

Yngve, his plate empty, leaned against the log behind him, emerald eyes cast skyward, murmuring, "A whole fortnight of no responsibilities."

Kyreen resumed eating, listening with half an ear to her friends as her mind wandered. A contest to be top trainee. Synnove's comment about one of them winning the competition had not been wrong. This group of friends, their bond strengthened by their recent mission, held the top spots in all areas. If she was being honest with herself, they four held the top four spots in all categories, except one. Kyreen was by far the top in horsemanship and had only been beaten twice all year by Ebbe in sparring. Yngve and Synnove constantly traded the first and second slots in tracking, while Ebbe and Kyreen went back and forth in swords. As expected, considering Viggo was his father, Yngve held top spot in archery. Even Synnove managed to consistently claim the fourth spot in her weakest area, sparring, but Kyreen had never finished higher than thirteenth in tracking. Not good considering only sixteen trainees made up their class.

"Speaking of chores," Synnove said, pulling Kyreen out of her thoughts and reaching for Kyreen's empty plate. "I best report to clean-up."

"My thanks," Kyreen replied, handing over the dish. Though she could not recall having eaten, her stomach churned, the food she had just consumed sitting heavy as she continued to ponder that prospect of her ineptitude being placed on public display in competition.

"Perimeter duty," Yngve commented, pushing of the log to propel to his feet.

"Me as well," Ebbe added, following his friend.

Alone, Kyreen glanced around the clearing. Other trainees had also moved away to fulfill their evening duties. Having just arrived back, Kyreen did not yet have her assignments. As that thought percolated, Kyreen realized with a jolt that she had not been scheduled to be back for another few days. She was not even supposed to be present. Would there be a place in the competition for her? Teeth nibbling her bottom lip, she looked over to where the camp's instructors took their meals. Most, Lang included, still loitered in the area, their evening meal concluded, engaging in conversation.

As though sensing her gaze, Lang looked in Kyreen's direction, their eyes locking. Kyreen remembered her vow to Aren. Despite the churning of her stomach, she made a snap decision to act. Before her brain could dissuade her to do otherwise, she was on her feet and halfway to the small group of instructors. The conversations ceased and all eyes turned to Kyreen upon her approach, only increasing her discomfort.

"Hail and well met," Kyreen greeted the collective, inclining her head respectfully.

"Kyreen, welcome back," Atle greeted her warmly, rising to his feet. "I hope your early return means everything went smoothly in the city."

"Yes," she replied. "The contracts with Brodyr Llafur have been signed."

"Good, good. The revenue will be a great help to our people," Atle stated, moving closer to Kyreen. "We have been finalizing details for tomorrow. I trust your friends filled you in on the details?"

"Mostly," Kyreen responded, her gaze on the Camp Master while her peripheral vision attempted to keep track on Lang. He and the other instructors had gathered their dinnerware to take to the cleanup station. So intent was her focus on the tall bearded Calanian, she very nearly missed Atle's next comment.

"With evening exercises cancelled in anticipation of tomorrow's competition, I recommend you spend your free time in preparation for the tournament."

Kyreen turned her attention fully onto Atle, thinking she heard something in his voice, but his gaze was indecipherable. She inclined her head once more, internally steeling herself to go after Lang, saying aloud, "Sound advice. Thank you, Camp Master. I bid you good night."

Atle returned the gesture, his eyes flicking towards the retreating group of instructors then back to Kyreen. So fast was his glance that Kyreen wondered if she was reading too much into the older man's gesture. Until she had fully turned and heard the older man murmur, "Best of luck."

Though his words could have been referring to tomorrow's contest, Kyreen felt he had intuited her plans. Jaw and stomach clenched, she hurried after Lang, timing her approach to coincide with his exiting the dishes area. Kyreen's paranoia had her believing that all the other instructors had peeled away, leaving Lang alone. One of them had even engaged Synnove in conversation so she did not hail Kyreen.

Unwilling to reach out and touch Lang to gain his attention, Kyreen opened her mouth but his name fell silent upon her tongue.

'Damn the man!' she thought. He had to know she was behind him, he had to have sensed her turmoil. Unable to find her voice, she finally coughed softly. A stiffening of Lang's shoulders was the only indication he had heard her.

Without turning to look at her, he muttered, "Not here," before striding towards the forest at the edge of the camp, away from the cliffs.

Kyreen followed silently. Though she concentrated on clamping down her emotions to prevent others from sensing, she fluctuated between nervous, and angry, and afraid. Afraid? This reaction surprised and worried her. She recalled the last time she had left camp to hold a discussion with Lang. Had Collin not interrupted maybe they could have resolved this last summer. Inhaling deeply, she pushed away thoughts of what could have been and focused on the now. Though her skills had improved vastly over the fall and winter months, Kyreen still felt ungainly and noisy compared to this man before her, silently making his way through the trees to the small clearing that was used for tracking practice. Knowing the confrontation she had been actively avoiding for weeks was close at hand served to calm Kyreen's nerves so that, by the time Lang stopped and turned to face her, Kyreen had regained some control.

In the dying twilight, Lang waited, silently regarding her. She could not decipher his expression nor could she feel any emotions. The void distracted her, a frown wrinkling her brow. How did he do that? It was as though he shut down his very essence. Did he always have such control or was it only around her? Could he hate her so much that he had to hid away the strength of that emotion?

"You wanted to talk," Lang commented drawing Kyreen out of her musings. "Or did you simply wish to stand around in the dark, assaulting me with your emotions?"

The man's tone more than his words fanned the angry embers that lay smoldering. The flare of temper burned away Kyreen's reticence and doubt.

"I want to know what your problem is," she snapped. "A number of people tell me I need to adjust my attitude towards you, that I need to work it out with you, but I cannot fix what I do not understand. I do not know why you despise me. From the moment I entered the Council Tent last summer, you have treated me with such hostility and I cannot figure out why. Your mere presence stirs up so much animosity inside of me that I cannot think straight in your presence. Not even the vilest of people that I have encountered—Markku, Soren, Falk—had the effect you have on me."

Kyreen paused for breath. Her eyes glittered with unshed tears. She clenched her hands by her side, striving to not cry, to not show weakness. That she had said so much, shared such private thoughts, appalled her. Swallowing the lump in her throat, she took a deep breath to continue.

"I made a vow," she confessed. "A vow to Aren that I would resolve this tension between us before the Spring Festival. That is the only reason I stand here and ask for your help."

She paused again and when Lang made no move to respond, she tentatively closed the distance between them, resolutely pressing down the uncomfortable tension in her bones. Lang squirmed and made to take a step back.

"No, do not go," Kyreen said, desperately grabbing at his hands, the contact of their flesh sending electric shock waves through her body.

"Have you not suspected?" Lang asked, his voice husky.

'Suspected what?' she thought, frustration surging.

"Oh, by the goddess! This would have been so much less complicated had you never left," Lang muttered. "Or never returned."

Old hurts resurfaced, but Kyreen ignored the pain, focusing instead on the anger once more.

"Yes, I agree," she snapped between gritted teeth. "I do apologize if my family's flight from the castle when I was but a child complicated your life."

Lang chuckled softly. "No, I mean... if you had been here... if we had grown up together... if we had known each other when..." His voice trailed off and he looked down at the hands Kyreen had forgotten she had clasped.

Belatedly she realized she could feel Lang's emotions. Anger nor hate filled him. Quite the opposite. He radiated a peace, a tranquility, a fondness. Kyreen gasped and abruptly stepped back, severing the contact.

She stared at Lang a long moment, her mind racing. Then she began to shake her head.

"No, no, no. You despise me. You attack me at every turn. We are adversaries," she muttered, pacing around the ash filled fire pit.

"There is a fine line between love and hate," Lang commented quietly, his green eyes following her movements. Something in his voice reminded Kyreen of the tone she used on spooked horses.

"When you feel my emotions, you give them the label," Lang continued. "The discomfort you feel is that I know you do not feel the same for me. Without reciprocity, I am stuck in limbo."

"You mean...?" Kyreen stopped pacing to stare at Lang. "We are... You and I... We are..."

"Bonded. Soul mates," Lang finished for Kyreen when he saw she would not, could not complete the sentence.

Kyreen sunk down, sitting upon a log, her head light, her breath stolen away.

Lang moved to sit on the log across the fire pit from her position. "I felt it the moment you entered the tent last summer."

"But why did you not..." Kyreen let that sentence die without completion. She remembered that night very well. It had been the first night she spent with Collin.

"I did try eventually," Lang said. "That evening by the lake? But that outsider interrupted. Right after that you left for Myrddin to help your friends. Then the skirmish happened and I was injured."

Kyreen held her head in her hands, her brain hurting as her mind raced, replaying scenario after scenario. All her interactions with Lang. Him calling her a distraction. Him asking her to stay out of the battle, questioning her intentions to stay, showing up every time she returned to camp.

"That is why you came to the Training Camp," she stated more than asked, raising her head to gaze at him. "To be with...to be near me."

"Aren was most gracious when I made my request," Lang admitted.

"Does everyone know then?" Kyreen asked, mortified at the thought, remembering Atle's words to her just moments earlier.

"Some have surmised," Lang replied, shrugging.

For a long while the two sat in silence as night fell around them. The evening mist had not yet reached the forest so overhead the stars shone brightly. To the east, a soft glow promised the impending moonrise. Kyreen felt the presence of her people in the camp, including Lang's. For once, she pressed away her hostilities, her prejudices, to just relax in his presence.

Finally, she broke the silence, putting a voice to the question hanging between them. "Where do we go from here?"

Lang did not answer for so long that she worried maybe he would not. Just as she opened her mouth to repeat the question, he replied, "I do not know. But this right here, you and me sitting in peace, without hostilities, is a balm upon me. Thank you."

An uncomfortable silence fell between the two. Kyreen continued trying hard to wrap her mind around this new reality.

"Kyreen, I do not expect us to resolve this...situation tonight," Lang commented. "For now, it is good for us to not be enemies, for the hostilities to end, to be in your presence without conflict."

"Not enemies," Kyreen repeated. "I do not know, Lang. That is an awful big jump."

She laughed so he would know she was teasing. After a heartbeat, he joined in. A moment later, the fatigue from the day of travelling hit and Kyreen stifled a yawn.

"Tomorrow is a big day," Lang said, rising to his feet. "You should get your rest if you hope to win."

Kyreen rose as well, stating, "I do not expect to win. While my skills are sufficient enough in most areas, I cannot master tracking. That will pull me out of the competition for sure."

The two began walking back towards camp, their shoulders not quite touching. Yet Kyreen could feel the heat radiating off of Lang's body. In companionable silence, Lang escorted Kyreen to her tent.

Once there, Kyreen impulsively reached out to squeeze Lang's hand as they bade each other good night.

"Thank you for your candor tonight," she said. "I hope we can continue the conversation again soon."

Reluctantly ignoring the urge to linger, Kyreen released his hand and ducked into the tent. As the hour was still early, Synnove had not yet returned, and Kyreen gave thanks for the solitude as she prepared for sleep.

With her animosity gone, she found she could feel Lang, even without probing. She knew when he turned to walk away to his own tent across the compound. He transmitted a calm that gave her comfort as she settled into her bedroll. With her mind racing to process the evening's revelations, Kyreen thought sleep would evade her, but a tranquility unlike any she had felt settled over her like a blanket and she drifted off almost immediately. While Synnove's silent entrance hours later woke her, Kyreen simply murmured a good night and drifted back to sleep. There would be time for talk in the morning.

Chapter 11

As was her habit, Kyreen woke early. After dressing silently, she slipped from the tent without waking Synnove. Through the dense pre-dawn fog, she sensed, rather than saw, Lang waiting nearby. Surprisingly charmed by his presence, she smiled and motioned her invitation for him to join her. They walked side by side to the border of camp, this time towards the beach cliffs. The lone sentry they met silently waved them through, her expression neutral. Everyone in camp knew of Kyreen's early morning ventures to the cliffs where she went to prepare for the day. Synnove had tried accompanying Kyreen a few times, but inevitably determined the extra sleep was a more agreeable way to prepare for the day.

Instead of working on her centering, Kyreen found a large, relatively flat boulder near the cliff's edge from where they could observe the surf breaking on the rocks below once the sun rose a little more. She settled on the chilly rock, beckoning Lang to join her when it became apparent he would not do so on his own.

"Good morn," she finally spoke, feeling shy after their previous meeting's revelations, unsure how to proceed.

"Good morn," Lang responded, smiling. Kyreen tried to recall if she had ever seen his emerald eyes shine so bright. "Are you ready for today's festivities?"

Kyreen's stomach churned anew. Whether from his gaze or his words, she did not rightly know. She groaned softly before replying.

"I was not supposed to be here to compete," she commented. "Is it too late to go back to Myrddin?"

"While you are correct, you were not scheduled to be in camp, your absence was not deliberate on the Camp Master's part. The games are set by moon phases as related to the Spring Festival," Lang responded, pausing to peer directly at her through the gray shadows. "I, for one, am pleased you have the opportunity to compete."

"To make an utter fool of myself, you mean," Kyreen muttered. A part of her marveled at the ease she felt around Lang. Now that she knew he was not plotting against her, she found herself saying things she would normally only reveal to Synnove in private. Yet another part fretted at how quickly that ease had happened, and at that other factor, the being bonded soulmates, which terrified Kyreen more than she cared to admit. Distracted by her internal chattering, Kyreen nearly missed Lang's next words.

"I do not know if you jest or are being serious," he said. "I believe you can win this tournament. There is not an instructor here willing to take that bet either, so I know I am not the only one with such an opinion."

"You bet on the trainees?" Kyreen asked, her face reflecting her concern.

Lang chuckled. "No, I jest. We do not wager, but we do talk. You are one of the top trainees, Kyreen, if not the very top."

Deep down Kyreen knew Lang was right, and hearing him say the words warmed her. Then a cold splash of reality poured over her.

"Tracking," Kyreen stated quietly. "Despite how well I place in the other areas, it is tracking which will doom me. No matter how hard I try this basic skill, that every Calanian toddler has mastered, evades me."

"That is your problem right there," Lang responded cryptically.

Kyreen quirked a brow at him, silently questioning.

"You are trying too hard," Lang explained. "The reason we teach the skill at such a young age is so that it becomes an integral part of our beings, so that it is as natural as breathing. The secret to evading is not to overpower but to fade away, blend your essence with that of your surroundings. Let go of all conscious thought, of worry, of stress. Let the spirit of your environs flow *through* you, instead of around you."

"We have a little bit of time before morning assembly," Lang remarked, standing with a glance towards camp before swiveling his gaze over to her. "Would you like to practice?"

Kyreen paused a long moment before nodding. The peace between them so fresh, she found she still had to override her default mode of defensiveness.

"Thank you," she murmured, standing and walking to stand in front of him.

"Close your eyes. Starting at the crown of your head, imagine yourself fluid, like a river, energy flowing down over your body like a waterfall." Lang's voice, soft and steady, safe and secure, drew Kyreen into a meditative state.

"Keep that image in your mind," he continued. "Now imagine your head, your neck, your shoulders, all a part of an immense waterfall cascading over your body."

Kyreen remained still, listening to Lang's voice as he continued walking her through the final visualizations. Once she had visualized all her body as part of the waterfall, down to her feet, he paused speaking for a moment, letting this sensation settle in before continuing. "Now imagine the current of this waterfall over you as currents of energy mingling with the energy of the world around us. The wind. The water. The rocks. Augmenting the spirit of the world around us passing through your body."

Kyreen gasped softly, the sensation of connection coursing through her body. The feeling so surprised her that her eyes flew open and the bond disappeared. A feeling of loss cascaded over her being like a bucket of cold water. The breath left her body sharply as though she had been punched in the stomach. This was accompanied by a wave of vertigo. Kyreen staggered back a step, slightly disoriented. Lang reached out a hand, grasping her elbow to steady her. The instant she stabilized, he pulled back his hand as though touching her burned him.

"We should head back," Lang said, stepping away before Kyreen could comment. "It is almost time for morning assembly."

Kyreen fell in step beside him, quietly pondering the last few moments. As they reached the edge of the assembly are, Lang paused.

"Atle nor I will be present at any of the events," he commented. "I tell you this so you will not be distracted by my absence."

Kyreen wanted to ask why, but merely nodded.

"Now I must take my place," he concluded with a smile, striding away without glancing back. More than a few of the trainees' curious glances followed him.

Kyreen's brow furrowed as she found her place in the assembly, her mind working through the implications of Lang's words. Synnove, already in place, cast Kyreen an inquiring look, but before either could speak the morning ritual began. Moving her body through the age-old motions, Kyreen's mind continued to work through Lang's parting words.

Atle was Ebbe's father. Though she had not witnessed more than a handful of interactions between the two these past few months, Kyreen could imagine they shared a strong bond, a bond that could be perceived as an advantage for Ebbe, support for him as he competed. The final piece of the puzzle clicked into place and Kyreen almost fumbled her transition from one pose to another. If indeed she and Lang were… she had difficulty thinking the word…bonded, then they too would share a connection that could be considered support for Kyreen during the competition. Though she doubted that she and Lang shared a particularly strong bond at this time, she realized that without consciously trying she could feel his presence nearby. As Lang had said of her the previous evening, his essence soothed her soul, a balm upon a wound of which she had not previously been aware.

Finally, as the group moved as one into the next position, Kyreen pushed away all conscious thought. Slipping easily into her meditation, she silently recited the words taught to her by her mother so many years ago. Though Kyreen was back with her people and no longer needed to remember her story for the Telling, she found comfort in the recitation. Today as ritual completed, Kyreen found herself a bit more centered, a bit more focused, a bit more ready for the day ahead.

After announcements, the group dispersed for morning meal. Though she did not speak as the two fell into step with Yngve and Ebbe, Synnove gave Kyreen a sideways look, her expression questioning. Kyreen, knowing that look meant an interrogation would be had later when the two were alone, merely flashed a grin at her friend, linking her arm through the younger woman's arm so that they walked with shoulders touching.

"Now I really want to know what you are playing at," Synnove murmured quietly for Kyreen's ears alone. "Who are you and what have you done with my dour tentmate?"

Kyreen chuckled and squeezed Synnove's arm without comment as they queued up in the meal line. Even had they been able to have a private conversation, Kyreen doubted she could easily express the change to Synnove. It felt as though a shroud had been lifted from her, that before today the whole world had been out-of-focus, viewed from behind a veil.

Directly after breakfast the trainees reported to the equestrian area. Fifteen horses stood saddled and ready. Kyreen noticed her gelding was not among the animals. Upon reflection, this made sense. To level the playing field none should use their personal mount. Aside from Kyreen only two other trainees had personal mounts. Horse ownership at this age was rare now. In past generations, it would have been much different. Riding an unknown horse did not bother Kyreen. With all these being Calanian bred and trained, she had no worries about an inferior mount. Names written on wood chips had been placed in two separate bowls and Magnar, working in Atle's absence, began drawing.

"Yngve. You are up first on horse 1," the Hunt Master announced immediately pulling the next set. "Tappen is second. Horse 2."

As Magnar called each trainee's name and number, that person would pull away from the group, collect the corresponding numbered horse, and move towards the starting line of the course. With her focus on hearing her name, Kyreen chose to ignore the course until she had gathered up her assigned horse, a leggy liver chestnut mare with the palest of flaxen mane and tail. The animal's coat was so dark she looked brown in the shadows. But once she was led into the sunshine, the deep burnished red shone bright. Coupled with her four long stockings and wide blaze, the animal was quite the flashy specimen. Kyreen placed a hand upon the creature's neck, her fingers sliding under the silky mane. Gazing into the mare's large liquid brown eyes, Kyreen realized it had been years since she had ridden any other horse than her gelding.

"We shall do just fine," Kyreen murmured softly to the mare, reaching up to scratch behind the animal's ear.

Taking her spot eleventh in line, Kyreen turned her attention to the course. The first event of the tournament would be tent pegging, where riders attempt to stab a peg positioned on the ground with a spear from the back of a galloping horse with the first round being a straightforward elimination round. Anyone who managed to collect the peg on each of five separate passes would advance to the next event, which Kyreen anticipated to be ring mustering. That event, where trainees would be competing against the clock and each other, entailed each rider collect rings using a spear, continuing to ride their horse back and forth along the course as many times as they could before the sand ran out of the hourglass. Different sized rings placed at different heights along the route awarded varying points. The smaller the ring, the lower the ring sat to the ground, the greater the points. The winner of that second round would be the one who accumulated the most points within the allotted time. Kyreen had confidence in her skills both with the spear and in the saddle. The unknown factor here would be her horse's willingness and physical ability. She stole a glance at her mount's hindquarters. Not as strong as her gelding, but she saw power in the muscles.

Kyreen watched the first grouping of five. The strategy in this first round was simple—spear the peg—a soft wood square no bigger than Kyreen's palm—with your spear from the back of a galloping horse. Any competitor with five pegs at the end of five rounds moved to the next round. Even if a peg was missed and they knew they would not advance, riders were motivated to continue for consolation points. As Synnove had explained last night over dinner, each of the five events in the tournament scheduled to take place today and tomorrow would award 15 points to the winner, 14 for second place, 13 for third and so on, all the way to no points for the competitor in last place. Kyreen earnestly hoped she never received that zero. Her primary goal in this competition being not to humiliate herself.

Though horsemanship had been something every Calanian knew and worked on from very early childhood, their current situation made it difficult for many of the youth to perfect the skills necessary for these feats of horsemanship. Thus, after the five rounds of tent pegging only seven competitors remained. Kyreen had not noticed the other competitors' performances as her loaner mare had been skittish on the start line next to the other horses. Fortunately, the mare had a good burst of speed and, once started, ran straight without any prompting from her rider. Kyreen was pleased to note her three friends had all advanced. None of the riders who had been in her heat moved to round two, so Kyreen would be the final competitor.

Yngve, quite the accomplished equestrian, having had the advantage of growing up in the Council Camp with ready access to horses, set the standard high for the rest of the competitors by racking up a hefty number of points. When it came time for Kyreen's first pass, another horse passed too close, spooking the loaner mare just as the pair took off. Very nearly losing her seat, Kyreen's spear was not positioned properly for the first row of rings. Fortunately, the score was not cumulative. Instead each pass stood alone, each competitor taking their highest round. Once Kyreen figured out her mount's temperament, her final two rounds were exemplary. The final tallies found her tied with Yngve, who grinned broadly at his cousin.

"This means tie breaker round," he announced, cheerfully patting the neck of his big sorrel gelding.

Kyreen did not appreciate the burst of confidence exuded by her kin. She cast a questioning glance at Synnove, standing nearby.

"Tough luck there," Synnove commented, walking over to stroke the nose of Kyreen's loaner horse. "This sweet girl is quick, but not really much of a racer. Yngve's mount is faster on the straight away."

The tie breaker turned out to be a combination of skill and talent. The two finalists would race side-by-side to the far end of the meadow, pull the waiting spear from the ground, spin their mount around and race back to the starting line where the spear was to impale a waiting apple set upon a tree stump.

As the course was being prepared, Kyreen fretted. Absently nibbling her bottom lip and stroking the mare's neck, her mind raced, trying to figure out a winning strategy. Yngve's mount was heavily muscled and as all the horses had already had several gallops, maybe there would be some fatigue there. Also, the gelding's bulk might prevent him from being as nimble as the mare at the turnaround. If Kyreen could get the mare to keep up until the turn, they just might be able to eke out a lead for the final straight away. The big question would be could they keep the lead.

Her brow furrowed in concentration, Kyreen led her mare over to the starting line. As she passed Synnove, the younger woman placed an encouraging hand on Kyreen's arm.

"Remember to spear the apple," Synnove commented quietly. "Arriving first is not the primary goal."

Kyreen smiled her thanks to her friend, silently admitting to herself that being so intent upon the race aspect she had, in fact, forgotten the end objective.

The leggy mare proved to be a racer after all and the turn, as Kyreen speculated, had been Yngve's downfall. By the time, he had pulled up the spear and turned the big horse around, Kyreen's mount had gained enough of a lead that Yngve's gelding could not recover before Kyreen speared the apple.

After the race, Yngve had quickly sought out his cousin to extend his heartfelt congratulations.

"I was in the lead. How did you get ahead of me?" he asked as they and their two friends began walking towards camp for midday meal.

"It was amazing!" Ebbe responded, uncharacteristically animated, his big hands gesturing wildly. "Kyreen had the mare spin around the spear while it was still in the ground."

"Then she grasped the shaft of the spear as the mare took off," Synnove continued the tale. "Thus, letting the mare's quickness pull the spear up from the ground for her."

"So, she did not slow down much at all, while your horse had to turn and restart," Ebbe added.

"What you may not have noticed," Kyreen broke in with a sheepish grin, "was that I very nearly lost my grip on the blasted spear because that mare is so explosive off the line."

The four friends continued chatting, gathering up their midday meal before moving to a secluded grouping of boulders under a canopy of pine trees. As Kyreen settled into eating, listening to the younger Calanians' banter, she realized she missed Lang's presence. She glanced over to the group of instructors, where usually he sat engaged in conversation when partaking of his meals.

Quietly she exhaled and returned her attention to her own group. Knowing that they were supposedly meant to be bonded but not really knowing what that meant made Kyreen more than a little nervous. She enjoyed her independence and worried about losing herself in the relationship. This last thought startled Kyreen so much she almost choked on her food. The relationship? She and Lang had exchanged amicable words for the first time ever just last night. That did not a relationship make. Her appetite gone, Kyreen put down her plate, resolving to think on something else. She still had swords this afternoon followed by tracking after dark.

"Kyreen, are you going to finish that?" Ebbe interrupted her reflections, motioning to Kyreen's half-empty plate.

Kyreen shook her head, passing the plate to her friend with a smile. Both Yngve and Ebbe were constantly finishing off Synnove and Kyreen's meals. Sometimes the young women would joke that food was the true reason Ebbe and Yngve stuck around them. But it was all in good fun, Kyreen knew. The four were close friends, with no romantic inclinations amongst them. Synnove had confided in Kyreen that Ebbe had someone he wrote to, someone a year younger who would be arriving at training in the fall. Kyreen had seen Yngve in the company of a fellow trainee on more than one occasion, smitten expressions on both of their faces. Suddenly Kyreen wished for this day's competition to be over, not because she dreaded the evening's tracking, but because she looked forward to the time she would be able to spend with Lang.

"Alright there, Kyreen?" Synnove asked, a small curious frown furrowing her brow.

Kyreen mentally shook the cobwebs from her thoughts, rising to her feet to join her friends as they readied for the next round of competition. "Never better," she said, half surprised to find it true.

Chapter 12

The afternoon's sword event held no surprises. Ebbe and Kyreen, as the number one and number two ranked trainees, won their brackets to face off in the final. Though Kyreen detested losing, Ebbe's good natured sportsmanship, as exemplary in victory as it was in defeat, took away any sting she may have felt when time was called and Ebbe won on points. After two events, she held a two-point lead on the husky youth and a three-point lead over her other two friends.

"That will disappear this evening," she commented during dinner in response to Synnove's enthusiastic congratulations.

"Do not be so sure," Synnove responded, giving Kyreen another cryptic look. "There will be no Soul Seeker in tonight's competition."

"Soul Seeker?" Kyreen asked, automatically passing her half-eaten plate over to Yngve in answer to his unspoken question.

"My thanks," Yngve replied, adding, "Nor will they use a Hunter, Synnove."

"I have no idea what that means either," Kyreen shook her head at her cousin.

Yngve and Synnove exchanged glances, then Synnove stood, handing her plate to Ebbe before turning to extend a hand to Kyreen. "Come," she said. "Walk with me?"

Kyreen took Synnove's proffered hand, allowing her friend to draw her to her feet. Synnove slipped her arm into Kyreen's and they began walking towards the tent area.

"You have such skills," Synnove said, "as demonstrated by today events, that I often forget you were not raised amongst us."

For the first time that day, insecurity flooded through Kyreen, the now familiar hurt returning to make her heart ache.

"Shh," Synnove whispered, tightening her grip on Kyreen's arm. "I do not say this to hurt you. It is merely an observation, my own realization that you may not be aware of things that I and the others learned from our families growing up."

"Late last summer, when we novice trainees arrived, I was so excited," she continued quietly, her path taking the pair in a circuitous route around the tents. "Not only is Training Camp something I have looked forward to most of my life, but it meant I would finally be with my best friends."

She paused to glance at Kyreen with a wry smile. "Drawing you for my tentmate was an extra bonus. For now, I count you among my best friends as well."

Kyreen nodded, holding her tongue, wondering where this was going.

"Anyway, I was happy for many reasons, but spending time every day with Yngve and Ebbe was the top of that list. Although the youth in our class may not have grown up in the same camp, we have known each other our entire lives," Synnove explained. "Every spring our families have gathered in the Great Valley for camaraderie and to celebrate the new year. When we were very young, we would play together. As we grew older, we worked alongside one another, planting in the spring, weeding in the summer, harvesting in the fall. Long before we came here to learn the skills of combat, we connected. We know each other's histories. Unlike you, we were not strangers thrust into a strange environment."

Kyreen pushed down the waves of frustration. Synnove had a reason for reciting this. There had to be a point, something Kyreen was missing.

"Yes, I apologize. I sound more like my mother every day," Synnove smiled compassionately. "I will get to the point. I bring up this background so that you will know how our people adapted over this past generation since the Battle."

Kyreen's brow furrowed anew, her unspoken question reflected in her eyes.

Synnove guided them to a boulder on the edge of camp. She sat, gesturing Kyreen to join her. The clearing was empty save for them two.

"You have heard it was a Calanian who worked with the Galorians to orchestrate the invasion of the castle, yes?" Synnove asked, drawing her legs up to her chest so as to wrap her cloak around her against the evening breeze, her chin resting upon her knees, resting her gaze in the distance.

"Aren alluded to such," Kyreen nodded, "though I know not the details."

"That, then, can be another story for another day," Synnove commented, her voice uncharacteristically soft and sad. "But I want you to know that he was not a stranger. He was a well-known citizen, a tradesman, well-liked even. He was my da's uncle and the reason my parents were absent when the invasion started. Mum was pregnant with my oldest brother and Papa's uncle convinced them that travel would be unwise."

Again, Kyreen held her tongue. Feeling her friend's sorrow, she reached over to squeeze Synnove's hand.

"This…betrayal was not the first for our people. There had been another, not many years before, which resulted in the king's murder," Synnove continued, returning the pressure on Kyreen's hand with a sad smile.

"That story I do know," Kyreen remarked, remembering her grandfather's portrait from the war room of the castle. Not for the first time, she wondered if it still hung there or if it had been destroyed in the ensuing years.

"Of course," Synnove replied. She inhaled deeply and Kyreen felt her friend's centering. Upon her exhalation, Synnove resumed her story.

"After the Battle, the small band of leaders that remained held council. That one of our own could plot to destroy us was heartbreaking and eye opening. It did not matter that he knew not of the planned massacre. He merely thought to dethrone your mother, not expecting the consequences to be so extreme. In the aftermath of the Battle, our leaders had to wonder why and how we could have come to this as a society. Calan had always been prosperous. The farms produced well. The tradesmen made profits. But as we had prospered and grown, we had also pulled away from our founding culture. Neighbors did not know each other. Threads of discontent, envy of another's successes, selfishness had crept in causing general discontent and dissatisfaction."

Kyreen listened as Synnove talked about how the leaders had planned out their reality as refugee's living on the land as nomads, designing their society to weed out any malcontents who might not fit in. Everyone worked together. Any grievances were to be aired immediately and handled by the individual camps, with only occasional, severe cases being brought to the Council during Spring Festival.

"We are not a perfect people," Synnove concluded. "We do have our troublemakers, but this system is designed to weed them out before they can cause any severe damage, for the most part."

Kyreen thought back to Hanoria, the isolated province in which she grew up. They governed by council as well, but without a single leader. While there were petty politics, the rules there had also been designed to keep the people safe.

"Forgive me, Synnove, if I missed your point," Kyreen said, "but what does this have to do with tonight's tracking competition?"

"Oh, right!" Synnove laughed, sounding more herself. "I did have a purpose for heading down this path. Egads, my apologies again! I fear I strayed just a bit. The policies, the structure of work and life for our people now revolves around community. Much like a bee hive, everyone has their duty to protect and serve. But our people also have a divine gift, something that is unique to only a few others. As Calanians, we all possess it, but as our society changed before the Battle, less and less attention was given to our inherent abilities, so much so that one of our most ancient traditions had been cast aside for the past few generations. When restructuring our society, the leaders decided to bring it back. This includes the rites of passage process which takes place over a summer when a youth reaches puberty. Through a series of boring lectures and guided meditations, youth prepare for the final divination quest. After completing the quest, the youth will have divined their special talent, which helps set them on their path. I am a Soul Seeker. I see people's inner essences like fireflies. Thus, I am extra sensitive to people's emotions."

"My turn for apologies," Kyreen grimaced. "Sharing a tent with me must be torture."

"Yes, you do emote more than most, but your company more than makes up for it," Synnove chuckled. "However, it is also why I can so easily find you during the track. Your brokenness shines like a beacon in my head."

The younger woman paused, turning her sapphire gaze to Kyreen thoughtfully. "Or at least it did. You have seemed different today. Not quite as broken, almost complete."

Uncomfortable with the direction the conversation had taken, Kyreen sought to bring it back on track. "Is that why Yngve is good at the track? Is he a Soul Seeker?"

"No," Synnove shook her head. "He is a Hunter, just like his father. When he concentrates on the hunt, Yngve can tune into his prey. It is not as reliable with humans, but very effective on game like deer. It is almost as though the Hunter calls their quarry to them."

Kyreen reflected on Synnove's words. As they had talked, dusk had fallen and groupings of dark forms move through the purple shadows.

"Two things before we need to go," Synnove said. "First, the quest is highly personal. You and I are good friends, as is Yngve, else I never would have spoken to you of our talents. It is not so much a secret as it is private."

"So, I should not go inquiring about it to everyone?" Kyreen quipped.

"That would be a blunder for sure," Synnove chuckled.

"And the other?" Kyreen asked, her eyes watching their classmates moving towards the tracking area.

"You need to figure out your talent," Synnove declared, rising to her feet.

"Maybe after the tournament? Is it complicated? Rigorous?" Kyreen wrinkled her nose as they started walking. "No, do not tell me. I have enough to think about without worrying about yet another test."

"Later then," Synnove conceded with a chuckle, slipping her arm through Kyreen's. "You are correct. Let us concentrate on the task directly ahead of us."

Kyreen nodded. She had been both trying to avoid thinking about and also dreading this event all day. At least it should be done and over very shortly.

Synnove and Kyreen, while not the last to arrive at the fire ring, were later than was their norm and had barely joined Ebbe and Yngve before Magnar spoke.

"Good eve," the Hunt Master said, pausing while the gathered Calanian youth responded in unison. "Tonight's competition will be a straight-forward elimination. One tracker shall hunt. If you are located, a tap on your shoulder, head, foot, body part, shall indicate your elimination. Take the chip given and remain in your spot until the all-clear signal is sounded. Anyone moving after detection shall be disqualified."

Kyreen glanced around the clearing, her anxiety beginning to intensify. Her mind began to race. A strategy. She needed a strategy. If she chose a hiding spot close to base she would have more time for centering, but she would be more vulnerable to being one of the first found. Ideally, she could move to avoid detection, but that really was not an option. Kyreen had never finished higher than thirteen.

As Magnar released the group with his well wishes, Synnove leaned to whisper into Kyreen's ear, "Control your panic. Emotions are easily tracked."

"Without either a Soul Seeker or a Hunter, it will be much harder for the tracker to locate you if you shut down," Yngve added quietly as they all moved towards the dark forest.

"And go high if you are able," Ebbe contributed, patting Kyreen's shoulder as he passed.

Then her three friends slipped away, silently melting into the shadows. Alone, Kyreen concentrated on moving through the underbrush, her mind automatically clicking off the time. The star light above offered a little relief from the complete darkness. A five hundred count might sound like a good head start, until you were faced with the countdown. As she delved deeper into the forest, trying to ignore the faint noises made by others also seeking a place to hide, Kyreen simultaneously concentrated on being quiet, calming her nerves, and deciding the best spot in which to wait.

When her internal count reached 300, Kyreen began searching in earnest for a secluded spot in which to settle. Ebbe's parting words rang in her mind.

"Go high," he had said.

Kyreen placed a hand on the trunk of a sturdy pine tree. With plenty of low hanging branches this would be an easy climb.

'And an easy mark,' Kyreen silently chided herself. Despite his words to the contrary the previous day, Kyreen did not believe Ebbe would purposefully lead her astray. Still the tree looked too easy and surely would draw the attention of the tracker.

Kyreen began moving again, this time actively searching for a tree without very accessible lower branches. With the count in her head at 425, Kyreen found her tree. From the ground, the tree looked inaccessible; its wide trunk bare of branches within reach, except for a neighboring tree with a single branch jutting into its neighbor.

Taking extra care to keep quiet, Kyreen climbed the neighboring tree and moved out onto the branch to navigate over to her target tree. Though she had never climbed at night, Kyreen had spent many afternoons in Hanoria crawling amongst the ancient forest trees surrounding Jorn and Ildri's homestead. Her muscles well remembered the motions as memories flooded her mind. Resolutely pushing away the mental images, Kyreen found a branch upon which she could settle, back against the study trunk, just as her mental count reached 500, which meant the hunt was on.

Suppressing the urge to reach out towards the base, to seek the essence of the tracker, Kyreen inhaled deeply. The strong scent of pine, the adrenaline of being hunted, the anxiety of being hidden opened a new deluge of memories, this time of her flight with her mother, of fleeing Calan, of maiming Falk. Gritting her teeth and squeezing her eyes closed, Kyreen mentally suppressed these new memories and emotions. Imagining a box into which she shoved these feelings then slammed down the lid, Kyreen took another deep cleansing breath. Pushing away the worried thought about wherever the tracker was, Kyreen allowed Lang's words from this morning to flow through her mind.

She imagined the waterfall washing over her head, her hair, her face, her shoulders. With each imagined part of her body, Kyreen's heart slowed and her breathing deepened. By the time she imagined her toes as liquid and the energies around her melding with her own energies, all the tensions of the day, of the competition, of this task had drifted away. As the feeling of connectedness deepened, Kyreen resisted the urge to grab ahold, instead relaxing even more, feeling the tree's essence, the forest's essence, even the night's essence weave with her own essence, melding and flowing until Kyreen could not determine where she began, where the forest began. She was one with the world around her and the world was one with her.

A hand upon her boot jerked Kyreen out of her trance. She gasped as the severed connection left her disoriented. Even as the vertigo hit and Kyreen struggled to maintain her balance, a round wooden token was thrust into her hand.

Kyreen barely registered the tracker's descent, the muffled sound of boots hitting ground below the only sign that he or she had left the tree. In the dark, Kyreen fingered the chit in her hand, battling the hot angry tears that sprung to her eyes. Disappointed in how quickly she had been discovered, Kyreen belatedly realized she could feel the raised numbers on one side of the round piece. Numbers? Surely that could not be right. If she were the first discovered, the number would be zero, for zero points.

As she ran her fingers over the burnt in symbols, Kyreen allowed hope to sneak in. yes, definitely two numbers. A one and a zero. Ten? Accounting for the initial zero points awarded the first trainee discovered, this meant she was the eleventh trainee found. Could that be correct? Kyreen turned her attentions outward, seeking cautiously without probing. Unsurprising the forest around her was silent. The nocturnal animals had long cleared away from this area due to the Calanians' nightly exercises. Gradually, Kyreen began to sense others around her, though she was unable to identify anyone or to discern specific emotions. She was, however, intrigued by the number of essences she felt between her hiding place and the base fire.

The distinct shrill hoot of a night owl, a species long extinct in these parts, pierced the night's silence. Kyreen dropped speedily to the ground, her descent neither stealthy nor deliberate. Moving through the forest she was slightly surprised to discover how far she had travelled from base. Reaching the clearing, Kyreen queued up to hand in her chit.

As she handed her chit to Magnar for recording, Kyreen was surprised to see Synnove off to the side, having already reported in.

"Do not worry," her friend reassured her when Kyreen approached looking concerned. "I took first."

"By being a sneak!" Yngve remarked good-naturedly, coming up to hug Synnove. "Good job there, Syn!"

"Not a move you could have done if they had brought in a Soul Seeker as tracker," Ebbe said, joining their group and patting Synnove on the back with his congratulations, "but you already knew that going in."

"What did she do?" Kyreen asked.

"Circled around behind the tracker," Yngve replied, pulling away from Synnove, with a glance towards a group of their fellow trainees who looked to be heading back towards camp, presumably to then go out to the cliff pools for the evening.

The two young women followed his gaze. As Kyreen registered one of the group, a blue-eyed brunette named Karine, looking their way, Synnove patted Yngve's arm.

"Go," Synnove said amicably. "You and Ebbe go on ahead. I will catch up after I walk Kyreen back to our tent."

The two young men waved farewell before hurrying to join their peers. Synnove, as was her custom, linked an arm through Kyreen's, as the two women followed at a more sedate pace.

"Because I am a Soul Seeker and Yngve is a Hunter, our camp leaders were limited in the type of tracker to be used in tonight's competition," she explained to Kyreen. "It is unusual to have both talents in the same class. Hunters are uncommon and Soul Seekers are very rare."

Synnove glanced around before leaning in close to Kyreen, her voice lowered. "Truth be told, I believe Yngve may have held back. He, too, should have thought to double back past the tracker."

"Maybe," Kyreen responded, chuckling softly. "Or mayhap he was distracted by a certain blue-eyed maiden."

"Possible," Synnove conceded. "But it seems distractions are not always a disadvantage. Congratulations on your performance, my friend."

Kyreen blushed, unsure if it was from her friend's warm praise or the unspoken insinuation. Before she could respond, the pair had reached their tent and Kyreen became aware of Lang's presence. Butterflies erupting in her stomach, Kyreen now understood why Synnove had not attempted to talk Kyreen into joining their peers at the cliffs.

"We must have a longer, more private chat. Soon," Synnove whispered, giving Kyreen a quick hug. With that farewell, Synnove waved to Lang and faded into the shadows.

Nibbling her bottom lip, Kyreen approached Lang. Though her attentions had been focused on her tasks throughout the day, she discovered in hindsight that she had been missing him.

"You were not near camp," she stated, not questioning.

"No," Lang responded. "Atle and I rode out of range following breakfast."

"My apologies," she nodded, suddenly shy. "I am unsure how to proceed."

"We can talk," Lange suggested. "How is the competition going?"

"Well," she replied. "I am in third overall. Yngve, unsurprisingly, is in first place. Synnove and Ebbe are tied for second. Thank you for your assistance with the tracking exercise this morning. I placed higher than I have ever before."

"Good to hear," Lang commented. "I do not believe your deficiency is from a lack of talent. No, I believe if you had not been forced to flee, if you had been raised amongst your people, there would be no question as to who the top student would be."

He paused to chuckle, "Of course you would have passed through this camp years ago and so much would have been different."

Something in Lang's voice tugged at Kyreen. She felt emanating from him, just around the edges, sorrow, distress and guilt. This last emotion confused her, but before she worked up courage to ask, Lange pressed away his emotions and continued talking.

"Let us stop standing around in the chill. Would you prefer the fire and people or the woods and privacy?"

"The woods," Kyreen promptly responded. This, whatever it was between them, was too new, too fresh, too unfamiliar. Kyreen did not want to share it, especially after her disastrous relationship with Collin.

Collin! By the goddess, the entire time she had been with Collin, Lang had known of this connection between her and him. No wonder Lang had not been friendly towards her.

Lang had begun walking towards the forest but paused when he saw Kyreen had not followed him. He turned to look at her in the dark, the soft light from the moon barely illuminating her face. Kyreen closed the distance between them, grasping his hands in hers.

"Lang," she said, quietly. "I am so sorry for my actions, for anything I did that may have caused you discomfort."

"You have nothing for which to apologize," Lang responded, staring down at their hands.

Kyreen followed his gaze, belatedly realizing it was she who clasped his hands. Lang had not returned the gesture. The guilt had once again leaked into his essence. She loosed her grip on his hands, taking a small step back.

"What is the matter?" she asked. "Is there something in my touch?"

"You have done nothing wrong. I enjoy you holding my hand," Lang replied cautiously. He paused and Kyreen felt his internal struggle before he continued. "I... We... You were very explicit in your feelings before, when we... at the Council Camp."

Kyreen's mind raced. She and Lang had not had many interactions, so it did not take long for her to remember that she had unequivocally ordered Lang to never touch her again.

"Oh," she murmured.

"Yes."

Kyreen exhaled softly. She could easily say the words to reverse her earlier sentiment, but did she want to? Yes, she felt different in Lang's presence. While she had enjoyed these last few interactions, she had not yet let loose of her wariness. Her physical attraction towards Lang had even diminished, maybe because she did not sense from him an attraction towards her. Unless...she peered up at his face in the shadows.

"Lang, have you been shielding yourself from me?" she asked with uncharacteristic—for her—directness, almost certain of the answer.

He nodded without comment.

Kyreen exhaled again. The energy that it would take, the concentration, she could not image the effort it would take to consciously pack away strong emotions.

When Kyreen did not respond, Lang turned away and continued walking towards the forest's edge. After a moment's hesitation, Kyreen followed, confident Lang knew where he was headed. Once in the embrace of the trees, she enjoyed the respite from the chilly breeze. Between the pale moonlight and night vision, Kyreen was able to keep up with Lang, but having to concentrate on stealth took all of her focus, preventing her from dwelling on the conversations behind and ahead of them.

When Lang stopped at a tiny clearing, Kyreen closed her eyes to get her bearings. She sensed the camp and people behind her as well as the youth at the heated mineral pools. The wind, though not as harsh, still whistled through the trees, chilling the left side of her face. So, they were north of the camp. She inhaled. The fragrant pine trees mingled with a strong smell of the ocean interwoven in the scent. The sound of the surf echoed louder here. She reckoned they were between the practice arena and the craggy cliffs overlooking the beach.

Opening her eyes, Kyreen saw Lang had sat down with his back to the clearing's single boulder, looming large and pale in the moonlight. Still without speaking, she settled on the ground beside him. She pulled her knees up to rest her chin upon them and wrapped her cloak around her. The boulder pressed cold upon her back, the bed of pine needles cushioned and the heat of Lang radiated beside her despite their bodies not touching. The wind swirled softly through the small clearing, playfully ruffling her loose curls.

"I do not want my emotions to sway your decisions," Lang commented quietly, picking up their conversation.

Kyreen nibbled at her bottom lip, unsure of how to respond. She appreciated Lang's concern. She herself felt overwhelmed by the thought that they were bonded, that it was their destiny to be together. Where was her free will in all of this? Did she not leave Hanoria because her foster father had betrothed her to Stian without her permission?

"I do not know what to do," she responded. "I am so confused."

"I know," Lang remarked.

Kyreen looked at him mortified, then saw his grin. She chuckled and he joined in. As they laughed together, she reflected on this exchange. She had been well on her way to feeling shamed by his response to sensing her emotions. Yet seeing his smile had chased away the negativity, had made the situation acceptable.

As their laughter quieted, Lang said, "Enough with the serious, would you tell me of your day? I missed not seeing the tournament."

So Kyreen recounted the competitions. Lang listened, interjecting comments and questions. The moon continued across the sky, while the stars above rotated and their conversation meandered. With recounting complete,

Kyreen let her voice fade and they sat in companionable silence, the night embracing them. Kyreen felt a tranquility deep inside her unlike any she had ever experienced.

"Lang," she said quietly without looking in his direction.

"Hmm?" he murmured. Though he still kept his emotions on lockdown, Kyreen felt a ripple when she said his name and found she enjoyed the sensation.

"May I lean against you?" she asked impulsively before her insecurity could stay her tongue. She stole a glance at his face, then, wishing to erase the animosity between them, she added, "I rescind my words from the Council Camp. You may touch me."

Lang turned to face Kyreen fully. Once again feeling from him an array of emotions, she turned her own body so that they sat facing each other, legs pulled up and crossed, knees touching. Lang took Kyreen's chilled hands in his warm ones, peering into her eyes without speaking, his expression unreadable. This did not feel romantic nor did it feel improper. After a long moment, he brought her hands to his lips, pressing a soft kiss to her knuckles before leaning back against the boulder. Gently he pulled Kyreen to his side, slipping an arm around her shoulders. Kyreen nestled in, marveling at how natural this felt to her.

"Thank you," he murmured against her hair. "I had to be sure you truly meant what you said."

"Be sure?" Kyreen frowned.

"I am a Truth Seer," he answered. "That is why I occupy the seat next to Aren on the Council."

Kyreen nodded without speaking, anticipating a story, waiting for him to continue.

"I am by far the youngest member of the Council. You may not realize it, but it was not that long ago that I competed for top student here myself," he paused, dropping his mouth down to whisper against her ear, "which, of course, I won."

Kyreen chuckled, his breath and whiskers tickling her ear.

Lang sat back upright, settling Kyreen against him before continuing. "After leaving training, I had planned on spending some time back home, in the Great Valley, working with the horses or helping in the fields, as is typical for a youth without specific trade skills. Then the Council's Truth Seer had an accident and died quite unexpectedly. She had fallen from her horse in the later stages of pregnancy. Her back was broken and she, of course, intuited from the healers that her prognosis was not good. Not wanting her baby to die, she begged them to open her to remove the child, a girl."

When he did not resume speaking, Kyreen asked quietly, "You were close to the woman?"

"Aye," Lang replied. "Though she was my mentor and cousin by blood, we were closer. She was more like my older sister. Her parents, my mother's sister and her mate, took me in after the Battle."

"Oh," Kyreen commented quietly.

"My father was a castle guard so we lived there full-time," Lang continued without prompting. "My mother hated the castle. She was from a farming family and grew up out in the country. She loved to take me and my younger siblings outside the castle walls, into the woods. We spent many, many days out there… before…"

After a few moments of silence, Kyreen asked, "How old were you?"

"Six," he responded, not needing her to clarify. "Da had not been on duty that night so he was there when the alarm bells woke us up. He gathered us all up to escort us to the evacuation area before he reported to the battle. My mother was pregnant, very much so. The castle was so full of people. The hallways crowded. She, my brother and my sister were separated from us in the crowd. Rasmus was four and Anika two. When Da and I reached the gate, he told me to go to the woods with the other children. He said my mother was sure to be right behind us, that she and my siblings would find me before too long, that he would seek us out after the fray settled down. He asked me to be brave, then kissed the top of my head and disappeared back into the castle."

Lang paused, softly rubbing his cheek against Kyreen's dark curls. "I never saw any of them alive again."

They sat in silence once again. Each thinking back to that fateful morning and of their lost family. For Kyreen, the memory had blurred over the years into a series of disconnected images. Some days she struggled to remember what her brother looked like. She could easily recall separate details like his eyes, a brighter blue than the customary Calanian sapphire, and his golden hair as straight as Kyreen's was curly, but she could not assemble all the individual features together. Now she wondered where he was, what he looked like as a man.

Lulled by the warmth of Lang's arm around her shoulders, the lullaby of the wind through the pines and the distant sound of the surf, Kyreen's eyes drifted closed. The fatigue of the day's competition slipped over her and soon she slept.

Chapter 13

Kyreen's eyes snapped open, her thoughts disoriented for an instant. Was she in the woods with her mother? Whose arm was around her? In less than a heartbeat, she came fully awake, remembering she where was and with whom.

Lang, either awakened when she twitched or having not fallen asleep, whispered, "Good morning."

She looked around. The inky darkness of night had given way to predawn greyness. She relaxed. It was still early.

"I worried I had overslept," she said quietly, adding with a smile, "good morning."

"I would not have let you oversleep," he assured her, his voice muffled as he spoke against her curls adding, "thank you."

"For?" she asked, brow furrowing.

"For the best night's rest I have had in a very long while."

"I enjoyed myself too," she said. Something in his voice affected Kyreen. Self-conscious she pushed herself away from him, running a hand through her cap of errant curls. "I really should get back to my tent. With luck Synnove is still asleep and I can avoid an interrogation."

She chuckled softly, her heart glad when Lang joined in. He still had his emotions well-hidden, but enough bled through for her to feel he was not offended by her words.

"Very well," he commented, smoothly rising to his feet, extending a hand to pull Kyreen up.

After brushing the pine needles from their clothing, the pair made their way back to camp without speaking. Though the sentry did not say a word, merely nodding as the two passed, Kyreen blushed with embarrassment, unable to stop the rush of emotions.

"You have such strong reactions to the most interesting matters," Lang commented quietly, leaning down to place his mouth against her ear.

His breath and whiskers tickling, Kyreen smiled, even as his words created another wave of embarrassment.

"Someday," she said, "I will tell you about Hanoria, the place where I was raised."

"Tonight perhaps?" Lang inquired as they approached Kyreen's tent.

"I would enjoy that," she responded, not as surprised to discover the truth in her words as she would have been just two days prior.

"I look forward to tonight then," Lang said, wrapping his arms around Kyreen.

"Me too," she answered, returning his embrace.

After what seemed much too soon, Lang pulled back. Placing a soft kiss on Kyreen's forehead, he turned and disappeared into the mist.

Smiling, Kyreen slipped into the tent, glad to see Synnove's form on her pallet. Kyreen's relief was short lived when her tentmate sat up even as Kyreen was settling onto her blankets.

"I cannot keep track of everything you need to tell me," Synnove teased, her voice full of glee. She began clicking items off her fingers. "Engla. The baby. Your trip to Myrddin. A lover in Myrddin? Your sudden proficiency in tracking. Nighttime trysts with Lang?" She paused, smiling over at her ill-at-ease tentmate. "I am pretty sure there is more that you are keeping from me."

"Synnove," Kyreen began, only to stop when her friend put a hand.

"But not this morning," Synnove said firmly. "Today is all about the tournament."

"Very well," Kyreen nodded, watching her friend pull on her boots.

"But soon, Kyreen, you and I will have a conversation," Synnove replied. She leaned over plucking a leaf from the older woman's curls, adding with an impish grin, "I cannot wait to hear about everything!"

Once again embarrassed, Kyreen snatched the leaf from Synnove's hand. "There is not much to say."

"Only someone with much to tell would attempt to cover it up with such a poor lie," Synnove teased, rolling toward the tent's exit. "Let us go. Morning assembly will start soon."

Kyreen watched Synnove exit, then looked down at the dry oak leaf in her hand. Impulsively she placed it upon her knapsack before slipping out after her friend, a smile on her lips and heart.

A short while later, after morning assembly and breakfast, the two women had a little time before the day's first competition. They were seated around the camp fire with their peers, the conversation trivial. About the fourth time Kyreen pushed her ebony curls out of her face, Synnove leaned over.

"I could braid your hair for you," she offered quietly. "It should be long enough for plaiting."

When Kyreen hesitated, the younger women chuckled softly. "By my word, Kyreen, today is about competition. I will not pester you with my burning curiosities."

Laughing, Kyreen acquiesced. So, the two went back to their tent for hair ties. Sitting outside, the morning sun starting to burn off the gray mist, Kyreen distinctly felt Lang's exit from camp. Instead of feeling distracted, she found she merely looked forward to his return.

"Thank you, Synnove," Kyreen said, lightly running her fingertips over the neatly woven braid. "It feels good to have it out of my face."

"We need every advantage we can get for archery," Synnove commented, not needing to add that Yngve was by and far away the one to beat in this category.

As predicted, Yngve did indeed take top honors in the archery event. Kyreen barely edged out Synnove and Ebbe for second spot with her friends rounding out the top four with 3rd and 4th respectively. As the trainees gathered for midday meal, before the afternoon's final event, it was Yngve in the overall lead with a single event left, sparring.

"I, for one, do not need to see the brackets to know I have not a chance to win in sparring," Synnove said without malice as she finished eating, handing her still half full plate to Yngve. "You two," indicating Kyreen and Ebbe, "will each have a bracket and I have no hope of advancing to the final round."

"I will never give up," Yngve commented, digging into Synnove's abandoned meal. "Although I believe I would prefer not to face either of them myself."

Ebbe's face folded into an uncharacteristic frown as he mentally calculated. "Unless all of you completely fail, my friends, I do not believe I can make up enough points to take overall points."

Kyreen ate slowly listening to her friends banter back and forth. The midday sun overhead warmed her back against the slight chill on the wind. For the first time in a long time she did not feel on edge about coming events. She could just as easily take second place to Ebbe in the spar. The thought of not placing first did not affect or worry her. These games of skill were exactly that – games. She would do her best as would her friends. The opportunity for camaraderie and fellowship was the highlight.

"All right there?" Synnove asked, drawing Kyreen out of her reflections. "Never better," she answered with a smile.

Noticing Ebbe eyeing her plate, Kyreen handed it over, glancing around the clearing. A majority of their classmates had finished their meals, and had begun dispersing.

"I believe the draw has begun," Synnove commented, rising to her feet.

Kyreen and the two young men followed suit. The latter hurriedly finished their extra rations and paused to drop off the soiled dinnerware before catching up with the women.

"I, for one, prefer to face Kyreen," Synnove commented, picking up on their previous conversation. "She is quick about it. No dawdling. The whistle blows. She pounces and then I am on my back."

They all laughed, even Kyreen. Synnove slipped an arm through Kyreen's, smiling up at her friend to ensure Kyreen harbored no hurt feelings.

"I will remember that technique," Ebbe said, pretending to ponder Synnove's information.

"She also does not leave bruises from throwing you down so blasted hard," Yngve added, rubbing the small of his back. "Try remembering that as well."

The friends laughed once again as they reached the sparring circle. Then their focus was directed to the newly posted brackets. As expected, Ebbe and Kyreen were ranked in the top two positions. The rest of the names had been drawn and placed randomly. Kyreen could not decipher the complicated divisions for consolation and rankings as one lost and continued.

"Then just do not lose," she murmured quietly to herself.

"That's always a good strategy, my friend," Synnove whispered into Kyreen's ear with a soft chuckle. "And remember to go easy on your poor tentmate."

She pointed at her name in the same bracket as Kyreen's. If both women won their first two rounds, as they should, they would face off in the third round with the winner moving on to the final, whereas Yngve and Ebbe upon winning their initial spars would meet in the second round. With each spar being held the main practice arena and Ebbe at the top of the bracket and her at the bottom, Kyreen's first match would be the last of this first initial round.

Therefore, she found a comfortable spot to lean against a tree and watch the spars.

As expected, both Ebbe and Yngve easily overpowered their first opponents. Synnove, while not as competitive, strong, or aggressive as her friends, also had no problems with her spar. Before too long Kyreen found herself in the ring facing Duabe, a young man from a blacksmith family, second in size only to Ebbe. Kyreen used his size to her favor in flipping him to the ground. Though she made her victory appear easy, it was much less so than it had been when the trainees had first arrived in camp. Kyreen silently marveled at the improvement, not just of her opponent, but all the trainees. She reckoned that her winning moves probably would not be successful in a few more months. But it was today so she enjoyed the accolades from her friends as she extended a hand to Daube to assist him to his feet.

"Well fought," she said. "You have improved since we last met."

Her sincere praise earned Kyreen a big smile from her opponent and a quirked brow from Synnove.

"Not that I am complaining mind you," Synnove murmured for Kyreen's ears alone as they made their way back to their viewing spot, "but since when does the stony Kyreen give praises?"

"I do not know," Kyreen shrugged, grinning. "It felt like the right thing to do."

The next bout, the first of the second round, the one pitting Yngve and Ebbe against each other, began, so the women turned their attentions to the ring. They did not wish defeat upon either of their friends and it was tense watching the two young men face off. Yngve had also improved over the winter months and managed to hold his own with his friend. Still when time was called, Ebbe had the most points and was declared the winner.

Kyreen watched the two friends as they exited the ring. The camaraderie and good sportsmanship between all the competitors continued to amaze her. She hoped if Ebbe defeated her today, she could react with the same good grace.

After Synnove won her next spar on points, Kyreen entered the ring. She had not studied the brackets, therefore was slightly surprised to find herself facing Yngve's love interest, Karine. For most of the season Kyreen had kept to herself, only Synnove's extroverted nature and stubbornness at making sure Kyreen was included in everything had kept Kyreen from being completely estranged from the rest of the class. So, while Kyreen had experienced a few dealings with Karine, she had not really interacted much with the other young woman. Thus, Kyreen was taken aback to feel a strong animosity rolling off of her opponent as they faced each other. Kyreen's brow furrowed, confused by her opponent's reaction. What could Kyreen have done to garner such animosity? Surely, it could not be jealousy over Kyreen's relationship with Yngve? Everyone knew of Kyreen's blood kin relationship to Aren, and therefore Yngve. Besides this emotion felt more of outrage than jealousy.

Distracted by the mystery, Kyreen missed the starting signal, thereby almost did not avoid Karine's first attack. Her frustration at the misstep caused Kyreen to be a bit too aggressive in her take down, knocking the breath out of Karine. Fortunately, no real damage had been done and nobody made a comment. Yngve did, however, give Kyreen a frown as he moved over to Karine's side.

The matches continued, giving time before Kyreen was scheduled to meet Synnove in the ring. Kyreen spent the time mulling over Karine's attitude while watching the matches with half attention. Finally, it was Ebbe's turn in his semifinal round. The young man he faced was not as tall or husky, but possessed quickness and strength. A few minutes into the match, Ebbe spun his opponent up and over his shoulder, knocking the other man out, ending the match.

"Ouch," Synnove muttered, wincing visibly. "Try to take it easy on me, Kyreen."

Kyreen glanced over at her friend, wondering if Synnove meant to be lax in the ring. She need not have worried. Synnove entered the ring focused and prepared to give the match all of her attention, just like everything else she did even though she had never been victorious against her tentmate. While the competition remained pure, Kyreen felt gratitude towards her friend who with her intimate knowledge of Kyreen's life could have easily distracted her with verbal barbs, a technique employed by some of the lesser skilled trainees. Not for the first time Kyreen wondered if their pairing as tentmates had been engineered or chance.

What Synnove lacked in strength, natural talent, and aggressiveness she more than made up for in quickness and tactical smarts. Fortunately for Kyreen, she was quicker than Synnove and had taught her tentmate strategy.

Thus, the match ended fairly quickly with Synnove on her back grinning up at Kyreen.

"At least I will not be bruised," she quipped as Kyreen pulled her to her feet.

Kyreen chuckled as they exited the ring, making way for the next round of matches to begin. She and Ebbe would face off in the champion match while Synnove would compete against Yngve in the consolation bracket.

She watched the consolation matches with divided attentions. The mystery with Yngve's girl still puzzling her and the upcoming match with Ebbe should have been her priority, but Lang occupied her thoughts. When in the ring Kyreen had no problem focusing on the task at hand. But, in the lull between matches, she found her contemplations constantly circling around to the tall, bearded Calanian. That Lang occupied her thoughts was not a new experience. The man had been a prickle upon her since Kyreen's arrival to Calan last summer. At least that had been Kyreen's perception. Now her conflicting emotions battled.

Kyreen had never truly pondered what is meant to be soul mates. On the surface, hearing people like her cousin Aren discuss it, being bonded sounded charming, romantic even. In practice Kyreen did not like the notion that she had no choice, that being bonded to Lang, that their relationship had been somehow engineered by some omnipotent being or mystical energy. Kyreen could not, however, deny the stirring of feelings that fluttered when she thought on her recent interactions with Lang. When her imagination wandered into lustful territory and Kyreen found herself fantasizing about how Lang's beard would feel upon her skin as they kissed, she stood up, both physically and mentally shaking herself off.

"All right there, Kyreen?" her tentmate asked, brow furrowed.

Kyreen nodded, grateful Synnove had not appeared to have picked up on Kyreen's emotions, or if she had, Kyreen's tentmate had chosen discretion.

"I need to move around," Kyreen responded.

"Do not wander too far," Ebbe called after her good naturedly, "I would dislike winning by forfeit."

Kyreen chuckled giving her two friends a wave as she moved off. Yngve sat on the opposite side of the ring, having taken to shadowing Karine ever since the match with Kyreen. Every so often Kyreen caught the young woman glaring at her. Kyreen resolved to ask Yngve about her after the tournament. Now was neither the time nor the place for out-of-ring confrontations.

Knowing she needed to be focused if she had any chance of defeating Ebbe in the championship match, Kyreen headed for an unoccupied area where she could meditate. After a few cycles, she felt much more centered, just in time as Magnar called for Synnove and Yngve to enter the ring. Kyreen moved back towards the ring to watch her friends. Being a double elimination match and having faced Ebbe so early meant Yngve had fought through several extra matches to get to that match. This left the two friends evenly matched as Synnove used her quickness to garner a couple of early points. When the time finally ran out, Synnove was declared the winner on points and it was Kyreen's turn to face off against Ebbe.

Chapter 14

As always, Kyreen's nerves calmed and a peace settled over her as she entered the ring. Though the young man still resembled the bright-eyed youth Kyreen had first sparred last summer, these last few months at Training Camp had strengthened more than Ebbe's body. Now he had experience and training to go with his size and strength. No longer could Kyreen rely on distraction or lapses to gain an advantage. Resolutely she reined in her thoughts. Now was not the time for woolgathering.

Normally Kyreen made an opening lunge with the start of a match in order to gain an early point, to put her opponent on the defense, but she had been practicing with Ebbe for months. He would be ready for just such an opening. As Magnar recited the obligatory remarks at the head of each match, Kyreen's mind raced over different possible opening gambits, devising and rejecting half a dozen in as many seconds. Then, just as Magnar signaled the start of the match, she latched onto one possibility. Unable to stop herself, a grin spread across Kyreen's face, which almost cost her the match. For Ebbe, who had been coiled ready to pounce on Magnar's mark, hesitated upon seeing his friend's expression. But his pause was not long and he committed to the lunge before the sound of Magnar's voice faded. Even so, that little hiccup caused Kyreen's strike to arrive just a heartbeat too soon as she dropped to the ground, deftly rolling under Ebbe's touch to strike his leg awkwardly before popping up behind him. She tagged him once more from behind, not hard enough to knock him down but hard enough to cause a stumble.

"Two points to Kyreen," Magnar proclaimed.

Now, Kyreen thought, all she had to do was evade Ebbe until the final sands in the timepiece ran out. Easier said than done she discovered over the ensuing moments. Ebbe and Kyreen circled, lunged, evaded, sometimes singularly, sometimes in a flurry, but each managed to whirl away each time without any retaliatory strikes. When the final sands sifted through the glass, Magnar declared Kyreen the victor on points and she released her pent-up tensions.

"Good show, Kyreen," Ebbe commented a beefy hand patting her shoulder.

"You, too," she responded cheerily. "I swear you make me feel like an old woman. The sand moved a tad too slowly there."

"Well done," Synnove said, hugging Kyreen tight as the two competitors exited the arena. "I knew you could do it."

Kyreen looked around in confusion. All of the trainees, Karine included though reluctantly, approached to offer congratulations. After the third person, Kyreen belatedly realized everyone was commending her not for the sparring win but for the overall tournament victory.

Ebbe grinned anew, wrapping Kyreen in a bear hug. "Synnove would not allow us to say anything."

"Rightly so," Synnove defended herself. "Kyreen would have overthought the whole thing and lost."

When Yngve the last in line hugged her tight, Kyreen whispered in his ear, "Cousin, I thought you had top points."

"That loss to Synnove in the end put she and me tied in overall points," Yngve responded, shaking his head.

"If Ebbe had won your match, it would have been a four-way tie between us four," Synnove added.

Kyreen caught a glimpse of Karine looking at their group. "I also thought you were angry with me," she told Yngve, who had the grace to look sheepish.

"No," he replied, "Karine is for some reason but I was merely…"

"…taking advantage of the situation," Synnove finished for him. She pushed Yngve towards Karine. "Go. We have some time before evening meal and Kyreen owes me a chat."

With a farewell wave to both women, Yngve and Ebbe moved off to join the group of trainees heading towards camp. Synnove slipped an arm through Kyreen's to guide them to a log upon which they sat. Magnar and the other camp instructors nodded to the pair as they too made their way out of the practice area.

Once alone Kyreen relaxed, grateful the competition was concluded, feeling odd that she had emerged victorious. Deep inside, a competitive spark flared as she realized Lang had also won top spot here a few years prior. He would be proud of her. Just like that, her thoughts turned to him, pushing away anything else.

"That right there," Synnove said, drawing Kyreen back to the present. "Your face lights up and you feel whole. That is entirely new and you did not bring it from Myrddin."

Kyreen hesitated, unsure about sharing even though Synnove was her tentmate and closest Calanian friend. How much could Kyreen say without revealing too much or lying? She nibbled at her bottom lip.

"And now it is gone!" Synnove threw up her hands. "Poof! Just like that. You are the most perplexing soul I have ever observed."

"Wait," Kyreen responded. "You mean you see souls? I know you sense souls, but are you saying that you see, that you visualize souls?"

"Sure, yes," Synnove answered shrugging. "Every soul gives off an aura of color. Calanians are green. Babies start off as a pale green and as the years go by the aura changes to a deep green."

"Others? What do they look like?"

"I have never seen anyone other than Calanians," Synnove responded with a shake of her head.

"Really?" Kyreen frowned. She had not ever fully contemplated just how isolated her people had become. "What about the guards at the castle?"

"With the armor and distance, I could not discern their auras. I am told other people emit different auras."

"Told?"

"As I mentioned before Soul Seekers are very scarce. Once my gift had been revealed I trained with the only other Soul Seeker, a distant cousin several times removed. She shared many of the ..."

Synnove's voice trailed off and she shot a grin at Kyreen. "You crafty dodger! Every time you do this! Not now! It is your turn to talk."

"What?" Kyreen returned the grin.

"You switch the topic, get me talking so you will not have to," Synnove responded good naturedly. "Soul Seeking can wait. Tell me about Myrddin."

So Kyreen spoke about Engla and the newborn babe. She even included how she had gone to the guild hall to fetch Collin due to Engla's birthing sadness.

"He is your former lover, is he not?" Synnove asked.

Kyreen blushed deep red, silently cursed her tentmate's memory. "Yes," she finally spoke, "Collin is the man who stayed with me at Council Camp last summer. We were intimate until Engla's arrival."

"What type of friend is she to steal away your lover?" Synnove asked with typical Calanian bluntness.

"Engla did not know," Kyreen replied, defending her oldest friend, "and I pray she never knows. Truth be told, she did me a favor marrying Collin."

Synnove nodded, then with a sly expression spreading over her face, asked, "How did you happen to have a key to the guildhall side entrance?"

Kyreen blushed again, now cursing her lapse in attention during the telling of the events in Myrddin. "Rhun had given me the key on a previous visit," she replied cautiously. Before Synnove could respond, Kyreen felt Lang return to camp, and a tension deep inside, one she had not previously recognized, released.

"So, it is him," Synnove remarked.

"It is who?" Kyreen tried to feign innocent when all she wanted to do was find Lang and...what? Embrace him? Kiss him? Her mind flew ahead and her cheeks flushed.

"Rhun, the guild master," Synnove stated bluntly. "He is your lover in Myrddin. But I had already surmised that from previous bits of conversation."

"Yes, him," Kyreen admitted absently, her mind clearly not on the conversation.

"Something else is the matter right now," Synnove said, peering suspiciously at Kyreen. "Your soul light is glowing."

"Lang," Synnove stated leaning back with a nod. "We all noticed his absence at the tournament. Unless it is Atle who makes your soul light shine."

"Oh, Synnove, stop!" Kyreen admonished, her cheeks deepening in embarrassment even as she laughed good naturedly.

"If you would keep me informed then I would not have to make up stories from various bits and pieces of information you let slip," Synnove stated, half-serious, half-joking. "Do you need to go meet him?"

Kyreen paused. Did she? She did not know. Should she approach him in front of others? What was protocol? Was she ready to be public about their relationship? Was Lang? What was their relationship?

"I have no idea," she finally confessed to her friend. "For so long I felt only animosity towards Lang and now...now he tells me we...he and I..."

"Are bonded?" Synnove offered. At Kyreen's nod she continued, "I am not surprised. You have both felt broken to me, plus there are the strong emotions you both exude around each other."

"You suspected this?" Kyreen asked incredulously. "Yet gave me no warning?"

"Do not get riled at me," Synnove stated, not unkindly. "It has taken me most of the winter to get you to speak more than a dozen words a day."

Kyreen knew Synnove spoke the truth yet still she felt uneasy. Was it the conversation or something else?

Synnove stood up suddenly, extending a hand to Kyreen. "Come," she said. "You have shared enough of your secretive life for one day. Let us find your man. Evening meal is upon us. Then I feel like joining the others at the springs. This weather has been gloriously sunny and beautiful these past two days, but Ebbe predicts snow by tomorrow eve."

Kyreen took her friend's hand and smoothly rose to her feet. Heading towards camp the tension in her heart began to lessen, completely dissipating the moment she saw Lang.

As Synnove had said, evening meal had begun. As Kyreen joined the queue, Lang, nearly to the front of the line, turned and caught her eye. He gave her a quick wink and a smile before turning his attention back to the conversation he and Atle were having.

Synnove held her tongue but arched an eyebrow at Kyreen. Then she launched into a discussion about something which Kyreen listened to with only half her attention.

By the time the meal concluded the sun had set and the wind had picked up, its chill holding a promise of the impending snow Ebbe had predicted. Kyreen bade her friends farewell as they dispersed to complete their evening chores before heading to the cliffs. Wrapping her cloak about her body Kyreen moved to the central fire to warm up.

Moments later she felt Lang's silent approach. Just days earlier tension would have filled her, but tonight his arrival warmed her nearly as much as the flames of the fire. Without speaking Lang stood beside her, their shoulders barely touching. Though she could sense the rest of the camp as they went about their evening duties, Kyreen felt most strongly connected to the man next to her.

As the silence grew Kyreen's mind wandered. Should she have greeted him upon his arrival? Was he waiting for her to speak? Had she missed something? Nibbling at her bottom lip, she stole a look at Lang's face, unable to discern anything from his expression. Concerned about offending him, she refrained from probing his emotions which were probably completely locked down and undetectable anyway.

Unexpectedly Lang's gaze shifted to her face, his green eyes twinkling as he grinned at her. "With all the anger gone from you, I do rather enjoy experiencing your range of feelings," he commented, the warmth and teasing of his tone taking away any sting.

"At least I have emotions," Kyreen grumbled, returning the grin.

And like that, the tension fled from her, and their conversation flowed. Lang congratulated Kyreen on her victory and she related the details of the day's competition. Camp life continued around them as the twilight dusk deepened into a dark starry night, yet no one approached the pair standing before the fire. At a lull in the conversation, Kyreen looked around, wondering how aware the others were of this connection. Were they consciously avoiding her and Lang, or maybe it was more subconsciously? A blush rose to her cheeks as she pondered the gossip that might be going on about the two of them.

"And there she goes," Lang quipped watching her face.

Though no animosity or judgement laced Lang's tone, Kyreen's anxiety intensified.

"I am sorry," she responded.

He shook his head. "No apologies needed. Maybe this is a good time to move somewhere more secluded, then you can tell me about this place you grew up."

Kyreen agreed and they headed away from the warmth of the fire. She thought their path would take them to the same small clearing where they had spent the previous evening. Instead Lang aimed for the sleeping tents, eventually pausing before one Kyreen could only assume was Lang's tent.

"The wind and temperature are a tad cooler than yester eve," Lang explained. "Either we can converse inside my tent, or I will gather up a blanket and we can go back to the clearing by the cliffs. Your choice."

"Cliffs," Kyreen quickly responded. The implications of being in his tent were too much for her to deal with at this time.

Lang gave her a questioning look before ducking inside, but he held his tongue. As they once more walked side by side, Kyreen warred internally at containing her emotions. By the time, they settled into what Kyreen had started thinking of as their clearing, she had her emotions under control.

"Now then," Lang said, settling back against the boulder draping the blanket over them, "I was present at your Telling last summer but to be perfectly honest I did not hear a word you said. Your arrival had set me so off-balanced it was all I could do to sit still."

"But you…" Kyreen struggled to remember his exact words, "…you deemed my story the truth then recommended immediate separation."

Even now knowing the true reason behind his dislike, the memory of his words hurt her more than she liked. Shivering Kyreen drew her legs up, wrapping her arms around them, setting her chin on her knees.

"Ouch," Lang winced. "Yes, I did make that recommendation. Though I knew your story true, I did harbor worry that your presence would be a distraction."

"For you or for our people?" Kyreen asked, ashamed she could not stay her accusatory tone.

"Both," Lang sighed. "Since we are being honest I would say mainly me, only partially our people."

Kyreen nodded, grateful for the honesty but still hurt. She did not wish to quarrel or bring up past bad behaviors. Goddess knew she had not always, or even ever, behaved rationally where Lang was concerned. Belatedly she wondered how much of her lingering hostility was from her past history with Lang or from her failed relationship with Collin. Once again, she flushed with embarrassment.

"I am so sorry," she said.

"For?"

She shrugged, tongue tied, and unable to verbalize the words in her mind.

"Last summer," she finally answered.

"Let us leave the past there where it belongs. Nothing can be done to change it," Lang commented. Kyreen sensed sadness and, again, guilt woven in his words. Before she could pursue it though he added, "Why don't we start with your Telling?"

So Kyreen recited the words of her story while the stars overhead emerged and the wind danced among the trees. At some point, Lang's arm slipped around her shoulder and she snuggled against his warmth. As she finished the Telling, Lang's fingers absently played with a soft curl that had escaped from her braid.

"I sense so much unspoken in your words," he finally commented quietly.

Kyreen nodded slowly against his shoulder. Here in the dark, nestled against Lang's warmth, Hanoria and her youth seemed so far away and long ago. Yet she did still feel ties to that far away province. Though Stian now lived at Jorn's farm, she could not picture him there. Always in her mind she saw her foster parents, not as they had been there at the end, but how they had been when she first arrived, already advanced in years but still vibrantly full of life. Ildri, her foster mother, had been so full of love and light, and Kyreen's presence had just multiplied those traits. Upon reflection Kyreen had to wonder who saved or doomed whom that cold First Day of Snows when Tyra left her in Jorn's care.

"It would be simple to dwell on the last years," she finally replied aloud. "When Jorn drank too much and Ildri…when her body remained while her essence had gone. But truly, had I not been of Calanian blood, had I not known what I had lost, had I belonged there, it would have been a wonderful childhood. Would they have been better off had I never entered their lives? That is a two-edged sword of good and bad."

"My apologies for dredging up sad memories," Lang murmured into her hair.

"Not all sad," she replied, relaxing into his embrace, stifling a yawn but not before he sensed her weariness.

"Sleep. There will be time enough for talk later," he whispered, drawing the blanket more securely around them and kissing the top of her head.

With a contented sigh, Kyreen happily complied, allowing her eyes to drift shut. Within moments she slumbered, while Lang continued to keep watch on the night, idly twirling one of her curls about his finger.

A light sprinkling of snow overnight had draped the landscape in white, but the pines overhead sheltered the pair from the snowfall. So, when Kyreen awoke to the warmth of Lang's body beside her under the blanket, she felt just as cozy as if she were in her tent. Cautiously she shifted to look up at Lang, who eyes were already open, watching her.

She smiled then snuggled back, nestling her head against his shoulder. She was content to stay right where they were in their cozy den. No reason to venture out into the cold wet snow. Blood rushed to her cheeks as her mind wandered, exploring the possibilities of what they could be doing instead of sleeping. Before her imagination could get the better of her, Kyreen silently chastised herself. This was the second night they had spent together, yet they had not even kissed. The thought gave Kyreen pause. While she could no longer deny her physical attraction to Lang, she had yet to feel any reciprocity from him. She could sense he enjoyed her company and their time together. But beyond that she felt no sexual tension or passion from the tall Calanian.

Could soulmates be platonic? The thought startled her. She had always assumed the bond was one of a bodily nature. Yet there was so much she did not know, so much she did not understand.

"It is much too early and too peaceful of a morn for you to be so upset," Lang remarked, his quiet voice, the rumbling of his chest beneath her cheek, pulling Kyreen from her thoughts.

She drew away from him, sitting up to look at him, her green eyes serious. The question escaped her mouth before her mind registered her words. "Do you desire me?"

As soon as she spoke, Kyreen's face blossomed red and she turned away, saying, "My apologies. Please do not answer that."

"Hey," Lang said quietly. He pressed a hand to her cheek, bringing her face back towards him. Slowly, he lowered his lips to hers. The kiss started soft, exploring, then deepened, leaving Kyreen breathless when he finally pulled back.

"Let us enjoy our time together?" he said, his voice husky.

"M'kay," Kyreen murmured.

Lang chuckled, "Come on. Morning assembly should be starting soon."

He rose smoothly to his feet, extending a hand to assist Kyreen up. Once she stood, he pulled her close, gazing down at her, a smile playing about his lips. As she looked up at him, the beauty of his features struck her breathless again. Did he know the affect he had on her? Surely, he must feel her arousal. She waited for another knee-weakening kiss, but instead he pressed a chaste kiss to her forehead before walking her back to the assembly grounds.

PART II

"I cannot believe I am about to say this, but I am happy to be leaving the cliffs," Synnove commented, tying up her bedroll. "Spring Festival is always such an exciting event with everyone all together in one place."

"I am looking forward to it," Kyreen responded, finishing up her packing.

The Training Camp's migration to the Great Valley had finally arrived. Once the Festival had concluded, the trainees would stay in the Great Valley for the remainder of the summer, unless the Council had decided to attempt retaking the castle. That was the topic on all the trainees' minds for the last fortnight, all except maybe Kyreen. After her victory in the tournament, her night life had settled into a much different routine than the previous few months. While training continued during the day, being exempt from camp duties left Kyreen with much free time to spend with Lang.

Synnove and Kyreen moved outside to begin dismantling their tent. All around other trainees similarly packed gear and tore down tents.

Kyreen inhaled deeply, enjoying the scent of the pines and the ocean. Though she had not said anything to Synnove, Kyreen would miss this place. Not for the first time she marveled at the last fortnight, how much she had changed. Her time with Lang had filled an emptiness she had never realized existed inside of her. As Synnove had described seeing Kyreen as whole, it had surely seemed such as Kyreen had flourished in all training areas even tracking.

On the fourth evening exercise after the tournament, when Kyreen had returned to the fire without detection, Magnar had pulled her aside after the others left.

"No more," he had told her, "may you be passive in the tracking. From now on you must seek as well as evade."

Once his words would have cut Kyreen even though he spoke with a smile. This time, however, she had been able to perceive this before the hurt flooded.

"Yes, Magnar," Kyreen had responded, anxious to leave for her nightly rendezvous with Lang.

"And Kyreen?" Magnar had halted her before she could slip away.

"Yes?" she had paused, her body tense more from habit than from his tone which had not changed.

"I am glad you have reconciled your differences with Lang," the Hunt Master had remarked.

Joy and warmth, tinged with just a touch of embarrassment, had flooded the young woman. She had returned his smile, saying, "Many thanks, Magnar. So am I."

Now the Hunt Master's voice broke through Kyreen's memories, pulling her back to the present. "A little less woolgathering, a little more work," he ordered.

Embarrassed, Kyreen glanced around, immediately relieved Magnar had been prodding not her but Yngve's girl at the adjoining tent site. Absently Kyreen realized she had never asked Yngve why Karine held a grudge against her.

"If you will take the tent, I can carry our packs," Synnove commented before Kyreen's thoughts could wander again. "Once we drop this gear off we are done. Well, you are. I am assigned to assist breaking down the kitchen."

"I feel so indolent," Kyreen remarked as they began walking towards the center of camp where the wagons waited. "I would help, but everyone pushes me away."

"I would relieve you of your burden of sloth," Yngve quipped, falling in step with the young women, "but I am not permitted."

"He knows because he asked," Ebbe added, the young men's tent resting easily on his shoulder as the friends strolled together, causing the four to laugh.

Gradually, over the last fortnight, the weather had warmed, the wind losing its chill and the grasses once again greening. The sun rising in the east warmed Kyreen's face while the breeze ruffled the few errant curls which had escaped her braid. She sighed softly, contentedly, enjoying the moment.

After loading their gear into a wagon, Kyreen's friends dispersed to their assigned duty stations and Kyreen found herself alone. Just to occupy her time Kyreen drifted over to where the horses had been gathered to be saddled. Amund, the camp's hostler, nodded to Kyreen upon her approach.

"You may grab your gelding if you wish," she told Kyreen. "He does not misbehave with others, but he does not exactly behave either."

"Yes, he has always been sneaky that way," Kyreen responded with a chuckle.

From her pouch, Kyreen withdrew an apple saved from breakfast just to lure her horse to her, but she need not have bothered. The gelding, expressing his joy at seeing Kyreen, easily parted from the herd to be haltered. As she went through the task of saddling the big sorrel horse, Kyreen chatted to her horse, enjoying the process. She believed both she and her horse were looking forward to being on the trail once more. They both had a bit of wanderlust.

"Later, Kyreen," Yngve called to her as he and another trainee rode out of camp. As a Hunter, he was tasked with scouting ahead of the camp's path to make sure it was clear for the wagons. Moving the camp was always a perilous undertaking.

Once her horse had been tacked Kyreen wandered off to the side, under a large oak tree to wait for the migration to begin. Eventually Lang, his horse saddled, joined her. Without speaking they stood shoulder to shoulder, watching the other horses being saddled. Kyreen's gelding sniffed Lang's mare, who head butted the big horse good-naturedly.

Once again Kyreen marveled in the calm she felt in Lang's presence. Though they had spent every evening together since the tournament, their physical relationship had not advanced beyond a handful of kisses that had left Kyreen breathless. In those moments, she could feel Lang's desire for her, a red fiery flame, that called to her desires. Almost immediately, however, Lang would shut down his passions, closing off from Kyreen anew.

When pressed Lang would ask for her to enjoy the time they had together in peace. Today Lang still had his emotions under wraps, but Kyreen sensed a new layer of apprehension. Though he gave no external sign of the tension, she had become attuned to the nuances in his, what little she could feel.

As the couple stood waiting, the other trainees began assembling as their chores were completed and their mounts saddled. Synnove nodded as she passed by them, walking with Ebbe and Karine, who glared icily without speaking. Because he was in her peripheral vision as Kyreen's gaze followed the group, Kyreen caught the motion of Lang clenching his jaw.

'So', she thought, turning a thoughtful gaze on Lang. 'Maybe Karine's attitude is not related to Yngve after all.'

Aloud she asked, "Do you know Karine well?"

"We have met," Lang responded neutrally.

"Do you know why she is so displeased with me?" Kyreen continued pressing, deciding to take the direct path.

Lang swiveled his head to gaze at Kyreen. She saw the almost imperceptible tightening around his eyes and knew his words before he spoke them. "Please let us enjoy today's ride?" he asked.

Kyreen, sensing anew the sadness and guilt inside him, acquiesced. Though she wanted answers, she also did not wish to be the cause of his discomfort.

"Very well," she answered, reaching a hand over to squeeze his gently.

Smiling a soft smile that did not reach his eyes, Lang grasped her hand in his lifting it up to his lips. Placing a gentle kiss upon her knuckles, he murmured, "Thank you."

Eventually all was packed and everyone set to go. A small handful of trainees and leaders remained with the wagons, which would travel a more circuitous route, arriving in the Great Valley later in the day. The rest would travel through the forest, arriving in the Great Valley shortly before midday.

Riding single file through the trees and on alert for any Galorians did not lend itself to talk. With Lang's horse in front, Kyreen's gelding was content to follow. So Kyreen relaxed, inhaling deeply the pine scent mingled with the musky odor of the horses. Hoof beats muffled by pine needles softly clumped, the sounds joined by creaking leather and an occasional jangle from a bit.

Her thoughts wandered, pondering on the upcoming Spring Festival. From her vague memories, she recalled it to be a celebration of the foaling season. From Synnove, however, it sounded like so much more. Spring foaling would be taking place, but so would preparing the fields for planting. General assembly would also happen, a time for leaders like Aren to report on the happenings of the last season and to prepare every one for the upcoming one. The activity which intrigued, and worried Kyreen the most, was the Courting Ceremony. According to Synnove, the festival had always included the courting, a time when all the eligible Calanians would come together in search of spouses. This was a highlight of the festival, since the Calanians were so infrequently all in one place. This gave young people the opportunity to meet other young people, dance and socialize and, with luck, discover love.

When Kyreen asked Synnove if she had plans to be courted at the festival, the younger woman had shot Kyreen a dark look.

"I will not be courted," Synnove had proclaimed icily. "I will do the courting, and yes I do have someone in mind."

Mentally noting that the courting rites of Calan were definitely different from Hanoria, Kyreen had inquired about whom Synnove had set her sights.

Synnove had grinned coyly. "Now that is a secret I cannot share not even with my best friend lest I jinx it. Will you be courting Lang?"

"What?" Kyreen's face had flushed red. "How come in one breath you proclaim you cannot talk about your beau then in the next ask about mine."

"You and Lang are not unknown," Synnove waved a hand. "We all know you two should be bonded. Just like we all expect Yngve's girl to court him this year. Those two have been drawn to each other since we were children. They may even covenant."

Kyreen's face had turned several more shades of red hearing Synnove's casual proclamation that everyone knew she and Lang should be bonded. Everyone it seemed save she. Now Kyreen nibbled at her bottom lip contemplating her relationship with Lang. She could not deny she enjoyed their time together or that she was attracted to him. Their nightly conversations flowed easily and she relished their camaraderie. But did she love him? Was she in love with him? What was involved with courting? How did one court? Synnove had mentioned dancing. Was there a dance or a ritual or words to recite? Suddenly Kyreen's anxiety skyrocketed. She pinched the bridge of her nose between her forefinger and thumb, silently reciting her morning meditations in an attempt to quell the panic rising in her chest.

Ahead of her, Lang turned in his saddle to cast her a questioning look over his shoulder. Kyreen smiled wanly and doubled her efforts to stamp out her anxiety.

'Think happy thoughts,' she silently chided. Breathing in deeply she turned her mind to the other aspects of the festival. All of the camps would be present which meant she would be able to visit with Aren and Viggo. Kyreen also looked forward to spending some time with Vidar, the old blacksmith. He had been childhood friends with her grandfather and had always had a story to tell. The foals would be dropping as well. Kyreen had requested birthing duty during the festival and hoped she would be able to assist with a few births. Foaling season had always been her favorite time on the homestead in Hanoria and she missed working with horses on a daily basis. Kyreen allowed her mind to wander along these topics as the caravan continued the trek through the woods.

Shortly before midday the terrain began to change. The trees grew closer as the forest closed in around the group of riders, and Kyreen recognized the thick brambles that protected the perimeter of the Great Valley. Then they had reached the gate and were through. Just as it had the summer prior, the vast verdant green valley took her breath away. As the others began urging their mounts forward to lope down the valley, Kyreen pulled her gelding to the side to take in the view. Tents and activity abounded on this side of the river, glinting blue in the distance. The Training Camp looked to be the last to arrive.

"Alright there, Kyreen?" Synnove inquired pulling Kyreen out of her thoughts.

"Just admiring the view," Kyreen grinned.

"You do that. Me? I am going to go find my family." Synnove gathered her up her reins to leave, then added, "I will see you at the training section to put up our tent once the wagons arrive."

Kyreen nodded, waving her friend away. "Sounds good. Now go!"

Watching Synnove and her mount take off, Kyreen had her hands full restraining her gelding. He did not understand why all the other horses were getting to run while he must stand still.

Kyreen felt Lang pull up next to her and turned to him. The smile on her lips faded when she saw his expression. The guilt and sorrow he had been suppressing overflowed.

'No,' she thought. 'I do not want to hear what he has to say.'

"Kyreen," Lang started to speak. "I have avoided this conversation too long. I fear maybe…"

Kyreen held up a hand, shaking her head. "Whatever you need to say, please do not. I want to enjoy my ride down to the camp."

"But I need to…" Lang started to talk but Kyreen spurred her gelding forward. Not needing any additional encouragement, the big horse sprang forward. For an instant Kyreen felt bad about her childish behavior but then the wind caught her hair and her blood raced with the dizzying speed. She leaned down low against her gelding's neck, the reins loose, her eyes stinging from the wind. After his initial burst of speed, the gelding settled into long loping strides that ate up the distance.

In too short a time, Kyreen found herself on the edge of the encampment where several trainees had been met by their family members. Kyreen spotted Synnove across the way with a dark-haired woman who wore Synnove's face in twenty years. Glancing around Kyreen spied Yngve embracing his younger sister, Gunda. Aren, Viggo, and their middle child Reidar were also present. Kyreen thought about going over, but decided she may as well face up to whatever Lang had wanted to discuss.

Sliding off the gelding, she turned to face the direction from whence she had ridden to watch Lang, having followed at a much more sedate pace, ride into camp. His green gaze peered at her and even from this distance she could feel his sorrow. Brow furrowed, she stood waiting as people and horses milled around her. When he reached the edge of the encampment, he slid off his horse and began walking towards Kyreen on foot. While still a few steps away, Lang's attention was diverted and his eyes moved to something off to her left.

"Papa!" a small girl not more than three or four years of age ran up to Lang, her arms opened wide, two braids streaming behind her.

"Jetta!" Lang exclaimed, snatching the little girl into his arms and pulling her close.

Over the child's dark head, Lang gazed at Kyreen, who stood frozen in place. She felt as though a bucket of ice water had been thrown over her. Before she could recover, a striking woman, her brunette hair glinting auburn highlights, walked up to Lang. Resting upon her hip was an infant child, not even a year old. Lang shifted the little girl in his arms so as to take the baby from the woman who softly kissed his cheek before the gathering up his horse's reins for him, so he could hold both children.

Dazed, Kyreen turned away before Lang could speak or the woman glanced her way. Swallowing the lump in her throat and blinking back hot tears, Kyreen somehow stumbled away, heading to the horse area.

Chapter 16

"Kyreen!" Gunda called, running to catch up with the older woman.

Kyreen blinked back the unshed tears before turning to her cousin's youngest child. Whether the excitement of the day or discretion, Gunda did not appear to notice Kyreen's distress as the two embraced before continuing to walk towards the makeshift stable area. Gunda immediately launched into telling Kyreen of the latest news. Finding the youngster's enthusiasm a welcome distraction, Kyreen listened with half an ear as the girl talked about her trip to the valley, and the two made quick work of untacking the big gelding. Much too soon for Kyreen's liking her gear had been checked in and the gelding turned out to graze amongst the other horses. The sight of the herd, all varying shades of chestnut glinting in the spring sun, tugged at Kyreen's heart, reminding her of the herd she had left in Hanoria.

"There you are," Synnove's voice brought Kyreen out of her reminiscing. Kyreen waited as Gunda and Synnove greeted each other warmly. Of course, they knew each other, Kyreen thought remembering Synnove's mention that Yngve had been one of her best friends growing up.

"I am on duty here, helping with the horses," Gunda commented, taking the reins of Synnove's mount. "Maybe we can visit more at dinner?"

"Of course," Kyreen nodded.

Synnove slipped an arm through Kyreen's and led them away from the horse area. Once out of earshot she leaned in to whisper, "It appears Gunda has picked her mentor."

"What?"

"A mentor. It is someone to assist with coming of age, sometimes a parent or sibling, but most usually another relative. The mentor is meant to be a listener, to give advice, to ease a youth's transition to adulthood," Synnove explained. "Gunda is about the age. If I recall correctly she is three or four summers younger than Yngve."

"I do not know why anyone would seek advice from me," Kyreen muttered, her heart aching anew as she recalled Lang and his…family was the only word she could use.

Synnove stopped walking, peering up at Kyreen with sharp eyes. "What has happened?"

Kyreen glanced around. They were standing in the midst of a large number of Calanians, all hurrying about their business, everyone seeming to have a task. Although the activity and crowd nowhere matched the intensity in Myrddin, Kyreen felt simultaneously claustrophobic and exposed. This atmosphere was not ideal for a private conversation.

Sensing Kyreen's reticence, Synnove began walking again, only now their path headed for the edge of camp. Though the trees on the plain were scarce, Synnove spied a small grove along the river's bank. As they walked towards their destination, sunlight glinting off the languid currents, Kyreen felt the anxiety drain away. The hurt, however, remained burning, cutting, aching.

"Did you know?" she asked her friend.

"Did I know what?" Synnove replied warily.

"That Lang had, has a family, a mate, children?"

Synnove stopped walking to turn her full attention to Kyreen. "A mate? Children?"

"At least that is what it looked like to me," Kyreen nodded. "After all a small child does not yell 'Papa' to strangers."

Her heart aching anew, Kyreen recalled the beautiful woman handing the infant over to Lang, her lips pressing a kiss to Lang's bearded cheek, Lang's obvious comfort holding both the children.

"No, I did not know," Synnove shook her head, after Kyreen recounted the scene.

The two had settled in the dappled shadows of the grove, sitting shoulder to shoulder, facing the slow-moving river. Both had their legs drawn up, chin on knees.

"I am at a loss for words," Synnove continued, her voice quiet and neutral. "There must be an explanation. I saw both your soul lights."

Kyreen angrily wiped away the solitary tear that had escaped her eye. Frustrated at herself for trusting, for caring, for being made the fool again. "Your soul lights were wrong," she said aloud. Her sorrow making her blunter than was her norm. "Now I know why he would not bed me."

Synnove gave Kyreen a sharp look. "You mean to say that in all this time, all these nights together, you have never once coupled?"

Kyreen blushed red again and she buried her face against her knees. "Yes," came her muffled reply.

"Oh," was all Synnove said.

After a few moments of silence Kyreen peeked over at her friend, who sat gazing thoughtfully out over the river.

"Your silence concerns me," Kyreen commented. "You are supposed to be telling me everything will be alright, that I was mistaken, that I should not throw myself into the water."

"It will be, you were, and the current here is not swift nor is the river deep." Synnove responded, her tone pensive.

"Synnove, what is it?" Kyreen gave up any pretense of joking.

"That you and Lang have not consummated your relationship," Synnove remarked. "I realize this topic embarrasses you, though I know not why, but you also seem to want my advice."

"Yes," Kyreen prompted, suddenly unsure whether she truly wanted to discuss this topic with her tentmate.

"Was it you or he who pulled away from coitus?"

Kyreen opened her mouth to respond but hesitated. Was Lang the reason their physical relationship had not progressed? Up until Synnove asked the question Kyreen had been positive it had been. But maybe he had been waiting for her to make the first move. No, she told herself, she had made the first move. She had initiated kissing on several occasions and, while he had initially responded to her advances, leaving her weak-kneed and breathless, always it was he who pulled away, not Kyreen.

"Him," she finally answered.

"Then I would guess he is still bound to the woman you saw," Synnove remarked.

"How can that be?" Kyreen asked, her frustration level rising again. "I thought he and I were bound. You saw it in our soul lights." This last sentence came out more sarcastic than she had expected, causing Synnove to flash her a look of irritation.

"You two are bonded," Synnove explained patiently. "Anyone can be bound. That is another part of the festival, covenanting and renewing the marriage ties."

"I give up," Kyreen sighed, standing up to scoop a flat stone to toss out over the water with a quick flip of her wrist.

"I will get our quarters settled. Yngve or Ebbe can assist with tent," Synnove said, standing to brush non-existent dust from her seat. "You take your time."

"Thank you. You felt him, too?" Kyreen asked without turning, her gaze fixed on a small herd of mares and foals grazing just the other side of the river.

"No," Synnove replied without humor. "I felt your tension and looked over my shoulder."

Kyreen nodded still without looking, so she missed the silent interaction between Synnove and Lang as he walked up. Though Synnove stood almost a head taller than Kyreen's Hanorian friend Engla, she was petite for a Calanian and Lang was the tallest Calanian Kyreen had met. That did not matter to Synnove. Neither did she care that Lang served as one of her instructors, at least not for today. Today he was the man who hurt her friend and made Kyreen shed tears. As she passed Lang, Synnove paused to glare up at him, her fierce expression and flashing sapphire eyes spoke volumes to let Lang know she held him responsible and that he had better rectify the situation.

Lang stepped aside to let the young woman pass. He waited, watching her retreat, until Synnove had reached the camp's edge before approaching Kyreen. Reluctantly he sighed, running a hand over his closely shorn black hair. There was so much he needed to say, so much he should have told Kyreen weeks ago when they first reconciled their differences.

At first, he had hesitated because he had wanted to enjoy the relief gained from no longer battling. After a few days, he could never find the right time. Then when they had arrived in the Great Valley and he had fully intended on speaking with Kyreen before descending into camp, she had taken off before he had been able to form the words. Even now, with her standing before him, the hurt radiating from her, he did not know where to start. That he had caused this pain made it even worse. He would rather she be angry and lash out.

"I believe Synnove is rather peeved with me," Lang quipped, trying to break the ice.

"Do not," Kyreen replied, her tone flat and emotionless. "Do not attempt to joke with me. Not now."

Lang moved to stand behind Kyreen, barely refraining from taking her hand. "Would you at least look at me?"

"My ears hear just fine," Kyreen answered. She bit the inside of her mouth using the pain to focus, to push down the anguish. She did not want to look at Lang for fear that she would lose her composure, that she might break, that her heart would shatter. Unbidden Kyreen recalled the scene from last summer on the lake shore when she last felt betrayed like this. She had sworn then that she would never fall down like that ever again.

"I do not know where to begin," Lang sighed, moving to stand shoulder to shoulder with Kyreen so he could at least see her in his peripheral vision.

"You have a child, children," Kyreen stated. "How is that so difficult to say?"

"Not difficult," Lang responded. "Complicated."

"By the goddess, I hate that word," she fought to keep from turning to face him. As long as she kept her gaze focused on the herd, on something neutral, she would not succumb to the tears.

"Jetta is not of my blood," Lang explained quietly. "Her mother, Marietta, was the Truth Seer, my foster sister, who died during the birth. Marietta had a mate, but he was killed in a skirmish with a Galorian patrol. It was their bond severing that caused Mariette's fall which led to her broken back. Before she died, Marietta asked me and Kasja to watch over her child."

"That seemed fairly straight forward," Kyreen commented, even as her heart ached anew hearing his story. "Nothing complicated there."

Lang resisted the urge to chuckle. Leave it to Kyreen to confront his deceit head on. She had a directness that was grounded in something unique. Certain things flustered her, and her embarrassment at things he considered natural amused him. Not for the first time he wondered what she would have been like had she never left Calan. Dead most likely, he reminded himself. Still, what if her personality had not been shaped by an outside world of which Lang had never experienced? This valley and the one bordering where the camps, the castle and the Galorians lay were the sum total of his world. He could not begin to imagine the city of Myrddin or even the vast ocean as he had only ever once seen the Great Sea from afar. Kyreen was travelled; he was not. His experiences differed so vastly from hers. Theirs was an odd pairing.

"The other child?" Kyreen's question drew Lang out of his thoughts.

"Esben. Yes, he is my blood, mine and Kasja's," Lang responded, unable to keep the smile from his voice. "He was born last summer, shortly before you arrived at the Council Camp."

"Again. Seems pretty straight forward," Kyreen's voice lacked any emotion as she resolutely continued to avoid his gaze. "What is so complicated about telling me you are bonded?"

"Kasja and I are not bonded," Lang stated firmly.

"Married, covenanted, bound, whatever word you use, Lang, you are partnered, you are spoken for, you are not free to... to do whatever it is we have been doing for the last fortnight," Kyreen ranted, very nearly losing the precarious hold she had on her emotions. She wrapped her arms about her body, so she would not throw them up in frustration or strike out at him.

"Kasja and I were bound," Lang admitted quietly. "But she released me last fall. After you arrived, I realized immediately who you were, what you were, and once I told her, she dissolved our union."

Surprised, Kyreen could not stop herself from glancing over at Lang. Though he still kept his emotions locked away from her she could read some of it on his face. Even in her anger, Kyreen found herself drawn to this man, both physically and emotionally. It frightened her, the depth of her attraction. She knew if she allowed herself she could drown in him.

"If that is true, then why hide her and your children from me? Why do you continue to shield your emotions from me? Do you not wish to be with me?" Kyreen hated hearing the need in her voice when she spoke that last sentence.

"At first I expected you to leave. Every time you left for Myrddin I wondered if this was the time you would not return," Lang said, running a hand over his hair to idly scratch the back of his neck. "By the time I accepted that you were here for good, you had moved to the Training Camp. I was in bad shape. The injury I sustained in the summer's skirmish was not healing properly. Kasja finally went to Aren and they decided that I should join the Training Camp as an instructor."

He paused to glance over at her, but she had returned her eyes to the grazing herd. She still did not trust herself or her emotions to fully look upon him. He continued, "Every time I approached you with the intention of making amends, I would say or do something to anger you. At least being in your general proximity tempered the anxiety, and my wound finally began to heal properly."

"You ask if I wish to be with you?" Lang commented. "The answer is yes, wholeheartedly. I cannot think of anything I want more than to share every day with you, except..."

"Except...?" she prompted after a few moments of silence, once again feeling bits of emotion slipping from his tight grasp.

"Except I also need to be with my children. They are my responsibility. I have a duty to them both that I must uphold. As it is, between my work on the Council and this past winter at the Training Camp, I have missed many milestones," Lang finally replied.

Kyreen understood responsibility. Between caring for her foster mother, handling Jorn's farm business, and managing her herd in Hanoria, she had shouldered her share of responsibility. Had Jorn not shirked his responsibility with Ildri, would Kyreen even be here? Probably not. For she knew it was only Ildri's death and Jorn's multiple deceptions with the failed betrothal, the sale of the herd, and finally the sword, that pushed Kyreen into action. If not for those events, as ignorant to the trials of her people as she had been, would Kyreen have ever left Hanoria?

Sighing softly, she made her decision of forgiveness.

"Your deception," she held up a hand when Lang opened his mouth to object, turning to fully face him, locking eyes.

"Your deception," she repeated, "while not a lie, your omission of the facts, your silence, your secrecy, that hurt me more than I care to admit. If this, whatever this is..." she gestured between them "...if this bond is to work, there can be no secrets, no shadows, no shielding. I have enough uncertainty in my world as it is. I cannot do us in half measures."

Lang nodded. "Agreed."

"Agreed?" Kyreen said meekly, her courage fleeing as her brain caught up with her words.

Lang gathered her hands in his, raising them up to his lips, pressing a firm kiss to her knuckles, his eyes locked on hers. "You are sure?" he asked softly.

"Not really," Kyreen nodded despite her words. "I am terrified."

Lang chuckled, putting his arms around Kyreen to pull her close. Kyreen melted against his body, sliding her arms around his torso. Resting her head upon his chest she reveled in the heat of his body against hers, the steady beating of his heart beneath her cheek.

They stood that way for a long time, Kyreen's mind racing with unspoken questions, her emotions erratic. She knew he could feel them all but as soon as she tensed with that thought, he would tighten his embrace a bit and murmur quietly. After another few minutes, she completely relaxed against him, allowing her thoughts and emotions to flow like the river beside them. Just as the currents of water had no right or wrong neither did Kyreen's feelings. Her hurt and pain were neither good nor bad, neither were her joy and delight. As soon as she had this epiphany, she felt something inside her release, whether physical or mental she could not say. In that moment, it was as if a new level of awareness opened up. Kyreen felt more sharply the presence of the Calanians in the nearby camp. So, too, could she feel the herd grazing peacefully across the river and nature all around her, the leaves on the trees overhead, the wind, the trees themselves, the grass, the water. Just barely Kyreen resisted her initial urge to analyze. Instead she pushed herself to relax, breathing in deeply, permitting the awareness to wash over and through her. She was grateful for Lang's presence holding her upright for without it she surely would have toppled over.

One more deep breath and she felt their bond. In her mind's eye Kyreen could visualize their connection, his essence and hers meeting, joining, entwining. Suddenly it was as though they had fused. She felt his spirit flowing deep inside of her, weaving deeply to her core. She also felt Lang's emotions, so very strong. His affection, his guilt, his joy, his pain, his desire. This last washed over her, eager and ravenous, immediately setting her body aflame, buckling her knees with its intensity.

With the vertigo pulling so strong, Kyreen had to open her eyes, surprised to find the world around them unchanged. The river currents still sparkled under the afternoon sun, the mares across the river languidly grazed. Pulling back slightly she smiled up at Lang, her face wet with tears she had not realized she shed.

Slowly he lowered his lips to hers, kissing her softly and thoroughly. When they finally parted Kyreen's knees buckled anew and she leaned against him, breathless. He wrapped his arms around her pulling her head to his chest once more.

When she could speak, her voice husky, Kyreen said, "I need to go help Synnove prep our sleeping quarters."

"I, too, need to get back," Lang replied, reluctance in his tone. "Aren has requested my presence at the hearing plenary."

"Tonight then?" Kyreen asked. "We will continue the conversation?"

Before he answered, she felt his hesitation, the guilt seeping back in. "It will be late. I promised Jetta I would tuck her in tonight."

"Very well," Kyreen said. Unsuccessful in stopping the flash of pain in her heart, she did not trust her voice to say much more than that.

"I do want you to meet them," Lang murmured against her hair. "Before the festival ends and they leave."

Kyreen nodded, a new wave of anxiety flaring. Reluctantly she pulled away. "For now, duty calls."

Lang gathered her hands in his, raising them to his lips, placing a lingering kiss on her knuckles, his fiery emerald eyes gazing into hers, igniting the warmth throughout her body.

Walking back to camp, side by side, Kyreen took in the surroundings. She had been so emotional earlier she had not been able to appreciate the coordination and logistics of this gathering of all the camps. Preparations for the evening meal were already well underway and she spied some of her fellow trainees working under the watchful eye of the head cook.

Kyreen left Lang at the main area serving as court today where Aren would be hearing grievances. Kyreen waved at her cousin, who glanced at Lang briefly before smiling at Kyreen, causing the younger woman's cheeks to blaze red. Walking away Kyreen chuckled to herself knowing there would be time over evening meal to catch up with her cousin.

"Everything settled?" Synnove asked as Kyreen walked up. The tent had been erected but their belongings still stacked outside.

"I believe it will be," Kyreen nodded. "Although you probably already knew that."

"Eh, it is my curse," Synnove shrugged with a grin. "Come on. Let us stow our gear. Then I want to introduce you to my family before evening meal begins. I am serving tonight."

"Oh, I have not checked the duty roster yet," Kyreen commented picking up a bedroll.

"I did. You have dishes tonight. Then you are with the mares tomorrow. Lucky you. I am relegated to maintaining latrines."

Chapter 17

After months of living together, Kyreen and Synnove quickly had their belongings arranged and the inside of the tent set up to their liking. Sitting on her bedroll, watching Synnove finish straightening her blankets Kyreen thought they could have been back on the marshes or anywhere else, except for the many presences Kyreen could feel. Though her connections were not as strong as earlier with Lang, she still sensed him and the others, like a second pulse.

"Do you feel everyone around you all the time?" Kyreen asked Synnove as they exited their tent.

"What do you mean 'feel'?" Synnove shot Kyreen a questioning look.

"I mean 'feel' all these people," Kyreen replied, sweeping one arm to indicate the camp.

Synnove stopped walking. "You 'feel' all these people? You 'feel' more than emotions?" she asked.

Kyreen nodded cautiously. "Yes. You do not? I thought everyone did."

"Not that way," Synnove slipped an arm through Kyreen's and began walking once more. "This is most interesting."

Kyreen was saved from responding as the women entered the center of camp. Synnove knew just about everyone they passed, either offering up a verbal greeting or simple nod of the head. She set a pace however which discouraged conversation. Kyreen on the other had only recognized a handful of people with whom she exchanged congenial silent nods. After a few steps, Kyreen realized Synnove steered them not towards the family residences but towards an area void of tents. A few people milled around a fire pit, the embers low in the warm spring afternoon, but ready to be stoked once the sun set and temperatures dropped. Synnove approached an older man, uncharacteristically short and rotund for a Calanian man, his black hair worn atypically shaggy, just like his bushy beard, both shot with streaks of gray.

"Synnove, heart of my heart!" the man exclaimed spying the two women approaching the fire pit. He hurried over to engulf Synnove in a long embrace.

"Papa," Synnove said upon their parting. "This is Kyreen. Kyreen, my father Orn."

Before she could react, the man reached over to engulf Kyreen in a rib cracking hug.

"Kyreen, well met!" the short, rotund man gushed. "My daughter has told us so much about you it is as though you are already family."

"Yes, it has been quite annoying. 'Kyreen did this!' 'Kyreen said that!' You appear quite normal despite Synnove's idolizing," a man's voice spoke from behind Kyreen.

Extracting herself from Orn's embrace, Kyreen turned to face the voice. Though the words had been contemptuous, the tone had been laced with amusement and affection. Kyreen found herself facing a young man, his age somewhere between hers and Synnove's. With Synnove's infectious grin and sparkling sapphire eyes, Kyreen recognized him to be Synnove's oldest sibling, Synnove's breathtakingly handsome older brother. His bearing and countenance exuded confidence, and tremendous charisma radiated from him, splashing over her in intense waves. Even as she opened her mouth to greet the young man, he captured one of her hands in both of his, pulling it up towards his lips.

"Did I say normal?" he asked, his dark blue gaze locked on Kyreen's face, his warm breath tickling the back of her hand. "By the goddess, Synnove, you never mentioned you were sleeping with the most exquisite creature to grace these woods."

As he finished speaking, Synnove's brother pressed a lingering kiss to the back of Kyreen's hand, his eyes never leaving her face. Despite her best efforts, Kyreen's heart rate quickened and her cheeks blushed red as heat flooded her body.

"Sten, you beastly creature!" Synnove scolded, slapping her brother's hands away from Kyreen, who felt immense relief once the contact between her and the young man had been broken. "Leave Kyreen alone! I forbid you to wile your charms upon her."

Sten laughed nonchalantly, pulling Synnove to him for a tight embrace, his eyes continuing to hold Kyreen's gaze. "Very well, sister of mine. Though you know as well as anyone the quickest way to pique my interest is to forbid me from it…or her." He winked roguishly at Kyreen, who felt her cheeks redden anew.

"Besides she turns such pretty shades of red," he added.

Synnove pulled out of her brother's embrace to frown up at him.

"I am serious, Sten," she warned, holding the look until her brother's gaze dropped Kyreen's eyes to meet his sister's.

"Fine. Relax," Sten patted Synnove's cheek before glancing back at Kyreen. "No hard feelings. I like to see how quickly I can earn Synnove's wrath. Just a little game."

"Well met, Princess," he murmured, reaching over to once again take Kyreen's hand in his and raising to his lips. "I am Sten, first born of Gisli and Orn, and I am your servant."

Though the intensity had diminished, Kyreen still felt a rush of adrenaline at the man's touch. Everything about him—his expression, his tone, his bearing, his words—exuded earnestness, yet she could not shake the uneasy feeling she was being deceived.

Synnove laughed, seeing doubt in Kyreen's expression. "You may as well quit while you can with dignity, brother. Kyreen is not one of your vacuous Calanian maidens. She has been in the world and perceives your trickery."

"Also, I am not your princess," Kyreen added, extracting her hand from Sten's, barely refraining from wiping it on her pants. "Not now nor ever again."

"Princess?" Sten's brow furrowed, then he waved a hand. "Oh, I meant nothing by that. I call all the beautiful young maidens princess. It is not like you are a..."

Now it was Sten's turn to be flustered, his eyes widening as Synnove and Kyreen grinned at him.

Before he recovered Synnove grabbed Kyreen's arm anew. "We are going to visit Mama," she called over her shoulder, steering them away from the fire pit.

"Kyreen, pleased to meet you," Orn called from the stage where he had gone after introductions. "Synnove, please bring her by tonight."

"Sten and Papa are getting ready for tonight's entertainment," Synnove informed Kyreen before the laughter took over. "You certainly put Sten in his place. His look! It was priceless. Thank you! Someone needs to do that more often."

Uncertain how to respond, Kyreen merely smiled and allowed herself to be propelled to their next destination, which was in the direction of the Council Tent, which Kyreen had failed to notice previously. Initially she thought Synnove was guiding them to the large red and white striped tent, but instead they headed for a much smaller blue and red striped structure.

"Hello?" Synnove called, pausing before the lowered flaps of the canvas entrance. Glancing at Kyreen, she said in a quieter voice, "It is never good to barge in and startle her."

'Her' Kyreen discovered mere moments later when the tent flap flung open was Synnove's mother Gisli, a tall, willowy brunette with sparkling sapphire eyes and an open, friendly smile. While Synnove had inherited her diminutive stature from her father, everything else she had apparently taken from her mother. Again, Kyreen thought, as they exchanged introductions and pleasantries, that she gazed upon a portrait of what Synnove would look like in twenty years.

With the formalities dispensed, Synnove dove right into the latest issue. "Mama," she said, "Kyreen never went through rites so has yet to discern her talent."

"Oh?" Gisli murmured, peering anew into Kyreen's face. "She is of royal descent, my dear. Therefore, I would guess her to have some leadership category."

"No," Synnove interrupted, her tone and expression impish. "She 'feels' people."

Gisli straightened, glancing at Synnove with a surprised expression. "Really?"

Feeling intrigued yet oblivious, Kyreen watched silently as her friend's mother ventured back into the shadowy interior of the tent, gesturing for the two young women to follow. A few scattered mage lights, similar to those Kyreen recalled seeing at the guild hall in Myrddin, lit the interior of the tent. Most of the light these lamps cast shone directly upon the three lone tables lining the walls of the tent. One table housed a wooded shelf that looked to have a hinged door which Kyreen later realized could be shut, rendering the bookshelf into a trunk to move the books. The other two tables had books and parchment scrolls strewn about in, to Kyreen's eye, a haphazard manner.

Gisli scanned the books on one of the tables, pushed aside a scroll and extracted a medium sized tome. Synnove threw a smile over to Kyreen with an expression Kyreen had come to recognize as Synnove's just-you-wait expression.

"Mama is a historian, but her favored specialty is talents," Synnove explained.

"The trouble with talents," Gisli murmured, flipping through the book, "is that our people grew lax not only with discerning talents but recording them. Here we go."

The Historian set the book down on the table, one finger pointing to a printed list. Synnove and Kyreen stepped up to flank Gisli, gazing down at the fine print.

"Here we go," Gisli repeated. "Rasmus the Tactician. Nanna the Gallant. Ebba the Bold. Arvid the Charming."

She looked over at Kyreen. "By the time Rolf, your grandfather, took the throne, talents were no longer being tracked. From my research, though, I would label him an adjudicator. Unfortunately, I do not have enough material to discern your mother's talent."

Kyreen looked down at the book, reading the names of her ancestors with a growing lump in her throat. Every day for as long as she could remember she had recited these names. Yet, here and now, seeing them listed on the page truly brought her forbearers into reality.

"I do not understand what this has to do with me," she said, after clearing her throat.

"Leadership talents are dominant," Gisli explained. "All of the royals have a variation of a talent that would be classified as a leadership skill. Yet it sounds like you have been endowed with an empathic talent, much like my Synnove has being a Soul Seeker. As a recessive talent, empaths come from two parents with the dormant talent. There is no record in the royals of this recessive talent."

Gisli's words hung in the air between the three women for a long minute, leaving Kyreen just as confused as she had been before the conversation. Then the older woman snapped the book closed and smiled at Kyreen. "Never mind all this history. While I find it terribly interesting and do love a mystery, in the whole scheme of the world, it really serves no purpose."

"Oh, Mama, you know that is not true," Synnove soothed her mother, slipping an arm around the taller woman's waist for a warm hug.

Gisli wrapped her arms around Synnove, tall enough that she could rest her chin on the top of the young woman's head. Kyreen glanced away at the books strewn about the table, uncomfortable about intruding on such an intimate moment between the mother and daughter.

After a long silent moment Gisli said, "My apologies. This festival has me feeling melancholy and I fear for this child with the impending announcement from the Council at the annual meeting."

Synnove squeezed her mother before pulling back to gaze up at Gisli. "I will be fine, Mama. You know I miss her, too. Kyreen met Signe last summer, remember?"

"Yes, I had forgotten," the older woman glanced over at Kyreen. "Signe felt honored to have been present for your Telling."

"I did not know your older daughter well," Kyreen replied, "but she handled her role on the Council commendably. Signe left an impression on me."

Gisli smiled, then the sadness fled her face as she grinned down at Synnove. "Maybe you are mistaken. She exhibits a good deal of diplomacy."

"I doubt it," Synnove chuckled. "I believe Kyreen to be a Connate. For a bit, I thought maybe Parturient."

"Interesting," Gisli looked over Kyreen, who suddenly felt like an experiment specimen. "Some of those abilities do overlap. Let me look up some references?"

"That would be wonderful," Synnove commented, stretching up to kiss her mother's cheek. "Duty calls. We will see you at evening gathering."

Kyreen managed a hurried farewell as Synnove swept her out of the tent. Blinking in the sun after the dim interior, she noticed people exiting the nearby Council Tent.

"Synnove," she said, slowing down her friend's walk. "Where are we headed?"

The younger woman glanced over at the exiting people, her distinctive grin blooming. "Nowhere that cannot wait," she replied, adding, "It is getting to be time for me to report for duty anyway."

With a wave of her hand, Synnove strode away, her steps quick without appearing hurried. Kyreen wrapped her arms about her body, uncomfortable and conspicuous in both her solitude and stillness. The last persons to exit the tent was Aren, who upon spying Kyreen walked over.

After embracing and exchanging greetings, Kyreen inquired about the hearings.

Aren ran a hand over her face. "Very few this year. A side effect from last summer's melee I believe," she replied, a shadow crossing her face before she smiled at her cousin. "But I do not believe you were waiting for me and for news of the yearly hearings?"

Kyreen blushed at the insinuation in her cousin's voice. "Truthfully, no," she confessed. "I had hoped Lang might be here."

"So, I thought," Aren stated. "As soon as the hearings ended, he went to spend time with his children."

Something in Kyreen's countenance reflecting the involuntary rush of hurt made Aren look more closely at Kyreen. "You have reconciled your differences?" Aren asked. "That is what it appeared like to me earlier."

"In a matter of speaking," Kyreen shrugged. "I have not yet processed the fact that Lang has children, has a mate."

"Had," Aren corrected. "Kasja released Lang last fall, else he never would have agreed to go to the Training Camp."

"So, you did know!" Kyreen exclaimed, not knowing whether to feel angry or betrayed.

"Only after Kasja approached me after last summer's battle," Aren replied. At Kyreen's silent reproach, she added, "I could not say anything to you, Kyreen. You held so much anger towards the man that had I mentioned bonding to you, you may have fled or worse bitten my head off."

Kyreen's anger deflated, knowing Aren spoke the truth. She had been unreasonable with regards to Lang. "My apologies," she mumbled.

"None needed," Aren chuckled, throwing an arm around her cousin's shoulder to guide them towards the center of camp. "I acted the same towards Viggo for almost a year before coming to my senses."

Kyreen laughed, allowing herself to be propelled into the bustling crowd.

Later, about midway thru evening meal sitting with Aren and Viggo and their children, Synnove and her mother, Ebbe and his father, Kyreen paused her eating to glance around. The mood of the encampment filled her with joy. Suddenly she realized that the veil of silence had been lifted. While the noise level of the Calanians still did not amount to much, there was a festive mood coursing through the crowd that infused itself into Kyreen. Returning to her partly finished meal, she listened to the conversations around her, absorbing quietly, not feeling apart yet not participating. This calm sense of fitting, of being right where she belonged, enveloped her.

"Kyreen," Yngve called over, bringing Kyreen out of her thoughts, "will you be joining us for sparktaske?"

Ebbe and Synnove both chimed in, urging Kyreen to come with them. She hesitated before answering. The game in question was a sport of skill, keeping a feathered and weighted object in the air by using mainly feet and legs, no hands. Kyreen had only played it a few times at Training Camp because it had a tendency to become boisterous. Yngve and Ebbe had been looking forward to the festival where they could participate without restriction.

"Sure," Kyreen finally answered, knowing Lang would not be available anyway. "I will go after cleanup."

Having committed and with her plate empty Kyreen stood up, excusing herself to go to the kitchen area to begin her assigned duty. Though she did not know any of the other people also on assignment, they all seemed amicable, settling into an efficient routine and the kitchen area was soon cleaned up, ready for the morning's crew.

Her duties completed for the evening Kyreen exchanged pleasant farewells with her fellow workers then began wandering towards the bonfire built up in the middle of the encampment. Many of the Calanians gathered around, their attentions focused on the slightly raised platform upon which Orn stood regaling the crowd with a story. Kyreen paused on the edge of the crowd to listen. Synnove's father told a familiar story, one Kyreen remembered from her own childhood, about an old ruler confronted with a difficult decision and his daughter who finds a unique solution, thus saving the kingdom.

"That old man, how he lives for these few days every year," Sten commented quietly, his voice low and much closer to Kyreen's ear than felt comfortable.

Annoyed at herself for allowing Synnove's brother to sneak up on her, Kyreen shifted away from the young man, murmuring, "He tells a good tale. I am enjoying the story."

Either oblivious or not caring, Sten moved closer to Kyreen, his body heat radiating, a hand hovering just below her elbow. "I have to confess, Princess," he whispered, his breath tickling Kyreen's ear, his presence overly intimate for her personal comfort level, "I cannot get you out of my mind. You have bewitched me."

Frowning Kyreen turned towards Sten to remind him not to call her Princess, but the movement brought her lips perilously close to his and, his sapphire eyes seizing her gaze, the reprimand fell silent. Just then the crowd burst into applause and Sten stepped back with a bright smile.

"That is my cue," he remarked casually, pulling the lute upon his back around to strum. With a wink, Sten turned to stride jauntily towards the stage his father had exited. Before Kyreen could recover he was stationed on stage, singing a lively tune. Exhaling softly, not quite sure about the game Sten had been playing, Kyreen turned to leave, but a soft hand upon her arm pulled her back.

Kyreen turned, surprised to see Orn. She flicked a glance at the stage where Sten sang. Had not Orn just been up there? Annoyance rose up again as she realized the older man had ambushed her just as his son had moments earlier. Before she could protest, Orin gently propelled them to a spot outside the ring of spectators. Kyreen noticed Sten's voice did not carry very far, even though he had been quite audible when she had been on the edge of the crowd.

"Kyreen!" Orn's voice, simultaneously quiet and enthusiastic, pulled her attention. "I am so glad to see you here, my dear. I had been hoping to catch you early in the festival. I have so many questions."

"Oh?" Kyreen replied, wondering silently what her tentmate's father needed to speak with her about.

Orn pulled Kyreen a little farther away from the entertainment area with a glance at the audience. Satisfied that their conversation would not intrude on anyone listening to Sten, Orn resumed speaking in normal tones.

"Yes. Ever since my daughter Signe wrote about your Telling, I have desired to speak with you. Then, when Synnove became your tentmate, I knew our paths were destined to cross. It has been difficult waiting all this time but I know it shall be worth it. My masterpiece for sure. An instant sensation."

"My apologies," Kyreen interrupted as politely and respectfully as possible when it became apparent Orn thought she know what they were discussing. "I am at a loss. About what are we talking?"

"Oh no, my dear! My apologies for not elucidating!" Orn chuckled, his beard waggling. "I very much desire to hear your story, your mother's story more specifically. For we all know her beginning and her tragic ending. It is the middle bits which are missing. Our people have ballads of our leaders and even of the Battle, but there has yet to be anything sung about our Queen Tyra."

Unexpectedly, strong emotions welled inside Kyreen, taking her breath away. She had not thought that the Calanians might be interested in their queen's story, in Tyra's story. She had forgotten that her history was also a part of her people's history.

"…for she is our last majesty, until this ordeal is ended," Orn was saying when Kyreen pulled her attention back to the present. Now the man peered up at her, clearly awaiting an answer.

"Yes, of course," Kyreen said, her throat tight. She coughed softly to clear it. "I would be honored."

"Very well," Orn rubbed his hands together, his smile broadening. "Shall we talk tomorrow over evening meal? In Gisli's tent mayhap? I know she would enjoy the tale as well."

Kyreen nodded but before she could speak he glanced over to the stage, saying, "That is my cue. Tomorrow then, my dear!"

With a pat on her arm, Orn turned and, moving with a grace that defied his bulk, wove a path through the crowd to jump onstage beside his son. Though one was youthful, tall and lean while the other graying, short and rotund, both men carried themselves in the same manner, with similar mannerisms, quite at ease performing beside each other. Kyreen felt herself drawn back towards the show, but stopped after the first step. Resolutely she turned, determined to seek out her friends.

Chapter 18

Following the youthful shouts of enjoyment, it did not take Kyreen long to find the cluster of young adults gathered in a clearing, torchlights illuminating the space. Kyreen held back watching the young men and women pass the weighted shuttlecock around and across the circle. It appeared the competition had not yet begun, that they were simply warming up. Some of the more talented youth added flourishes as their feet or knees lofted the projectile across to another participant. Multiple conversations were transpiring and laughing bounced about as the shuttlecock made its way around the ring.

Synnove, spying Kyreen, extricated herself from the group and strolled over. Her cheeks flushed and eyes sparkling in the torchlight, she grinned at her friend. "Alright there, Kyreen?" she asked.

"I am," Kyreen replied, glancing over at the throng of young adults. "Though I am not up for a competition tonight."

"I understand," Synnove said, turning to stand shoulder-to-shoulder with Kyreen.

For a few minutes, the friends stood in silent observation before Synnove broke the silence. "The Courting Ceremony occurs in four night's time."

"I have heard," Kyreen nodded.

"You asked me earlier about who would be courting me," Synnove stated cautiously.

"And you nearly bit my head off with your reply," Kyreen chuckled, imitating Synnove's voice. "'I will not be courted. I will do the courting.'"

Synnove chuckled softly. "Yes, well, that got me thinking. That place you grew up in."

"Hanoria," Kyreen offered.

"Yes, Hanoria. They seem to have a very …different mindset from Calanians."

Kyreen glanced at Synnove. Her friend was speaking uncharacteristically cautious. "What is on your mind?"

"You do know that you are supposed to be the initiator, right?" Synnove commented. "It is our choice, as women, to decide with whom we shall covenant, who shall father our children. It sounds to me as if this was not how it is done in Hanoria." Synnove shuddered at the thought of her father, or worse her brother, controlling her future.

"Yes, I knew it," Kyreen answered after pondering a moment. "But I had not thought on it."

Synnove nodded. "Very well. Now you need to think on it. If you do not court Lang and do not do it during the festival, then you will have to wait another year."

"What do you mean?" Kyreen asked sharply. "I thought covenanting was a formality, not a requirement."

"It is, for most," Synnove answered. "I have been thinking about you and him, and I fear, my dear friend, that you are bonded to a traditionalist."

"Meaning?"

"Meaning your relationship with Lang will not go forward until you are covenanted," Synnove shook her head. "Very few still hold to that directive, and I could be mistaken, but it explains why he has pulled away from consummating your relationship."

Kyreen's cheeks blushed at discussing this with Synnove. Her eyes drifted back to the group of youths, no longer punting the shuttlecock. It appeared warm ups were complete and competition would begin soon. Yngve's girlfriend's eyes locked on Kyreen's, her face severe.

Averting her eyes, Kyreen glanced at Synnove. "Do you know why Karine holds such contempt for me?"

"I am not sure," Synnove shrugged. "I can find out for you."

"Kasja is Karine's sister," Lang spoke quietly from behind the two women. "Karine believes I have betrayed her sister, and that Kyreen is to blame."

Synnove glanced over her shoulder, surprised by Lang's presence. Then she looked at Kyreen who had not moved, who kept her gaze forward on the young adults preparing for their game.

"You knew he was there," she hissed.

"I did," Kyreen admitted, turning to grin at her friend. "It is not often I can pull something over on you. So, I am petty when it happens."

Synnove rolled her eyes before giving Kyreen a quick hug. "I shall take my leave. Good night, Kyreen," she said, nodding at Lang and adding, "Spar Master."

Lang stepped up to stand next to Kyreen as they both watched Synnove rejoin her peers. A part of Kyreen filled with envy at how seamlessly her friend could transition between situations. For some reason, this made Kyreen think of her foster father Jorn. Though he had been deeply in love with Ildri, in the end their love had not been enough to fulfill him. Jorn had always wanted more, children, farmland, money. Though this envy Kyreen had felt towards Synnove just now resembled only a shadow of what she used to sense from her foster father, its existence troubled her.

"That is never good," Lang commented quietly, eyeing Kyreen as she nibbled thoughtfully at her lower lip. "Are you troubled?"

Kyreen shook her head, turning her gaze to him with a smile. "No, simply woolgathering on topics better left in the past."

She slipped an arm through Lang's and turned them away from the gaming youth and scalding gaze of Karine.

"Where shall we head?" she asked. "I imagine wandering outside the camp is discouraged."

"Not as much here as in Calan proper," Lang replied. "But I do know a place that is not only private but out of the weather."

"Lead on," Kyreen remarked, intrigued. While the clear night sky overhead twinkled with stars, the brisk breeze still held a bite.

A few minutes later, Kyreen ducked under Lang's arm holding back the flap to the Council's tent. Straightening up to look around, her heart pounded as though their presence here were forbidden. The lamps had been set low leaving the interior of the tent awash in shadows. The massive wooden table, surrounded by a variety of mismatched chairs, monopolized the center of the space. A handful of armoires, also of varying sizes and designs, lined the perimeter of the tent.

"This entire place must be difficult to pack up and move," she murmured, wondering why the thought had never crossed her mind before tonight. "Why keep all this?"

"Your mind thinks in a such an unusual manner," Lang chuckled, leading her to one of the side tables. "I hope you do not mind sitting on the rug. The chairs, as you may recall, are not all that comfortable."

"Not at all," Kyreen replied, settling down with her back against the sturdy furniture. "After all, you only promised private and out of the wind, not comfortable."

Lang chuckled again as he settled beside her. Kyreen sighed softly, leaning her head on his shoulder. These stolen moments every night, alone together had become the best part of her day. She craved not just the physical contact with Lang, but mostly the five words she had come to love hearing from him.

"Tell me about your day," he whispered into her ear.

So, she did.   He would listen, quietly interjecting questions or comments. Then he would tell her about his day, or at least that had become their evening routine. Tonight, as she finished up her tale, Kyreen sensed a restlessness within Lang. Though he gave no exterior sign, it felt to her as though he were drumming his fingers.

"You have something on your mind," she stated, not asking.

"Several somethings," Lang admitted. "I apologize for my distraction. Please continue."

"My day's telling is complete," Kyreen replied. "Did you wish to speak about your day, or mayhap something else?"

"To be honest, I am fatigued," Lang said, the regret in his voice apparent as he pressed a kiss to her curls. "We should probably retire to our tents."

Unbidden, Kyreen's thoughts turned towards Lang's sleeping arrangements. This morning—was it only this morning? —she would have been certain he would be sleeping in the Training Camp area. This evening, however, she had visions of him sharing a tent with his children and his…Kasja.

"Hey," Lang whispered, pressing a finger to Kyreen's chin turning her face to his. "I will be sleeping just down the row from you, quite alone." He dropped his lips to hers.

Kyreen both loved and hated that he could read her so easily. Her insecurities embarrassed her. Her inability to hide them seemed both a blessing and a curse.

After a long hot-blooded kiss, they departed the tent. All around, the camp had quieted down as people turned in for the evening, though a small group remained around the entertainment stage. As Kyreen and Lang strolled by, Sten's gaze found hers. He gave her a courtly bow and blew her a kiss, which caused her to chuckle softly.

"Have I competition for your heart of which I should be aware?" Lang whispered playfully, his whiskers tickling her ear.

"You know better," Kyreen teased back. "Synnove's brother is a terrible flirt. I believe he is what my foster mother Ildri would call a 'pot stirrer.'"

"So true," Lang replied tightening his arm about her shoulder.

Too soon, Kyreen found herself crawling into her bedroll, the taste of Lang's lips still upon hers. Smiling in the dark, she rolled over, almost immediately drifting off to sleep as the day's activities had left her drained. When Synnove entered a short while later Kyreen barely registered her arrival.

The next morning Kyreen roused herself early in order to ride across the river to the semi-permanent camp where the mares ready to foal were being held. The wooden structure nestled on the edge of the woods sat about an hour's ride from the main camp, near enough to camp for commuting, yet far enough away to isolate the newborn foals and their mothers from the bustle of the festival. Two other Calanians walked up as Kyreen finished saddling her gelding. The middle-aged man introduced himself as Raum and the young woman as Ylva, his daughter, who looked to be a couple of years older than Kyreen, had a still-sleeping and swaddled babe strapped to her back.

Even though she desired to be off and had been looking forward to the solitary ride, good manners required Kyreen wait for them to saddle their mounts once Raum had mentioned they were also heading to foaling duty.

Despite her reluctance at the company, Kyreen found the ride with the two to be quite pleasant. Raum did most of the talking. Upon discovering they were travelling and working with Kyreen, the princess, Ylva had become bashful, barely uttering a word the entire first half of the trip. During a lull in Raum's running monologue pointing out interesting tidbits about the Great Valley, Kyreen attempted to draw the quiet woman into the conversation by inquiring about the bundle upon Ylva's back. The young woman's face broke out into a big grin as did the proud grandpa's. With the tension broken, the new mother eagerly spoke about her baby for the rest of the ride.

Once at the foaling area, Kyreen lost herself in the tasks at hand. After the three full-time hostlers, who had been up overnight, retired into the woods for some sleep, two others gave the morning report. A half-dozen people had been posted full-time with the herd of 75 mares in foal this season. Eighteen had already dropped, three had been in active labor overnight, with another seventeen exhibiting signs of impending labor. Since most births occurred without complications, the staff mainly observed, stepping in only on the few extreme cases with issues.

"That mare there," said Moa, a tall lanky woman with silver shot through her ebony braid, motioning to a big boned sorrel resting in a patch of sunshine at the forest's edge, "she has a bit of a cantankerous history. Her foals are always big and require some assistance. Plus, she likes to wander away to give birth in the trees. Could one of you take her?"

Kyreen watched Raum and Ylva exchange glances. This mare appeared to have an unfavorable reputation. Feeling up to the challenge, Kyreen lifted a hand, saying, "I can do it."

"Very well," Moa replied. "All I ask is you keep a close eye on her as the day goes on. If at any time, she breaks away, follow her. Do not attempt to keep her here in the clearing. Until then, jump in wherever you see best to help. Aren tells me you had a herd and are well versed in the foaling."

Kyreen nodded, slightly flustered at the notion of Moa and Aren discussing her and her past life. "Yes. My herd was much smaller. I only ever had a dozen or so foals in a season."

"Our plan right now is to double the breeding herd next season," Moa continued. "Those contracts you helped negotiate last harvest are helping generate much needed revenue for our people."

Not for the first time, Kyreen remembered that she was not as anonymous to the Calanians as she liked to believe. Of course, everyone knew her name as the princess. It appeared she also had a reputation as Aren's emissary with the guild Brodyr Llafur.

More than a little embarrassed, Kyreen gave silent thanks when Moa switched subjects, handing out assignments. For the rest of the morning Kyreen worked alongside Ylva checking out the mares waiting to go into labor, while the others concentrated on assisting the mares in active labor or other low skill chores.

Ylva turned out to be an amicable work partner. She did not feel the need to fill the silence as the two women fell into a companionable routine. Ylva would halter and hold a mare while Kyreen conducted the inspection, running her hands across the swollen belly, checking under the tail, then feeling the legs for swelling or lameness.

After the fifth or sixth, Ylva asked, "How do you do that?"

"Do what?" Kyreen replied, her hand pausing on the rump of a light sorrel mare with a painfully distended belly.

"You are calling the unborns by their gender," Ylva explained. "So far, a colt, two fillies, another colt, then this filly."

"I do not know," Kyree shrugged. "I have always been able to discern gender."

"What a wonderful talent," Ylva commented her voice wistful.

"It has its purposes," Kyreen responded uncomfortably, extremely thankful when the shout for midday meal arose.

Half-way through the meal, Kyreen noticed the troublemaker mare ungracefully lurch to her feet and begin shuffling towards the forest. Excusing herself from the group, Kyreen began tailing the slow-moving mare, making sure to keep far enough back so as not to spook the already agitated creature. After a few minutes of wandering the mare found her spot, slowly walking in a circle, tamping down the underbrush to create a nest area into which she laboriously settled down. Kyreen edged into the little clearing, slowly lowering herself to the ground. The mare turned her big liquid brown eyes to the young woman. With her herd in Hanoria, Kyreen knew each of her mares intimately and worked hard to ensure each mare's comfort during the labor process. With this mare, since she did not know the animal, Kyreen decided to slowly normalize her presence.

From this distance, Kyreen could feel the foal – a colt – struggling to be free of his mother. He fought powerfully and Kyreen had no worries about his life force during the labor process. She did want to check out the foal's positioning, but to do that she needed to be able to physically examine the mare. So, she began talking to the horse in quiet soothing tones, not thinking much about her words, knowing those did not matter. For a while she recited stories from her childhood, then launched into her Telling. By the time Kyreen had finished that recitation, the shadows around them had lengthened and Kyreen had moved to within an arm's length of the mare.

Kyreen allowed the silence to build around them as the afternoon passed. The mare continued to exhibit signs of impending birth becoming restless, struggling to her feet to pace around the small patch of trampled undergrowth, only to pause and drop back to the ground.

Moa made little noise as she approached, yet neither Kyreen nor the mare expressed surprise when she walked up to kneel down on one knee beside the younger woman. Twilight had fallen purple and gray in the forest and the mare had just risen to her feet once again.

"How is she?" the horsewoman asked, her voice hushed.

"Restless," Kyreen responded, taking the proffered plate of food from Moa. "Thank you for this. I did not realize how famished I was."

"You are welcome," Moa responded, her gaze never leaving the mare now edgily shifting her weight from hoof to hoof. "I appreciate you keeping watch over her. We delivered three more foals today and four more have entered active labor. The night shift shall be fairly busy."

"What sort of trouble are you expecting with this one?" Kyreen asked.

"With three of her last four births the foal presented backwards," Moa answered promptly. "That coupled with the size of the foal makes her a higher risk."

"I had a couple of those," Kyreen commented. "Always a tense time. I take it all her foals delivered alive and otherwise healthy?"

Moa nodded, rising to her feet. "Aye. Big strapping lively foals all of them."

She glanced down at Kyreen. "Raum and Ylva have already left for the camp, but you are free to head back if you wish. I can go fetch one of the overnighters."

"If it is alright with you," Kyreen replied with a shake of her head, "I would like to sit with this one during her journey. I am looking forward to meeting this colt."

"I thought you would feel that way," Moa smiled. "I will leave you two to it. If you require assistance, call out. Sleeping quarters are close by and we are isolated enough here that there should not be any danger."

Once alone, Kyreen settled with her back against a tree trunk, thoughtfully gnawing on the food Moa had brought. The mare continued her uneasy shuffle. The moon, almost full, slowly rose, an ethereal glow over the tree tops. Once finished with her meal, Kyreen began speaking to the mare once again, this time more to keep herself from dozing off than to soothe the laboring creature. Knowing her tone to be more important than her words, Kyreen talked about any topic that came to mind. When the pale disc hovered almost straight overhead, washing their little area in eerie moonlight, Kyreen gave a small sigh of relief when the mare stilled. She felt the increased tension from the colt. A few moments later the mare staggered back to the ground, her movements breaking the foal's birthing sac. Kyreen, still speaking in soft, soothing tones moved over to the mare's side. Gently stroking the creature's distended belly, Kyreen leaned over to examine the birth canal, doubly thankful. First for the bright moon overhead illuminating the entire scene, and second to see the birthing sac appear with only a single hoof protruding out. She released a soft sigh of gratitude as it appeared the colt had dropped into the proper position.

For the next several moments, the clearing fell silent with only the soft grunting sounds of the mare as the contractions continued to ease the colt out, the birthing sac glowing in the moonlight. The second hoof shortly followed the first, both slipping out slowly until both front legs were exposed to the knee. Kyreen began counting off the time as the mare continued to strain yet the foal's feet did not move any further. Just as the young woman began to feel concern, the legs slid out a bit more, followed by the colt's nose. Breathing a small sigh, Kyreen continued her quiet observing as the colt's head fully escaped. She then moved in a little closer to ensure the birthing sac had indeed broken just as the colt's shoulders cleared the birth canal and he slid almost completely out of his mother. With a final pat to the new mother's haunches, Kyreen moved back to her observation post. Silence settled around the clearing once more as the mare and foal rested. After a few long moments the mare righted herself, nosing her baby and began washing him with her tongue, which roused the newborn. Kyreen watched as the mare lurched to her feet, neck bending as she continued to lick at the colt, who began attempting to stand. After a few mis-starts he finally managed to rise up on four spindly shaky legs. Kyreen exhaled the breath she had not realized she had been holding when he remained upright and began sniffing at his mother's side, searching for the nourishment his instincts told him would be present.

Chapter 19

A couple of hours later, as the night gave way to morning, the eastern sky bruised purple with the promise of dawn, Kyreen, the colt in her arms, led the mare out of the forest. Setting the foal on the ground where the mare could sniff him over, Kyreen approached the fire at the center of camp. One of the overnighters rose to his feet, meeting her halfway.

"Any problems?" the man, Gerik she vaguely recalled his name, asked.

"None," Kyreen responded. "I was wondering about feed for the mare."

By the time Kyreen had acquired a flake of alfalfa for the mare, the sun had begun to rise. Moa, emerging from the forest, walked over to Kyreen, her sharp eyes appraising the newborn foal napping beside his mother currently munching the sweet hay.

The two women exchanged greetings then Kyreen gave her report. With the sunrise, she had her first look on the colt's coloring, a dark chestnut like his mother, deep robust red accented by four white anklets and a small whorl of white at the center of his face. The young woman smiled watching his little stub of a tail flicking back and forth as he now nursed greedily.

"I am happy to hear the birth went so smoothly," Moa commented at the end of Kyreen's report. "Come let us break fast before you head back to camp."

Kyreen hesitated, and the older woman paused in her movement to add, "Unless you would prefer to stay for this shift. You do not have to. You were out all night."

"I know," Kyreen replied. "I did get a few snoozes during the night and would enjoy staying, if that is alright with you."

Moa chuckled. "I will never turn away eager help. Not everyone shares your affinity for working with the herd, Kyreen."

The two women walked over to the prep area to gather up food. To Kyreen's delight, boiled eggs were one of the options.

"I have not had these since I left Hanoria," she commented enthusiastically, deftly peeling the hard-outer shell.

"We have a flock of chickens over on the farming compound," Moa explained. "Not enough is produced for all the camps, but it is a nice benefit for those of us living in the valley year-round."

Something in Moa's voice made Kyreen pause in her action and look over at the older woman, who watched Kyreen intently.

At Kyreen's silently questioning gaze Moa continued, "Have you considered what you will do after your Training Camp stint has concluded? Your skills and experience are gladly welcomed here if you desire to work with the breeding herd."

"Thank you," Kyreen responded. "I had not given much thought to the future."

The arrival of Raum and Ylva stopped any further conversation on the subject. After hearing the overnight reports, Moa handed out the day's assignments. Kyreen had been taken off the lower skilled task of checking the pregnant mares. Today she worked with a full-time hostler to check the foals and their mothers. The woman, a reserved blue-eyed brunette named Agda, took lead while Kyreen held back making notes in a journal. Once the pair settled into a rhythm, the job went fairly quickly and, also, gave Kyreen time to ponder Moa's offer of joining the horse camp. While she enjoyed working with horses, was it what she wanted to do full time? Starting the herd in Hanoria had been a whim of circumstance with that first set of horses. Then it had been a distraction, relief from farm work. In the end, it had become work to keep everything coordinated so the revenues would stay up. Kyreen could not say she would enjoy it as her vocation. She did not even know how being with the horse camp would affect her relationship with Lang. As she thought on it, she wondered how long the valley would continue to be the horse headquarters. After her mission to the castle, Kyreen had not heard anything, but harbored a guess that the announcements from the Council tonight would include a plan for attacking the castle via the tunnels.

What then, she wondered. What would happen if her people were successful in driving the Galorians away and retaking their lands? Would Lang still be bound to the Council? Would she be expected to take a more active leadership role? Kyreen grimaced at the thought of not only becoming the Calanian leader but also of taking her place on the throne. She had not been here, had not experienced the suffering, the decades of anguish. She had suffered through her own trials, but nothing compared to that of her people. So, if not the throne, then what exactly did she want if her people's lives returned to normal?

All these thoughts clamored through Kyreen's brain as she recorded the information spoke by Agda, who did not speak other than to report her statistics which Kyreen appreciated.   She also respected how the other woman calmly yet efficiently conducted her examinations in such a way as to cause the least amount of stress to the mares and their newborns. Just before midday, Agda and Kyreen completed their task and walked back to the encampment. Once hearing of nothing amiss, Moa dismissed Agda to assist the others still logging the pregnant mares before turning her attentions to Kyreen.

"You may wish to head back to camp and catch some rest before tonight's meeting," she said. "Most of us will be riding back as soon as reporting is complete. We are leaving a skeleton crew here overnight."

The lack of sleep catching up with her, Kyreen acquiesced without protest. She wasted no time getting her gelding saddled and departing before anyone had the opportunity to join her. Once a fair distance away from the horse camp, she let the reins loose so the gelding could set his own pace. Inhaling deeply, she relished the sunshine beaming on her face, the clean fresh air, and the peace of solitude. With her exhalation, Kyreen felt the release of a tension she had not been aware she held. Then much too soon the camp came into view and she felt the presence of her people, a light strumming on her soul, the tautness, creeping back in.

Pulling the gelding back down to a slow trot, Kyreen headed towards the equine quadrant, exhaustion sweeping over her quick and sudden. Stifling a yawn, Kyreen surprised herself by feeling gratitude upon spying Gunda on duty. Slipping from the saddle, she hugged the youngster in greeting.

"Do you mind?" Kyreen asked, handing Gunda the reins. "I am beyond fatigued."

The girl's face broke out into a large smile. "It would be my honor," she replied, giving Kyreen another hug. "Thank you, cousin."

Kyreen watched her walk away with the gelding, too tired to dwell on the guilt welling up about shirking her responsibility. The horse would receive exceptional care from Gunda. Then she turned to smile at Lang just walking up. Without speaking, he pulled her to him for a long, warm embrace. Kyreen leaned into him, relishing his steady heartbeat under her ear.

"Careful," she murmured, "I may fall asleep standing here."

His laughter rumbled against her cheek. "That is what you get for sitting up all night with a laboring mare, like she needed your assistance. Mares have been foaling without you since the beginning of the world."

Lang carefully turned Kyreen towards the Training Camp's quadrant. Keeping his arm draped about her shoulders, they began to walk slowly towards the tents. As drowsy as Kyreen felt, it took her a moment to realize they had stopped before an unfamiliar tent. She looked up at Lang her eyes and furrowed brow asking the question on her mind.

"My tent," Lang commented. "Here you may rest undisturbed until dinner. Your tent is up towards the front of the camp, lots of noise there."

Nodding, too tired to argue, Kyreen crawled into the tent. Lang helped her with her boots as sleep overtook her and she curled up on top of Lang's bedroll. The spring sun had warmed the interior of the tent, and she breathed in the comforting scent of Lang that permeated the space. In no time, Kyreen slumbered deeply, so deep she did not feel Lang lie down, carefully wrapping his arms about her, his breath soft against the back of her neck.

When Kyreen awoke the bright sunlight no longer beat upon the tent. Instead muted shadows washed across the interior and Kyreen found herself alone. As she tugged on her boots, however, she felt Lang's presence outside the tent.

He stood as she exited, the cheerful greeting on Kyreen's lips checked unspoken from the grim look on Lang's face.

"Did you have a good rest?" he asked, pulling her into a tight embrace.

"Yes, thank you," she responded pulling back to gaze up at him to ask quietly, "what has happened?"

Lang glanced around to ensure they would not be overheard before answering, his voice low. "Galorian soldiers have been spotted along our perimeter barriers to this Valley."

"But this is so removed from the castle," Kyreen frowned. "Well beyond their usual daily patrols."

"Exactly," Lang nodded. "I had just returned from a special council meeting when you awoke. Our timeline has been moved up."

They began walking towards the center of camp where the smell of the evening's meal made Kyreen's mouth water. It had been a while since this morning's breakfast. As they walked in silence, Kyreen contemplated

Lang's words. The timeline being moved up most likely meant the Calanian forces would attack the castle before summer solstices, maybe much sooner.

The two remained quiet through the food line gathering up their evening meal and had just found a place to sit when a voice called out for Kyreen.

She turned to see Orn hurrying her way and realized with a jolt that she had forgotten their meeting scheduled for the previous evening.

"My apologies," she blurted before Synnove's father could speak. "I was delayed last night."

Orn waved a hand offhandedly "Do not concern yourself, my dear. Lang here let me know you had duties."

Kyreen glanced at Lang, who shrugged with a sheepish grin.

"I worried," he said. "When you did not appear I sought out the duty chief who directed me to the woman you rode with…Ylva? She told me you were sitting with a mare about to foal."

"Bringing life into this world," Orn murmured. "What a noble undertaking."

Kyreen smiled wanly at Orn, her mind preoccupied with the implications of Lang's words, that he had been waiting for her return, that he had gone looking for her, that he had been speaking with others about her. Her thoughts made her stomach churn and she could not decide if her feelings were those of discomfort or delight. She had spent so much of her life trying to escape notice that anytime she found herself the focus of attention she could not help feeling exposed and vulnerable.

"Is now a good time for us to speak?" Orn's question pulled Kyreen back from her thoughts.

She looked to Lang who nodded, giving the rotund bard all the encouragement he needed. Orn took hold of Kyreen's elbow and began escorting her away from the dining area. Kyreen glanced over her shoulder to give Lang a silent apologetic farewell. He smiled and blew her a kiss. Feeling better about abandoning him, Kyreen turned her attention to salvaging her meal and not losing any of her food as Orn sped through the crowd. As they strode past the queue for food Kyreen spied her friends, who all waved to her. Synnove added an apologetic look of her own when she saw who escorted Kyreen.

"Here we are," Orn said cheerily, lifting up the entrance flap and waving Kyreen into the tent. "In we go."

Kyreen had been halfway expecting Synnove's mother to be present but the interior of the tent was empty. Orn bustled in as though he were well-acquainted with the space. He pulled two chairs up to the table with the least number of scrolls and books. Still he had to transfer a number of items off the surface before Kyreen could set down her plate and cup. Orn then gestured her to sit before he took the other chair.

"I feel bad eating in front of you," Kyreen admitted reluctantly, her stomach growling.

"Nonsense!" Orn waved a hand before patting his belly. "It is not like I could not benefit to skip a few meals. Besides I already dined. One of the main benefits of having an adoring public. The head cook always serves me up first."

Orn chuckled and Kyreen settled into her Telling. Orn listened attentively, occasionally requesting a clarification and asking very few questions, but even then, it took Kyreen more time than she had expected. By the time she finished, she had a tugging urge to get back to Lang.

"If we are done," Kyreen said reaching for her dirty dishes, "I shall be heading out."

"Yes, dear. I appreciate you taking time to speak with me." Orn took both of Kyreen's hands in his. "Leave those for Svante. I am sure she is lurking about somewhere."

Kyreen recognized the name of Synnove's youngest sibling, a sister who Kyreen had yet to meet. Before she could protest leaving her mess for someone else to clean, Orn had pulled Kyreen to her feet, propelling them both towards the tent door and towards the center of camp. Dusk had fallen while the two had been inside and a brisk wind from the northern snowcapped mountains meandered through the camp. Kyreen drew the hood of her cloak up as Orn, his hand on her elbow, guided them to the edge of a crowd gathered about the raised dais.

"Bother!" Orn grumbled. "I had rather hoped this would be over by now."

Belatedly, Kyreen remembered tonight's gathering when the Council was to give their annual report and announce plans for the upcoming summer. Feeling slightly annoyed, more at herself for forgetting than Orn for avoiding, Kyreen tugged her arm free of Orn's grasp. A gust of wind blew her hood back from her head as she stood on tiptoe to see the individuals standing on stage. All the council members, including Lang, lined the back of the dais, while Aren stood towards the front addressing the crowd.

"So, did you give the old man what he desired?" Sten's voice murmured quietly in Kyreen's ear, his warm breath tickling. He had moved up behind Kyreen so that his hands grasped her elbows and the length of his body pressed against her backside. His presence so startled Kyreen she very nearly cried out. Only years of practice kept the sound from escaping her lips, though her entire being tensed up.

The combination of his lips warm against her ear, his fingers grasping her elbows, and the heat from his body pressing into hers made Sten's words seem obscene as though she and Orn had been engaged in something nefarious. The intimacy in his actions caused Kyreen great discomfort and she made to move away from him. This only caused Sten to tighten his grip upon her arms.

"Not so fast, Princess," he whispered. "My father had you all to himself for a good while. Now it is my turn."

Sten tugged at Kyreen's arms. When she resisted, he leaned in whispering anew. "Unless you wish to interrupt your cousin's report and cause a scene."

Chapter 20

With great reluctance Kyreen allowed herself to be led away. For all his grumbling, Orn kept his attention so intent upon the activity on the stage that he did not notice Kyreen's departure. Sten led them back the way Kyreen had just come from with his father. He kept one hand firmly on her elbow, throwing his other arm around her shoulder so that they walked hip to hip. Aside from the discomfort of the intimacy Sten's touch caused her, Kyreen did not feel otherwise alarmed. She did not sense any animosity or intent to harm from Sten. Quite the opposite he exuded jubilation.

At the Archival Tent, Sten ushered Kyreen in, commenting, "Here we will not be disturbed."

As she entered Kyreen noticed the interior had been tidied up in the short time since she had left with Orn. The chairs were back in place. The scrolls and books Orn had moved were again setting upon the table, and the dishes Kyreen had abandoned were gone.

Sten, after casting a final glance around outside, closed and fastened the tent flap, then turned to face Kyreen. His deep sapphire eyes glinted, the pupils dilated, and his cheeks were flushed. Kyreen belatedly wondered if perhaps Synnove's brother might be under the influence of alcohol or some other drug.

"Princess, you do not know how long I have waited for this moment," he said closing the space between them to gather her hands in his.

Intrigued, wanting to hear him out and remembering he was Synnove's brother, Kyreen permitted the touch even though she strongly desired to slap his face.

Taking her silence as permission, Sten smiled brightly. Most Calanian men were handsome specimens with sharp features, dark hair, green or blue eyes vivid against pale skin, their bodies strong and lean, but, even when judged against Lang, whom Kyreen had always considered to be exquisitely handsome, Sten stood out. His wavy dark hair, a little longer than the norm, begged to be stroked; alabaster skin drawn taut over chiseled cheekbones and square jaw framed sensual lips; his blue eyes glittered an invitation to plunge into their carnal depths; his smile shone brilliantly, comforting, reassuring. The hands that held hers were not rough with callouses, yet neither were they too soft and the pressure with which he held her hand hit the perfect balance between limp and too firm.

All this went through Kyreen's mind even as Sten continued talking. "Ever since my sister wrote about you I knew you were my destiny. Waiting to meet you has been agony."

"Sten, I…" Kyreen began only to be stopped by a finger pressed to her lips.

"Please let me finish," he interrupted, his tone soothing like a parent about to explain an important fact to their child.

Kyreen closed her mouth, nodding for Sten to continue. He smiled another of his bright smiles that tugged at Kyreen, inviting, drawing her in. Inwardly she tensed, steeling her resolve to prevent that to happen, while keeping her outward appearance relaxed.

"You and me, Princess," Sten said. "We together would be a beautiful couple, a powerful couple, the most beautiful and most powerful couple in Calan."

Shocked, Kyreen's eyes widened and she made to take a step back, but Sten merely followed, drawing closer. As they were roughly the same height Kyreen found herself staring into his sapphire gaze.

"Just think," Sten continued. "With you on the throne and me by your side, what a formidable team we could be."

Kyreen shook her head in disbelief, which merely made Sten tighten his grip on her hands, pulling them up to his lips. His breath warm on her skin as he continued speaking. "The Council is sure to recommend an attack on the castle, maybe sooner than later. With you controlling that creature in the dungeon, it should be an easy victory. Once the Galorians have been driven out, this time next year, the festival and our people will be back within the castle and you will be crowned our rightful queen."

"But Aren," Kyreen finally found her voice only to be cut off by a sharp shake of Sten's head.

"Aren will not be queen," he stated firmly. "For too long she has been domineering us, sending us to our deaths. Everyone holds her responsible for their loved ones dying whether in battle or from illness. Too many fathers and mothers, brothers and sisters, sons and daughters. Aren will never be our queen."

Sten's voice, so full of assurance, almost convinced Kyreen that his words could be true. Then she remembered his bardic vocation and shook off the enchantment.

"Aren should be on the throne," Kyreen stated, surprised to find she believed that to be true. Once their people were settled back in their land, Aren should be the one leading their people. Having made that determination, something deep in Kyreen unclenched.

"No, Princess!" Sten asserted. "You are the rightful heir! You are descended from our last queen! You belong on the throne!"

Sten paused, inhaling deeply, collecting himself before continuing with less frenzy. "Not only would Aren on the throne be a constant reminder of the nightmare our people have endured these many years, she is not a diplomat. She is a fine warrior and an excellent general. I do not harbor hard feelings for the old woman. I am merely stating she is not what our people need as we transition back to a more stable existence, back to civilization."

Sten paused again. This time to bring one of his hands up to Kyreen's face, his palm cupping her jaw, his thumb caressing her cheekbone, as he gazed into her emerald eyes. "Our people need a new face, a fresh face, a young and beautiful face on their throne. Someone well-traveled, well-connected to the outside, who can bring our country into the modern age, who can gain us a seat in the Myrddin Court. Our people need you, Princess."

"With you by my side?" Kyreen inquired.

"Yes! Exactly!" Sten replied, once more grasping Kyreen's hands in his. "With me by your side, as your Prince Consort, you would be, dare I say, our greatest monarch ever. I have great support skills, outstanding people skills, and I could keep you very, very well satisfied."

This last bit Sten delivered slowly, lowering his voice even as he drew Kyreen's hands to his lips. With his sapphire gaze locked onto her emerald one, he pressed a soft kiss full of promise to her bare skin. A flash of heat soared up through Kyreen, making her gasp softly. With a passionate smile, Sten carefully turned one of Kyreen's hands over to press a sultry kiss to her palm, never breaking eye contact.

Kyreen tingled all over, her breath quickening, her rapid pulse banging in her ears. She snatched both her hands out of Sten's, gaining an immediate respite without skin contact. She took another step back, a table pressing into her hips.

"So," she said, her voice cracking. She licked her dry lips, cleared her throat, and tried anew. "So, this is about tomorrow night's courting?"

"Yes, Princess," Sten replied, clearly enjoying Kyreen's discomfort. "I believe we should covenant before this summer's campaign."

Covenant with Sten? Kyreen could not even conceive of the notion that she should court and covenant Lang, a man with whom she clearly had a connection, and now Synnove's brother was proposing that they, two veritable strangers, take the vows of covenant? She found herself at a loss for words.

Sten, taking Kyreen's silence as her consideration of his proposal, stepped forward closing the space between them anew. Before she could react, he had slipped his arms around her, pulling her into him, her hands pinned against his chest, trapped.

"We would be perfect together," he murmured, before covering her mouth with his in a deep kiss.

Heat flared up again inside Kyreen, her body responding instinctively to the promise of his lips and mouth. For an instant, Kyreen could visualize Sten's dream. A gold jewel-encrusted circlet on her head, her overseeing courtly duties by day, the two of them entwined together at night. Abruptly she shook herself with a mental slap. What was she thinking? Sten cared nothing for her as a person. He only wanted her as the Calanian queen.

Their lips still connected and nowhere to go, trapped between the table and Sten's body pressing against her, and her hands pinned, Kyreen twisted in Sten's embrace, tearing her lips from his. Gasping in relief from the loss of contact, she shook her head to clear it and continued twisting until she faced the table. Deftly before he could react, Kyreen drove an elbow into his abdomen, grabbing the largest hardbound book on the table and spun around, knocking Sten upside the head.

With a surprised look, Sten staggered back and Kyreen swung again this time with her open hand, connecting the blade of her hand against his neck. Sten's eyes widened, then went dim as he dropped to his knees then toppled to the side.

Kyreen exhaled, heart pounding, then turned to return the book to the table. Leaning her palms on the table top, she took a few deep cleansing breaths to get herself under control.

"You should not be here when he wakes," a soft voice said from behind Kyreen, who spun around fresh adrenaline pumping through her veins. A small figure stepped out from the shadows of the tent wall. Clothed in trousers and an overly big tunic, her dark hair shorn close to the skull, the young teen appeared male, but Kyreen ventured to guess she gazed upon Synnove's younger sister.

"Svante?" Kyreen inquired cautiously.

"I prefer Svein," the girl replied quietly with a typically masculine name.

Taking in the girl's appearance and her short hair with her soft proclamation, Kyreen nodded, extending a hand. "Svein, well met. I am Kyreen, friend of your sister Synnove."

Svein grasped Kyreen's hand, responding, "Well met, Kyreen."

She glanced down at her brother prone on the tent floor. "I meant what I said you should not be here when he wakes. Sten does not take rejection too well. He so rarely encounters such situations."

"How much did you hear?" Kyreen inquired looking down at the motionless Sten with a grimace.

"Only the last bits," Svein replied, motioning to the shadows behind her. "There is a small opening I use to bypass the main door."

"I agree I should be going," Kyreen stated. "Will you be alright with him?"

"Oh yes," Svein replied cheerily. "Sten would not harm me physically. All his anger will be focused on you and yours."

"Very well," Kyreen said reluctantly. "If you are sure."

"Go, go, go," Svein shooed Kyreen with gestures reminiscent of her father.

Kyreen ducked out of the tent, the brisk wind slapping her immediately. The adrenaline coursing through her veins began wearing off and she felt a little wobbly as she hurried towards the center of camp. The meeting and announcements seemed to have ended as Kyreen began encountering groups of people almost immediately which helped keep her from sprinting. For some reason, she felt an urgency to find Lang, her inner panic growing with each step she took.

"Kyreen!" Synnove grabbed her friend's arm as Kyreen rushed by her. "What is wrong?"

"Lang," Kyreen whispered, not wanting to ever tell Synnove what just transpired between her and Synnove's brother. "I need to find Lang."

"He is probably still in the quad," Synnove answered, gesturing back the way she had just come. "Would you like…?"

Synnove did not finish her question as Kyreen had already taken off. Shrugging, the younger woman hurried to catch up with the friends she had been walking with when she had spied Kyreen rushing towards them with a wild look in her eyes.

Kyreen resumed her brisk walk. She barely controlled herself from sprinting, pushing back waves of panic, as she skid to a halt at the edge of the quad. Across the way, she spied Lang with Aren, Viggo, and another person. Though Kyreen only saw this person from behind, she guessed the woman was Lang's former partner Kasja. The four stood in quiet conversation. Kyreen raised a shaking hand to her mouth, biting down on a finger to keep from calling out, unwilling to cross over to the group.

From across the clearing Lang frowned, his eyes finding Kyreen. Sensing her distress, he sprinted toward her, reaching her just as her knees gave way and she fell into his arms.

"Lang," she rasped her voice barely audible. "I cannot…breath. I am …so …scared …worried… frightened…"

"Kasja!" Lang called out, gently setting Kyreen to the ground.

Tears filled Kyreen's eyes as she watched the tall beautiful woman, the mother of Lang's children, his former lover, walk towards them accompanied by Aren and Viggo. Why had he called out to Kasja and not one of the others? This had not been how Kyreen wanted to meet Lang's former mate. As the trio arrived, Kyreen's panic subsided and she found her ability to breath returned. Covering her face with a hand, Kyreen exhaled shakily.

"Thank you," Lang murmured reaching a hand up to squeeze one of Kasja's hands.

At Kyreen's inquiring gaze, Lang dropped the other woman's hand and rose to his feet, pulling Kyreen, now feeling much better, to her feet as well. "Kasja, Kyreen. Kyreen, Kasja," he introduced the two, gesturing between them with one free hand, the other arm he kept wrapped around Kyreen, holding her close.

"Kyreen, well met," Kasja smiled brightly taking one of Kyreen's hands in both of hers.

At the other woman's touch, Kyreen felt the last of the panic drain from her. Startled, Kyreen barely refrained from snatching her hand away, murmuring, "Well met."

The calm exuded by Kasja washed over Kyreen, who stared at their hands entwined. She wanted to feel annoyed at the woman's tranquil smile, she wanted to be angry at Lang for bringing Kasja over, she wanted to lash out at someone, but every time one of these negative emotions welled up inside her, a new wave of calm washed it away. She tried frowning but even keeping that expression took effort.

Kasja, it seemed, had no issue frowning which she aimed at Lang. "You have not told her about me?"

Lang shrugged. "It never came up in conversation."

"Two days ago I did not know you even existed," Kyreen commented casually, instantly mortified that she spoke her thoughts aloud.

Aren failed at hiding her smile. "It takes some getting used to being around Kasja."

"I apologize," Kasja spoke softly to Kyreen. "I am a Demulcent, a soother. I pacify discord and anger and, in this case, panic."

"Panic?" Aren and Lang both asked simultaneously.

Kyreen looked at the four people staring back at her with questioning gazes. She shook her head, trying to ignore the strong emotions fighting to break free.

"I do not know what came over me," she said. "I was in the Archival Tent with…Synnove's brother, Sten. When I stepped out I began feeling uneasy, that I had to find Lang, that something terrible was about to happen."

"About to happen, not had happened?" a voice asked from behind Kyreen.

Chapter 21

All five turned to look at Gisli standing just on the edge of the clearing. She walked forward, her sapphire gaze sweeping over the group before landing on Kyreen. Synnove's mother placed a hand softly on Kyreen's arm.

"Yes, it was an impending doom," Kyreen answered.

Gisli shook her head, clicking her tongue. "Synnove was correct. I had hoped she had been mistaken. I mean it has been years, decades even since..."

"Gisli," Aren interrupted the Historian gently. "Synnove was right about what?"

"About Kyreen being a Connate."

The four people around Kyreen inhaled softly. Kyreen glanced from face to face, wanting so hard to be worried but unable to feel any concern.

Gisli continued, explaining to Kyreen, "A Connate is not only one of the empathic traits, it is the pinnacle of all empathic traits. A Connate feels everything around her. The longer a Connate is around people, the more sensitive she is to their moods. To be honest I do not know how Kyreen has not..."

"That is enough," Aren interrupted Gisli once more. "Thank you for bringing us this information, Gisli. We can take it from here."

"Yes," Gisli replied. "I may have some notes on techniques to control the input so Kyreen can..."

"How about I go with you to the archives?" Viggo suggested, taking the Historian's arm and guiding her away from the group.

"Tell Svein hi for me," Kyreen called out to the retreating pair, "and tell Sten, if he is awake, I am sorry."

As soon as the words escaped her, Kyreen slapped a hand over her mouth. Did she really just blurt out like a drunken idiot? Resolutely, she ignored Lang's questioning gaze, instead turning her attention to her cousin. Aren had an amused expression on her face, apparently enjoying Kyreen's uncharacteristic frankness.

"For some," Aren explained, "Kasja's presence acts as a liberator, much like alcohol does. I imagine it is doubly so for you, cousin."

"That is all fine," Lang commented, "but what caused the panic in Kyreen in the first place?"

"I have a theory," Kasja said, looking around before adding, "but I do not believe we should discuss such things at out here in the open."

Aren nodded, then proceeded down the path her husband and Gisli had just taken. Kyreen followed, sandwiched between Lang and Kasja. She kept looking over at the beautiful woman, wanting to say something, just barely managing to stay her tongue by forcing her gaze over to Lang. But then she would feel the urge to blurt out something to him, so would stop her mouth only by dragging her gaze back over to Kasja.

The third time Kyreen directed her gaze onto Kasja, the woman grinned at Lang, saying, "She does have some superior will power. A bit stubborn, I imagine?"

"You have no idea," Lang muttered.

"She is right here and can hear you," Kyreen stated, staring up at Kasja. "She thinks it is rude to speak about people as if they were invisible. She also thinks you are very tall and incredibly beautiful."

As Lang and Kasja both chuckled, Kyreen grimaced. She then focused her attention on her boots, biting her tongue, letting the pain occupy her befuddled brain.

Thankfully, the Council Tent came into view and Aren ushered them all inside. Kyreen's cousin uttered a low series of words and the lights rose slightly.

"I believe the protections of the day are still in place," she commented, taking a seat and gesturing the others to be seated as well. "Our conversations will not be heard."

Lang pulled out a chair for Kyreen who smiled at him as she sat. "You know I am not drunk, right? I can get myself into a chair without assistance."

She winced, resting her face in her hands, "Sorry!"

He patted her shoulder, taking the chair beside her. Kasja discreetly sat a few chairs down from Kyreen, which placed her squarely in between Kyreen and Aren.

As soon as everyone had been seated Aren turned her gaze to Kasja, saying, "You have a theory? I would like to see if it matches mine."

Kyreen turned in her seat to watch Kasja, her hands clenched together in her lap, consciously working to keep a hold on her tongue. A flash of memory ran through her mind of her and her twin brother sitting at a table very similar to this one, so young and small they shared a chair, so frightened of the chaos around them, their tiny hands clasped together. Sadness washed over Kyreen only to immediately scatter. Her brain knew something was wrong, but she could not react. A lone tear escaped Kyreen's eye, trailing slowly down her cheek as she pushed away the discomfort so as to better concentrate on the words Lang's former mate spoke.

"…as long as everyone remained in the quad, within the sphere of my influence. Then, once the people began dispersing, their emotions returned. Kyreen, having spent the last couple of days with all of us, getting in tune with our emotions, began receiving all that input without any warning, without a filter."

"I agree," Aren responded once Kasja finished speaking. "I can imagine our people are anxious about the castle campaign, especially now that we have moved up the timeline."

"Everyone on the Council is anxious," Lang commented. "That does not mean it is the wrong course of action. We all realize this is a necessary course of action to return us all to our homeland."

"I know," Aren responded, rubbing a hand over her face. "I am just so tired."

"People are tired, too, of you sending their loved ones to die," Kyreen's mouth continued to speak without her usual filters. As soon as the words escaped her mouth Kyreen cringed, exclaiming, "Aren, my apologies! I do not believe that. It is something I heard tonight."

Though her cousin had much practice controlling her facial expressions, Kyreen could tell that her words had wounded Aren, so Kyreen told them what had transpired with Sten in the Archival Tent while the Council's annual report had been being presented. In her current state, she delivered the report virtually unedited, causing Kyreen great discomfort at times, until Kasja's influence washed it away. By the time she reached the part where Sten kissed her and she had to describe her vision of being queen, tears streamed freely down Kyreen's cheeks. She could not tell if her crying stemmed from knowing her unfiltered words caused pain or from the utter helplessness she felt in her inability to censor herself.

"Aren, I do not want to wear the crown," Kyreen concluded. "I do believe you are the rightful queen and should lead our people once we retake our homeland. I do!"

"I believe you, cousin," Aren responded quietly.

Unable to stop, Kyreen turned to face Lang in the chair beside her. She gazed tearfully into his eyes. "Lang," she said quietly, "I cannot court you and I cannot covenant with you, not now."

Lang's eyes widened, his mouth opened to reply but Kyreen pushed on before he could speak.

"It is not because I wish to court or covenant Sten," she said, shuddering a bit at the thought. "Simply I am not ready for such a commitment. I am still struggling greatly with being a Calanian. There is so much change going on I am learning new aspects about our people, about my family, about myself. Like this Connate talent. I can barely cope somedays, so there is no way I can in good conscious make a commitment to you like a covenant. I mean I enjoy our time together. I may even love you but this bond it scares me. I do not want to lose myself..."

"Hey," Lang said quietly, grabbing Kyreen's hands in his to stop her from continuing. "I do not and have never expected a covenant, not yet. Eventually maybe, but now is not only the wrong time, but it is too soon."

Even as her mouth opened to reply, a part inside of Kyreen cringed in mortification that she would utter these words not only in front of her cousin but also Lang's mate, former mate she mentally corrected, saying, "Then why have you delayed consummating our bond? I have felt your desire. Why the hesitation if not for covenant?"

Now Lang ran a hand across his face, mumbling, "By the goddess, I have made a mess."

"As much as I would like to, now is not the time for me to say, 'I told you so,' Lang, but it is time for Aren and me to excuse ourselves," Kasja suggested quietly.

"No!" Kyreen spun around to face Kasja, her eyes wide, a flare of panic surging then subsiding. "If you leave, the panic will return. Please do not let that happen."

"I fear Kyreen is correct," Viggo commented from the tent entrance. He walked over to drop into the chair beside Aren. "The only way for the talent to reset is for Kyreen to isolate herself for a few days."

"I do not understand why this is happening now," Kyreen said. "I spent all winter at Training Camp without an issue."

"From what I gleaned from Gisli, you may have had some effects but the Training Camp population is the smallest, maybe one hundred people with all classes combined," Viggo explained. "Festival grounds currently have about two thousand people here now."

"One thousand, nine hundred, fifty-two," Aren stated. "According to the census numbers reported tonight."

"And Kyreen is connected to each one," Viggo added.

"The Festival concludes tomorrow night, right?" Kyreen asked. At Aren's nod, she continued. "Then I can go spend a few days at the birthing compound, only a handful of people are there."

Aren nodded, "That sounds like a good plan. For tonight however…"

"Kyreen is welcome to stay in my tent with me and the children," Kasja offered. "It is not large but we do have room for one more bedroll."

Kyreen bit her tongue to avoid opening her mouth. She already felt uneasy with the evening's events, she could not imagine what she would feel like once relieved of Kasja's influence.

After a long moment's pause, making certain no other words would come pouring out, Kyreen murmured, "Thank you."

Aren rose to her feet, signaling an end to the evening's conversation. The others all stood as well. Kyreen turned to Lang, thinking he had been very quiet. Indeed, he had a thoughtful expression on his face.

"Are you alright?" Kyreen asked quietly as the others began moving towards the tent exit.

"I will be and so will you," Lang answered with a smile. He looked at Kasja. "Do you mind heading out with Kyreen? I need to speak with Aren."

"Not at all," Kasja replied with a glance to Kyreen. "I will wait for you outside."

Lang waited for Kasja to walk away before pressing a soft kiss to Kyreen's lips. "Go with Kasja and I will catch up."

"Very well," Kyreen answered, pressing a final kiss to his lips before heading out with a farewell wave to Aren and Viggo.

Kasja, as promised, stood outside the tent, arms wrapped around her drawing her cloak tight against the brisk wind. Though her hair had been braided into a single plait that hung halfway down her back, a few tendrils had slipped out to curl about her beautiful face. She smiled at Kyreen when she stepped out of the tent.

"I imagine you may wish to stop by your tent before we retire."

"Yes, thank you," Kyreen responded as the two women fell in step towards the Training Camp section. "Tonight was not the introduction I would have imagined had I been given the chance to think about meeting you."

"Do not judge Lang too harshly," Kasja commented. "He has a good heart, but terrible communication skills."

"So I am learning," Kyreen replied with a chuckle. She cast a sidelong glance at the other woman. "I want to dislike you, but I cannot. Is that your effect or is it because you are just as beautiful on the inside as you are on the outside?"

"Maybe a bit of both," Kasja laughed, her voice low and throaty.

"I do not understand why you are being so nice to me," Kyreen said. "I do not believe I could be so graceful were I in your place."

"Oh, I do not know," Kasja replied, as they stopped before Kyreen's tent preventing further conversation on the subject.

While it felt late to Kyreen, it was still early in terms of the young adults. Thus, she started slightly to find Synnove already tucked into her bedroll for the evening. Hastily, Kyreen explained about her panic attack, just barely managing to avoid the topic of Synnove's brother and his proposal.

"I do not know how long I will be with the mares," she concluded, as she finished packing her bag and began rolling up her bed.

"But you will miss the Courting Ceremony tomorrow," Synnove commented. She had sat up on her bedroll, her hair, released of its braid, billowed about her face in wild curls. "What about you and Lang?"

"That is still unsettled but he is not waiting for a covenant," Kyreen shrugged. She finished tying the bedroom, pausing to glance at her friend. "I do hope your courting goes well."

Synnove grinned. "It has been. That is why I turned in early tonight. To be rested for the ceremony. I have everything in place and he is ready."

"That I doubt," Kyreen grinned, opening the tent flap. "I do not believe any man could ever be fully prepared for you, my friend. Farewell."

"Farewell, Kyreen. Safe travels," Synnove called quietly, settling back down on her bedroll.

Outside the tent Kyreen stood, shouldering her gear, saying, "I am ready,"

The women walked in silence a few moments. As they passed the quad, Kasja spoke.

"I love Lang," she said quietly. "I have known him a very long time. His sister was my best friend. He is a fine man, a considerate lover and an excellent father, but I am not, have never been, and never will be in love with him."

After a brief pause, Kasja continued, "I was bonded once. We knew early on, in my twelfth year, his thirteenth."

Kyreen listened as they walked through the quiet encampment. Some youth still played sparktaske but they were far enough away that their voices were muffled.

"He fell ill the winter before we had agreed to covenant during the next festival. The healers could not save him. That season many families lost loved ones to the illness that spread through all of the camps, except for the farm camp where I happened to be." Kasja paused before a tent, gazing down at the entrance a long moment, then turned to face Kyreen. The bright moonlight glimmered in her dark blue eyes full of unshed tears.

"You asked why I am nice to you," she said her voice hushed. "Lang gave me the gift of motherhood, something for which I will be eternally grateful. I want to give him the gift of bonding, something I have experienced yet could never share with him. Even without our covenant, he will continue to be the father of my children and we will continue to be close friends."

Kyreen swallowed the emotional lump in her throat with great difficulty before she could speak. "Then I thank you."

Kasja glanced over Kyreen's shoulder. "I believe that is Lang walking this way. Let me go relieve my sister, who is with the children."

As Kasja knelt to enter her tent, Kyreen turned to greet Lang. A part of her had worried she and Kasja would need to be in close proximity, however, the woman's influence seemed to still work if Kyreen were a few feet away.

When Lang reached her, he slid his arms around Kyreen, pulling her to him for a passionate kiss. As they parted, the tent flap behind them opened and a figure stepped out.

"You make me ill!" Karine muttered quietly as she brushed by the couple, her shoulder bumping harshly into Kyreen's arm.

Kyreen's eyes followed the young woman's exit for a short moment then moved back to gaze up at Lang. As she opened her mouth to speak, he leaned in for another kiss, staying her comment and completely pushing away her thoughts of Karine.

When they parted at last, Lang pulled her into a hug, his beard tickling her ear as he spoke quietly.

"I have never been a jealous man, but when you spoke of being in Sten's arms and of kissing him, I believe it was only Kasja's influence that kept me sane. I wanted to find the man and pummel him senseless."

"He kissed me," Kyreen replied, trying to pull back to look Lang in the face, but he merely tightened his embrace, one of his hands moving up to stroke her hair.

"I know," he murmured. "Bad phrasing. I apologize. You have done nothing wrong. I did not mean to insinuate you had."

Kyreen relaxed into his embrace, relishing the warmth of his body and the comfort of his touch.

"I spoke with Aren," Lang whispered in her ear. "If you are agreeable, she has approved my furlough. I can take you out across the Great Valley. We could be alone together."

"But your duties on the Council, your children," Kyreen replied, adding, "my duties with the foals."

"Kasja and the children will be leaving with the other families the morning after courting and the Council is in recess until we resettle in Calan. The foals will come whether you are there to deliver them or not."

Kyreen hesitated. Exactly why she could not pinpoint. With Kasja so close, many of the emotions which guided Kyreen's actions were being suppressed. On the one hand, she relished the idea of spending uninterrupted time with Lang, but the idea also terrified her, or at least it would if she could feel terror right now.

Sensing Kyreen's reluctance, Lang said, "I owe you multiple apologies, Kyreen. I should have told you about Jetta and Esben, and about Kasja and our union. It was my silence that fueled my reluctance to complete our bond. I did not wish to enter into our relationship without being forthcoming about my family, yet I could not bring myself to speak about them. For that I apologize."

"Thank you for that," Kyreen responded, her head resting upon his chest, the beat of his heart under her ear steady and reassuring. "But I had already decided to forgive you that first afternoon when we spoke by the river."

Lang pulled back, pressing a fingertip to Kyreen's chin, tilting her face up to his. After another long kiss he murmured, "Then you will go with me in the morn?"

Kyreen hesitated again, then nodded. His lips reclaiming hers suspended any further discussion.

A short time later Lang lifted the tent flap so Kyreen could slip into the structure. He continued to hold the door so moonlight illuminating the interior as Kyreen unfurled her bedroll in the spot indicated by Kasja. The three adults communicated with their hands and expressions so as not to disturb the two sleeping children. Once Kyreen had her bedding arranged, Lang waved farewell to the women and allowed the flap to drop. Kasja murmured 'good night' and Kyreen responded in kind. As the two women settled in for the night Kyreen worried she might not be able to fall asleep after her nap earlier in the day, but in no time at all she drifted into a deep, dreamless slumber.

Chapter 22

The next morning Kyreen opened her eyes to be confronted by a set of deep emerald eyes peering at her face. When the infant, Lang's son Esben she recalled, saw Kyreen was awake, he gurgled gleefully sitting back to clap his hands. She winced when he squealed his delight. Almost immediately the tent flap raised and a little girl, Jetta, scooted into the tent. She stood looking down at Kyreen still reclining in her bedroll. The girl's expression, while not unfriendly, was on the stern side. For a few long moments Kyreen and the little girl stared at each other while the infant boy played with Kyreen's blanket, his little fists drawing handfuls of fabric up to his mouth. Kyreen tried not to think about the drooling and slobbering as she continued staring at the baby's older sister. Her stomach tried and failed rolling with anxiety so she knew Kasja had to be nearby. Children had always made Kyreen nervous. She never knew what to say or what they might say back to her. Babies she could handle. They did not speak.

Finally, Kyreen said, "Good morning."

"Good morning," replied the little girl.

"I am Kyreen."

"I am Jetta."

"Jetta, well met," Kyreen extended a hand, which after a slight hesitation, the little girl took in her own for a handshake.

"Well met, Kyreen," Jetta responded, her expression and tone very serious.

Kyreen glanced over at Esben who looked back at her with huge green eyes and both fists in his mouth. "He probably should have a better breakfast other than my blanket, would you not agree?"

Jetta looked down at her brother, a smile breaking out on her face. Then she remembered her attempt at being grown-up and the smile went away.

Kyreen reached over to pull Esben's hands from his mouth and disengage the soggy blanket from his grasp. Undeterred, the infant pulled Kyreen's hand to his mouth and began gnawing one of her fingers. She rolled up to a sitting position so as to extricate her finger, only to have the infant grab for her other hand and draw those fingers towards his mouth. Finally, Kyreen settled on scooping the baby up and settling him onto her lap so he could lean back against her, playing with his feet while she found her boots.

"So, Jetta," Kyreen said, as she awkwardly worked on pulling on her boots with a squirming baby in her lap, "did you sleep well?"

"Yes, I did."

"Did you have any interesting dreams?"

"No, I did not."

Much to Kyreen's relief the flap of the tent pulled back. She glanced over to see who entered, her smile widening when she recognized Lang. Self-consciously she ran a hand over her hair, pressing back the errant strands which escaped her braid overnight.

As for Lang, his heart tightened with affection at the domestic scene before him. Kyreen freshly awake cradling his son in her lap, conversing with his daughter.

Jetta's face lit up when she saw her father. Forgetting any thoughts of being stoic, she launched herself into his arms to a squeal, "Papa!"

"Hey, Pumpkin," Lang responded, wrapping his arms around his little girl, his eyes on Kyreen. Silently, he mouthed 'Good morning' before backing out of the tent with Jetta clinging to him.

Kyreen managed to roll towards the tent's entrance without dislodging Esben. Gathering the baby in one arm she exited the tent and stood upright without stumbling or dropping the child. The sun had risen, barely, and not many were yet stirring in the early hour. A few other families had begun emerging with their little ones.

Shifting Esben to one hip, Kyreen looked around for Kasja, standing across the way, speaking with one of her neighbors. The other woman smiled at Kyreen and waved a greeting while nodding at whatever the neighbor said. Kyreen shifted her gaze to Lang, who had swung Jetta onto his back where she clung easily, chattering to him about something Kyreen could not follow. He reached out for Esben, who eagerly went to his father, then Lang pressed a chaste kiss to Kyreen's cheek.

"Good morning again," he murmured quietly, his breath warm upon her skin before he stepped back.

Tingles ran up Kyreen's spine and she smiled back at him replying, "Good morning."

"Shall we go break fast?"

"Yes, yes, yes!" Jetta replied cheerily.

Kyreen glanced over at Kasja, who quickly excused herself with the neighbor and joined them. The two women walked behind Lang as he trotted in front pretending to be Jetta's horse. Kyreen could not help smiling at the spectacle, a side of Lang she never could have imagined.

"As I said last night," Kasja commented, "he is a fantastic father. I know he dislikes being away so much."

"Why do you and the children not stay with him at Council Camp?" Kyreen asked. "Other families are there."

Kasja grinned wryly, "My talent is not conducive to politics nor war. Nobody can trust their feelings in my presence."

Kyreen nodded thoughtfully. She had not thought much about it but from her own experiences last night, she understood the reasoning.

"I feel uncomfortable intruding upon your family," Kyreen commented abruptly, adding with a blush, "still having trouble controlling my tongue this morning."

"You should not worry," Kasja replied. "You are a part of our family now."

Kyreen's throat tightened as tears pricked her eyes. She blinked a few times and swallowed the lump in her throat before replying, "Thank you. Again, I say that I do not know that I would be so graceful were I in your position."

Kasja reached over to loop her arm through Kyreen's so that they walked with shoulders touching, a move Kyreen had only usually experienced with her closest friends or relatives. The other woman leaned in so as to speak softly, "We have all lost so many family and friends over the years that we cherish the connections we do make. I have faith you would act with grace, Kyreen. Lang could not be bonded to anyone less."

The women continued to walk in silence, their gaze focused on the man in front of them completely focused on his children. As they queued for their food, Lang glanced back, his grin widening at the view of the two women, their arms still interlocked. In the coming years Kyreen would often reflect on this moment, how his smile melted her heart, how this was the moment she fell completely and totally in love with this man.

As the women joined Lang and the children in line, Kasja reached to take Esben from his father, saying, "Jetta, you need to stand up in line."

Kyreen hung back watching the family unit organize to collect their food. Her heart melted anew when Jetta, one hand in Lang's, turned towards

Kyreen with a shy smile and took Kyreen's hand in her little hand, drawing Kyreen into the family circle. Lang grinned at the tears shimmering in Kyreen's eyes and gave her a wink.

Once through the food line, they found a mostly empty area to settle in to eat their meal. Jetta sat in between her father and their new friend. She concentrated on her porridge, not paying attention to the adult's mundane conversations. Esben sat in his mother's lap, trying to grab the spoon as she fed him.

"Kasja," Lang asked between bits, "what are your plans for the day?"

"It is my turn being with the babies and children," Kasja responded, familiar enough with Lang's tone to add, "We have plenty of people today. Tomorrow, when we ready for the migration, my presence is more necessary."

"Could you and the children accompany us a little way out?" he inquired. "Maybe we could take midday meal together out on the plains?"

"I am always up for a ride," Kasja answered. "I had planned on walking out with you two at least to the river. What say you, Kyreen?"

Caught with food in her mouth, not expecting to be drawn into the conversation, Kyreen had to swallow before replying. "That sounds good to me. A picnic would be lovely."

Her mother saying 'ride' had caught Jetta's attention. When she heard Kyreen, the little girl's face lit up anew. "A picnic?" she said, gazing up at Lang. "Please, Papa, may I go?"

"That settles it," Lang chuckled, ruffling his daughter's hair. "Yes, you may, Pumpkin. As soon as we finish eating we can get ready."

Kyreen spotted Synnove in the meal line and commented, "I should let Synnove know my plans have changed."

She rose to her feet with her empty dishes in hand. Both Lang and Kasja were still eating as were the children. Kyreen glanced over at her tentmate then back at Kasja. "Do you know how far I can go before…before the emotions return?"

Kasja looked over at the line, answering, "You should be fine. My influence weakens the farther apart we are but also emotions should not be quite as high this morning."

A short while later, Kyreen cinched up the saddle on her gelding as Lang finished tacking a mare for Kasja, who had the children with her procuring food for their impromptu outing. Lang's mare stood patiently nearby, already saddled. Kyreen secured her gear to the saddle then turned to watch Lang, as she ran a nervous hand over her freshly braided hair. Lang, noticing the movement, tightened the cinch then moved over to Kyreen.

"The panic has returned?" he asked gazing down on her face with concern.

"Just a feeling of unease," Kyreen shrugged. "Uncomfortable but not unbearable."

"Let me see if I can distract you," Lang replied, with a mischievous twinkle in his eyes. "I never did have the opportunity to greet you properly this morning."

Wrapping his arms around her, he proceeded to kiss Kyreen thoroughly, completely distracting her from everything except the prospect of spending the next few days completely alone save for each other. When they parted, Lang kept his arms tightly around her so Kyreen could rest her head on his chest. Breathless from the kiss, she relaxed into the embrace enjoying the steady beat of his heart under the quick pounding of her blood rushing in her ear.

A few minutes later Lang shifted so that his arm stayed around Kyreen's shoulder and she could turn to see Kasja and the children approaching. Lang hurried to relieve Kasja of the bag of food while Jetta skipped up to Kyreen, her two dark braids bouncing, her sapphire eyes sparkling.

"Are you ready for an adventure?" Kyreen asked the little girl.

"Yes, I am," came the quick reply.

Kyreen reached for the bag as Lang walked up. "I can take this," she said. "You may need both your hands."

"Thank you," Lang replied before scooping his daughter up and lifting her high over his head, spinning around before settling her gently in front of his saddle. He placed the reins in her hands with a soft order to sit still while he helped her mother with the baby.

Kyreen secured the food bag to the back of her saddle with the rest of her gear. The gelding turned his head to gaze at her as though admonishing her for loading him down like a common pack mule. Kyreen gave the star on his forehead an affectionate rub before swinging up into her saddle and glancing over at her companions. Lang, having held Esben so Kasja could mount her mare, had just settled into his saddle and gathered the reins from Jetta.

They headed northeast out of camp. Kyreen closed her eyes, lifting her face to the sun. The spring day appeared to be shaping into an unusually warm one. The wind, however, still held a bit of a bite and made everyone wrap their cloaks about their bodies as the horses broke into an easy jog, which discouraged conversation between the adults. Jetta, however, chattered constantly to her father asking questions of and receiving answers from Lang that Kyreen could not overhear. Eventually those two pulled ahead, leaving Kyreen and Kasja trotting side by side. After a few miles, the camp having disappeared behind them, Kasja pulled her mare down to a walk. Kyreen reined in her gelding.

"Oy," Kasja groaned with a grimace. "I am too long out of the saddle and too old to trot that long."

"Someone enjoyed the ride," Kyreen responded with a nod to the slumbering baby in Kasja's arms. "I am impressed you could carry him and keep in the saddle. Besides you are not that old."

Kasja smiled, "Thank you for the kind words. I am closer to your cousin's age than yours. I was eleven when the Battle occurred. I was also one of the more fortunate in that both of my parents survived as did my three younger siblings. Not many of us had such a blessing, but then we lost my mother when she gave birth to Karine."

"I practically raised Karine as Father was one of the horticulturists tasked with feeding our people. He helped design our farmlands here," Kasja swept a hand towards the fields across the valley floor where people, little specks in the distance, worked tilling and planting. "That is why Karine is so protective of me, and so angry with you and Lang. She is young and does not understand the complex ties of love. I do hope once she experiences a bond, she will understand that I have not been wronged."

"She and Yngve have grown very close this year at Training Camp," Kyreen commented.

"Yes, she has mentioned him to me on numerous occasions," Kasja responded with a grin. "I shall be interested in seeing how courting goes this evening. Aren has always been a bit protective of her first born."

The two women chuckled, exchanging knowing looks, as Lang rode back up having turned around when he noticed they had fallen behind. He looked between the two women who appeared to be bonding over a confidence and said, "I think maybe I should have kept riding. Do I want to know?"

"Simply a bit of chattering," Kasja responded, giving Kyreen a wink. "But not about you, so have no worries."

"Good to hear," Lang breathed a sigh of relief. He turned his mare around so that the horses walked together three abreast with Kyreen's gelding in the middle.

"I was thinking," he continued, "that we may need to stop for midday meal soon. With both children, your ride back to camp will be slower and you need to be there for Karine since she is courting."

"Good idea," Kasja replied. She squinted looking forward, then pointed. "See those trees? If memory serves, the river has curved back and they grow upon its banks."

As the sun pushed past midpoint to begin its downward journey into evening, Kyreen stood, stooping over, in the green grass, Esben's two tiny fists gripping each of her index fingers as she helped him stand, keeping him from toppling as he slowly shuffled along on bare feet, his gaze set on the river several hundred feet before them. Behind the pair, Kasja lounged, spread eagle, on her back, soaking up the sunlight and the respite from childcare. A little way downstream, Lang walked with Jetta masterfully keeping the little girl away from the water while letting her believe she set their course along the river bank. Occasionally, Jetta would bend down to point at something and Lang would squat down to discuss the item or pick it up for inspection.

When her back began protesting, Kyreen hoisted Esben up and settled him down on her hip. As he played with her free hand, trying desperately to pull her fingers into his mouth, Kyreen turned slowly to survey the land spread out around them, savoring the warm sunlight and the frisky breeze, and the calm inside her. Some of the serenity came from Kasja for sure but also Kyreen had felt the shift when they had pulled away from the encampment.

Movement from Kasja drew Kyreen's attention as the older woman rose to her feet to begin packing up the remnants of their picnic. Kyreen walked over to offer assistance which Kasja waved off.

"You have Esben occupied," she said, smiling at her son. "That is assistance enough."

Kasja knelt down to withdraw a small packet from the food sack, as she glanced over to where Lang and Jetta appeared to be inspecting a gray river rock. She looked over at Kyreen with a sheepish expression.

"I hope you will not think me too forward," she said, rising to offer the brown package to Kyreen, "but I did not know if you had found time to procure any rue."

Kyreen took the proffered package thinking of the tiny amount of the contraceptive plant that she had left over from her last trip to Myrddin several weeks prior. Even Kasja's influence could not prevent the blush from spreading across Kyreen's face as she mumbled, "Thank you. What I have is a couple of months old."

Kasja shook her head. "Rue is more effective the fresher it is. I love that little one there," she added, nodding in the direction of Esben in Kyreen's arms, "but Lang and I had not planned on having children quite so soon. With Lang on the Council, we had hoped to wait until our people were back in our homeland. Esben is the result of some old rue."

"Thank you for the advice," Kyreen replied, working hard to keep the baby from snatching the package from her hand.

"Here let me relieve you. I am done packing," Kasja said, taking her son from Kyreen. "Most of this will go on with you two anyway."

Kyreen looked down at the packet, reluctant to continue on the subject, but unable to stop herself from saying, "Speaking of rue, how do you stand it? The taste is foul and the texture revolting."

Kasja cocked her head to one side with an inquiring look, then her eyes widened and she asked, "Are you chewing it raw?"

Kyreen nodded wordlessly, grateful Kasja only grinned and did not laugh as she explained to Kyreen that the plant leaves were meant to be brewed as a tea.

"Go ahead and make a batch tonight as soon as you make camp. Lang can drink it too. Rue tea will not adversely affect men. If you drink it again in the morning and continue every evening and morning, without skipping, you will be protected from pregnancy," Kasja explained, adding, "I am sorry no one ever explained this to you before."

"Aren gave me my first bunch and probably assumed I was familiar with its application," Kyreen responded, feeling the fool then added with a wry smile, "My mother taught me a great deal about herbs and their medicinal properties over the two years we were on the run. I suppose birth control was not something she thought to explain to her five-year-old."

Kyreen grinned at Kasja, who grinned back. Both women were still chuckling softly when Lang and Jetta walked up. Once again Lang glanced between the two, wondering what they could be discussing, looking so at ease with one another. As much as he had enjoyed this day with his family, right now looking at Kyreen, her eyes sparkling in the afternoon sun and the breeze rifling through the stray ebony curls framing her face, he only wanted to be alone with her in his arms.

Shortly Kasja and the children were headed back to camp. Jetta, perched behind her mother, turned around every few steps to wave back at her father and Kyreen, who stood waving back at the little girl. Then Kasja urged the mare into a jog and Jetta had to hold on to her mother with both hands.

As soon as they were truly alone, Kyreen felt Kasja's influence leave and so many emotions slammed back into her conscience. Shaking her head, she began attempting to sort through the feelings of guilt, embarrassment, and insecurity, then Lang gently turned her so they were facing each other.

"Any panic?" he asked quietly.

"No," Kyreen shook her head.

"Good," he said, taking her face between his hands and dropping his lips to hers. "The rest are your normal feelings and can wait," he murmured in her ear once their lips had parted. "I have been aching to kiss you all afternoon."

After another deep kiss full of promise, they began the next part of their journey. Lang pointed to the dim shadow staining the forest's edge at the base of the northern mountain range as their destination. Then he urged his mare into a jog and Kyreen did the same with her gelding.

Chapter 23

Just as the sunlight had begun to soften and the shadows lengthened, their destination came into view. Without either of them feeling the need to talk, they cared for the horses in silence before placing them in hobbles to graze for the evening. Kyreen felt momentarily guilty for not bringing any oats along but then remembered the gelding had been spending many days at pasture and today was probably the only hard travel day until they headed back to camp.

"You will survive," she murmured to him, rubbing behind his ear before heading back to the clearing where Lang had begun unpacking their gear.

After witnessing the ease with which Kasja and Lang had worked together with their children, Kyreen felt an awkwardness as she attempted to assist Lang in setting up camp. Finally, she announced she would go collect wood for the fire. As she turned away, Lang softly grabbed her elbow, forcing her back around to face him.

"Kasja and I have had many years of practice working together," he told her, cupping her face between his hands. "Even before Marietta's death forced us into a family, we had spent many, many days exploring this valley with our siblings. Do not be frustrated. This is the first of many outings for us. There are bound to be some missteps."

Kyreen nodded and he gave her a long kiss. When they parted, he added with a grin, "Besides I am so particular about setting up camp, building the fire pit, storing food, and such that nobody can ever help me."

Unsure if Lang spoke truth or simply wished to assuage her wounded feelings, Kyreen walked away feeling better nonetheless. When she returned with an armful of wood suitable for a fire, Lang made quick work of getting the fire started. He then pulled out a pot to which he added water from a water skin they had filled at the river.

At Kyreen's inquiring look, he said, "I thought you would be making up some rue tea."

When she turned red, he chuckled. "Kyreen, I never know whether to be alarmed or amused by your reactions. I know what rue tea is for and, with our misunderstandings put to rest, am fairly sure intimate relations will transpire at some point. I thought we had clearly established that this is not the time for us to enter into covenant. Thus, logically, it is definitely not the time to have a child."

He paused to look over at her, adding, "You are expecting us to consummate our bond, are you not?"

Which simply made Kyreen's face deepen to a dark rosy color. She buried her face in her hands, torn between the urge to laugh or to cry. Instead she just sat there with her hands covering her face taking several deep breaths. When she felt she had control over herself, she lowered her hands and looked across the fire at Lang, who glanced up from the pot of water just starting to boil. Without a word Kyreen pulled out the packet Kasja had given her and walked it over to Lang. He took her hand and rose to his feet.

"I do not say these things to embarrass you," he said.

"I know," Kyreen replied. "I spent so many years avoiding conversations about such things that even though I know in my head they are natural, in my heart I hear my foster mother reprimanding me."

"Did you not have conversations about contraceptives with your previous lovers?" Lang asked, his tone as nonchalant as if he were inquiring whether she had ever eaten an apple.

Blood flooded Kyreen's face anew. She could not decide if this bout of embarrassment arose from the fact Lang asked about her previous lovers as in the plural or that she had never considered having such a conversation with those men.

"No, do not turn away," Lang admonished, his tone not unkind. He gestured between them, adding, "As you said yourself if this, whatever this is between us is going to work, there can be no secrets, no shadows, no shielding. We have to be able to talk about everything."

Kyreen bit her tongue, fighting the urge to lash out at Lang that he had no business lecturing her on communication. He, after all, had failed to tell Kyreen about the existence of a mate and children for a fortnight.

"And now you are angry with me," Lang mumbled, squatting back down to begin preparing the tea.

Kyreen stood staring down at Lang for a long moment, torn between the urge to stroke his hair and apologize or to turn and run into the darkening woods. Eventually, she compromised by walking to the opposite side of the fire and settling back down on the ground.

"It is not as if I do not know you have been with other men," Lang commented quietly, his gaze firmly on the pot of tea he brewed. "There was that outsider who traveled with you last summer, then I heard something about the guild master from Myrddin, when you went to Gladys last fall for the contract talks."

He looked up, all amusement and mirth gone, his expression raw and vulnerable.

"I meant what I said last night. I have never been a jealous man, and I am not still, but what I feel for you grows deeper with each passing day. I have never experienced anything like it, not even fatherhood. When you walked into that tent last summer, it was as though a piece of me that had been missing my entire life, a piece I never knew I was missing, had suddenly fallen into place, making me whole. Being at odds with you all this time has been agony, but being with you also scares me. I have never felt this much. This connection between us is something new for me. Had we met under usual circumstances, we would have been hormonal youth without any common sense. As it is we are adults with rational brains, trying to navigate something never meant to be rational or logical."

He looked down at the tea. "And now I am rambling and want to stop. Are you still interested in tea?"

Silently Kyreen pulled her cup from her pack and walked over to Lang. After he had filled it, she settled down on the ground beside him. Their shoulders touching, each quiet in their own thoughts, they drank the tea. Once she had drained her cup and saw Lang had as well, Kyreen set the cup aside and turned towards Lang.

She opened her mouth, fully intending to share her thoughts with him. Gazing at him though, the firelight glinting off his beautiful face, she changed her mind and decided to trust her instincts. In a move that looked much smoother in her mind than in execution and which surprised them both, Kyreen shifted towards Lang, throwing a leg over him so she straddled his lap. Taking his face in her hands, before she lost her nerve, she kissed him deeply pressing her body against his. The fire warmed her back but the heat that flared up inside burned fiercer as Lang returned the kiss. His hands running along her shirt found the edge, then slid under. The contact of his hands to her bare skin fueled the heat coursing through her veins, drawing a soft moan from Kyreen.

For several long moments Kyreen lost herself in the kiss, in the feel of his hands on her body, in the heat of their connection. Then Lang moved his head back, breaking the kiss, his hands pulling out from under her tunic.

A quiet whine of protest escaped her as she opened her eyes, wondering what could be wrong.

Lang gazed into her eyes, the desire apparent in his. His voice husky, he quietly asked, "Are you certain?"

Kyreen stared back at him, resisting the urge to kiss his lips again, as her brain struggled to form coherent thoughts. When she could speak, her voice also laced with desire that matched the fire in her eyes, she whispered, "I am not a hormonal youth. I am certain."

In answer to her words, Lang reached around to her braid, his fingers releasing the tie, then deftly undid the plait. He combed through her dark hair, relishing the wild curls framing her beautiful face. Then, his eyes never leaving hers, he wrapped one arm around her tightly using the other to push their bodies upright. He grinned at her soft squeal of surprise and relished the feel of her legs wrapping around his hips, her fingers gripping tightly at his shoulders. Moving towards the fire, he slid both of his hands under her buttocks to better hold her close as he kicked dirt over the small fire before heading towards the bedding he had lain out earlier.

Sometime later, after the sun had set and the glow over the trees announced the impending moonrise, Kyreen opened her eyes. Warmly ensconced in Lang's arms, she smiled with a small sigh. The peace of their solitude washed over her, followed by a fresh heat as Lang brushed his fingertips along her naked body. Moaning softly, she snuggled back into him. His hand reached up to sweep her mop of ebony curls away from her neck, his breath warm as he leaned forward to press a number of soft kisses along the nape of her neck before murmuring quietly, "Are you hungry?"

"Not for food," she quipped playfully, only to be immediately contradicted by a loud growl from her stomach, noisily reminding her that midday meal had been several hours ago.

"Liar," Lang hissed in her ear, his voice laced with laughter. With a final soft kiss that landed haphazardly on her ear, he sat up and began rustling around for their hastily discarded clothes.

"I am not sure, but I believe these are yours," he said, placing a pile in her lap. "I suppose I will know when we put them on."

Once clothed, Lang stood and stretched before turning to look down at Kyreen, saying, "If you do not mind leftovers tonight so I do not have to build up the fire again, I promise to fix you a delicious supper tomorrow."

"It is a deal," Kyreen responded, pulling on her last boot and rising to her feet.

"I hope you like trout," he said, giving her a kiss then turning to gather food.

Kyreen had never had trout, though she had heard of it. As she discovered the following evening, she did indeed like the fish as prepared by Lang. She did, of course, wonder if her enjoyment came solely from the flavor, or her ravenous appetite, or the joy of the day she spent with Lang.

After breakfast that first morning, they had left the horses to graze while Lang led Kyreen into the forest. Though it had been a few years since he had visited this area, the lay of the land had not changed much and he soon found the trail. Walking single file, their path leading them up in elevation, the pair travelled in silence, partly from training, partly from a comfort between them that did not need to be filled with talk. Kyreen, never overly verbose, relished the silence of their journey.

At one point Lang stopped suddenly, putting up a hand to signal silence from Kyreen. Startled she looked around, wondering if a Galorian patrol could possibly be out this way. Then she followed his gaze through the underbrush where a doe, caught washing her newly born fawn, gazed at them, frozen, her eyes huge and liquid brown. After a moment Lang, quietly and slowly, resumed walking, Kyreen following. Once clear of the doe's area, Lang glanced back at Kyreen, his gleeful expression melting her heart and reigniting the heat in her body.

As though he could read her thoughts, Lang turned around to pull her into his embrace. After a long kiss, he murmured, "Not much farther now."

"M'kay," Kyreen mumbled, unable to form anything more coherent.

True to his word, they soon exited the woods at the banks of a medium sized stream, running fast with the early snow melt. Large rocks bordered the river, huge trees overhead created dappled shadows over the entire scene. Lang put down his pack and began rummaging through the contents.

Kyreen slowly lowered her pack, gazing about the clearing. This place more than any other she had visited in Calan reminded her of the woods in Hanoria where she had spent so much of her childhood exploring. Some of the giant trees had yet to begin sprouting leaves while the evergreens stood tall and full. The sound of the stream running across the rocks echoed off the trees. The spring sun, barely halfway up to noon, shone bright in the cloudless sky but offered little warmth at this altitude, especially with the jaunty breeze rifling down the river corridor.

Kyreen inhaled deeply, savoring the crisp clean air. The smell of pine trees mingled with smells of the water and the sunshine, for Kyreen truly believed sunshine held a scent all of its own. She relished the tranquility of their solitude while savoring the exhilaration radiating from Lang. She turned her attention to his activities which involved his dagger and a stick.

"A spear." Lang answered when asked by Kyreen what he formed. "There is a nice shallow area over there that is wonderful for gigging."

While Lang went to take care of finding their dinner, Kyreen found a sunny spot on a boulder big enough upon which she could recline. After pulling a small book from her pack, she placed the bag under her head as a pillow then cracked open the novel she had borrowed from Rhun on her last visit to Myrddin.

Rhun. Kyreen placed the book on her stomach, her gaze staring up through the trees without really seeing them. Nibbling at her bottom lip Kyreen wondered what she would say to Rhun when she next saw him. She had not given the guild master a thought since before she and Lang had begun spending so much time together. She cared for the big man and always enjoyed their time together, but they had both always known their relationship could never be permanent. He led the most prominent guild in the largest city in the realm. She lived in the woods with her displaced people, plotting to regain control of their homeland. Kyreen conducted some mental calculations, realizing with a start that she had a meeting scheduled with Rhun in just a few days, ten if her math could be trusted.

This quarterly meeting had been scheduled to take place in the small village of Gladys, which saved Kyreen travel time. Although truth be told she would have preferred meeting in Myrddin so she could visit Engla and the baby. She would need to pen her friend a lengthy letter to catch her up on all the news Kyreen had to share. Going to Myrddin would be much simpler.

Sighing Kyreen decided to forget about anything aside from reading her book and enjoying the beautiful day. When Lang walked up much later, he found Kyreen completely engrossed in the novel.

"Here I am slaving to catch dinner while you laze about doing nothing," Lang teased, sitting down beside Kyreen.

She squinted up at him, his face in shadows from the sun behind him, trying to decide if he truly were teasing or if something more colored his words. She pushed down her insecurities, deciding to go with the first and replied, "I was not doing 'nothing.' I was exploring a dragon's lair with plans to rob the creature of its pilfered treasures."

Lang plucked the book from her hand and, closing it without marking her place, set it to the side so he could loom over her prone body. With his hands placed on either side of her head he leaned down to kiss her before she could protest.

Nuzzling at her neck, one hand stealing under her shirt to fondle her breast, he murmured, "I can think of something more productive we could be doing right now."

Kyreen laughed. For a moment, she wanted to ask him how their making love could be considered productive, but Lang's continued kissing and fondling drove that thought and all other thoughts from her mind as her body responded to his touch.

Afterwards Kyreen nestled against Lang, the boulder rough under her hip, the breeze cooling her heated skin. She sighed a soft sigh of contentment then Lang sat up abruptly. As she, too, sat up in alarm, glancing about for danger, he began gathering up their clothes.

"Get dressed," he said, tugging his shirt over his head. "I want to show you someplace."

The place in question lay almost an hour's walk through the forest, paralleling the mountain range. Just as they entered the small clearing, Kyreen had begun to wonder just how far Lang expected them to travel today. She felt chilled from their trek in the shadows, yet sweated from the exertion of the hike through thick underbrush. Lang stood at the edge of the tree line beaming at Kyreen, but what she saw before her did nothing to improve her mood.

"This was one of my favorite places growing up," Lang gushed, turning to view the lake nestled in the small tree-lined valley, surrounded by dark rocks. The smooth surface of the water reflected the handful of fluffy white clouds hanging in the sky overhead. The only movement in the lake came from a small spring trickling into it on the far side. Lang continued speaking, his tone reflecting the joy he felt returning to this place.

"For some reason, the water is warm all year round. We think a hot spring feeds in here but the water is very deep. One summer, on a dare,

Kasja's brothers and I kept trying to dive down to the bottom, but none of us could ever find it."

To Kyreen's horror, Lang began shedding his clothes anew. Only this time she desperately wanted nothing to do with his nakedness, and wished fervently to be anywhere but here. Without awareness that she had moved, Kyreen backed into a tree trunk, her eyes fixed on the extreme, to her mind, expanse of water. Her hands reached behind her gripping at the rough bark, the tree both hindering her escape into the forest and helping her remain standing on weak knees.

Lang, oblivious to her emotions due to the excitement of his own, turned towards Kyreen clad only in his trousers. His words dying unspoken upon his lips, he frowned, perplexed by her reaction. Setting down the boot he had just removed next to its mate, he walked over to where Kyreen stood, pressing against the tree, her face unnaturally pale, her emerald eyes round in fear. He gathered her hands in his, prying them from the tree trunk she clung to. Her skin cold against his, she actively attempted to pull away.

"Hey," he said quietly, his tone calm and soothing. He pressed his lips to the back of both her hands before continuing. "What is the matter?"

"I..." Kyreen's voice faltered. She licked her dry lips and tried to swallow the lump in her throat. Still her voice came out as a hoarse whisper. "I cannot go...I mean I never...I cannot swim."

Lang pulled back slightly in surprise, as though the concept had never entered his mind. In his thoughts, swimming came as naturally as riding a horse, a skill that everyone possessed. He and his siblings and their friends had been swimming for as long as Lang could remember. Even before the Battle, he had memories of his mother teaching him to swim in one of the ponds in the woods surrounding the castle. Before he could think about the consequences, he asked, "How can you not know how to swim?"

Immediately, he regretted his choice of words as Kyreen's eyes filled with tears. She jerked her hands from his, wrapping her arms around her body, her gaze dropping down to the ground.

"Swimming is not something we did in Hanoria. The waters there never warmed," she said quietly. "Besides, nudity would never be condoned."

"But this past winter, on the marshes, surely you went to the hot springs," Lang responded, straining to remember all the evenings he had trailed her, just to relieve the agony of their unfulfilled bond, and now realized that, while she joined her friends at the beach, she had never ventured into the springs.

"I only went once," came her soft reply. "When Atle sent me, after you and I had quarreled. I went alone but Synnove joined me shortly. I do not think she noticed me clinging to the rocks when she arrived. It was not until she had slipped in and stood up that I realized how shallow the water was. I felt such the fool."

Her voice trailed off, leaving unspoken that she again felt the fool here. Lang wrapped his arms around her, pulling her close, a hand cradling the back of her head, his face lifted to the sky, gazing up through the trees as his mind worked out how to solve this without further hurting Kyreen's feelings.

"Would you be open to me teaching you to swim?" he asked cautiously.

She stiffened, replying, "But there is no beach. You said yourself the water is deep."

"It is deep here, but across the way, where the snow melt runs in, there is a sand bar, not too deep," he assured her, softly stroking her hair, absently wishing it were not contained in the braid.

For a long moment, they stood there embracing as Kyreen pondered his question, fighting the panic that flared anytime she thought about entering the water. Lang could feel her heartbeat quicken as she thought. Patience, he continued to remind himself. He had to be patient with Kyreen. She looked so Calanian that Lang kept forgetting that their past, their childhoods, their experiences had been so vastly different. Not for the first time he wondered at their bonding.

"Very well," Kyreen finally spoke. Joy radiated through Lang as he sensed how uneasy she felt about the prospect and he realized the precious gift of trust she had just given him.

Now, safely back at their base camp enjoying the deliciously prepared fish, Kyreen ruffled a hand through her still damp curls and reflected back on the day with good feelings. Lang had proven to be a proficient, patient instructor, getting her to relax in the water, even practicing swim strokes. She knew she should not have been surprised by this as she recalled how he had guided her regarding the tracking exercises and how he had interacted with his daughter at the river. Lang was a kind, compassionate man who would be a wonderful father to their children.

Kyreen paused, her fork midway to her mouth, shocked at the thought. Their children? Had she really just thought about that? Kyreen had never been one to dwell on or obsess over the thought of procreating. Though her close female friendships had been limited to just Engla and Synnove, both women had quite often referred to their future children as though motherhood had been a foregone conclusion. Kyreen on the other hand had never felt that pull. Even now, with her feelings for Lang continuing to blossom every day, she could not completely commit to the idea of children. Not right now. Not before their people were back in their rightful home. Not before Aren could be crowned. Not before Kyreen discovered what happened to her twin. There were so many unknowns in the future, how could she entertain the thought of having a child at this moment?

"No, nope, not letting this happen," Lang stated, breaking into her thoughts. He took her plate, empty of the meal she did not remember finishing, from her hands and pressed her tea into them saying, "No angsty wool gathering allowed on this holiday."

Kyreen grinned at him, draining the last bit of drink from her cup, before rising to her feet.

"You prepared the meal," she said, relieving him of both their dishes. "The least I can do is clean up."

As she turned away, Lang grabbed her, pulling her close, wrapping his arms about her from behind, pressing his body to hers. His breath warm and moist on her ear, he whispered, "I will help. For the sooner we finish securing the camp for the evening, the sooner we can retire, and maybe, just maybe, we might get to sleep before the sun rises in the morning."

He was correct. It was very nearly sunrise when they finally drifted to sleep.

Chapter 24

On their third morning, Kyreen woke up alone. Sensing Lang's presence nearby, she did not feel alarmed. Instead she gave a big stretch of her body as she yawned, contemplating rolling over to go back to sleep. Lang, it seemed, could operate on very little sleep. While Kyreen enjoyed their evening activities immensely, the effects of their late evenings and early mornings were beginning to wear on her. For Lang also rose early and, once he rolled out of bed, the man did not stop for the entire day. Not only did it seem he had planned on showing Kyreen all his favorite spots in this single visit, he also took care of the meals, showed Kyreen the various edible spring vegetation, as well as caught trout or maintained a small trap line for rabbit like the one he roasted the previous evening. After dinner, as Kyreen had cleaned up, Lang had worked on treating the rabbit skin, explaining to Kyreen how he planned on making a rabbit fur hat for Jetta to wear next winter.

After a short internal debate, Kyreen rolled from the bed to dress and find Lang. He looked up with a smile from the breakfast he prepared.

"Good morning, sleepyhead," he teased good naturedly.

She just rubbed her fingers across his skull, relishing the feel of his bristly short hair under her fingertips before dropping a kiss to his upturned lips, murmuring, "That looks delicious."

He handed her a plate saying, "Eat up. Today is going to be busy."

"More exploring?" she asked, having been hoping for something more relaxing.

"Not really," he replied, nodding towards the valley floor. "There is a weather system moving in soon. Probably just rain and wind but I would prefer being some place more sheltered, in case it turns nasty."

Kyreen glanced up at the sky, noticing for the first time the churning gray clouds. Out over the valley, the sky raged dark and angry. While Kyreen finished her meal, Lang began packing up their gear and making the area look as pristine as it had when they had arrived.

By the time they had loaded everything onto the horses and mounted, the wind had picked up, the sky overhead a dark gray promise of impending rainfall. Lang pointed his mare east away from the incoming storm and set a brisk enough pace that they managed to stay ahead of the storm. After a few miles, they turned north to enter the mouth of a U-shaped valley. A fair-sized stream traversed the middle of this smaller valley, fed by waterfalls peppered around the edges. Lang paused to point out the entrance to another smaller valley in the distance.

"There is a cave system all through this area and one of the entrances is just up through there," he said before urging his mare into a quicker lope.

A cave? Kyreen thought, spurring the gelding into a lope to follow Lang. The wind had picked up quite a bit by the time they travelled to the new, even smaller valley, yet the rain held off until Lang reined his mare to a stop at the yawing entrance. The temperature, which had been dropping during their trip as well, had reached a less than temperate level. Kyreen drew her cloak tighter, reining to a halt beside him.

Lang slid to the ground and led his mare to the cave entrance through which two wagons could easily go in side-by-side. Kyreen halted just shy of the opening, her brow furrowed.

"What is it?" Lang asked, glancing back, his tone friendly, not matching the shortness of his question.

"Are you not worried about bears?" Kyreen asked. At the gelding's nudging, she moved to just inside the cave entrance, out of the rain just beginning to pelt down. The inside of the cave expanded out and up into a spacious chamber.

"About what?" Lang responded as he began unloading the mare's packs.

"Bears. Huge, shaggy creatures with really long, really sharp claws. Predators? Territorial? Nasty tempers in spring after hibernating all winter?"

Lang shook his head. "Never heard of them. The only predators around here are wolves but we pretty much ran the packs out of the Valley."

"Ran them out?" Kyreen asked.

"When we began cultivating the valley there were several wolf packs, but they hunted the deer," Lang explained as he unsaddled his horse, "so we had to cut down their numbers in order to save our food supply."

Not entirely convinced, but preferring the dry cave to the torrential downpour outside, Kyreen started unloading the gelding. After stacking the gear and removing the tack, she rubbed her horse down well.

"What shall we feed the horses?" she asked.

"I am fairly certain there are provisions in the back," Lang answered.

Though it was barely noon, the storm outside had darkened the day so the interior of the cave was in shadows. Lang walked to a sconce in the wall Kyreen had not previously noticed. Reaching up he wrapped his hand around a sphere at the top of the torch. Very gradually the sphere began to glow. Shortly it shone a bright white light illuminating the interior of the cave.

Lifting the torch from the holder, Lang grinned at Kyreen and said, "Shall we go see what is in the coffers?"

The supplies stockpiled in the cave amazed Kyreen, both with the quantity but also the efficiency of the system. As he rummaged, pulling out what they would need, Lang explained the system to her.

"This area is used for fishing, trapping and foraging by those living full-time here in the valley, especially in late summer when all the berries are ripe. That was always my favorite trip," he said, handing Kyreen a flake of hay for the horses. "People venture out here several times a year, the youth mostly, sometimes as young as ten," he added, picking up an armful of supplies and walking back to the front of the cave with her. "I believe the adults devised these trips as a way to keep us occupied during the time between planting and harvest, but it was so much more. We learned survival and cooperation and self-sufficiency."

Kyreen divided the sweet-smelling hay between the horses, enjoying listening to Lang's memories. He spoke with such delight about his youthful adventures. Thinking back on her own upbringing, she knew she had been blessed with loving foster parents, who had never restricted her from roaming the forest around their homestead. She, too, had had her friendship with Engla, but her friend's visits to the homestead had been very limited. What Kyreen had lacked in her childhood had been the camaraderie that Lang had experienced with his friends who accompanied him on his adventures.

Once the cave had been arranged to Lang's satisfaction, he went to the entrance to stare out into the rain which showed no signs of slowing. The only sounds in the cave were from the downpour and the horses munching hay. For a few moments, Kyreen lingered towards the back of the cave, watching Lang watch the rain. Though he stood completely still, hands on his hips, she felt the restlessness rolling off him.

Silently, she contemplated his back, internally debating. She knew what she wanted to do. She knew he would have no objections. Yet she stood rooted in place, unable to close the short distance between them.

Lang felt the indecision in Kyreen and fought his initial instinct to turn around. He knew what he would see if he did. Kyreen looking at him, her emerald eyes wide with doubt, her teeth nibbling her lip, perhaps a finger nervously twisting a stray curl. Her periodic shyness with him these last couple of days confused him. He knew she desired him and, when they made love, her inhibitions melted away. It was in these quiet times, when she had opportunity to overthink, that she pulled away from him, acting as if they had committed something wicked with their lovemaking. Her attitude confused Lang, more accustomed to Calanian women who were decisive and straightforward with their pursuit of lovers.

Even as he reminded himself once more to have patience, he felt Kyreen step towards him. A moment later, she tentatively placed a palm flat upon his back. He leaned into her touch, resisting the new urge to turn around. Emboldened, Kyreen slid both hands around his waist, stepping up once more to press the front of her body to his back, resting her cheek between his shoulder blades, the linen of his shirt rough against her skin. After a few short breaths, she began to move her hands, slipping them under his shirt so as to slide her palms across his bare abdomen.

Lang inhaled sharply, desire igniting at the feel of her skin on his. Kyreen froze at the sound of his intake. For several heartbeats, neither of them moved. Then, slowly, her fingers resumed their exploration of his body, gradually moving lower and lower. When she began to place soft kisses along his back through his shirt along his spine, Lang groaned and, unable to resist any longer, turned in her arms to kiss her. Without breaking the contact of their lips, he scooped her into his arms and moved them to the pallet of bedrolls.

The storm outside the cave continued to rain and blow throughout the rest of the day. When Kyreen opened her eyes after dozing off, the shadows in the cave had deepened, an artificial dusk created by the weather and she again awoke alone in their bed. This time, however, she did not sense Lang's presence. Faintly alarmed she sat up to look around. Both horses stood where they had been earlier. Just as Kyreen began reaching for her clothes, she felt Lang, outside the cave. A moment later he rushed in from the torrential downpour. Standing just inside the entrance, he stood, rivulets of water pouring off his body. Once he decided the majority of water had sluiced away, he moved into the interior, grinning over at Kyreen.

"Good afternoon," he greeted her.

"Hello," she responded, pushing back the anxiety that flared whenever she felt Lang had made a judgement about her idleness.

"I went out to set a trap line for dinner tomorrow. Tonight we can scrounge through the pantry," he said, grabbing a cloth to dry off his hair. "I was thinking with this storm it would be a good time for us to ..."

"Lang?" she interrupted.

He paused mid-word to look over at her sitting on their pallet, legs pulled up, chin resting on her knees, the blanket tugged up to cover her body.

"Can we just...I do not know, sit together for a bit, maybe talk?" she asked meekly.

"I suppose," he replied, walking over to sit down beside her and started tugging at his boots, "but we talk all the time."

"No," she said quietly. "You talk. You talk about the woods, your adventures, your friends, growing up in the valley, teaching me about things I should have learnt as a child, and I love to hear you. But for weeks at the cliffs, you rarely spoke all those evenings we spent together except to tell me how your day had been. I love your stories, I truly do. I would also love to have a conversation, talk back and forth between us."

She paused, trying to gauge his feelings, watching him closely as he finished shedding his wet clothes. She lifted the blanket so he could slide in next to her, his skin cool against her. As the silence grew between them, she unintentionally began to nibble her bottom lip.

"That is why I talk," Lang said. "Whenever you have a chance to think, you go somewhere negative. I thought if I kept us busy, if I kept the silence away, if I could keep you satisfied physically, that you would not become so distressed."

"Distressed?" Kyreen repeated quietly. "I know I worry more often than I should, concerned that I am messing up because I do not want to disappoint you. I have enjoyed our time both at camp and here. I want to continue spending time with you, making memories. I feel I know so much more about you than I did a couple of days ago, but I do not feel like I know you."

Lang frowned, "What do you mean you do not know me?"

"I know about your family, your friends, your history," she answered, speaking slowly as she struggled to find the right words, "but I do not know why you feel the need to always be busy or what you see yourself doing once we have ended this war or what your favorite book is and why."

Silence fell between them once again. Kyreen resisted the urge to nibble her bottom lip before adding, "When I get thoughtful it is not a bad thing. It is how I figure out this world around me. It is what I have done my entire life, when everything kept changing every day, when nothing felt normal and I did not know if it ever could be normal again, when I felt so alone. I know I do not belong in Hanoria, I never did, yet it is most familiar to me. I have no place in Myrddin either, with its crowds of people. There are days I wonder if I belong here with my people, if I can ever fit in. But I do know that being with you feels right and I do not want that feeling to go away."

Wordlessly, Lang wrapped an arm around Kyreen's shoulder and pulled her into his lap, tugging the blanket about their bodies to ward off the chill brought in with the storm. His embrace bore nothing sexual, merely a shared intimacy. Kyreen rested her head on his shoulder as they both stared out into the rain.

"I do not have a favorite book," Lang said quietly. "I can read, we are all taught to read, but I have never found enjoyment in reading. Besides books are scarce and there are always chores to be done."

Kyreen digested this information silently. The winters in Hanoria had been long and fierce, so unlike the milder, more temperate winters here. Jorn's stories, and those in the books his friend Havard would bring, had served as distractions when she could not venture out into the woods. So many worlds, so many adventures, so many characters, she had discovered through those tales. She felt connected to those fictional lives, as though their experiences were her own. She could not imagine not having these stories in her life.

"Could I read aloud to you?" she asked tentatively.

She felt Lang hesitate, imagined him thinking about all he felt needed to be done.

"Just this afternoon, while the storm rages," she added.

"Very well," he acquiesced.

Before the words had left his lips, Kyreen sat up, eagerly reaching for her knapsack. She withdrew a small, slim novel, carefully wrapped in oil cloth. The book was a collection of Hanorian fairy tales that Rhun had gifted her at their second meeting last year. Kyreen had been delighted to discover that most of the tales within the book's cover were similar to those she had heard from her foster father over the years. Now she carried the book with her always and still loved to read it, hearing Jorn's voice narrating the stories in her head, reminding her that not everything in her childhood had been bad.

Lang watched with a smile as Kyreen settled back, drawing his arm about her shoulders, so she could nestle against his side. Her obvious delight was contagious. He relaxed and leaned back, listening to her voice, visualizing the words she spoke. They sat like this for several hours, as the storm outside continued and evening slipped over the world.

The next morning dawned sunny and clear as though the storm had washed away the grime, leaving the world shiny clear. Lang, per usual, rose with the sun, leaving Kyreen to slumber. The smell of breakfast, however, roused her from her sleep. Still drowsy, she fumbled into her clothes, then padded barefoot over towards the fire.

"Is that ham?" she asked, running a hand through the wild mass of curls on her head.

"Yes, it is," Lang responded cheerily. "Now eat up quick. Daylight is burning and we have a lot of ground to cover."

Kyreen nodded, taking the proffered plate of food. As she settled down on the ground beside Lang to eat, he leaned over to plant a kiss on the side of her head.

"Make sure to bring that little book with you," he whispered in her ear, more than his breath sending tingles down her spine. "You dozed off in the middle of that last story and I need to find out what that bloke does after those magic beans grow."

Kyreen grinned at him and resumed eating her food with more enthusiasm. Between mouthfuls, she asked, "What do you think he does?"

"If it were me, I would chop the damned thing down straight away," Lang replied, getting to his feet to begin cleaning up, "but that would make for a very dull and very short story so I gather he climbs up and finds all types of trouble."

Later that morning, after they had trekked up the mountainside to check Lang's trap lines, the couple stopped by one of the snow runoff springs for midday meal. While Lang assembled the food, Kyreen read the rest of the story aloud to him. Once the tale and their meal had been completed, Lang asked Kyreen what she would prefer to do with their afternoon.

"If we hike north a bit there is another swimming hole, not near as big or warm as the other one in East Valley, but still swimmable," Lang said. "Or we can follow this stream up the hill. There is a nice plateau up there that overlooks the entire valley. Terrific views. We would not stay for the sunset though unless we wish to hike back to the cave in the dark or we could spend the night out in the woods."

Kyreen chose swimming. With Lang's help, she had overcome her fears and had begun enjoying being in the water. Soon they had cleaned up, and packed up, and began their hike.

As they were not in the trees, but passing along a grassy meadow, Kyreen walked beside Lang. Her heart skipped a beat when he reached over to take her hand in his. Overhead a few white clouds littered the blue sky. All around them, green shoots proclaimed it spring. Kyreen relished this feeling of rebirth all around them. Then she spied something that caused her to stop still.

Lang halted, glancing back at her, his eyes full of concern. "What is the matter?"

"Maybe nothing," Kyreen replied, pulling her hand away from his to begin walking across the meadow towards the tree line where a huge branch rested. It looked to have broken off from a nearby tree. Kyreen slowed down, approaching the limb cautiously.

"Do you know of any bees hive around here?" she called to Lang over her shoulder.

He scrunched his face, trying to remember, then nodded. "Yes, I believe so. Are there any now? You best stay out of their way."

"I think maybe this branch had a hive before it broke away," she replied approaching the fallen limb.

When Lang reached her, Kyreen had her knife out, using the implement to cut one of the exposed cylindrical combs. She divided the chunk in two, offering the larger half to Lang, who took it with a quizzical expression.

"Honey comb," Kyreen said, bringing the treat to her mouth. After a taste, she smiled. "Luscious!"

Tentatively Lang took a bite of the comb, enjoying the sweet explosion on his tongue.

"Where are the bees?" he asked.

Kyreen poked around at the edge of the ragged hole in the tree branch. The wood peeled back easily exposing a huge dark comb system inside. "I am not sure. It appears the branch rotted. The bees nested here a while, maybe as long as four or five summers. Yesterday's storm must have torn the branch from its tree. Maybe the queen flew off this morning and her colony followed. I see a few dead bees and all this dark comb inside is the brood nest."

She sat back on her heels, absently sucking at the comb in her hand as she surveyed the abandoned hive. "We should harvest this comb," she said finally, glancing back at Lang. "This is quite a find. If we do not take it some animal will. Probably a skunk, since you say there are no bears around."

Lang shrugged. "You sound like the expert. I have no experience with hives except to have the good sense to give them a wide berth."

"Ildri and I use to collect honey several times a year," Kyreen responded. "She was quite adept with the bees. Once a fortnight, we would take the honey and her breads to market. Before the farm started making a profit those sales kept our family afloat, though neither Jorn nor Ildri would admit to it."

Lang watched as Kyreen efficiently cut away several chucks of comb, setting them on the piece of bark she had peeled away from the branch. When she reached the dark combs, she paused. Breaking off a small chunk she took a bite, then rose to her feet and walked over to Lang. She held the bit of comb, dark honey oozing out, to his lips her gaze both an invitation and a question. Without speaking Lang carefully took the comb from her hand with his mouth. This honey tasted different, tangy, not as sweet, but still delicious.

After licking the honey from her fingertips Kyreen glanced back at the tree branch and the pile of comb stacked beside it, saying, "I may have been too ambitious. I am not sure how to get this back to the cave."

Lang slipped his arms around her to lean in for a kiss, savoring the honey sweetness which lingered on her lips. "There is an empty food sack we could fill. As you said, that pile is quite the haul," he replied. "We very rarely harvest honey."

After loading up the honey comb and securing it in a tree for safekeeping until their return trip, they continued on to the pond. When they had finished swimming, Lang requested Kyreen read one more story before they headed back to the cave. That night, once the meal had been completed and cleaned up, as Lang finished securing the cave for the evening and the horses could be seen grazing by moonlight, Kyreen reflected on this day, so ordinary yet so perfect. For the first time in a very long time, a feeling of contentment settled over her and she looked towards the future with anticipation.

"Woolgathering again?" Lang teased, sitting down beside her. "Anything I should worry on?"

"You should be very worried," Kyreen teased back mischievously.

She leaned over to kiss him, and he pulled her into his lap. Very shortly all contemplations about the future or anything else had completely slipped from her mind.

Chapter 25

The next day while Lang went to check the trap line, Kyreen pressed the honey comb to transfer the sweet amber liquid into containers Lang had found in the storage area. Finishing up just before midday, she decided to do some training outside of the cave with her sword, something she had not done on her own for quite a while. From what she had gleaned, most Calanians stopped daily ritual practice at adulthood, but the movement and meditation brought Kyreen so much calm and focus, she doubted she could ever stop doing it. Though the sunny morning still held a chill, before too long a light sheen of perspiration coated her forehead as she moved through the sets, mentally reciting the Telling as her mother had taught her so many years ago. Today, as she attempted to meditate, a lump grew in her throat and tears pricked her closed eyelids, as she remembered Tyra. As with her brother, Kyreen could not recall her mother's face exactly, just bits and pieces like her sparkling emerald eyes, her wildly curly hair, her gentle good night kisses, her calloused hand soft against a child's forehead.

From the shadows of the tree line, Lang watched as Kyreen glided through the movements. He had never seen her practice with the sword as trainees performed the camp's morning ritual unarmed. Even from this distance the weapon's beauty could not be denied. The tapered hilt—its brass, silver and copper braid hidden beneath Kyreen's hands—rested between a silver rose pommel and brass scrolled guard. The two parallel edges narrowing to a pointed end glinted in the sunlight. The ancient runes etched along the razor-sharp blade blurred as she continued her movements. The fluidity of Kyreen's transitions and the steady pace she set made the exercise look more like a dance. Though he felt he could watch her all day, he also felt the urge to be closer to her and knew as soon as he walked up she would cease the exercise. In the end, he did not need to make a decision, for as soon as she drew back to center, Kyreen slid the sword into the dark leather sheath strapped to her back. When her eyes opened she immediately turned to find him, her smile lighting up her face.

Lang held up the brace of conies in his hand, walking towards her. "Rabbit for dinner?"

"Sounds good," she replied leaning up to press a kiss to his lips.

As had become their routine, while Lang set to cleaning the carcasses, Kyreen fetched her book of fairy tales and read out loud to him as he worked. He loved the sound of her voice and the way she affected different voices for the various characters. She made the stories come to life for him in a way he had never experienced by reading to himself.

Once the carcasses were prepped to be cooked for evening meal, Lang moved inside the cave to assemble a light midday meal. After Kyreen put away the book she brought out some of the dark honey comb she had set aside for the meal.

"It is quite tasty on the hardtack especially when coupled with an apple," she said, demonstrating the combination and handing it to him.

"Very," he agreed, playfully grabbing her hand so as to lick her fingers. Then with a kiss to the back of her hand, he released her and handed her plate to her. "Shall we eat outside?"

Settled just outside the cave in the sun, they ate in silence. Both horses, their coats gleaming golden red, glanced up briefly from their grazing to watch the two, then went back to the grass. The mare's flaxen mane and tail contrasted starkly with her sorrel coat. The gelding, while less flashy than other Calanian bred horses, the whorled star on his forehead his only white markings, made up for it with perfect conformation. Kyreen had always enjoyed just observing him in repose.

She thought back all those years when Jorn had purchased the mare and stud colt. Kyreen had been so surprised when her foster father had agreed to the extravagant purchase. Sometimes she wondered how much the pain reliever weed she had fed him had affected the old man that day. This gelding, born of that straggly mare, had been the first foal Kyreen had ever helped deliver into the world. At the time Jorn had suggested selling him as a yearling. Though Kyreen had known the sale would have brought in much needed income, she simply could not bear the thought of parting with this particular foal, and Jorn had not pressed the issue. Fortunately, the harvest that season, aided by the ox also purchased that year, had kept him occupied. Kyreen savored the sweet honeycomb as she reminisced about her herd. She would definitely keep Moa's offer of working with the herd in mind, but it would have to wait until after this summer's campaign concluded. Kyreen could not imagine the plans to retake the castle failing. Keeping the Galorians from attacking in the future though would present another separate issue.

"You wear your thinking face," Lang whispered, his whiskers tickling her ear. "Woolgathering?"

"A bit," she replied, popping the last bit of the honeycomb and apple into her mouth.

As they cleaned up, her thoughts turned more towards the upcoming campaign. She imagined Aren and the Council were busy making plans and discussing strategies. Quietly she broached a topic that had been on her mind since the previous day. "Lang, how much longer until we return to camp?"

"Already tired of my company?" he responded with a grin. Snaking an arm about her waist to pull her into him, he nuzzled at her neck playfully. Instantly heat flared as her body responded to his touch.

"You know that is not true," she replied, running her fingers through his short hair to guide his face up to hers for a leisurely kiss. When their lips parted, she added, "I just feel strange taking a holiday while everyone else prepares for battle."

"I told you the Council is on recess," Lang responded, cupping her face in his hands. "Most of us with family had planned on spending time with them until the other camps cleared out."

Now Kyreen felt even worse. Lang should be with his family. She should be back at training. When she voiced her concern about training, Lang shook his head.

"You were not at the annual report and did not hear," he said. "Because the timetable moved up, training is done for the season. Even if the Council had not made this determination, your time at training had come to a conclusion for sure. You are vital to the summer campaign."

Kyreen sighed. "I feel like I am not pulling my weight."

"The whole campaign hinges on you and that creature in the tunnels," Lang replied quietly. "I think that is pulling more than your weight."

Kyreen shrugged, pulling away from him to walk to the cave entrance. She gazed out over the meadows, the grazing horses, the rolling hills, the blue cloudless sky. When she spoke, her words were so quiet that Lang walked up to stand behind her, simply to hear her voice.

"You make comments about being productive," she said, wrapping her around her body. "How productive have I been these last few months? What have I done? What have I contributed? I bumbled through training, my friends are the only reason I could keep up. If Aren were not my cousin, would I have been offered a spot at the Training Camp? Sten's only interest in me was my title, or the title he thought I should have. I may have been born to the last queen of Calan, but I am not a princess. I do not belong on the throne. I just want to fit in. I want to earn my place, not get by on the charity, or worse the pity, of others."

Lang walked around to face Kyreen, gathering her hands in his, pulling her arms away from her body. He ducked down so as to look into her downcast face.

"Where is this coming from?" he asked. "You are here because you belong here. You are Calanian. You do not need to prove yourself to anyone, but if you need proof that you have been productive I will tell you. You went after that mercenary from Faldor, the one who led the Galorians in the Battle, the one who assassinated our queen. You negotiated the trade deal to bring much needed revenue to our people. You talk about fumbling through training, yet you took top prize in the tournament."

"That all sounds good when you say it," Kyreen responded. "Then someone says something or does something and I am lost. I do not know what it is or how to do it, and Synnove, or now you, have to explain it to me like I am a brain-addled child."

As she spoke, Kyreen's voice raised and she tugged her hands from Lang's so as to gesture into the cave. "Take for example those torchlights. You touch them and they begin to glow. I touch them and nothing happens. I saw lights like those in Myrddin but in a secret passage, never out in public, and in the Council Camp's tent. If I did not know better I would say these lights were magical but I know they cannot be because magic does not exist. To even pretend that it does can get you executed because magic has been outlawed for millennial."

"If magic did not exist, why would it be outlawed?" Lang asked quietly.

Something in his voice broke through Kyreen's raised emotions, much like the first night they had conversed and he had made a comment about the fine line between love and hate. He was telling her something, something important, but she could not wrap her mind around it.

Finally, she asked, "Are you telling me magic exists?"

Lang nodded without speaking.

Kyreen slowly sank to the ground, her mind reeling. Closing her eyes, she pinched the bridge of her nose, trying to sort through the many emotions rattling around inside her. The food she had just consumed rolled restlessly in her stomach.

"You truly did not know?" Lang asked, sitting down beside her.

Kyreen shook her head, leaning against him, eyes staring out over the horses.

"Your reaction," he added, "it seems more than surprise."

"Many of the stories I grew up on had magical creatures and sorcerers who wielded power," Kyreen replied. "They were always evil and the heroes always had to overcome, overpower, and outsmart the magic. Sometimes with the deities' help, sometimes without, but always magic was not good and had to be defeated."

"While there are a few dedicated mages, most of us are not sorcerers," Lang responded, not defensively. "For the most part, we do not study or cultivate magic. We use magic for conveniences like safe lighting or basic protection spells."

"Every day, something new," Kyreen muttered. "Why did this not come out at Training Camp? Why did they not get used there?"

"That experience is meant to be primitive without amenities."

"Still," Kyreen commented, her frustration level rising. "Not one mention in all these months."

"It is not an anomaly here, Kyreen. No one would have thought to inform you," Lange explained. "We are taught basic spells during childhood, but, as I said, we do not expand beyond those handful. Maybe after everything concludes, you can borrow one of the history books from the Archives."

"I will," Kyreen sighed again, resting her head upon his shoulder.

They sat in silence for several minutes before Lang said, "Getting back to the original conversation, I had thought to stay out another several days," he paused when she tensed, "but if you will give me one more day we can go pick up the trap line tomorrow and head back the following morning."

Kyreen thought on this for a moment. She had enjoyed their time together and a part of her already mourned its ending, but a larger part of her felt driven to get back, to finish planning, to get started. She could not fully relax knowing the task which lay ahead.

"Thank you," she finally whispered.

"If you like," Lang said, "I could teach you how to illuminate the torches."

Kyreen sat upright, slipping into his lap, sliding her arms around his neck. Leaning in she kissed him deeply then, pressing soft kisses along his jawline, she whispered softly into his ear, "Maybe later?"

Smiling, he wrapped his arms around her, their discussion concluded for the time being.

Once the decision had been made to return to camp, time seemed to speed up for Kyreen. Though she had been the one pushing to get back, she now felt an almost desperate need to not squander any of their remaining time alone. Everything they did had a finality to it that tugged at her heartstrings. Their final hike up the mountain. Their final swim. Their last time making love on the shore of the lake.

Reclining on the sun warmed boulder, resting side by side, gazing up at the sky, a perfect shade of blue, void of any clouds, Lang must have sensed her anxiety.

"Do not mourn our last few hours," he said. "We will come back soon. I can bring you here in late summer, so we can gorge ourselves silly on berries."

Grinning, Kyreen rolled over to kiss him. "Promise?"

"Promise," Lang replied, smiling up at her, loving the way her wild curls hung down creating a veil to the outside world.

She leaned in to kiss him again, all her worries quickly chased away.

Chapter 26

Crossing the river two days later, Kyreen felt the camp inhabitants' presence. She involuntarily tensed, worried about the overwhelming negative feelings, but the sensation settled into a steady buzz, like the hum of cicadas on a warm summer eve, one she had become oblivious to before.

The trip back from Little Valley, as Lang had called it, had been uneventful. After an early breakfast, the pair had been in the saddle as the sun rose. About an hour into the ride Kyreen realized they were heading due west, not heading south. When questioned Lang had said he wanted to swing by the farming village before going to the camp, except the word he used was "home." He wanted to stop by home before going back to camp.

The sun in the blue cloudless sky had begun its downward trajectory when the first fields came into view. By the time they entered the compound that serviced the few farming families, the sun hung low on the horizon casting long shadows. Several people walked up to meet them. Lang slid from the mare's back, hugging and greeting everyone as they arrived. Kyreen slipped off the gelding's back and, leaning against the gelding, stood off to the side watching. People continued appearing as news of Lang's arrival carried through the village. It seemed everyone came out and Lang knew them all. Before long Kyreen felt overwhelmed, unable to keep all the conversations straight.

Watching Lang interact with these people, strangers to her, was enlightening. Kyreen often forgot Lang's young age, just three years older than herself. Yet he held a position on the Council and had served as the sparring instructor this past winter. Kyreen had always thought of the Council members and Training Camp instructors as Lang's peers but seeing him here, so spirited and gregarious, she could now tell how withdrawn and reserved he had kept himself with those two groups. She supposed maybe Lang had grown his beard, which most Calanian men did not sport and which she personally loved, to make himself appear older. She wondered idly how young he would look and how much more stunning he would be without the beard obscuring the lower part of his face.

When the chaos of Lang's arrival began to calm down, Lang brought a woman over to Kyreen. Tall and willowy with more silver than sable in her long braid, she offered Kyreen a hand, heavily calloused from hard labor and a warm, inviting smile. Lang introduced the woman as Anika. Kyreen recognized the name to be Lang's aunt, the woman who took him in after the Battle.

"Kyreen, well met," she said. "Kasja has told us so many nice things about you."

The mention of Lang's former mate startled Kyreen until she remembered that Kasja too hailed from this small farming community.

"Is she still here?" Lang asked glancing around. The hope in his voice tugged at Kyreen and her guilt for keeping Lang from his family surfaced anew.

"No," Anika replied. "She and the children only stopped in overnight, as I suspect you are doing?"

"Yes, Mama," Lang responded apologetically.

"No worries," Anika patted his arm. "I am happy to see you when you can make it."

Anika, the pride shining in her blue eyes, looked at Kyreen. "We miss our Lang but know he does important work on the Council."

"With Kyreen's help, we should be able to retake the castle," Lang said, pulling Anika into one arm and Kyreen into the other, "so maybe we can return home by fall. Now enough talk. I am famished."

As she walked along with Lang and Anika, who continued to speak with each other about the community goings on, Kyreen thought on Lang's last statement. This valley was quite apparently the home of Lang's heart. Of course, he would wish to return here. This village had a permanence about it, so unlike the nomadic camps which moved within the formal borders of Calan. Feasibly, this village might continue to operate for a while to provide food as the Calanians resettled their lands after almost two decades of disuse. The big question for Kyreen had to be did she want to live here? She had always envisioned herself in the castle, living within the walls of the last place, really the only place, she had ever felt at home. Watching Lang here in his home, interacting with his kin, so completely at ease, once again roused the envy buried deep inside of her. She so craved to fit in, to belong, and sometimes the hurt of witnessing that belonging in others had begun to pain her. Resolutely she pushed down the feelings. She would not succumb to that darkness, at least not tonight.

"You have been quiet," Lang whispered in her ear as they queued up for food. "Should I worry?"

"Always," Kyreen teased, choosing her reply carefully, knowing he could tell if she was less than truthful.

To her surprise, he kissed her right there in the line. Always their public displays of affection had been chaste kisses or hugging. As she and her body responded, Kyreen also felt two familiar presences nearby, one friendly, the other not so friendly. Once her and Lang's lips parted, Kyreen glanced around, her face breaking out in a smile spying her cousin at the rear of the line.

"Yngve," she called out, forgetting her shyness and dashing over to him.

"Hail, Kyreen," Yngve greeted her with a big hug, lifting her momentarily off her feet. "I did not expect to see you here."

"I could say the same about you," Kyreen answered, her gaze moved to the young woman standing beside Yngve, not hiding the discontent from her gaze. "Hail, Karine."

The young woman regarded Kyreen a long moment, hostility radiating. Just when Kyreen thought she would move on without speaking, Karine returned the nod, quietly replying, "Kyreen."

Yngve took Kyreen's elbow to pull her aside out of the line and presumably away from Karine. Kyreen, so happy to see a familiar face, allowed him to do so without protest. Her glance towards Lang was rewarded by his waving her on before he resumed his conversation with a tall, gangly young man in line.

"So, you and Lang?" Yngve said. "You were not at the Courting Ceremony. Synnove was vague on why you left."

Kyreen briefly explained her hurried exit from the Festival then turned his words back on him saying, "So you and Karine. I was not at the Courting Ceremony. You took vows?"

"We did," Yngve nodded. "Mama was not pleased."

"I can imagine," Kyreen remarked.

"But she came around once she realized our bond," the young man added. "She cannot deny its pull, plus bonding is a rare gift now."

"How so?" Kyreen inquired, wondering to herself if she would call it a gift.

"Before the Battle, most covenants were bonded couples," Yngve explained. "Now less than a third are bonded. People are not covenanting as much, as they are waiting to have children, and when they do covenant, the pairing is less likely to be a bonded couple. The theory is we have lost so many young people."

"Interesting," Kyreen remarked. She had never thought of Yngve as the scholarly one. Synnove always had the information and history.

Her face must have reflected her surprise because Yngve grinned sheepishly. "Karine gathered all this information to present to Mama," he said. "We knew she would object."

"As long as you are happy," Kyreen replied, knowing her cousin was just by looking at him. "So why are you two here instead of at the Training Camp? Is there some rule against covenant couples training?"

"No, with the battle schedule moved up, training is over. We were all given a few days furlough and Karine wanted to come home," Yngve glanced around, his face and voice carefully neutral. "Once the campaign ends this summer, we will most likely come back here to settle."

"Really?" Kyreen remarked. "I would have thought you would stay in Calan. We are almost certain to retake the castle this summer. There will be some rebuilding for sure. I guess I always assumed you would be a tracker, work the castle guard as your grandfather did, as your father should have."

Yngve shrugged. "Karine is a farmer. My skills will be helpful here."

"I believe Lang would prefer coming back here as well," Kyreen said, wistfully. "I am not sure if I do."

"Then tell him," Yngve asserted. "He will go wherever you wish to go. It is your right."

Kyreen looked over to where Lang stood, gathering up food on two plates, while carrying on conversations with those around him. After all this work to reclaim their homeland, she wanted to live on Calanian soil. Could she simply tell him she did not wish to live in the Great Valley? Would he be happy away from his kin?

She sighed. Now was not the time to worry about life after the summer's campaign. She grinned up at her cousin. "You best get back in line with Karine before she strikes me dead with her gaze."

"She would not do that," Yngve said with a brief frown before waving farewell with a good-natured smile and striding off.

Kyreen walked over to assist Lang with one of the plates he was balancing. They moved over to sit with his aunt and other family members. With her food to keep her busy, Kyreen did not feel pressured into participating in the conversations, which all centered around the planting.

For a moment, she recalled the lively conversations Jorn and Stian had engaged in over the years. She hoped her friend was doing well on the farm that her foster father had deeded Stian last summer. She had no doubt Stian had done as she asked and reestablished the herd, but his true interest always centered in the soil, in the fields. She made a mental note to ask Engla about him in her next letter.

Once the meal had been completed, most of the adults moved to circle the center fire that had been stoked while the youth took care of the cleanup. Sitting on a log beside Lang as the sun went down gave Kyreen a small glimpse into what life on the farm could be like for her, working hard during the day, relaxing at night. Everyone had a job here, and though no one had gone out of their way to speak to her besides her cousin, Kyreen had not felt any animosity or negativity aside from her young cousin's new mate.

One of the older men, his short hair silver, his face lined with age, began to sing, drawing Kyreen out of her thoughts. The wordless melody he voiced sounded vaguely familiar to her but she could not place it. Another man joined in, his tenor harmonizing beautifully with the first man's deep bass. Kyreen could almost recall the name of the melody, but lost her train of thought when Lang added his baritone to the song. He grinned at her surprised expression without missing a beat. A few others, men and women, joined in the vocalizing, then a few more began singing words to the song. Kyreen closed her eyes, focusing on the sound, dredging up an old memory of her and Quillan sitting in the castle kitchen, with all the kitchen workers standing around the table vocalizing and singing this very song. She also caught glimpses of castle guards in her recollection. Her breath quickened, a visceral reaction to the memory.

She felt Lang take her hand, so opened her eyes to look over at him. He frowned slightly at the unshed tears shimmering in her eyes, but she shook her head with a smile, squeezing his hand and mouthing the words, 'I am fine,' knowing he could sense the truth. As the sun set and night settled, the group finished the first song and immediately moved into the next. This continued for a while, people joining and leaving as necessary. After several songs, Kyreen had lost count how many, Lang gave her hand a quick squeeze then rolled up to his feet. She followed suit, smiling her farewell to various people as Lang led her away from the fire.

As soon as they were clear of the firelight, the shadows cloaking them, Lang pulled Kyreen into his arms for a lingering kiss that left her breathless, which she figured did not matter as she probably could not have formed a coherent sentence. Weak kneed, Kyreen leaned against him as he began trailing kisses along her jawline to her ear, his beard tickling her skin.

"By the goddess, I have been aching to do that since suppertime," he whispered playfully, his hands beginning to roam across her body.

"Mm-huh," Kyreen responded. For the most part, she immensely enjoyed the effect he had on her, but a small part remained alarmed at how quickly he could turn her mind and her body to mush.

Lang pressed his lips to hers once again, then scooped Kyreen into his arms, her squeal of surprise muffled in the kiss. Breaking the kiss, he began walking.

"This is quicker than trying to get you to walk," he whispered playfully, letting her know he knew the effect his kiss had on her.

Kyreen took advantage of the opportunity to slide her arms around him so as to kiss at his neck. Gently nibbling the sensitive skin there she grinned as his pulse jumped beneath her lips.

"Watch yourself, woman," he murmured, his voice husky. "Would not want me to stumble."

"I trust you," she whispered, continuing her ministrations.

Shortly Lang stopped before a lone tent set up on the edge of the trees. Kyreen slid to her feet, coming to stand before him. He pulled her in for another long, sensual kiss, before raising up the tent flap. They ducked into the tent, all talking ended for a long while.

Now as she and Lang began unpacking the gear off their horses, Kyreen glanced around the Training Camp. With all the extra Calanians who had gathered for the Festival gone, the area seemed deserted. Setting her knapsack on the ground so she could begin unsaddling the gelding Kyreen paused, returning her gaze to the line of tents shining white in the midafternoon sun. Her brow furrowed slightly.

"I wondered when the thought would cross your mind," Lang chuckled from behind her. When she turned to look at him, he grinned but remained silent, continuing to rub down the mare.

Kyreen resisted the urge to respond to his verbal teasing. Returning to the job at hand, her mind raced. She had been thinking about taking her gear to the tent she shared with Synnove when the thought occurred that she would most likely be sharing Lang's tent. Even now, she felt the blush beginning to creep into her cheeks. She had just spent the last several days alone with Lang, very intimately alone. Now the prospect of publicly acknowledging their relationship here, among her classmates, caused Kyreen trepidation. She leaned her forehead against the gelding's side.

"It is not an issue for anyone but you," Lang said softly. Having finished grooming his mare, he had slipped behind Kyreen to slide his arms around her. Placing a soft kiss on the side of her neck, he whispered, "But it is your choice. If you do not wish to share a tent with me…"

"No," Kyreen interrupted quietly, pulling his arms tighter around her body. In the short time they had spent together, she had become accustomed to drifting to sleep in his embrace. She could not imagine giving that up. "I simply had not given thought to …to the logistics."

As her mind continued to ponder, she felt her face redden anew.

"The logistics?" Lang questioned. Then he chuckled, the sound vibrating against Kyreen's body hugged tight to his. He dropped his lips to her ear, his voice light and teasing. "You silly goose! You never cease to surprise..."

"And apparently amuse," Kyreen interjected.

"The tents are spelled," he informed her. "How else do you think our people have spent the last two decades in such intimate proximities?"

Kyreen shrugged in his arms, thinking to wrest out of his embrace in her embarrassment, but he merely tightened his grasp, snuggling his face against the side of her neck.

"I am such the idiot," she muttered. "Of course, they are. I suppose everything else is magicked, too."

Lang paused his play, gently turning her around to face him. He gazed deep into her eyes, quietly asking, "What have you against magic? It is a natural part of our lives."

"For some," Kyreen muttered, dropping her gaze, the two red spots on her cheeks deepening in color.

In response, Lang merely pulled her to him, hugging her tightly. He did not have an answer for her frustrations. Back in the cave he had shown her how to work the illumination spell used for the torches, but Kyreen had not been able to get the small spheres to glow. The light spell was such a small basic bit of magic even children as young as his daughter Jetta had mastered it. Absently, Lang stroked Kyreen's hair as they both thought about her failed attempts at spell casting.

Kyreen relaxed into his embrace, struggling to control the exasperation rising up inside her. Now that her eyes had been opened, she could see signs of magic and spells all around her. Lang had said magic was natural, but Kyreen could not feel that way. In Hanoria accusations of witchcraft or sorcery were taken extremely seriously, resulting in public trials and, if the accused, usually a woman, was found guilty, public execution. Though Kyreen had grown up hearing rumors about sorcery, she had never heard a first-hand account from anyone who had witnessed or performed magic. Nor had she experienced it first-hand until Lang held a dark sphere in his hand and recanted a few words to make the sphere glow. Then he had shown her the protection spells he cast every night to secure their campsite and the cave.

"Come on," Lang said softly, breaking into her thought. "Let us get our gear put away. I imagine Synnove will be thrilled to see you."

Chapter 27

Once again Lang had been correct. Synnove squealed, hugging Kyreen tightly when she saw them walking towards the center quad after stowing their belongings in Lang's tent. Now their tent, Kyreen reminded herself before being nearly tackled by Synnove. After a neutral, not unfriendly, nod to Lang, Synnove slipped an arm through Kyreen's and began walking them back towards the quad where Ebbe sat peeling potatoes.

"Hail, Kyreen," he said, looking up with a grin, a knife in one hand, a partially peeled vegetable in the other. "Forgive me if I do not get up."

Kyreen waved with a grin, saying, "Forgiven."

"I was keeping Ebbe company," Synnove commented, settling down to sit with her back against a tree. "Without classes and training, the days seem to drag."

Kyreen took a seat next to Synnove, leaning back against the trunk. She watched Lang sit down on a log across from her and Synnove. He and Ebbe exchanged greetings as Synnove began to speak. Kyreen kept her gaze on Lang and listened to her friend talk about the Festival happenings that Kyreen had missed. Once he saw her looking at him, Lang held Kyreen's gaze, a mischievous smile playing about his lips. Kyreen's body tingled in response and she struggled to not look away, determined not to squirm, but she felt the blush creeping into her cheeks.

Synnove stopped speaking, looking between the two of them, asking, "You do realize I can see you right?"

"What?" Kyreen answered. "We are just looking at each other. I am listening, I promise."

"No," Synnove responded. "I can see your soul lights glowing and getting brighter by the second. By the goddess, Kyreen, you two are just as bad as Yngve and Karine, who by the way are covenanted."

"I know. I saw them at the farming village," Kyreen commented, reluctantly breaking eye contact with Lang to look over at her friend, only to have her attention drawn back over to Lang when he stood.

"I am distracting you," he said, walking over to lean down and kiss her cheek. "I will go check in with Atle. Catch up with you at supper?"

Kyreen nodded, happy when he leaned down again to place a chaste kiss upon her upturned lips.

Ebbe rose as well with his pile of potatoes. "I should get these to the cooks," he said, adding, "and no offense, Synnove, or to you, Kyreen, but I have no desire to hear any more about precious Eilert who I am sure is to be Syn's next topic."

There was no malice in their friend's voice, just good-natured teasing. Synnove and Kyreen waved farewell to Ebbe and settled back against the tree trunk.

"Eilert?" Kyreen asked. "Why does that name sound familiar?"

"I think you met him last summer," Synnove answered. "He had council rotation with Signe."

"Oh yes," Kyreen recalled the name, but not the young man's face. "Is he the one you courted during the Festival?"

Synnove nodded, her blue eyes sparkling. "He is. I believe we will be ready to covenant next year, especially if all goes well with the castle siege."

"Is he still here?" Kyreen glanced at the activity around them. The atmosphere here was much more relaxed than it had been when they had been camping at the cliffs.

"No, he is attached to the Council Camp as a guard," Synnove answered. "Eilert will most likely join the castle guard proper once we are back in Calan."

"Do you think you will stay at the castle then?" Kyreen inquired. In all their months of sharing a tent the subject of the future had never arisen. It seemed surreal to Kyreen that the Calanian people were poised to retake their land after so many years. Considering she had only lived this way for several months, Kyreen could not imagine how it would feel for the young people who never knew of life before the Battle, let alone those like Aren and Lang who did remember.

"No, I do not know for sure," Synnove answered Kyreen's question drawing the woman's attention back to their conversation. "I mean, Svante is apprenticing under Mother and Papa has Sten following in his footsteps so there is no pressure on me to become a historian or a bard."

Kyreen sensed a reluctance in her friend, which was quite unusual for the extroverted young woman. "What do you wish to do?" Kyreen asked.

"Travel," Synnove replied with a sheepish grin. "I know we are meant to be a solitary country, not welcoming. Many say it was the opening of trade and welcoming of outsiders which led to the Battle, but I do not care. If Aren, or whoever takes the throne calls for diplomats I plan on applying."

"What about Eilert?" Kyreen asked. "Will it not be difficult to be separated?"

She thought about Lang and her upcoming trip to Gladys for the trade meeting, which she had not yet mentioned to him. Now she worried how their bond would affect her when she travelled. The last time Kyreen had gone to Myrddin she had been noticeably anxious to return and that was before they had spent so much time together. Even now, with him just out of sight, Kyreen felt a restlessness tugging at her, compelling her to go find him, even though she could feel him not too far away.

"No worries there," Synnove was answering Kyreen's question. "It is not like we are bonded."

"Then why did you choose him to court?" The question was out of Kyreen's mouth before she could think about it.

"Because I am of age. Because he is a good, solid man, not to mention handsome," Synnove replied. "For years, I wished for a bond, fantasized about it even, hoping to be bonded with Ebbe or Yngve. I am tired of waiting on destiny. I will find my own partner."

Kyreen grinned at the determination in her friend's voice, and believed her. If Synnove wanted to travel, to be a diplomat, Kyreen had no doubt her friend would get there.

"I suppose my natural question would be, why not choose Ebbe? He is a good man, not bad looking either," Kyreen commented.

Synnove looked at Kyreen, her eyes narrowed. "Ebbe is not interested in me, although I may have to watch him around Eilert. I thought you knew that."

"And how would I know that?" Kyreen asked. As she spoke she realized that on a subconscious level she had known. It simply had not mattered. It still did not matter, not to Kyreen, but she wondered if it mattered to others here. In Hanoria, for a man to be attracted to another man was considered an affront before their gods and would sentence a man to a life of abuse if he were not publicly shunned or worse executed. Most chose to move away before being exposed.

"If you had joined us in the pools maybe you would have," Synnove teased. "Of course, now it makes sense why you felt compelled to stay closer to camp. Everything is well with you and Lang?"

Kyreen blushed. "You know it, so why ask?"

"It is polite to inquire, besides as my brother pointed out, you turn such pretty shades of red," she answered, elbowing Kyreen companionably. "Speaking of which, Sten was quite agitated when he learned you had left. He seemed under the impression he would see you at the Courting Ceremony."

Kyreen felt her blush deepen which made Synnove raise an eyebrow. "Oh, Kyreen," she said. "You did not let him get to you?"

"Not completely," Kyreen shrugged.

She proceeded to tell Synnove a shortened version of what had transpired in the Archival Tent. While she did tell Synnove about Sten's kiss, Kyreen did not reveal her vision or reaction to either the kiss nor the vision. Without Kasja's influence, this retelling was both shorter and less emotional.

"I knew he was playing at something," Synnove grumbled. "In all his letters, he inquired about my tentmate, how were we getting along, what you were like. I should have known!"

"No need to get upset," Kyreen stated, patting Synnove's arm. "He did no damage."

"This time," Synnove muttered. She took a deep breath then, exhaling, stood up. "Duty calls. I have set up and serving duty. Will I see you after dinner?"

"I will make sure to find you," Kyreen responded also rising to her feet. "Lang and I leave in the morn to go to the Council Camp. When do you head back in?"

"Not for a while," Synnove replied as they began walking. "The plan is to pack up and leave most everything here, then head straight to the rally spot by the castle shortly after the next full moon."

After bidding Synnove farewell, Kyreen headed towards the tent she would be sharing with Lang. She had briefly debated seeking him out, but decided instead she could use this time to finish up the novel she had borrowed from Rhun. Though it was not lengthy, she had not had much solo time during which to read lately. She knew the guild master would most likely be bringing her more books so wanted to be able to return this borrowed one then as well. A part of her also worried what Rhun's reaction would be once he learned of her current relationship with Lang. While she doubted it would damage the business relationship between her people and his guild, it very well could destroy their friendship. Kyreen certainly hoped not as she dug through her knapsack. She thoroughly enjoyed their conversations, the range and the depth as they discussed so many topics, the books they read, philosophy, the varied politics of their two vastly different lives.

Spreading out a bedroll, Kyreen reclined on her back in the tent using the knapsack as a pillow, enjoying the warmth of the tent's interior after the chill of the shade and breeze of outside. She also, selfishly, wanted to avoid any interruptions from being outside and visible. Her fellow Calanians had issues with solitude and most would engage her in conversation if she were seen alone. Exhaling a contented sigh, Kyreen opened her book. Within minutes she had been transported away to another world full of dragons and other magical creatures, a world with a young man about her age, struggling to find his way back to the princess he loved, having completed the quest that would gain him her hand in marriage. So engrossed in the tale, Kyreen did not feel Lang's approach. Thus, she was doubly surprised when he lifted up the tent flap to reveal the soft shadows of the impending sunset.

"I should have known," Lang remarked, dropping to his knees to scoot inside.

Though he smiled, Kyreen thought for sure she heard an edge to his tone. Guiltily she closed the book and set it aside. Sitting up she ran a hand over her hair, sweeping errant curls away from her face. She pulled her legs up cross legged out of his way.

"My apologies," she said. "I lost track of time."

"You certainly did," Lang answered, reaching outside of the tent, pulling in a plate of food before securing the entrance flat. "You missed dinner. Atle and I were one of the last through the food line. Synnove seemed worried but I assured her you were most likely squirreled away, your nose in a book."

He handed her the plate and utensils, his eyes twinkling. Kyreen took the proffered food murmuring her thanks, before apologizing. "I am sorry."

"Why are you sorry? You have done nothing wrong," Lang replied, pulling his legs up into cross legged position so that their knees were touching.

Kyreen took a bite of the food keeping her eyes lowered so as to avoid answering his question. Lang put a finger under her chin so as to lift her face up. Reluctantly she raised her gaze to his.

"No turning away," he said quietly, his tone gentle. "No secrets, no shadows, no shielding."

Kyreen chuckled despite the unshed tears in her eyes. "Are you going to turn my words against me forever?"

"Anytime and for as long as I possibly can," Lang joked, then his smile faded. "Tell me what bothers you?"

Kyreen shrugged taking another bite of food. "I feel guilty being here instead of out there."

"You need not," Lang replied, taking her free hand in his, lifting it to his lips. "You had no obligations. We had no plans. As a matter of fact, Ebbe and his mates were feeling restless so Atle and I arbitrated a few spars. That is why we were late to supper. I had been worried you would be sitting alone waiting on me. So, I am happy you found something to occupy your time. Did you enjoy your afternoon?"

"Oh yes," Kyreen remarked. "It is an interesting book."

"Well then," he responded. "No harm. No need for apologies."

As Kyreen finished up her food, Lang flashed her a smile with a mischievous glint in his eyes. "Ready for some other form of entertainment?"

Heat flared in her body and her face reddened as Kyreen smiled back at him. "I do have an obligation this evening after dinner. I told Synnove I would meet with her. It should not take long to say farewell."

"Then why don't I wait here," Lang said, leaning back, his hands behind his head, legs stretching out. "I can spend the time devising new ways to make you blush for me."

His word caused Kyreen's face to turn red again. Looking down at him, she wanted nothing more than to peel his clothes off his body and take him up on his offer of entertainment. Instead she crawled over him towards the tent entrance, a move made clumsy by Lang grabbing her and pulling her body down onto him so as to give her a kiss. Laughing, Kyreen pulled away, collected her dirty dishes, and backed out of the tent. As the flap fell back into place, her last vision was of Lang reaching for her discarded book and opening it to the first page.

Chapter 28

If the mood amongst those in the Training Camp had been relaxed, the atmosphere at the Council Camp was anything but calm. Kyreen felt the tension seep into her being as they approached late afternoon the following day. The sensation grew as they drew closer. By the time she dismounted and handed the reins over to Gunda, Kyreen had a throbbing headache right at the base of her skull.

She tried to hide the discomfort from Lang but he could taste the lie when she asserted she felt fine.

"Why is it so strong already, still, now?" Kyreen asked Aren once she and Lang had tracked her cousin down. Not surprisingly, they found Aren in the Council Tent. She adjourned the day's meeting and sent the council members away when Kyreen and Lang entered the tent. As the tent's entrance flap fell back into place after the last council member exited, the edge of Kyreen's headache eased up. She could feel the magic in the tent's interior, presumably protection spells to make the space more secure. Although Kyreen still could not perform even the most basic of spells, she had become aware of the feel of magic around her.

"Tensions are still high. The reports coming in from our people watching the castle have been unusual," Aren replied, pinching the bridge of her nose. A gesture Kyreen noted which Aren had been doing quite often of late. She also noted Aren had begun looking worn, her hair which had been ebony black last summer now had generous streaks of silver and the fine web of lines on her face had deepened dramatically. Sten's word about Calanians needing a fresh, youthful face to lead them rang out in Kyreen's mind. Resolutely she pushed these thoughts away so as to concentrate on the conversation.

"…unusual amount of traffic into the bay," Aren was saying.

Lang frowned, mulling over this news. Kyreen could see why Aren would like having him on the Council even without his talent. Now that she did not have the hostility coloring her opinion, Kyreen knew Lang to be not only a good listener, but a born problem solver. He wanted to find solutions.

"This traffic," he asked, "is it an increase in goods shipping out or coming in?"

"Nothing is coming into Calan, nor being transported into Galor," Aren responded. "The traffic going into the bay is occurring at night. We have not been able to draw close enough to determine what is being taken to the ships."

"These shipments originate in Galor?" Lang inquired, rubbing a hand over his short-cropped hair.

Kyreen's gaze drifted to a map spread out over the middle of the table. Apparently, the Council had been working out the logistics of the impending attack on the castle. The logistics of timing and location being coordinated between all the camps made Kyreen's temples throb, just another indicator to her that she did not need to be in charge.

Galor was a completely landlocked country. Passage through Calan to the bay was its only real viable access to the outside world. Kyreen vaguely recalled overhearing that Galor had no natural resources such as ore, lumber, minerals, or even crops. She wondered briefly if this was because the Galorians had stripped away all of their natural resources or because the land had always been barren. Surely it had to be the former. Else why settle there in the first place? Now staring at the map, Kyreen realized how little she knew about these people, these Galorians, whose blood ran through her veins.

Lang had been contemplating the map same as Kyreen, leaning back in his chair, balancing on its back two legs. With his brow furrowed Kyreen could almost see the gears turning as he examined the map. Finally, he shook his head and looked over at Aren.

"I am sorry," he said. "Galor has nothing to export. With their rocky soil, they barely harvest enough to feed their…"

"What?" Aren and Kyreen asked simultaneously when Lang paused.

"It would not make sense," he muttered, mostly to himself, eyes back on the map. "Except…"

"Except what?' Aren prompted. "We have only one theory and I am curious if it matches."

"People," Lang responded, his gaze drawn back to the Calanian leader. "The only commodity Galor could reasonably export is people."

Aren nodded. "That is our conclusion, although you arrived to it much more quickly than we did," she paused to flash the pair a genuine smile. "I am happy for the two of you, but I am also happy to have you back here."

Her gaze turned to Kyreen. "That includes you, cousin."

Not completely believing the sentiment, Kyreen still inclined her head and murmured, "Thank you."

"So why are the Galorians sending out their people?" Aren asked. "That we cannot figure out."

"It would help to know if they are leaving willingly or by force." Kyreen interjected thoughtfully.

"What do you mean?" Aren asked.

"If Galor has no other means of income, what would keep them from selling their people?" Kyreen responded. "Maybe they are desperate for revenue?"

"They did start harvesting lumber," Lang commented. "At least until we stopped that activity."

"Slavery has been outlawed in the realm for ages," Aren countered. "There is no market."

"Not across the Great Sea," Kyreen replied, remembering her conversations with Rhun. "There is always a demand for slaves in the New Territories where slavery is still permitted. Pirates are a big danger to the sailors both in port and on the water. Raiding parties will disable a ship, then take all the cargo and crew to be sold at one of the less respectable ports."

Aren's face wrinkled in disgust. "That is deplorable. I cannot imagine any leader condoning such practices."

"Kyreen is correct," Lang said, now leaning forward to stare down at the map. "Who is instigating this and where are they going?"

Aren's gaze shifted to Kyreen. "You have a meeting scheduled in Gladys in a few days. It would be good to find out if they have heard anything of Galor recently."

Kyreen nodded, avoiding looking at Lang. She took comfort in the fact she did not feel any strong reaction from him.

"Now back to Kyreen's talent," Aren said, settling back in her chair, looking at them both. "Besides the normal anxiety over this impending attack on the castle, people are worked up over what happens afterwards."

"Why did I not feel it last summer?" Kyreen asked.

"I think it is because you had not been around us for very long," Aren replied. "But to be honest I am not familiar with your ability. It has been a while since a Connate has been officially recorded, maybe a couple of generations. There had been a couple in your grandfather's time, but nothing had been written about them. Gisli told me exactly but I cannot remember the details. I would like you to start working with her. She believes she has some idea of how you can control it."

Aren stood up. "Right now, it is time for supper and I am anxious to spend time with my family, not thinking about this campaign."

Lang stood, but Kyreen remained seated. "Is something the matter?" he asked.

"I am not looking forward to going out there," Kyreen admitted, feeling like a coward. "In here the pain is minimized. I can think."

"I understand," Aren replied. "You may stay here for the evening if you like."

"I can go get supper," Lang offered. "Then bring our gear in here for the night. Tomorrow we can work out a more permanent solution."

"After meeting with Gisli," Aren asserted.

"Thank you," Kyreen murmured, feeling self-conscious. "I apologize for being too much trouble."

"Oh, that your issues were all I had to face," Aren commented, patting Kyreen's arm as she walked towards the entrance. "You are not nearly as much trouble as you believe yourself to be, cousin."

"Be back soon," Lang whispered with a soft kiss to Kyreen's forehead, then followed Aren out of the tent.

Alone and restless, Kyreen stood up and began walking about the interior of the tent. After a couple of rotations, she paused at the head of the table, just behind the chair that Aren had occupied. A cloth banner which bore the Calanian royal crest – a tricolored hilted sword, an image of the exact one Kyreen carried, with a red rose resting upon the hilt, a verdant green stem wrapped about the blade—hung from the tent poles. Evidently this same image had been drawn on Kyreen's right shoulder blade as an infant marking her as an heir to the throne. She did not understand all of the politics of hierarchy laws that had deemed her and Quillan heirs to be marked but not Aren, who in Kyreen's mind should be next to ascend the throne.

The protections about the tent which helped shield the peoples' feelings from Kyreen also impaired her senses, for she was surprised to hear the tent entrance being loosed. She turned with a smile, saying, "That was quick. I did not expect you back so…"

The words and her smile faltered when the flap lifted and Kyreen saw who entered. From his bright smile and friendly expression, one would not have guessed that the last time Kyreen saw this man he had been unconscious from a blow of her hand.

"Sten?" she asked as he refastened the tent flap. "What are you doing here?"

"I saw Aren and him leave," came the answer as Sten finished securing the bindings. "I thought this would be a good time for us to talk. There! Now we will not be interrupted."

Sten straightened up and turned. He fixed his sapphire gaze on Kyreen like a wolf on a rabbit and moved towards her. Involuntarily Kyreen found herself backing away, keeping the table between them.

"Talk?" she asked, incredulously wondering if this was a joke. "We have nothing to discuss, Sten."

"Oh, come now, Princess. Surely you have had time to think over my proposal," Sten continued speaking as he circled the table.

Kyreen, her gaze locked on his, was surprised to discover she had stopped moving. The smiling bard quickly closed the distance between them. He reached out brushing the back of his hand to her cheek. Kyreen found herself unable to pull back.

"I do apologize, Princess," he said, his sapphire eyes holding her in place. "I realize now that I came on much too strong at the Festival. I am sure you felt overwhelmed by everything. My sister mentioned your panic attack. I hope you can forgive me."

Frantically Kyreen's mind raced. Something Sten had done or was doing to her made it impossible for her to move or look away.

"When I heard that you had left in the company of Aren's second, I feared she may have discovered our plans," he continued speaking, stepping up so that their bodies pressed together, he ran his hands down her shoulder and arm to clasp her hand in his, drawing it up to his mouth. "You have no idea how relieved I was to hear you had returned unharmed. I have missed you, Princess."

Softly he pressed his lips to the back of her hand, his eyes never leaving hers. Heat flooded Kyreen's body, an involuntary moan escaping her lips. Sten's smile widened slightly as he turned her hand over to begin pressing soft moist kisses against her palm.

"Yes, we will make a powerful couple, Princess," he purred quietly. Kyreen felt magic fill the space around them as he continued. "Beautiful and powerful. You and I together. Do you agree, Princess?"

"Beautiful and powerful," Kyreen heard herself answer. It was like watching someone else. Her mind felt foggy and she had difficulty remembering why she had been so upset a moment earlier.

"Say the words for me, my Princess," Sten whispered, continuing to press his lips to her skin slowly working across her palm, up her wrist, to linger over her rapid pulse, his tongue softly caressing the sensitive skin.

"We will make a beautiful and powerful couple," Kyreen stated, staring into his deep blue eyes, hoping she had said the right words, hoping he would be happy with her, hoping he would continue kissing her.

"Very good," Sten murmured, letting her hand go, allowing it to fall limply by her side. He grasped her shoulders in his hands. "Lovely, Princess."

"Lovely," she repeated, disappointed he had stopped kissing her hand, wondering what she had done wrong.

Her distress must have shown on her face for Sten chuckled softly squeezing her shoulders. "Now then, no pouting, Princess. You are doing wonderfully. I am very, very pleased with you."

Kyreen smiled brightly, so happy at his compliment.

"I need you to listen very carefully," he said. Leaning in close, his voice dropping volume, Sten placed his mouth to her ear.

Kyreen nodded, her eyes widening, intently listening to his every word. After he finished speaking Sten pulled back, stared into her eyes once more, then lowered his lips to hers.

"Kyreen?" Lang said.

Kyreen jerked awake, her back stiff from the angle that she had been sitting in the armed chair. Shaking her head, she ran a hand across her braided hair and looked over at Lang standing at the entrance, his hands occupied with two plates of food.

Kyreen hurried over to help him, breathing a small sigh of relief once he had stepped in and the flap settled back in place, blocking the outside world.

"My apologies," she said, crossing back over to the table. "I must have dozed off."

"No, I apologize," Lang responded. "Aren and I ran into Gisli on the way to supper. We spent some time making arrangements for you to meet with her."

Something about his sentence buzzed at the back of Kyreen's mind. Something about Gisli. Something she could not quite remember. Shaking her head, she turned her attention to the food on her plate, surprised to discover how famished she felt.

Later, after they had eaten and Lang had brought in their gear, Lang watched Kyreen as she set out their bedrolls. She had been too quiet during supper. At first, he attributed it to the day's travels and the effect the camp had on her. But when he had asked her what was bothering her and she had answered she was fine, he had experienced a conflict unlike any he had ever felt. Kyreen believed she was fine but also, she was not. There was both truth and falsehood in her words.

When she stood up after smoothing out the bedroll, Lang stepped up behind her, sliding his arms around her waist, placing a soft kiss behind her ear. The way she stiffened he thought maybe he had simply startled her, but then she shrugged pulling away from him.

"Kyreen?" he said softly, his brow furrowed with concern. It took all his restraint not to reach out to her.

She turned to face him, only her eyes were cast downward. Wrapping her arms around her body she murmured, "I cannot…. can we not…I mean…I am tired. Can we go to sleep?"

Once again, conflict radiated from Kyreen. Confused Lang nodded. "Sure. Would you like to read a bit before sleep?"

Kyreen shook her head, immediately sitting down to tug off her boots. Within seconds she had stripped down to her underclothes and slipped into the bedroll, lying down with her back to him.

Lang watched her for several long moments. His mind raced over the last several hours trying to discern what he might have done to upset her, but not only could he not figure out his blunder, neither could he feel any distress from her at all. Kyreen did not project any anger. In fact, she exuded no feelings at all. Sighing he made preparations to lie down beside her still form.

The next morning Kyreen awoke feeling sluggish and groggy. If she had asked him, Lang could have told her she tossed and turned all night, murmuring incoherently. As it was her face looked drawn with dark circles under her eyes. Aside from a quiet good morning greeting, the couple did not speak as they dressed and packed away their gear. Aren had made arrangements for the tent to remain their sanctuary until after breakfast. Then Lang would escort Kyreen to the Archival Tent to meet with Gisli before returning for the day's council meeting.

All through breakfast Kyreen watched Lang from the corner of her eye as he silently observed her eating. She did not understand why he had to hover so close over her. It was as if he did not think she could feed herself. She wished he would go away and leave her alone. As soon as the thought crossed her mind, a sharp pain pierced her right temple causing Kyreen to wince visibly. She closed her eyes to concentrate on blocking the pain but visions of dark blue eyes filled her mind. So, she opened her eyes and saw Lang watching her with concern.

"I told you already this morning that I am fine," she snapped, wincing as another sharp pain jabbed her temple.

Dropping her spoon, Kyreen slammed her chair back and stood up. "I am heading to see Gisli," she said tersely. "Do not get up. I am perfectly capable of finding it by myself. I do not need a nursemaid."

Hurrying out of the tent, Kyreen brushed by Aren without stopping. The morning sunshine and the people's emotions slammed into Kyreen, adding to the pain in her head, but she continued on blindly for several steps before a soft hand on her arm made her pull up.

"Princess?" came the soft inquiry.

Instantly the tension inside Kyreen receded. She blinked a few times as she turned her face toward Sten. She smiled sociably, placing a hand atop his on her arm.

"Hail, Sten," she said warmly, so happy that the pain of just moments ago had dissipated. "I am headed to speak with your mother."

"May I accompany you?" Sten asked.

Kyreen's smile widened. Suddenly there was nothing she desired more than to be walking by his side. He had the most beautiful blue eyes, and his hand was so warm against her arm.

"Please do," she acquiesced, leaning her head against his shoulder as he linked his arm through hers. With him so close she did not mind the buzz of the people's essence throbbing at the base of her skull. As they made their way towards the Archival Tent, Kyreen thought she and Sten made a beautiful couple, a beautiful and powerful couple.

Chapter 29

That evening as Lang stood in line for supper, Gisli approached him, a piece of parchment in her hand. Lang took the paper from the tall Historian, frustration blooming anew inside him. All day he had been uncomfortable and restless, worried about his connection to Kyreen. Attempting to give her the space she clearly needed after this morning's outburst, he had resolutely pushed through the day's council meetings without comment or even trying to seek her out in the Archival Tent after the meeting had adjourned.

"I fear Kyreen and I have much work to do," Gisli said, smiling at him with a slightly vacant look in her blue eyes. "Kyreen does send her apologies for the inconvenience. Since the Archival Tent is warded there is no need for her to return to the Council Tent this evening."

Without waiting for a reply, the woman turned and strode away. Lang watched Gisli disappear before turning his attention to the piece of parchment in his hand. Unfolding the paper, he fully expected it to be a note from Kyreen explaining the situation. Though Lang had never seen Kyreen's handwriting, he did not believe the tiny cramped letters came from her hand even before reading the words scrawled onto the page. Scowling he scanned the note one more time before striding over to the center fire to toss the paper into the flames. Once the page had burned to oblivion, Lang turned his gaze onto the crowd of people sitting eating then to those queued for food. Spying Aren in line, Lang approached her.

Seeing the look in her second's eye, Aren frowned. "What is wrong?"

Glancing around, Lang leaned in close whispering, "We need to talk."

Stepping back, his gaze moved to Viggo, watching with concern etched across his face, and Lang added, "You, too, please. I believe you may be of help."

It took all of Lang's restraint not to sprint to the Council Tent, but he managed. Aren and Viggo trailed him inside, standing as he let the door flap fall into place. Once he had secured the fastenings he glanced around the empty interior of the tent.

"Lang, what is with all this mystery?" Aren asked, her initial alarm dissolving into irritation at missing not only supper but time alone with her family.

Lang held up a hand, shaking his head. He continued to sweep his gaze around the tent.

"I cannot see you, but I think you are here," he said, his voice tight. "Show yourself."

A moment later the lights of the tent flared up and a slight figure emerged from the corner of the tent. Aren knew most Calanians. It was her job as their leader, and she took it seriously. But the youth before her had changed drastically over the months since Aren had last laid eyes on her at the Internment Ceremony last summer. With closely shorn hair and wearing a tunic much too big for her, Aren would have been hard pressed to recognize the youth without Lang's identification.

"Svante?" Lang questioned.

"I told you to come alone," Synnove's youngest sibling responded, her voice flat and emotionless, not reflecting any anger. "And I prefer Svein but I thought you would be more inclined to come if I used the name they gave me."

"Your note told me not to trust anyone too," Lang said. "But I trust these two."

"You should not. He can get to them just as easy as anyone else." Svein made no move to approach them or to sit down.

"You said Kyreen is in danger," Lang said.

"He has her enthralled," Svein answered. "Just as he has Mama and thinks he has me."

"Enthralled?" Aren and Viggo asked simultaneously.

"When? How?" Lang followed with his question.

"I think he laid out the foundation during the Festival but she broke the spell before he could get it completely set," Svein explained. Looking down at her hands clasped in front of her, her voice faltered as she continued, "That was the night I broke his hold. I believe seeing her fight him off, evade him, did something. I do not know if his magic weakened or if I gained strength."

As Svein's voice faded, Lang's mind raced. So many emotions swirled within him, anger being foremost. He clenched his fists tightly, barely restraining himself.

"Are they at the Archival Tent?" Aren asked, placing a gentle restraining hand on Lang's arm.

"No. He took Kyreen away sometime before midday meal."

Lang pressed back the panic that bubbled up. Suddenly he realized why he had been on edge all day. He covered his face with his hands.

"Goddess, I did not notice," he muttered.

"What?" Aren asked.

"Last night. When I got back with our food, Kyreen started acting strangely. I thought I had done something wrong," he answered. "I should have known she never would have withdrawn so completely. She could not have. Not on her own."

"The bond?" Viggo asked.

"It was as if we were strangers," Lang nodded, rubbing a hand across his hair. "Then this morning when she snapped at me. I should have known. I should have recognized something was wrong. The absence of her emotions. How could I have not noticed? She is always so full of emotions."

"You have to tread carefully," Svein cautioned.

In his panic, Lang had almost forgotten the girl's presence. She continued with her warning. "I cannot tell you if he has anyone else enthralled. I only know of Mama. He had some others during the Festival but released them before it ended."

She looked away adding as an afterthought, "I think they were practice. He had spelled me sometime during the winter, after solstice. I never broke free until the Festival. He does not notice me much anymore so I have been able to pretend. When Mama breaks free, he has to keep respelling her. It makes my head fuzzy."

Aren pinched the bridge of her nose, trying to think. Prioritize. What needed to be done first. All she could think about was her own daughter, not much younger than this one standing before her. Enthralling was a dark magic, strictly forbidden. If someone had worked such a spell on her daughter, Aren could not say what she would do to them. Judging from the look in Lang's eyes and the hostilities radiating from him, he was ready to go after Sten and Kyreen this second.

"Where do you think he is taking her?" Aren asked aloud.

"He did not say," Svein answered, pausing before adding, "I would guess to the man he talks to in the scrying bowl."

Aren felt her blood run cold. "Sten was scrying with someone? Is it an outsider?"

The last time Aren had heard of a Calanian scrying, her world had collapsed. It was how the traitor had communicated with the Faldorian mercenary and Galorian emperor before the Battle.

Svein was shrugging her narrow shoulders. "I never heard or saw the other one, just Sten talking into the bowl."

"I can try tracking them," Viggo said. "Of course, it would be faster in the morning light."

He looked at Lang, knowing were it Aren in the dark, enthralled, he would not want to wait for morning. Judging from the look Lang gave him, Lang had no intention of waiting.

Aren nodded. "You go, both of you. I need to figure out what to do with this one here, and her mother."

Lang turned to leave, but on an impulse turned around. Moving quickly, he closed the distance between he and Svein. Grabbing both the girl's hands in his, he squeezed them and smiled down at her.

"Thank you," he said. "Thank you for not waiting. I am in your debt."

With a final squeeze, he dropped her hands and sped out of the tent. Viggo kissed Aren's cheek and followed Lang. Suddenly alone with Svein, Aren looked over at the girl and silently wondered why her world had become so complicated.

Kyreen's eyes fluttered open. It was morning. She was outside. Furrowing her brow, she tried to remember where she was. Sitting upright she pulled the blanket up to her chin wondering why she was sleeping outside without any clothes on. The last thing she remembered clearly was leaving the Council Tent after yelling at Lang. Why had she been angry with him? She could not remember why exactly. Maybe she should get dressed and go find him to apologize. As she reached towards the pile of clothes beside her, she heard a rustle behind her and a warm hand pressed against her bare shoulder.

"Princess?" came the soft inquiry.

Kyreen glanced up over her shoulder, smiling warmly. "Hail, Sten. Do you know why I am sleeping outside? I thought I would find Lang and ask him."

Sten ran his hand down Kyreen's bare arm. Gazing into her emerald eyes, he pulled her up out of the bedroll to stand up before him. With his free hand, he brushed an errant curl away, then cupped his hand to her face.

"We are taking a trip, Kyreen," he said, infusing the magic into his words and his touch. "You are mine. Remember?"

"Oh yes. I forgot for a moment," Kyreen replied, happy that he had reminded her, happy to have him touching her, happy to be his. "We make a beautiful and powerful couple, Sten."

"That we do, Princess, that we do," Sten responded, allowing his gaze to drop from her eyes, greedily surveying her naked body standing so docile before him. "As much as I would like to dally, how about you get dressed so we can get going? I know of someone very anxious to meet you and we still have a very long ride ahead of us."

As the sun reached its apex, Viggo led Lang into the small clearing where Sten and Kyreen had spent the night. True to his Calanian training Sten had erased all evidence of their stay but Viggo could still see the camp clearly. He saw where a small fire had been. He saw where the two horses had been hobbled for the evening. He saw where a single bedroll had been lain out. Rubbing a hand over his face, Viggo kept that information to himself thinking as long as Lang did not inquire it might be alright.

"What is wrong?" Lang asked, looking down from the back of his mare. Watching Viggo walk about the small clearing, Lang's agitation had his horse upset and she pranced in place nervously.

"I do not wish to say," Viggo answered, swinging back into the saddle.

"Tell me!" Lang insisted.

"You do not want to know this. Trust me." Viggo responded, giving Lang a stern look before wheeling his mount around. "They headed this way."

Lang looked after Viggo's retreating back, the glanced back at the clearing. His imagination could fill in what Viggo had not wished to speak aloud. Fresh anger coursed through his veins as Lang spurred the mare forward to catch up with Viggo.

Several hours later, just before the colors of sunset arrived, Viggo pulled his horse to a halt, motioning Lang to be quiet. Both men slipped silently to the ground.

Viggo leaned in to whisper to Lang. "Their horses are walking even slower through here. I think he may be looking for a place to camp. The man is not hurrying at all. It does not appear he expected to be followed."

Lang nodded. Had Svein not sent him that note it very well could have been this afternoon before anyone suspected Sten and Kyreen of leaving camp. As it was, Lang's insides were tied up in knots at the thought of Kyreen enthralled and under this man's influence for the past two days. He took a deep breath. Being angry and alerting Sten to their presence would not be a wise thing to do.

"We should leave our horses here," Viggo was saying, "lest they call out to the other horses."

Lang nodded, impatient to close the distance between them and their target. Though hobbling their horses only took a few short moments, to Lang it felt like an hour. As they headed out on foot the sky above them through the trees was of two colors – the color purple of twilight and the fiery gold of sunset. Neither of the men took any notice.

Chapter 30

Kyreen's head hurt again. No, not again. Still. She could not recall how she arrived here, nor could she remember where here was. She pressed her fingertips into her temples, the pressure offering a temporary respite from the sharp, piercing pain. It had just been morning, had it not? Now it looked to be sunset. Where had the day gone? Where had she gone? Where was her gelding and what horse did she groom?

"Princess?" a hand grasped hers.

Kyreen turned and smiled. "Hail, Sten! I fear I may be lost."

Sten pulled Kyreen's body to his by snaking his free hand around the back of her neck, pressing into her bare flesh. Lacing the fingers of his other hand through her hand, he stared into her wide eyes, the trust reflected there arousing him, the power he held over her coursing through his body. He allowed the magic to build up then he sent it forth into Kyreen through his touch and his voice.

"You are not lost, Princess. We are on a journey," he said quietly, his voice softly seductive. "You and I together. Remember?"

Her body relaxed against his as her smile widened. "Yes, I do remember. Thank you," she replied, gazing into his beautiful blue eyes, thankful he was here to protect her, to care for her, to love her.

Sten's smile lifted as he watched her pupils dilate and felt her body melt against his. Her breath quickened and her lips parted, just begging to be kissed.

"What do you remember, Princess?' he purred, his lips hovering just above hers, teasing.

"We are a couple," she responded. "A beautiful and powerful couple."

"Exactly." Sten pressed his lips to hers, wrapping both arms about her body, pulling her tight.

After a moment's hesitation, her arms slid about him, her nails digging into his back through his shirt as she clung to him. A deep moan rumbled from the back of her throat.

Breaking the kiss Sten took a step back. The hurt and disappointment in her expression only fueled his desire.

"Not so fast, Princess," he clucked his tongue at her, scolding. "There is work to be done before we play. Finish caring for the horses while I gather some firewood."

Kyreen nodded and went back to rubbing down the chestnut mare in front of her.

From the tree line, Viggo and Lang had watched Sten approach Kyreen, then kiss. When her arms wrapped around the bard, Viggo had thought he would have to restrain the man beside him but Lang had been able, barely, to keep from running out. Viggo worried Sten might be able to sense their presence from the rage radiating off of Lang, but Sten appeared relaxed and confident that no one could possibly be following him. When Sten walked away and Kyreen resumed grooming the chestnut, Viggo motioned for Lang to follow him farther back into the trees.

"We will have to move in fast, use the element of surprise," Viggo whispered. "You get Kyreen and I will…"

"No!" Lang interrupted vehemently. "Sten is mine."

Viggo shrugged, knowing he would feel the same were situations reversed. He also knew he would be too emotional, more likely to mishandle the grab, although nobody would ever be able to change his mind. So, it would be with Lang. Therefore, instead of arguing, Viggo acquiesced.

"Based on what we witnessed, he uses touch and words to enthrall," Viggo added. "I would recommend you do not let him grab a hold of you."

Lang nodded, ready to head into the clearing.

"Wait until he is returned and the horses are no longer blocking a clear path," Viggo cautioned.

"Fine. Just pat my arm when you are ready," Lang responded, his entire body quivering.

The two men silently moved into place, observing Kyreen as she finished grooming one horse and began on the other.

Pulling the saddle from the sorrel gelding with three white stockings, Kyreen placed it with the tack she had removed from the other horse. The chore felt familiar but something about it also felt strange, like something was off, distorted like when you saw yourself reflected in water. She rubbed at her temples then went back to grooming the horse's coat. She needed to finish quickly. She could not remember exactly why but something drove her to work fast. As she knelt to hobble the gelding, Sten emerged from the trees with an armful of wood. Spying him, she relaxed with a smile, remembering it was Sten she had been waiting for. She was happy he had returned, happy that they were on a journey, happy that together they made a beautiful and powerful couple.

Leading the hobbled horse over to the other one already grazing in the outer edge of the clearing, Kyreen started walking back to Sten, anxious to be near him, hoping he would be pleased with her. The sun had disappeared below the tops of the trees, leaving golden stripes of fire in the sky while draping everything below in purple shadows. Sten had stoked the fire and now stood beside it, watching her walk towards him. The look on his face made her stomach churn and her pulse quicken.

Without any warning, someone grabbed Kyreen from behind. Though she reacted immediately, on instinct, the arms held her tight lifting her feet off the ground, not allowing her to gain any purchase with which to escape.

Even as she struggled against her unseen assailant Kyreen watched as a form bolted from the shadows to tackle Sten to the ground. Fixing her gaze on Sten, she redoubled her efforts, swinging her head back, trying to bash her captor's face. Writhing, she gave a wordless shriek of frustration as the arms holding her never lessened their grip. Sten and the other figure had risen to their feet, grappling clumsily. At Kyreen's cry, the other figure had stopped, glancing over his shoulder. She thought she might recognize the other man, but she kept her gaze trained on Sten, unable to glance away even for a second. She had to get to him.

Then a bright light blinded her. As her eyes closed, a deafening pop echoed across the clearing. The arms holding Kyreen lessened their hold, but she only sank to the ground, cradling her head in her hands, curling into a fetal position.

When Kyreen next became aware of her surroundings she found herself lying on the ground, her head aching as though someone had split it open. Clumsily she attempted to sit up without opening her eyes. Gentle hands assisted her upright. Taking a deep breath, she attempted to open her eyes. Gratefully the world was dark save for a small fire across the clearing.

Kyreen squinted up at the figure looming over her. "Lang?"

Speechless he dropped to his knees, wrapping his arms around her. She looked around the small clearing with a fire burning in its center and two horses grazing just beyond the circle of light cast by the firelight. Her frown deepened when Viggo slipped out of the bushes, hurrying towards the pair.

"We are too close to the castle," he reported quietly as he began dousing the fire. "I followed him as far as I dared before turning back. Between Kyreen's scream and that explosion, I fear we may have attracted attention."

"Castle? Who did you follow?" Kyreen asked as Lang pulled her to her feet. "Why did I scream? What explosion?"

"Take her back to our horses," Viggo ordered, beginning to gather up the gear Sten had abandoned after igniting the flash explosion that covered his disappearance into the woods. He glanced over at Lang, who had not moved. "Go! I will get this cleaned up and catch up."

Viggo looked at Kyreen who seemed disoriented. "Lang, you need to get her moving. We are not safe here."

Nodding Lang grabbed Kyreen's elbow and spun her towards the bushes he and Viggo had used for cover. The second time she stumbled Lang scooped her up over his shoulder. Kyreen's head hanging down reignited the headache anew, so she concentrated on pressing a hand to each temple as Lang trotted them back to his and Viggo's horses. Once there he unceremoniously dumped Kyreen to the ground with a mumbled apology. Then he quickly collected the horses and got them both unhobbled.

Standing before Kyreen, who had not moved, he gazed down at her wanting only to take her into his arms. Instead he handed her the reins to Viggo's horse.

"Can you ride or will I need to strap you in?" he asked, purposefully putting an edge in his voice.

His insult had the desired effect. Kyreen snatched the reins from his hand glaring up at him. Rolling to her feet, she swayed slightly but managed to stay upright. When she moved over to the horse's side, Lang turned to swing up onto his horse's back but glanced back before doing so, to see Kyreen simply standing by the horse, making no move to get into the saddle.

"Kyreen?" he said softly moving to stand behind her.

"The stirrups are too long," she replied, quietly. "I know they need to be shortened, but I do not know how to do it. I need to go that way."

She pointed in the general direction that Sten had been traveling when he fled the campsite. Letting the reins slip from her fingers she turned in the direction she had been pointing and made to start walking that way. Lang grabbed her arm, just as Viggo rode up with the two other horses. He quickly took in the scene, sliding off the back of the horse. Yanking Kyreen away from Lang, Viggo slapped her firmly across the face, before grabbing her by the shoulders and tugging her towards the chestnut mare she had been riding earlier. Lang watched in wonder as the older man positioned Kyreen next to the mare, grabbed the woman at her knee to hoist her up into the saddle, all in one smooth motion. Instinct took over for Kyreen once she was seated, her feet slipping into the stirrups.

Viggo thrust the mare's reins into Lang's hands. "You lead her," he said quietly. "She may still be under his influence."

Without any more talk, both men swung up into their mounts' saddles and began the trek back to the Calanian camp.

A couple of hours before dawn, Viggo stopped in a small clearing that he knew well, having used it during past hunting trips. Though he was anxious to get back, he knew they and their horses needed some rest. While he tended to the horses, Lang saw to Kyreen, who had yet to speak or react any further during their nighttime ride. She kept rubbing her temples and wincing as if in pain. When Lang attempted to hand her some of the food found amongst Sten's gear she had simply shaken her head and turned away. As Viggo finished caring for the horses, Lang had settled Kyreen down in a bedroll. Once it was clear she would stay down, Lang joined Viggo. Standing side by side one gazed down at Kyreen while the other scanned the dark trees around them.

"Thank you for that back there," Lang said quietly. "For getting her up on that horse. I...I did not know what to do."

"Kyreen is in shock," Viggo replied. "She is going to need our assistance to navigate her way back to us."

"How did you...know she would stay on the horse?" The question slipped out before Lang could think about it.

Viggo was quiet so long Lang thought maybe Aren's mate would not answer the question. Lang had not had opportunity to spend much time with Viggo. While Lang worked closely with Aren, they were not of the same generation nor social circle, what little of that there was left with the Calanians.

"Kyreen is acting like many of our people did after the Battle," Viggo's quiet voice brought Lang back present. "In those first few days after the initial push, my father and I spent most of our energies finding and evacuating survivors. My father showed me how to get them onto horseback which made it easier, faster to get them out."

The men stood in silence a few more moments before Viggo clapped Lang on the shoulder. "You go sleep. I am good for a couple more hours. I will wake you before dawn. I want to be back on the trail at sunrise."

From the bedroll, Kyreen listened to the men's voices, too quiet for her to make out the words, but still she took comfort in their presence. The overwhelming compulsion to head in the opposite direction from the one they had been travelling had finally faded away. With it the headache had also receded. Now her brain felt bruised like an apple that had been bounced around a bit too much. Kyreen's body also ached in places she tried not to wonder about too much. She slowly raised a hand to a spot towards the back of her neck that had been throbbing particularly hard. Gently her fingers explored the indentations as she puzzled over what the injury could be from. Whenever she tried to remember the events from today and yesterday, she would get brief visions before it would all just slip away like a fish in a stream.

When Lang settled down on a bedroll beside her, Kyreen wanted to roll over into his embrace. Maybe his touch could help her feel normal. Instead she lay extremely still, breathing slowly, listening and waiting for him to reach out to her. When he did not, she began to wonder what she had done to repel him. She vaguely remembered yelling at him this morning or was it yesterday morning? Maybe she had said something particularly hurtful. She should probably apologize. But his breathing had become shallow and she believed him to be asleep. As for her, Kyreen did not know when she would be able to sleep again. Though her body and her brain both cried out for rest, every time Kyreen closed her eyes she saw those same dark blue eyes and a feeling of claustrophobia so strong fell over her, she felt like she could not breath. So, she spent the rest of the night feigning sleep and listening to the soft footfalls of her cousin's mate as he paced the perimeter of their camp.

Chapter 31

Aren felt Viggo's return the next afternoon and quickly called a recess to the Council's latest planning session. By the time she met up with the group, they had left the horses in Gunda's care and Viggo had them headed towards the medic tent. Without slowing down, Viggo put his arm around Aren, who after all their years together easily slipped into his embrace as they walked in tandem. He kissed the side of her head, grateful as always for her presence.

Glancing over her shoulder to Lang and Kyreen trailing behind them, Aren inquired, "How is she?"

"In shock," Viggo murmured quietly.

"And Sten?" she asked, almost afraid of the answer.

"Gone," came the quiet reply. "We caught up with them near the castle but I am not convinced that was his destination."

Before Aren could ask anything more, they arrived at the tent, located on the very edge of the encampment. It was empty save for a locked footlocker and two cots. Aren worked the lights as Viggo turned to Lang.

"Kyreen may wish to clean up," he said to the younger man. "How about you bring her some hot water? She may also wish for food and tea now."

Lang nodded. Casting a final worried glance at Kyreen, he ducked out of the tent.

Aren waited until the flap fell back into place before facing her husband to ask, "What was that about?"

Viggo shrugged. "He was hovering. Kyreen needs a little space right now. I need space from him, too."

He moved over to stand by the silent woman. Keeping his distance, he gestured towards the footlocker, quietly saying, "Would you care to sit while we wait?"

"Thank you," Kyreen replied.

As soon as she had settled, Viggo pulled Aren to the opposite side of the tent. He slid his arms around her and pulled his wife close so it looked like they were simply sharing an intimate hug. In reality, he was shielding their faces from Kyreen.

"I did not lie to Lang. We need to make some rue tea," he whispered into Aren's ear, "with blue cohosh."

Aren stiffened at the mention of the herb with abortive properties. "Are you sure?"

"Fairly," he responded, giving her a very brief summation of their expedition, concluding, "A quick search of Sten's gear did not reveal any contraceptive herbs."

Aren did not need Viggo to explain to her the implications of his revelation. What better way for Sten to insinuate himself into the royal family than to father a child with the next queen? For so long Aren had concentrated on keeping her people safe so that one day they would be strong enough to rise up against those who exiled them. Now that day loomed close and Aren found herself unprepared for the politics that had begun to emerge. Perhaps she had been overly naïve to believe that her people would simply return to Calan without the political power plays that had led to the Battle.

"The tent needs to be spelled," Viggo was saying. "Put some security wards on it. As Svein said, we do not know who could be under Sten's influence. Without knowing exactly which spell he used, we cannot know how far his reach is, or if he will return."

Aren nodded. This trait in Viggo, his ability to step in, to think clearly in crisis, to lead during distress, had been her own saving grace over the years. She had come to rely on his swift, sure action when chaos reigned, especially in the early days of their exile.

"Anything else?" she asked.

"Is Vidar traveling with our camp or did he stay in the Great Valley?"

Aren's brow furrowed at the unexpected question about the elderly, blind blacksmith. "I believe he remained in the Valley," she responded.

"How quickly can he get here?"

Unsure where Viggo was heading but willing to trust him, Aren calculated the time it would take to send word to the Training Camp and then for Vidar to be transported here, adding extra time to account for the Council's move scheduled in two days.

"Three days if we pushed it. Four would be tight. Five more ideal," she said, adding, "Kyreen is scheduled to leave for Gladys morning after next, if she is up to it."

They both turned their faces to glance at Kyreen, still sitting complacently on the footlocker, hands resting motionless in her lap.

Watching her cousin stare unseeing at the tent wall, Aren wondered if Kyreen would be fit to attend the trade meeting.

"I would suggest sending for Vidar. Have him here when she returns," Vigo commented, pulling Aren back into his embrace to whisper into her ear. He no longer worried about Kyreen overhearing this part of their conversation, he simply enjoyed the opportunity to hold his mate.

"Why Vidar?" Aren asked, knowing there to be a reason which currently escaped her.

"I do not trust Gisli to work with Kyreen. Not now. Not knowing how Sten had her enthralled," Viggo responded. "Vidar had kin who were Connates. He may have some advice for Kyreen to learn how to control the talent."

With Viggo's words, Aren recalled Gisli telling her this during the Festival. The Historian had been excited about the chance to speak with a Connate. Admittedly Aren tuned out most of the woman's ramblings but had paid enough attention to recall specifically two facts that stood out. First, Vidar's aunt and sister had both been Connates, the last two recorded. The other item, a sobering revelation, Gisli stated most Connates, overwhelmed by the input received, succumbed to madness before puberty ended. Both Vidar's aunt and sister had lived into their twentieth year before madness drove them to take their lives.

Calmed both by her partner's plan and embrace, Aren felt ready to face this latest crisis. She glanced at Kyreen again, or more specifically, the footlocker. "The herbs we need should be in there," she said, reaching for the key she carried on her person.

"One more thing," Viggo commented quietly as they moved toward Kyreen.

He motioned for Aren to follow him so that they stood slightly behind and to the side of the sitting woman who paid them no attention. Silently Viggo gestured towards Kyreen's neck, where peeking out from under the collar of her tunic, just at the base of her neck Aren could see part of an angry red mark. Leaning in for a closer look she was shocked to recognize the indentations of a human bite mark. She drew back a few steps, leaning into Viggo.

"Do you think Lang has noticed?" she whispered.

"If he has not by now, he will at some time," Viggo replied. "I think we should try to find out how much Kyreen remembers."

Aren nodded.

"It may also be a good idea to give her a sleeping draught after. She did not sleep at all when we stopped."

"I can imagine," Aren said. "Let us get her moved to a cot."

By the time Viggo and Aren had moved Kyreen and retrieved the herbs, Lang returned with the supplies Viggo had requested. While Viggo made up the tea, Aren left to find a caster to ward the tent, and Lang took the food to Kyreen who sat on the edge of the cot. She shook her head, pushing the plate away.

"I have no appetite," she murmured.

"You need to eat," Lang responded, plucking a piece of bread off the plate and offering it to her.

"I told you I am not hungry!" Kyreen retorted, slapping his hand away. The bread flew out of Lang's hand, falling to the ground. Kyreen stared at it her eyes filling with tears. "I am sorry! I did not mean to."

Her forlorn tone rattled Lang. He scooped the bread up, plopping it back on the plate. "It is alright. See? No harm done."

Kyreen looked at him, her eyes shimmering with unshed tears. "What did I do, Lang?"

"What do you mean?" he asked with a frown.

"I cannot remember anything but I must have done something. You had to chase me down, escort me back, isolate me here, and you will barely look at me, not to mention you have not...when we stopped in the night, you did not...why do you avoid touching me?"

Lang, who had been squatting by the cot, sat back on his heels. He ran a hand over his head, at a loss for words.

Viggo, with the tea prepared, had been watching the exchange between the young couple. Divining this would probably be as good a time as any to interrupt, he stepped forward, pressing a cup into Kyreen's hand.

"No," she asserted, vehemently shaking her head and pushing away the cup. "I do not want anything."

"What you want is not my concern," Viggo responded, pressing back. "What you need is this cup of tea. I am not Lang. I will not acquiesce so easily. If necessary I am prepared to forcibly pour this down your throat."

Whether it was Viggo's verbal threat or the stern tone of his voice, Kyreen relented. She grasped the cup in both her hands, drawing the cup to her lips. She gazed up at Viggo, over the rim, keeping the cup pressed to her closed lips, but he was not fooled. Pressing a finger under the cup, he tipped it so that Kyreen could either drink the liquid or be soaked. She chose to drink.

The tea tasted different. Kyreen grimaced, swallowing the hot liquid. While it did not taste bad, she could not say she enjoyed it either. She recognized the rue, having been drinking it twice daily for a while. What she did not know was the other herbs, what gave it the not unlikeable tang. As she tipped back the last of the tea under Viggo's watchful gaze, Aren returned accompanied by an older Calanian woman, introduced as Brigit.

At Aren's direction, Brigit began pulling items from her bag - a small bundle of sage, a sachet of dried flowers, a raven feather, a small sack of polished rocks, a vial of saltwater. She turned to Aren almost apologetically saying, "I can work better without an audience."

When it became clear Lang was not going to offer, Viggo assisted Kyreen to her feet, not sure if she needed the help. As they passed the bowl of water Lang had brought for Kyreen to bathe in, something on the water's surface caught her eye. She flinched backing into Viggo.

"What is it?" he asked quietly, his hands resting on her elbows.

"I do not know," she replied, shaking her head. "Just my imagination."

Viggo did not say anything, just looked thoughtfully at the bowl as they continued for the exit. Outside Kyreen squinted in the afternoon sun, looking even paler than she had the previous day. She hugged her arms around her body, chilled despite the warm sun beaming down on their little group. Kyreen had never been one to overindulge in alcoholic beverages. Seeing Jorn's compulsion had cured her of any desire to imbibe, though she did enjoy a small glass of mead with Rhun. Right now, however, she felt like she imagined a drunk would feel. Her head still ached. The tea Viggo had forced her to drink rumbled noisily in her empty stomach. Kyreen still could not tell if it would stay down or not. Her body ached all over and she felt simultaneously chilled and feverish.

"It will not be long," Viggo murmured, keeping a soft hand on Kyreen's arm as she began to sway softly.

Lang watched Viggo, wanting to step in, to take care of Kyreen but he could not bring himself to do so. She had asked him what she had done wrong, convinced it was she, not he, who had blundered. Why he did not speak up immediately to appease her guilt he did not know.

Finally, the tent flap lifted and Brigit indicated they could reenter the space. Kyreen felt a great deal of relief upon entering, but then she caught a whiff of the residual magic. Though it smelled different than what she remembered, the scent was similar enough that the aroma triggered something inside her. Kyreen's entire body began trembling, her eyes widening in fright.

Viggo wrapped his arms around Kyreen, pulling her close. He glanced at Aren, then pointedly looked at Lang, who stood staring at Kyreen, unsure of what he should do.

"Do something about him," Viggo muttered. Aren recognized from her mate's tone that he was about fed up with Lang's behavior. Not that she could blame Viggo. She herself had begun feeling irritation towards her second in command.

"Lang," she said. "Let us go to the council meeting."

"I really do not feel...I should..." Lang stuttered uncomfortably.

"Go," Viggo commanded, his voice leaving no room for argument, but as Lang turned away Viggo gave him a stern look. "Soon, before this is over, Lang, you and I need to have a talk."

Once everyone else had left, Viggo had Kyreen sit on the cot. Her tremors had calmed and she did not look so spooked. Pouring another cup of tea, Viggo put a helping of sleeping herbs into the liquid.

"Here," he said, handing her the cup. "This will help you sleep."

Kyreen shook her head vigorously. "No, please do not make me."

"Take it," he urged compassionately. "I will stay with you. You are safe."

Reluctantly Kyreen took the cup. Wordlessly she drained the contents and allowed Viggo to assist her in lying back on the cot. Once she was settled, he sat on the ground beside the cot, taking her hand in his.

"Tell me what you remember," he commanded, his voice not unkind while still having force. "Beginning with your return from the Valley."

"I remember arriving at camp with Lang. We met with Aren, then they left for supper," Kyreen replied, her tone thoughtful as she recalled the events from the previous couple of days. "I was looking around the tent, at the banner, thinking about the mark on my..."

"What?" Viggo prompted when her voice trailed off.

"I...I cannot...I remember the entrance...Someone came in..." Kyreen's voice tightened.

Viggo stroked her arm softly. "Everything is alright. You are safe here. Relax and keep going."

"I fell asleep. Lang woke me up with the food," Kyreen's voice leveled out once more, her hand in Viggo's relaxing. "I was famished and exhausted so went to sleep directly after eating. But I slept horribly. In the morning, I yelled at Lang. I do not know why. I just felt so angry so I left to... to go..."

"To go where?"

"To...see Gisli..." came the tentative reply. "But I cannot remember going to her tent."

"What do you remember?"

Kyreen shook her head. "Nothing,"

"Do you remember being in the clearing, grooming the horse?" Viggo prompted once more.

"Yes, that is it," Kyreen responded, thankful for Lang's absence so he could not feel the lie she told Viggo. "One minute it was morning, then suddenly it was evening."

Kyreen yawned a great big jaw cracking yawn. Viggo patted her hand.

"You rest," he said. "A good sleep will make you feel better."

Once Kyreen's breathing had evened out and he was certain she slept, Viggo rose to his feet to carry her empty cup over to the footlocker setting it next to the teapot. The bowl of now cold water caught his eye. For a long moment, he frowned down at the glassy surface. Then in a swift movement he picked up the bowl, walked to the far corner of the tent and spilt the water into the dirt.

When Aren entered much later, she had Gunda with her carrying a third plate of food. Viggo, back at his post, sitting on the ground beside the cot, Kyreen's hand resting softly in his, frowned as the entrance closed behind his mate and daughter.

"Where is Lang?" he asked.

Gunda started a little, hearing a tone from her father that she had never heard before. Even at his angriest when she or her brothers had misbehaved never did he have such sternness in his tone. She set the plate of food down on the footlocker with a glance to her mother.

Aren nodded. "Thank you for your help," she said. "Now go eat supper with your brother."

Quickly Gunda complied without speaking. Viggo knew he would need to apologize to his youngest for scaring her. Right now, though, he was so livid he could barely contain his temper.

Rising to his feet, Viggo headed for the tent entrance. Only Aren's hand to his arm made him pause. He gazed down into her beautiful green eyes, but even their bond did not quench the anger.

"He is virtually untested," Aren said softly, not needing to say Lang's name. "Do not judge him too harshly. He is young."

"He is older than I was when we bonded," Viggo growled.

"We were forged in a hotter fire, made older by our lives, my love," she reminded him, appeasing very little of the anger coursing through his veins.

"That may be," Vigo admitted. "But he is old enough to know better. I would not permit one of my children to act as he has, nor would I allow anyone to treat my child as he is treating Kyreen. She is our kin. We are her family, Aren. It is my duty to call him out."

"You should not go so heated," Aren suggested. "Why not wait until morning?"

"No," Viggo shook his head adamantly. "Lang needs to be present tomorrow when she wakes and I do not mean merely physically present."

He pressed a kiss to her soft cheek, saying, "I will use the walk to calm down and I will be back before my food cools completely."

Once outside Viggo took a deep cleansing breath. The early spring evening air chilled his lungs. Striding towards the quad, something in his walk or expression discouraged any conversation from the smattering of people he met along the way. He found Lang sitting with a group of people, though from the way the young man slumped and played with his food, he had not been interacting with anyone. Lang glanced up glumly when Viggo stopped before him.

"If you do not wish to cause a scene, you will follow me," Viggo announced curtly, keeping his volume down so as not to draw unwanted attention. He turned and walked towards the woods, pausing at the edge of the tree line to wait for Lang to put away his plate of uneaten food, earning him a disgruntled frown from the head cook for wasting food.

Viggo had used the walk to clear his head. For Aren had been correct in that he needed to be calmer before addressing Lang. When he thought they had moved far enough away so as not to be overheard or interrupted, Viggo turned to watch Lang, who had been trailing back. The younger man's expression and entire comportment merely served to anger Viggo anew.

"That right there needs to stop," Viggo remarked, scowling. "You have nothing to sulk over, Lang. You are not the injured party."

Lang frowned and opened his mouth to protest but Viggo held up a hand, continuing.

"Kyreen has done no wrong here and you will quit treating her as if she did. You will stop tiptoeing around and you will stop holding yourself from her. She has been abused enough, both mentally and physically."

Viggo paused when Lang gave him a sharp look. "Yes, mentally and physically. I had thought to leave some things unspoken, to allow Kyreen the courtesy of discretion, but you decided to act like a petulant child whose favorite toy was taken away."

Viggo paused again, this time to check his temper before he said too much. Aren had also been correct that Lang was untested. What she had been reminding Viggo was that Lang had grown up in the safety of the Great Valley, where children had a relatively peaceful, almost normal life free from the stresses of surviving in the Calanian woods, ever alert for patrols or worse raids especially in those first few years. Also, the farming families had never suffered hunger, like those who had remained in Calan. But Viggo also reminded himself that this man before him had fought and been injured in battle last summer. So, Viggo counseled himself to be sure some of the anger he felt was not from the fact his eldest had just covenanted with a girl from the farming families, a petty, vain creature who irritated both Viggo and Aren.

When Viggo resumed speaking, his tone had softened. "Kyreen needs your strength right now. She has suffered a trauma that has damaged your connection. With your bond being so new it could have severed it completely. Hopefully not. The point being Kyreen is fragile as is your connection. It is your job to figure out how to help her heal without smothering her."

"I do not know how," Lang responded. When Viggo had initially summoned him, Lang had been irritated by the older man's presumptions to lecture him. Now his anger had dissipated leaving Lang full of doubt, a relatively new emotion for him. He added, "I do not know what Kyreen wants."

"Kyreen does not know what she wants," Viggo replied. "I do not know exactly how enthrallment works but Sten puttered with her mind. He took away her free will, made her do things against her nature. Fortunately, it seems she does not recall much, which could be a blessing."

"I keep seeing her kissing him," Lang shook his head. "I cannot shake the image."

Viggo's anger flared again, but he managed to control his voice. "Imagine what that must feel like to her if she has any memories? You need to…Kyreen needs you to treat her as if this did not happen, reassure her that your feelings for her have not changed."

"They have not!" Lang asserted.

"Then let her know that!" Viggo snapped. "How you react when she needs you most will be the link that cements your bond or shatters it. You need to check your ego and do what is best for your mate."

"No secrets, no shadows, no shielding," Lang muttered.

"What is that?" Viggo said.

"Nothing," Lang shook his head.

"Are we in accord?" Viggo inquired.

At Lang's nod, Viggo turned to begin the trek back to camp. He never looked back to see if Lang followed.

Chapter 32

Aren had begun to worry when the tent entrance opened and Viggo entered. Before she could ask, Lang also ducked in. Both men's faces remained carefully neutral, showing neither anger or worry.

"I will stay the night with Kyreen," Lang said. Aren could not be sure if his words held a sheepish tone or if it was her imagination. He added, "You should go be with your family."

Viggo picked up a plate of food, handing it to Lang. "I interrupted your supper. Kyreen will most likely sleep the night."

"Thank you," Lang took the proffered plate, adding, "for everything."

Viggo nodded, grabbed one of the remaining plates for himself, leaving without further comment.

Aren and Lang silently watched Aren's mate exit. Once the flap had dropped in place, Lang looked over to Aren and said, "He is quite persuasive."

"You have no idea," Aren chuckled.

After Aren departed a short while later, Lang sat on the footlocker chewing his food and thoughtfully gazing at Kyreen as she slumbered, Viggo's words running through his head. She slept on her side, back to the room, appearing to be at peace. As he reflected Lang felt the irritation from earlier building back up. Only this time instead of letting it control him, he took a long hard look at the emotion. Nothing Viggo had said had been wrong. Lang squirmed uncomfortably as he realized Viggo in fact had been spot on in so many ways. Everything Lang had been doing was for his own comfort, doing things to make himself feel better, trying to make the event go away without giving thought to what had happened, thinking only how Sten had wronged him. He had not given consideration to Kyreen's feelings. Now he imagined his own reactions had it been him, how he would have felt had someone invaded his mind and forced him to do acts against his will. The food in his stomach churned uneasily as Lang pondered this point for quite a while.

Lang finished up his meal, having a new-found respect for Aren's mate. Since joining the Council, Lang had not had much opportunity to interact with the man, who was renowned throughout the camps for his tracking and hunting abilities. To be honest, Lang had found Viggo to be a bit forgettable, always around but the man seemed never truly engaged, and he certainly never participated in idle chit chat. Viggo did a good job of taking care of Aren, all the while never bringing attention to himself in the process. Lang had never heard a negative or derisive word said about Viggo, quite the opposite. More than once, Lang had heard someone comment on how Viggo had assisted with an issue, a problem, a challenge.

With a soft sigh, Lang rose, crossing to stand over Kyreen. His heart ached anew seeing her laying there sleeping, thinking about her ordeal, and regretting, not for the first time, that he had been unable to protect her. He turned to the corner where his and Kyreen's gear had been placed. Rummaging through her pack he pulled out a small rectangular object wrapped in oil skin. Carefully he unwrapped the little book of fairy tales then sat down on the ground beside Kyreen, his back leaning against the cot.

Opening the cover, Lang paused at the inscription scrawled on the title page.

> *Kyreen –*
> *Safe journeys.*
> *Always, Rhun*

Rhun. The guild master from Myrddin. He had gifted this book to Kyreen, this book that delighted her so much. Did her pleasure derive from the stories or from the giver of the book, Lang asked himself, his fingertips idly running over the handwritten words.

Lang realized how much truth had been in Kyreen's statement their first day in the cave during the storm. He knew facts from Kyreen's life but what did he know of her? He resolved to do better about talking less and listening more, to work on their connection. He saw Aren and Viggo's bond with a new appreciation and determined that nurturing his bond with Kyreen would be his priority from now on.

Turning the page to the first story, Lang began to read aloud, his voice bouncing softly off the tent walls.

The first time Kyreen awoke hearing Lang's voice she wondered if she were dreaming. Then she recognized the words and realized he was reading from her book. Smiling, she let her eyes drift shut once more, drifting back into a dreamless, drug induced slumber. Twice more during the night she floated awake, his voice comforting and sending her back to sleep.

The fourth time her eyes opened the tent was silent. A soft glow from the tent walls told her it would soon be sunrise. Rolling over she saw Lang still sat upright, leaning back against the cot, his head lolling to one side. Kyreen stared at the back of his head, longing to run her fingers through his bristly dark hair. The sleep had helped her headache recede so that only a small residual soreness remained. While she lay on her side contemplating the back of his head, Lang jerked awake. Instinctively Kyreen closed her eyes, feigning sleep. She heard rustling, presumably him closing up the book then she felt him stand up. Straining her ears and keeping her eyes closed, she listened to him walk across the tent floor, then more rustling. She guessed he was stowing her book back in her bag. For a long few moments silence filled the tent. Kyreen imagined Lang stood looking at her thinking she was sound asleep. Just before she gave in to her urge to open her eyes, a noise came at the tent entrance.

More rustling, then Aren said, "Good morn, Lang. Were you able to some sleep?"

"Enough," he answered. "Kyreen seemed to rest easy, which is good news."

"How are you feeling this morning?"

Lang paused a long moment before answering, "Try as I might I struggle with the image of Kyreen kissing Sten."

Kyreen fought to contain her reaction. Why would Lang bring up that kiss? She had not seen Sten since that night of the Festival when she had left him unconscious on the floor of the Archival Tent. Or had she? Kyreen focused on Aren's words as her cousin counseled Lang.

"Kyreen was enthralled. She had no control over her actions. There is a reason enthrallment is prohibited. It takes away a person's free will."

"I know," Lang responded. "But…"

"You cannot hold her responsible," Aren insisted. "As it is she broke free two times in a span of two days. In speaking with his mother and sister, neither of them were able to do that. Gisli only managed to awaken three times in the time he held her. Kyreen is stronger than most, but if she believes you hold her to blame or think she could have avoided Sten's enchantment, you may very well break her heart."

Kyreen wrestled to hold back the sob building up inside and rein in her emotions. Silent, hot tears leaked from her closed eyelids. Between the flashes of foggy memories and this eavesdropped conversation, Kyreen pieced together most of what had transpired. She struggled to contain her imagination from filling in the blanks.

"Come with me to fetch breakfast?" Aren's words may have framed into a question, but her tone did not. "Kyreen will be fine until we return."

Lang moved quietly but enough of their connection remained so his soft kiss to Kyreen's head did not startle her. A moment later she was alone in the tent. After another few heartbeats, Kyreen opened her eyes and cautiously sat up, then stood. Her body protested slightly after having been prone in one position for so long, but loosened up after a few quick stretches. Kyreen knew that soon she would need to exit the tent to relieve herself but for now she could wait. Gingerly her fingers once again explored the painful spot on her neck. Finally admitting she stalled and that she only had a few more minutes alone, Kyreen pulled up her tunic to inspect her torso. Hot tears sprang to her eyes, as she gazed down on the vast arrangement of bruising. This final fragment, coupled with the conversation Kyreen had just overheard and her fuzzy memories, allowed her to piece together the events of the previous two days. Resolutely Kyreen put down her shirt and sat back to wait.

When Aren and Lang returned, accompanied by Viggo, they were relieved to find Kyreen awake, alert and famished. Sitting on the edge of the cot eating her porridge, she tried to ignore the building tension in the room, but eventually felt the need to lower her bowl.

"I am feeling much better," she said, her gaze moving between the three faces. "I would feel even better if everyone would quit treating me like I might break. I will not. I promise."

"Does that mean you will be ready to leave for the trade meeting in the morn?" Aren asked, sipping her tea.

"No!" Lang exclaimed before Kyreen could respond. Both Viggo and Aren glanced sharply at him, but Kyreen kept her gaze firmly on Aren.

"Yes," she replied quietly. "I will be ready."

Aren nodded, prepared to begin talking details of the meeting. She knew when Kyreen was ready to discuss what had happened with Sten she would. For now, Aren had dozens of issues to deal with today, about five of which needed to be top priority.

Lang, however, had another idea. He shook his head at Aren. "This is wrong. You cannot seriously think to send Kyreen off now. Surely someone else can be sent in her stead. Kyreen is much too fragile. She cannot…"

"Watch yourself," Kyreen interrupted, her voice quiet and steely.

Lang stopped talking and looked at Kyreen. Over the last few weeks, since they had reconciled their differences, he had forgotten how quiet her voice got when she angered, how brightly her eyes glittered, or how tight her lips pressed together.

"You do not speak for me," Kyreen continued, glad to have her anger to grasp on to. It felt better than the self-pity. "We are not covenanted. Even then I would warn against it."

Viggo suppressed a smile, lifting his tea to his lips. He had only come to the tent this morning to check on Kyreen. From her reaction now, he had confidence she had begun to heal. She may not be whole for some time, but at least she was acting more like herself. He coughed quietly, rising to his feet.

"If you all will excuse me, I have duties to attend to," he said. Inclining his head to Kyreen, then Lang, he kissed his mate's cheek then exited before any could respond.

"Maybe I should leave, too," Lang mumbled, looking down at his empty bowl.

"You do as you feel you need," Kyreen replied. "Just as I will do as I feel I need."

He stood up and both women expected him to leave without speaking. He surprised them both, however, by walking over to Kyreen. Placing a soft kiss on the top of her head, he murmured, "I simply want what is best for you."

Both women remained quiet several moments after his departure, then Aren cleared her throat.

"So, Gladys?" she asked. "Are you sure?"

Kyreen nodded. "I think it may help to clear my head, get back to normal."

"I would appreciate you asking Rhun about the Galorian exodus," Aren said, pausing as though she wanted to say more.

"Yes?" Kyreen prompted.

"What will you tell him?"

Kyreen noticed Aren's wording left the 'him' undefined. She momentarily wondered if that had been purposeful, then decided it did not matter.

"I will tell Lang that I have made the decision to go," Kyreen asserted. She had no desire to discuss her relationship with Rhun, although from

Lang's comment, her relationship with the guild master had not been nearly the secret Kyreen had thought it to be. She ran a hand over her hair, realizing it probably looked a mess and needed braiding. She stood, saying, "If there is nothing else, I need to go clean up."

The rest of the day Kyreen spent in preparation for her impending trip. Aren had a bundle of documents prepared. A shipment of herbs was also packaged up to be delivered. As the meeting would be in Gladys, not Myrddin, Kyreen would not be taking any horses for sale, thus it had been decided she would travel alone. At least it had been the plan before the previous few days had transpired.

When Kyreen had been summoned to the Council Tent to get the trade documents, Lang followed her outside afterwards. Kyreen had discovered she could take limited trips outside of shielded tents before her headache would intensify. When he touched her elbow, she felt a reluctance to stop, not because of the pain in her head but her heart. She did not know what to say to him to erase the sadness in his eyes. She mourned their diminished connection, almost more than her lost memories. Keeping a hand on her elbow, Lang gestured for her to keep walking. The silence between them continued all the way back to the medical tent Kyreen had been using.

Kyreen breathed a quiet sigh of relief when the flap fell down. Crossing to the knapsack she had left on the cot, she carefully stowed the documents she had picked up from Aren. Turning she was not surprised to see Lang carefully watching her.

"Tell me what is on your mind," she said, mentally girding herself for a discussion about why she should stay here.

"I understand, maybe even agree, that you need to go to Gladys," Lang admitted, much to Kyreen's surprise. "What I cannot abide is you going alone."

Her anger, sitting just below the surface, erupted anew.

"Do you think me helpless?" she snapped, daring him to say the words out loud dreading that he might.

"No, it is not that at all," Lang said. "It is Sten's sorcery which concerns me."

"You think he will be back?" Kyreen asked, a ball of fear erupting in the pit of her stomach. Determinedly she lifted her chin. "I refuse to allow him to keep me cowering in this tent."

Lang resisted the urge to grab Kyreen by the shoulders and shake her. That man had stolen her away, his powers were strong, and given Kyreen's inexperience with magic, Lang did doubt she could protect herself from another attack. Not that he would ever say those words out loud.

Taking a deep cleansing breath, Lang tried once more. "When Viggo and I caught up with the two of you, we…I attempted to restrain Sten. Just the few seconds in which we grappled, he attempted to enthrall me. Fortunately, he decided to set off that incendiary device and escape. I felt the power of his magic and…"

When his voice trailed off and it became apparent Lang would not continue, Kyreen quietly asked, "And?"

Lang swallowed, licking his lips. "It frightened me. Now removed from the situation, by light of day, I feel a fool, but I also feel a coward."

Finally, he gave into the urge he had been holding back. Crossing the distance between them he wrapped his arms around Kyreen, pulling her close, relishing the feel of her against him. After a moment's hesitation, Kyreen slid her arms around Lang, returning the embrace.

For a long time, they stood there in each other's arms. Kyreen rested her head upon Lang's chest, listening to his steady heartbeat, soaking in his essence. Being in his arms provided her with more healing than any amount of sleep, food, or talk. The tenuous hold of control that she had been clinging onto seeped away. Her body began to tremble, slowly at first then escalating. Eventually, Lang sank down to the ground, pulling her into his lap, cradling and rocking her. As he held her, Lang felt his anxiety also slip away. When she finally pulled away so as to gaze into his eyes, her face surprisingly void of tears, they both felt drained, but their connection had returned, albeit weak. Lang had not realized until that moment how much a part of him their bond had become. Similar to the first time he had seen Kyreen last summer in the tent, something deep inside of Lang clicked into place.

Slowly Kyreen leaned up, reaching her lips to his, ignoring the tickle of fear squirming in the back of her mind. She kissed him tentatively at first. Then, when he responded in kind, she deepened the kiss, continuing until her emotions for Lang washed away that last tiny bit of fear. When finally, their lips parted, she hugged him tight. This time they embraced with more joy, less desperation.

"I have to go to this meeting," she finally spoke softly.

"I know," he replied.

"You may request from Aren that I do not travel alone," she added quietly. "It is true he may decide to show up."

Lang tightened his arms around her, relief flooding his body. "Thank you."

PART III

In the end, Kyreen rode out of camp the following morning accompanied by the magic user Brigit who had spelled the tent. Aren felt that since the woman already knew a portion of what had transpired she would be a good candidate.

"Besides," Aren said as she walked with Kyreen and Lang to Kyreen's horse, "she has the added benefit that magic slides off her. She is immune to it."

Both Kyreen and Lang gave Aren a startled look. The Calanian leader had chuckled softly. "Please do not share that information around."

Now heading towards the border, Kyreen had doubts about her decision to travel to Gladys. Resolutely she pushed back those thoughts. Sten was not the only danger in these woods. Running into a Galorian patrol could prove just as disastrous.

Though Brigit looked to be closer to Aren's age, maybe a couple of years older, she deferred to Kyreen, allowing the younger woman to set the pace and choose the route. Having a companion made Kyreen a little more watchful on top of her initial concerns which kept wiggling back into her thoughts. All in all, relief coursed through Kyreen when the road out of Calan came into view and she stopped to check in with the guard for an update.

"There have been no patrols through here today," Kyreen commented to Brigit as they resumed their journey. "So, if you and your mount do not object I would like to speed up a bit."

At Brigit's nod, Kyreen spurred her gelding forward. As he settled into his familiar distance eating lope she relaxed a bit in the saddle, letting her mind drift a little to her tasks ahead. Before she knew it the little village of Gladys came into view.

Pulling up, Kyreen slid off her horse before they entered the town proper. She gestured for Brigit to dismount as well. Galorian patrols had rarely ventured into town or frequented the establishments here but Kyreen preferred to exert caution. It had been Rhun's connections from the guild which permitted them to meet at the village's only inn which also served as its only pub as well. Kyreen vaguely remembered that the innkeeper's wife's nephew was a guild member. Although she could not recall all the details, Kyreen did not wish to bring trouble down on this proprietor.

When all in the streets appeared normal, Kyreen took them to the stable across the street from the inn. Inside, being rubbed down, was a steel gray gelding with a black mane and tail. Seeing it caused Kyreen's pulse to quicken nervously before noticing the wide white blaze striping the animal's forehead. For a second Kyreen had thought it to be Collin's horse. She did not think she could handle seeing him right now. Thinking of Collin reminded Kyreen she had not written a letter to Engla. She shook her head to clear away the cobwebs.

The stable master approached and Kyreen focused on securing board and feed for their two horses. Once negotiations had concluded Brigit offered to stay to oversee care of the horses.

"That way if you like, you can greet the guild master," the older woman suggested.

Kyreen thanked the mage and exited the stables. As she crossed the road, however, her feet slowed. At the base of the steps leading up to the inn, she came to a complete standstill. Nibbling at her bottom lip, Kyreen stared at the unopened door. Her stomach churned, reminding Kyreen that they had not stopped for midday meal. Although now, as her nerves surfaced, that decision may have been a blessing. Hoisting the bag draped over her arm up onto her shoulder, Kyreen steeled herself and entered the inn.

Calling the establishment an inn might have been an exaggeration. Formerly a private residence, the front rooms had been gutted to create one big space throughout which a jumble of mismatched furniture – tables and chairs – had been littered. On the far wall, across from the door in which Kyreen entered sat a large hutch upon which morning meals would be lain out. Flanking the hutch sat two doors, both feeding into the kitchen in the back of the building. To Kyreen's right a flight of stairs led to the upper floors. One floor up housed the meeting rooms, one of which Rhun would have booked for their discussions, along with two suites, one of which he also secured for his use.

Kyreen knew Rhun's decisions to rent these spaces had nothing to do with the guild master's ego but with his generosity. While he would have been content in a small single bed room from one of the upper floors and to meet Kyreen in the public ground level area, he and his guild had the funds to pay for these other spaces and, with the remote nature of the village, Rhun's money had become a welcome injection of income not just for the inn but many other vendors like the baker, stable master, and vegetable peddler, to name a few.

Recalling Rhun's generous nature gave Kyreen courage to turn her gaze to the left, where the massive stone fireplace held a crackling fire lit more for ambiance than for heat. Grouped haphazardly about the hearth sat several comfortable arm chairs of varying size and color. In one particularly large wingback chair covered in a blue floral pattern, the fabric on the chair's arms fraying around the edges, sat Rhun reading a book.

The door swung shut behind Kyreen, casting the dining area into shadows as the windows facing the street had never been expanded when the interior had been converted and did not permit much natural light in. With the bell over the door chiming, she knew he had to have heard her arrival so she stood in place a moment allowing her eyes to adjust, and waiting for him to acknowledge her presence.

From his seat by the fire, Rhun finished scanning the paragraph he had been reading before Kyreen's entrance. He merely scanned because he knew he would not remember any word he saw after hearing the inn door open. Rhun had been looking forward to this meeting for some time, since Kyreen's last departure from Myrddin if he were being honest. He had concerns at times about how much he enjoyed Kyreen's company and how much she occupied his thoughts in her absence. Glancing up her beauty, as always, struck him, then he noted the dark circles under her eyes and the tight grip of her hand on the bag slung across her shoulder, reminding Rhun not for the first time how vastly different their lives were.

While Rhun's position as the guild master had its stresses, most of the job had settled into a daily routine, and very rarely, as in never, had it been life threatening. He knew the same could not be said for the life Kyreen lived. In addition to the hostile Galorian soldiers, her people had to survive the elements and dangers of their nomadic lives in the elements of the Calanian wilderness.

Realizing she waited for him to make the first move, Rhun marked his place in the book before rising to his feet. Something in the way she stood, in her wide green eyes, in her paler than normal complexion warned the big man to approach with caution, when all he truly wished to do was throw his arms around her for a hearty greeting. Rhun instead extended both hands toward Kyreen, forcing her to reciprocate the gesture, unclenching her death grip on the bag. Discarding his first instinct to bring her hands to his lips at Kyreen's visible flinch when their skin touched, Rhun instead gave her icy fingers a warm squeeze saying, "Good afternoon, Kyreen. I did not expect you so early."

Before he could stop himself, Rhun leaned in to place a chaste kiss upon her cheek. Pulling back, he registered her almost imperceptible flinch and felt the tightening of her body.

"We made good time," Kyreen replied, slipping her hands from his grasp so as to once again squeeze the strap of her satchel.

We? Rhun wondered. Only when delivering horses to Myrddin had Kyreen travelled with companions. Watching her now, he decided his questions could wait as Kyreen looked as though she might bolt back through the door at any second. So, he smiled and with a soft hand to her elbow propelled her towards one of the kitchen doors.

"Which means you most likely skipped a meal," he said. "Let us find Guenther or Hilde. I am sure they can fix us some food."

Allowing Rhun to move her through into the kitchen without protesting, Kyreen relaxed, feeling immense gratitude for the guild master on so many levels, but mostly for his lack of questions. The purity of his concern for her, too, void of any pity, felt so refreshing. Kyreen was glad now that she had made the choice to come to Gladys. A few minutes later, seated back in the dining area, a plate full of food before her, Kyreen experienced more gratitude for the guild master, for she had not realized how famished she was.

The bell over the door sounded, announcing Brigit's arrival. Kyreen paused her meal for the introductions, then Rhun disappeared into the kitchen to procure an additional plate for the newly arrived Calanian.

"Everything well with the horses?" Kyreen inquired, spreading a thick layer of berry jam on a thick slice of bread.

"Yes," Brigit answered, her gaze moving around the room.

Kyreen could not discern if the mage looked for something specific or was merely taking in the hodge podge of furniture and decorations adorning the space. Figuring the spell caster could speak to her if she had questions, Kyreen turned her attention back to her food.

"This area appears safe," Brigit announced a moment later. "I will need to inspect your meeting space and sleeping accommodations."

As Kyreen looked around, wondering belatedly what exactly made the space safe, Brigit dug into her bag, pulling out an oddly shaped stone attached to a leather string. At first the stone appeared to be milk white but when the light struck it, the stone began to shimmer with iridescent sparks. Brigit extended the necklace to Kyreen.

"I ask that you wear this for when I am not present. I apologize I did not think to give it to you before you came over here earlier," she said as Kyreen took the necklace, pulling the leather cord over her head. "The opal is spelled to alert me if magic is performed on you."

Kyreen smelled the magic of the amulet as it settled against her bare skin. With a clenching of her fists, she quelled the terror that rose inside of her with that aroma. Fortunately, Brigit's protection magic smelled slightly different than whatever black magic Sten had performed, so Kyreen was saved the embarrassment of a full-on panic attack.

Walking through the door with Brigit's food, Rhun witnessed Kyreen tucking the necklace under her shirt. He glanced back at Kyreen's companion, figuring her to be a spellcaster, which made more sense than Brigit being Kyreen's guard. It had been very apparent to him that Brigit had little experience in defense. While both Kyreen and Rhun had gravitated to seats backing to the fireplace, Brigit had taken the chair directly facing Kyreen. Thus, the woman now sat with her back not only to the stairs but also with all doors outside her range of vision.

Setting the plate of food down before the mage, Rhun wondered why Kyreen travelled with a spellcaster. Though technically the use of magic in the realm had been outlawed generations ago, people still casted. Prohibiting magic was akin to prohibiting breathing. The laws could be passed but the people would continue the practice. Admittedly one had to be careful how and when and in who's presence one practiced magic, though, as the rewards for turning in a suspected mage were inviting. Hence the authorities offered an additional bonus reward if the suspect is discovered in the act of performing magic. This helped to lessen the number of false reports submitted by disgruntled customers or jilted lovers looking to lash out with hurt feelings.

Settling back down in his chair, Rhun picked up his mug of ale, having opted for a liquid refreshment, and took a sip. Before the silence at the table could escalate to uncomfortable, he set his dark eyes on Brigit, saying. "Is this your first visit to the fair village of Gladys?"

"Yes, it is," came the response.

For several minutes Rhun led the conversation with Brigit, letting their talking about mundane topics fill the air. When Rhun mentioned dinner for that evening Brigit had shook her head pushing away her empty plate.

"No dinner for me tonight," she replied. "This food here will suffice. I cannot recall having ever eaten so much in one sitting. Right now, all I want is to retire to my room after I spell Kyreen's quarters and the meeting room. Then I have some reading to do."

"Which reminds me," Rhun commented getting to his feet. "I need to speak with Guenther about your accommodations. Only a single room had been reserved."

"I hope he will be able to find room for you, Brigit, else you may have to bunk with one of us," the guild master quipped, glancing around the room. Then he added with a wink, "On second thought, it might be more enjoyable if all the rooms are booked up."

Both women chuckled. Watching Rhun walk towards the kitchen, Brigit waited until the door closed behind him before turning to Kyreen with a mischievous grin.

"Now for an outsider, that man is extremely good-looking and charming," she told Kyreen, keeping her volume low. "I cannot help but wonder how he would compare to one of our own in lovemaking."

Kyreen, in the process of finishing her mug of tea, nearly choked. Her face flushed red as she coughed to clear her airway. She wondered if Brigit knew of the past which Kyreen and Rhun shared. If she did not, Kyreen was not going to illuminate the spell caster otherwise so she merely shrugged with a shake of her head, still clearing her throat.

"I may investigate myself," Brigit commented with another furtive glance at the door through which Rhun had disappeared before looking back at Kyreen, "unless of course you have plans."

"Not those type of plans," Kyreen admitted, taking a big gulp of her lukewarm tea.

Fortunately, Rhun returned shortly with the innkeeper who took Kyreen and Brigit up to their single bed rooms on the third floor. Rhun had given up trying to get Kyreen to take the other second floor suite, though he did insist on paying all the expenses for the Calanian people as part of their negotiated contract. Had he offered simply to pay Kyreen's expenses, she would have found a way out of it, but that he included all Calanians, she did not. Her people needed all the revenue possible from their business dealings and Kyreen refused to allow her pride to hurt the people's limited resources.

Once her belongings had been deposited in the small room, Kyreen exited her room, finding Brigit walking up the hallway.

"I need to check your room for reflecting surface," Brigit explained. "Then I would like to ward it with a protection spell."

Kyreen nodded without comment, unlocking her room door to allow the woman passage, saying, "I will ask Rhun which meeting room we are using tomorrow."

Brigit gave a wave, her attention focused on the task before her.

Kyreen found the guild master back in the blue wingback chair, though the book rested unopened in his lap. She paused on the landing to look at him for a moment. Brigit had been correct. Rhun was good looking. His smooth ebony skin glowed in the firelight, his profile highlighting his strong chin, sensual lips and high cheekbones. She knew his eyes, now trained on the merrily crackling fire, to be warm dark pools that saw so much more than the big man ever let on. She further knew the body under his clothes to be toned and muscled. A smile flitted across her face and her cheeks flushed at her memories of his body, his hands, his mouth. Shaking her head, Kyreen resumed her descent into the common area.

Rhun glanced her way, noting both the blush and the smile. As he rose to his feet, his concern for Kyreen rested in the shadows darkening her gaze. That she could look upon him with both that smile and such sadness in her emerald eyes made him continue his cautious manner.

"Brigit would like to see the room we will be using tomorrow," she said.

"Of course, let me show you," he responded.

Together they ascended to the second floor. As they entered one of the meeting rooms, Brigit appeared from the third floor. While the caster gazed around the room, Kyreen remembered the borrowed book.

When she mentioned it, and offered to fetch it from her room, Rhun said, "That sounds good. I have a few things for you as well. Meet me in my quarters when you are available?"

Brigit glanced over her shoulder at the two talking in the doorway. "I am fine. Neither of you need to stay around," she said. Kyreen could not tell if there was anything behind the magic user's words. Deciding she was simply being paranoid, Kyreen hurried upstairs to fetch Rhun's book. When she entered her room, the lingering scent of fresh magic assaulted Kyreen's senses, triggering a panic attack.

Closing her eyes, Kyreen silently recited her daily meditations until the tremors left her body. So, anxious to be away from the magic, Kyreen realized halfway back to the stairway that she had neglected to retrieve the book from her pack and had to return to the room.

Chapter 34

When Kyreen's tentative knock sounded at his door, Rhun let loose the breath he had been holding. Kyreen had taken so much time in retrieving the book he had begun to wonder if she had decided not to return, or worse taken off as he had feared she would since she first entered the inn. When he opened the door, Kyreen looked even paler than she had downstairs. Reflexively he placed a hand on her shoulder, drawing her into the room.

Once the door had closed, he turned to watch her move across the room. After setting the book down on the desk beside the stack of books and white pastry box Rhun had set out, she turned around as if to leave. Looking a bit surprised to see him leaning against the door, Kyreen took a tentative step back, a hand nervously rubbing at the back of her neck, her gaze roaming around the room as she avoided his eyes.

"Did you enjoy the book?" he asked.

"Yes, it was good."

"How about that ending?"

"It was fine."

"It was fine," Rhun repeated without inflection. He apprised her a moment then said, "May I ask you something, Kyreen?"

"Of course," she responded, her stomach churning dreading what he might ask.

"Do you consider us to be friends?"

Taken aback, Kyreen blinked at him. "Friends?"

"Yes," Rhun nodded, crossing his arms. "Am I your friend?"

"Yes, of course," she responded nervously, unsure what he meant.

"Good to know. I wanted to make sure before I asked my next question," he paused as though waiting for a response from her. When none appeared to be forthcoming, he continued. "Why are you travelling with a magical escort?"

"Much has happened since we last saw each other," she finally replied, twisting her hands together.

"So I gathered," Rhun commented, his gaze dropping to her hands. "How about you fill me in?"

"Very well..."

Rhun held up a hand saying, "Over on the couch where we can get comfortable. That is if I can move away from this door and you promise not to bolt."

Kyreen chuckled, the sound warming Rhun's heart. She nodded and moved to sit on the far end of the couch, her cheeks reddening again as she remembered the last time she and Rhun had occupied this sofa together.

Rhun took a seat on the opposite side of the couch, ensuring enough space between them that he would not involuntarily reach out to touch her and send her dashing.

"There is so much," she said quietly, almost to herself. "I am not sure where to start."

"The beginning is always good," Rhun encouraged, struggling not to show his impatience. He had seen this sort of behavior before and, in his experience, a man was always to blame. It disheartened Rhun to think a man could be responsible for the change in the vivacious, sensual woman who had departed his bed just a few weeks prior. He had believed Kyreen to be impervious such a thing.

Closing her eyes, Kyreen thought back over the last two months. Surely it had been longer than two months? She remembered the tournament which seemed another lifetime ago. Then she noticed Rhun gazing at her, waiting for her to speak.

"Now it seems so inconsequential," she said quietly, "but I won the annual tournament, over all the other trainees."

"That sounds impressive," Rhun replied. "Hardly inconsequential. The guild holds such tournaments frequently. Good for morale and bonds the men."

So Kyreen told Rhun about the events that made up the tournament. He listened attentively, making comments, asking questions, laughing where appropriate. As she spoke, Kyreen's anxiety lessened, her body relaxed, and some of the shadows left her eyes.

"So, after you won," Rhun said, "your prize was exception from camp chores?"

"That is correct," Kyreen nodded.

"What did you do with your spare time?"

The smile on her face dropped a little, but Rhun noticed her eyes remained lively. Two red spots appeared on her cheeks, and her face rearranged into a sheepish expression. Whatever it was she had to say was an embarrassment but not what caused her anxiety. He waited while she formed her response, almost certain what she was about to reveal, although the 'who' surprised him immensely. Not much surprised Rhun.

"I have...I mean...I spent it with someone," she finally said, adding so softly Rhun thought he had misheard, "Lang."

His eyebrows arched and he barely controlled a laugh of disbelief. "I beg your pardon? I believe I heard you wrong. Who?"

"Lang," she responded, still almost inaudible.

This time Rhun did not hold back. He threw back his head and guffawed. His laughter was contagious and soon Kyreen was laughing alongside him. They continued for a long time. When the chortling would die down, their eyes would meet and the peals of laughter would resume.

Finally, she wiped her eyes and choked back the last chuckles. Taking a deep breath, Kyreen smiled over at Rhun.

"Thank you," she said. "I needed that."

He nodded his head, his dark eyes twinkling and his lips twitching as though he might start laughing again until she added, "I was worried to tell you. I thought it might...I thought you would...that we might no longer be friends."

Rhun leaned forward placing a hand gently on her knee. "That would be a travesty. I value your friendship immensely and would be loath to throw it away just because you have found someone to love."

He sat back asking, "It is love, is it not?"

Kyreen thought on the question, nibbling at her bottom lip, before nodding. "I believe it is," she replied. "You are not disappointed?"

"I will not lie. I do enjoy our physical exploits," he paused to enjoy her fresh blush, "but we knew from the beginning that is all it could ever be. You would not do well living in Myrddin and I would never move to Calan. It is just how things are. As I said, I value having you as a friend, especially now that I am guild master and I supervise the few men I can still call friend."

"Thank you again," she replied softly, swallowing the lump in her throat.

"Now," Rhun said, the smile leaving his face, his voice quiet. "Will you tell me what is wrong?"

For a long time, she stared at him, her entire body still. He watched as the shadows crept back into her eyes, then she began to tremble. Restraining his urge to comfort her, verbally or physically, Rhun waited until she finally answered. It took her three tries to find her voice, even then she spoke so low he had to strain to hear her words.

"I want to, truly I do," she said, her eyes filling with hot tears that spilt in fat drops as she spoke, "but I cannot remember."

"Then tell me what you know," he replied, his stomach tightening.

"Someone enthralled me and took me away from camp. We think he was taking me to Galor but he escaped when Viggo and Lang caught up," she explained. Rhun noticed she kept her fists tightly balled in her lap, her tone carefully level.

"Someone?" he inquired. "Someone you knew?"

She nodded, "Yes, but not well. His name is Sten. He is a bard and Synnove's brother."

"Your tentmate's brother enthralled and abducted you?"

Kyreen nodded.

"What are you leaving unsaid?" he asked, careful to keep his reactions under control.

"I awoke a couple of times. Once the first morning after he first enthralled me when we were still in camp and then on the second evening in the forest right before Viggo and Lang showed up, but…"

"But?" Rhun prompted.

"There was one other time that I have not told anyone about," she struggled to get the words out, her voice dropping to a faint whisper. "It was the second morning. We were on the trail, in the woods. I woke up…"

"You woke up," Rhun said quietly.

"I was…I was alone, but…" she closed her eyes, afraid to say the words aloud. Because until she spoke the words aloud she could pretend it had never happened. "…I was naked."

They sat in silence while Kyreen's words hung in the air between them.

"There are times mostly at night when I am almost asleep that I have these flashes of… images… of him, of me, of us," she finally continued speaking. "But the images are not the worst part. The worst part is how I feel when those images flash through my head."

She paused again, her body trembling even more. Finally, she took a big breath and continued. "I felt then, and feel now when I have these images…happy."

"Happy?"

"Yes," she nodded. "Like I am the luckiest person in the world. Overjoyed to be…that he wants me. I have this…this insane thought…"

Rhun waited patiently, watching her internal struggle reflected in her face. Familiar with Kyreen's empathic nature, he kept his own face impassive, his body relaxed, and wrangled back his emotions so she could not feel the anger searing inside of him.

"It will sound ludicrous," Kyreen shrugged.

"Try me," Rhun encouraged quietly.

"I keep thinking…" she cast her gaze towards the ceiling, "Oh by the goddess, that he and I make a…a beautiful and powerful couple."

With the words out, the tears began to flow in earnest. Kyreen turned to face Rhun on the couch, her expression despondent. Slowly he opened his arms in silent invitation. Without speaking she scooted into his embrace, relaxing against him as her tears soaked through his shirt.

Sometime later a knock at the door roused Rhun. He closed the book he had been pretending to read, placing it on a side table. Glancing down at the now sleeping Kyreen, stretched out on the couch, her head resting in his lap, he carefully extricated himself. The woman slept soundly, never moving. Quietly Rhun moved to the door, opening it just enough to see the innkeeper with a tray of food that Rhun had forgotten he requested be sent at sunset.

"Good eve, Guenther," the guild master said in hushed tones. "If you could give me a moment?"

The innkeeper nodded. "Of course, sir."

Rhun slid the door closed quietly. Then he crossed over to the couch and gingerly slid his arms under Kyreen. Standing, grateful that she slumbered on, he carried her into the bedroom. After setting her down and covering her with an extra blanket from the cupboard, he eased shut the door between the bedroom and the parlor. Giving a quiet sigh, Rhun crossed over to allow the innkeeper access to the suite, his stomach rumbling quietly looking forward to enjoying the meal.

Rhun had just placed the last chunk of bread in his mouth when the door to the hallway burst open. Before the intruder had stepped two paces into the room, Rhun was there, a dagger in one hand, his other wrapped around Brigit's neck. Recognizing the Calanian before striking, Rhun withdrew his hand, but kept the dagger ready.

"That was foolish," he commented mildly, after swallowing the bread he had been chewing.

"Where is she? The princess?" Brigit asked, her eyes frantic.

"Kyreen?" Rhun looked towards the closed door separating the parlor from the bedroom. "In there. Asleep."

Brigit rushed to the door, flinging it open just as she had the hall door. Rhun, ready to threaten the mage if she woke Kyreen, tensed, spying a shadow lurking beside the bed bent over a still sleeping Kyreen. As he rushed forward, pushing past Brigit, Rhun registered the shadow to be a cloaked man, who now stood upright, one hand stroking Kyreen's cheek. As Rhun reached the foot of the bed, the man looked up drawing the guild master into his blue-eyed gaze. Rhun felt himself slowing down, coming to a complete standstill.

Then the cloaked stranger yelped as if in pain, turning his gaze to the doorway where Brigit had just thrown a spell. Rhun gasped as the connection between them was severed. The stranger hissed something in a language Rhun had never heard then dissipated into smoky tendrils that snaked over to the sideboard table disappearing into the porcelain bowl.

"Rhun? Brigit? What is happening?" A groggy Kyreen asked, sitting up on the bed, rubbing her neck.

Brigit rushed to the washstand. After peering into the bowl, she growled angrily, her hand sweeping it to the floor shattering the porcelain and spilling water over the rug. The mage spun around angrily stalking to the bed.

"How am I to keep you safe if you lie to me?" she ranted. "I asked you downstairs about him. You said you were not interested. You did not have to lie to me."

Rhun realized the 'him' Brigit referred to was himself, not the cloaked figure. Seeing Kyreen's confusion he stepped in, saying, "Maybe you could calm down? She did not lie. Her nap here was unplanned."

Brigit spun on Rhun as he had intended. In his opinion, he was much more better equipped to diffuse the mage's anger right now than Kyreen.

"This is not your affair," Brigit said. "It concerns the Princess and…"

"Do not call me that," Kyreen commanded angrily, swinging her legs around to sit on the edge of the bed. "And do not speak to him in that manner. He is a friend."

"He is an outsider," the caster spit out the word like poison, turning her gaze to Kyreen.

"So am I," Kyreen replied quietly. "I am not the Princess. Not anymore. Are you working with Sten?"

Brigit straightened, visibly surprised by the question. "If you are asking me if I participated in his enthrallment, then no. If you are asking if I am working to keep Aren from taking the throne, then I must answer yes. It is no secret."

Kyreen blinked at the straightforwardness of Brigit's answer. "Aren knows you conspire against her, yet she sent you with me to keep me safe?"

Rhun stood back, leaning against the doorframe. Kyreen's royal status had slipped from his mind over these past few months. Just another reason their relationship could never advance. He did not envy her the path she had to walk. Politics was never easy, especially for someone like Kyreen who had no desire to participate in the first place.

"Aren knows I work to have you crowned," Brigit was saying. "So she knows I will keep you from harm…if you let me."

"Would one of you tell me what happened?" Kyreen asked, her gaze moving between the two.

Rhun continued his silent observation as Brigit explained how the amulet had alerted her to the magic. First, she had checked Kyreen's quarters, then the downstairs dining area, before making it back up to Rhun's suite. Brigit's and Rhun's eyes met as she skipped over the part where Brigit barged in and Rhun very nearly killed her.

"What I want to know," Brigit concluded, "is how he found you. Checking for portals was just a safety protocol. Without a talisman, he should not be able to transpire here, to find you."

"A talisman?" Kyreen asked, pulling the amulet given her by Brigit out from under her shirt. "This is the only jewelry I wear."

"It could be something as small as a pebble," Brigit said, speaking more to herself. "Clearly not in your knapsack. That is upstairs. Possibly something in a pocket? Something personal. Something he gave you. Something that allows his magic to bring him to you."

"What about the bite mark on her neck?" Rhun asked from his position in the doorway.

Both women looked at him, speaking simultaneously.

"The what?" asked Brigit.

"It is a bite mark?" Kyreen said, raising her hand to her neck again.

"I noticed it after you fell asleep in there...on the couch," Rhun indicated to the parlor with a jerk of his thumb and a pointed look to Brigit, then peered at Kyreen, his voice softening. "I guess there is a little more to the story?"

"I did not know what it was," Kyreen responded quietly.

Brigit moved over to Kyreen, gently pushing aside the ebony plait and lowering Kyreen's shirt collar to fully expose the angry red mark. After muttering a stream of obscenities that would have done any of Rhun's guildmates proud, the mage nodded. "Yes, I believe this could work as the connection."

"That wound is fresh now," Rhun reported, struggling to hide his concern. "When Kyreen was asleep before he arrived, it was partially healed, mainly dark bruising."

Brigit looked like she wanted to break something else. Instead she stood upright and took a deep cleansing breath. When her eyes opened, she appeared much calmer.

"Kyreen, I can put together a poultice that applied to the mark might help to block Sten's magic so he can no longer locate you," she said, then paused glancing at Rhun then to Kyreen. "To be honest, everything Sten is doing, the enthrallments, the location spell, transpiring across the realm, that is all theoretical. We are mainly practitioners of protection wards. Only recently we were able to work out effective healing spells. Nothing we do is like this magic Sten has access to. I do not know if I have any protection that will stop him."

"If he becomes solid I can slow him down," Rhun said. "Just tell me how to keep away from his spells."

"Avoid his gaze and bare skin contact," Brigit replied. "Though I would prefer he have no access to the...Kyreen."

Rhun's lips twitched as though he had heard something funny, then he responded, "I would prefer my dagger at his throat and his blood upon the floor, but I can accept either of these two scenarios."

He pushed his body off the doorframe, rubbing his hands together. "Alright then what is the plan?"

"I have the components for the poultice in my room," Brigit said. "It will take me about an hour to prepare it. I presume Kyreen will be staying here for the night."

Rhun looked to Kyreen who said, "If you do not mind."

He grinned at Brigit, "You presume correctly."

"Then I will bring it up here and also cast a few protection spells."

Rhun caught Brigit's elbow as she walked by him towards the door. "I would not speak so freely about magic outside this room," he suggested.

"Understood," she answered.

Releasing Brigit, Rhun looked down at the pieces of the shattered bowl and the soaked rug. "Now I need to figure out what to tell Guenther about this."

From the hall door, Brigit called out, "Tell him I threw it in a fit of anger upon finding Kyreen in your bed."

Rhun turned to look at the mage, her hand poised on the knob. She arched her eyebrows, adding mischievously, "He will have no trouble believing that. Besides, it is the truth!"

Then she winked and slipped out. Chuckling Rhun turned back to Kyreen still sitting on the bed. "Saucy," he grinned. "Are all Calanian women?"

"You have no idea," Kyreen smiled. She stood and moved over to the porcelain shards scattered on the rug. Rhun intercepted her before she could begin picking up the pieces.

"No, leave it be," he said, steering her into the front room. "I will not have 'The Kyreen' toiling away like a common chamber maid."

Kyreen shook her head, laughing. "I wondered if you would catch that. I am mildly surprised you did not say something."

"I almost did," Rhun replied, releasing his hold on her elbow, gesturing for Kyreen to take a seat on couch. "But your little mage seemed a mite agitated."

Kyreen glanced over Rhun's abandoned plate asking, "Anything good here?"

Rhun paused in the doorway to the bedroom. "All the food here is good, when it is fresh and hot," he replied. "I can fetch another plate or there is a box on the desk you may want to look in. You missed seeing it when you arrived earlier."

She flashed him a bright smile, which would have delighted him had it not been for those dark circles that remained under her eyes. He watched her for a moment as she perched on the edge of the desk, carefully untying the twine on the white box. The look in Kyreen's eyes when she lifted the chocolate covered pastry to her mouth, followed by her soft moan as the sweet confectionary disappeared, brought the first true smile to Rhun's face since Kyreen had walked into the inn earlier that day.

Chapter 35

The rest of the evening passed without incident. Rhun suggested Kyreen take the bed in the bedroom and he would sleep on the couch, but she insisted he stay in the same room with her. Dawn found him dozing on the bed, fully clothed, with Kyreen snuggled against him. They had talked long into the night about books and guild politics, about anything except what had occurred in Calan and earlier that evening. The third time Kyreen drifted off, Rhun had insisted she take off her boots and slide under the covers. He had known how tired Kyreen was when she did not comment on the fresh lilac scent of the linens.

Now, in the predawn shadows, he pondered her predicament. In light of all she had going on in her life right now, their meeting to discuss the contract between the Calanians and his guild seemed trivial. Rhun knew he should cut the meeting short, send Kyreen back, but he was being selfish, wanting her to remain here.

Kyreen stirred, sleepily. Raising her head, she grinned at him. "Morning."

"Good morning," he responded, giving her a quick one-arm hug before slipping off the bed.

She watched him, instantly missing the warmth of his body. Sitting up, she ruffled a hand through her loose curls before swinging her legs around. Bending over the edge of the bed she found her boots and began tugging them on. She could not believe how much better she felt this morning. Part of the reason was the poultice Brigit had applied to the bite mark had taken the sting out of the wound. For the first time in days, it did not ache. But the main reason for her good feelings was Rhun. Though they would no long be lovers, he had proven himself a good friend last night. She realized with a start that he had somehow become her best friend. So much of Kyreen's life had to be shielded from Engla, not to mention the complication of Collin being Engla's husband. As for Synnove, Kyreen still had not decided how to break the news to her about Sten's recent activities.

Drawing on her final boot, she glanced at Rhun leaning on the door frame. Through her mop of hair, she flashed him a smile.

"What?" he asked.

"Nothing," she answered, rising to her feet. "I was just thinking how grateful I am for you."

She walked over to stand before him, taking both of his hands in hers. Gazing up at his face she said, "Thank you for everything."

Rhun gazed down at her, so many things running through his head that he wanted to say. In the end, he simply pulled her to him for a tight hug saying, "You may not be so happy with me after I tell you I think you should leave."

She tensed up in his arms. "Why leave?" she asked.

"I think your place is in Calan," he answered. "We can look over the documents during breakfast, but there is nothing urgent."

Kyreen thought about his suggestion. In light of all that had been happening, he was probably right. She sighed and he knew she would consent.

"Just one thing, that is rather urgent and more than a little strange," she said, remembering the Galorian issue.

As they walked downstairs to breakfast Kyreen explained about the mysterious transports out of Galor and the theories of the Council. Rhun had not heard any news from Galor, but as he pointed out none of his guild's contracts had ships sailing that far north. He speculated the ships were either going across the Great Sea or maybe to a port other than Myrddin.

"When we next meet, I should have some information for you," he said, in between mouthfuls of scrambled eggs. "Unless I feel you should know sooner."

"That would be excellent," Kyreen replied as she spotted Brigit coming down the stairs. "Let me go let Brigit know about our change in plans."

Shortly after midday, the two women had packed up and were ready to ride back to Calan. Brigit bade Rhun farewell then discreetly mounted her horse and began walking it towards the edge of town.

Rhun and Kyreen watched Brigit for a moment without speaking. Kyreen, already thinking about the journey ahead, Rhun wondering what else might be waiting to test Kyreen, how much would change before their next meeting. When she turned to him, he placed a hand on the scabbard fastened to her gelding's saddle, his expression somber.

"You carry your sword," he said, "but not always on your person."

She nodded without comment.

"If I may make one request of you," he paused until she nodded. "You would do well to keep yourself armed no matter how safe you feel you might be."

"You are correct," she responded, her eyes drifting to the tri colored hilt.

Rhun pulled her to him, wrapping his arms around her for a tight embrace, whispering in her ear, "And when he shows up, kill him straight away. I felt his power. He is not to be trifled with. Do not hesitate."

Kyreen hugged the big man tight, reluctant to bid him farewell, but feeling the pull back to Calan. "Thank you so very much," she told him, "for everything."

"Safe journeys," he murmured, placing a kiss on her forehead.

Kyreen swung up into the saddle, cast Rhun a final farewell smile, then urged the gelding into a jog to catch up with her travelling companion. For the rest of the afternoon the two rode their horses hard, pushing to reach the Calan border before sunset. Since the Council Camp's move would prevent them from making camp by nightfall, the two women camped the night at the border with the two guards, one of whom happened to be a former classmate of Brigit's. While the others stayed up late reminiscing Kyreen turned in early hoping to catch up on some sleep, but she spent the night tossing and turning, every noise in the forest waking her, so that by morning she felt horrible once again. Before they headed out Brigit changed the poultice, commenting to Kyreen that the bite mark had begun healing without signs of infection.

As the two rode into Council Camp, Kyreen's headache returned, but not as severe as it had been on her previous visit. Still Brigit noticed the tightness around Kyreen's eyes as Kyreen tried pushing back the pain.

"Do not fight it," Brigit suggested. "Let it flow over you, just run off. I could teach you some healing spells that might help although they only address minor injuries."

"Thank you," Kyreen replied, "I would say it might be worth a try but I cannot perform a simple illumination spell so maybe not."

"Illumination magic, really?" Brigit asked. "Do you know why you cannot?"

"I have not given it much thought, considering all that has been happening," Kyreen shrugged.

"If you are willing, I could work with you," Brigit offered.

Kyreen paused in the unsaddling of her gelding to gaze at the older woman. Now that Kyreen knew of Brigit's allegiances, she was reluctant to accept any help from the mage. On the other hand, if Kyreen could break through this magic block, she may be better equipped to deal with Sten. She knew physically he could not harm her. It was his magic which made him so dangerous and powerful. She grimaced. Thinking the word 'powerful' conjured up images not fitting on such a sunny spring morning.

"I would be willing," Kyreen finally replied, "but Aren will know of what we do."

"I would not wish it otherwise," Brigit answered. "I do not equivocate or play in shadows."

After unpacking their gear and caring for the horses, the two women started walking towards the Council Tent. They had not taken more than a dozen steps before Lang met them. Without speaking he drew Kyreen in for a long embrace.

Behind Lang's back, Brigit gave him an appraising look over before grinning playfully at Kyreen, still encased in the man's embrace. "I do give you a nod for your taste in men, Kyreen. Scrumptious!"

Kyreen, becoming accustomed to the mage's bawdy comments, rolled her eyes. She hoped Lang would not take offense.

"I will leave you be," Brigit waved. "I need to check in with the head practitioner."

Kyreen gave the mage a wave, then relaxed against Lang. That he had not hesitated, had not gazed at her with sad eyes, did not hold back his emotions now, made her feel at peace. Though she could sense his concern amongst his feelings, it no longer dominated his emotions.

Pulling back to greet him verbally, Kyreen found herself unable to as he pressed his lips to hers. The kiss melted away all other thoughts, making her weak-kneed.

When they finally parted, Lang softly brushed a stray curl from her cheek, saying, "By the goddess, I thought I might go crazy when I felt your return. I finally had to walk out of the council meeting. You are back early, not that I am complaining mind you."

Not wanting to ruin the moment with the truth or a lie, Kyreen smiled and pulled his face to her for another kiss. Talking could wait a few more minutes. For now, she enjoyed this almost return to what they had been before. Ever a realist, Kyreen knew too much had transpired for their relationship to ever go back to the carefree abandon of their time in the wilderness of the Great Valley. She could only hope to shed the stiffness and caution of their most recent interactions.

After a few moments Kyreen pulled away extremely self-conscious that they stood near the middle of camp, although most people were off doing their assigned duties and the area was mostly deserted.

"As much as I enjoy this," she said, her smile taking any sting out of her words, "I am certain you should be in a meeting and I need to take these papers to the council clerk."

Lang wrapped an arm around Kyreen's shoulder and began walking.

"The Council will be breaking for midday meal shortly," he murmured, nuzzling her neck. "Would you like me to show you where we will be staying? Put away your gear? Maybe shed the scabbard…and a few articles of clothing before we report in?"

Kyreen shrugged her shoulders, twisting away from Lang's exploring lips. She hated herself for doing so, but she felt trapped, his warm breath on her neck triggering a flood of panic. Struggling to breathe, she stood bent over on the path, hands clutching white knuckled to her bags. When Lang stepped toward her, it took all Kyreen's will power to hold up a hand with a shake of her head instead of bolting back down the path from where they had come. Her pounding heartbeat merely worsened her headache. She vacillated between closing her eyes to block light and visual stimulus or the need to keep her eyes wide open for assurances that Sten had not somehow found her and materialized in front of her. The more she tried to reason with herself that she was being foolish, the more anxious she felt. It was like telling the flame not to consume the wood.

Though it felt like an hour, Kyreen's panic receded after only a few moments. Other than Lang, who looked on with great concern, nobody had passed them by and nobody was near enough to have noticed.

When she could finally think straight, Kyreen reached out to take one of Lang's hands in her own. She cleared her throat several times before finding her voice. "I am sorry," she whispered.

Lang ran his other had across his hair. His heart broke to see Kyreen like this. So too did it make his blood boil with anger at Sten. How Lang longed to get his hands around the bard's neck. Lang felt driven to do something, anything to make Kyreen feel better. He had never been good with words, preferring actions. Now it seemed everything he did turned out wrong. He had no idea where to even begin to make this right between them.

As though she could read his thoughts Kyreen said, "Time will help. If you could, just give me some time?"

She gazed up at him, her green eyes so wide and sorrowful. Now he felt like a cad for his earlier proposal. All he wanted to do was gather her up in his arms and protect her from any more harm. Instead he gave her hand a soft squeeze and leaned over to pick up one of the bags she carried.

"Come with me," he said. "I will show you where we will be…"

They had started walking towards the grove of the trees when Lang let his voice trail off. Kyreen looked over at him.

"Where we will be…sleeping?" she asked.

"Only if you wish to stay with me," he answered. "If not we can find you another spot."

Now that the camp had moved closer to the castle in preparation for the assault, the tents used in the Great Valley had been left behind. Kyreen had not given any thought to whether or not she and Lang would continue sleeping together, having thought it to be a forgone conclusion. Now to hear Lang suggest she find another spot, doubts came rushing forward. Was it possible Lang preferred she go elsewhere? His greeting just a few moments ago suggested otherwise. Kyreen pressed a hand to her forehead.

"I do not know," she said aloud, wishing not for the first time that she would wake to find this all a bad dream.

They continued in silence through the trees. After Kyreen deposited her personal gear, she shouldered the satchel with papers for the Council. Turning to leave she noticed Lang watching her with guarded eyes.

"What have I done now?" she asked, the pain in her skull allowing her frustration to creep into her tone.

"Nothing," he responded, moving out of their designated sleep area. "I thought you would be leaving the sword too. When did you begin carrying it?"

'When Sten attacked me in my sleep,' Kyreen thought but did not say out loud.

Instead she replied, "It makes me feel safe."

Following Lang, watching his stiff back, Kyreen thought about what she would report and what she would leave unsaid. Belatedly she regretted not discussing this with Brigit on their journey back. Surely by now the mage had told her superior about Sten's appearance, which meant it would only be a matter of time before the incident made it to the Council's table. Thoughtfully she nibbled at her bottom lip, grateful for once that Lang walked ahead of her and did not see.

By the time the couple exited the forest, the council members had also begun emerging from their tent, just as Lang had predicted. While Lang waited outside speaking with his friend Geir, Kyreen went inside to drop off the papers. Aren, in discussion with one of the council members, spotted Kyreen's entrance. Excusing herself she walked over to greet Kyreen.

After hugging, Aren gazed upon her cousin with concern. Kyreen's natural pale complexion had adopted an even paler ghostly pallor, accentuating the dark smudges beneath her eyes. Though Kyreen smiled, it never reached her haunted eyes.

"You returned sooner than expected," Aren commented. "I sense no alarm however."

"No emergency," Kyreen replied, feeling her own concerns about her cousin. The stress of the recent events coupled with the impending attack had begun wearing on the Calanian leader. Kyreen wondered again how much she should share.

This internal debate must have reflected in Kyreen's face for Aren smiled with a squeeze of her cousin's arm. "I am strong no matter the gray that has appeared in my hair. Yes, I am tired but I am not near defeat."

Kyreen glanced around the now empty tent, unsure if her reticence came from her desire to keep from further alarming Lang or any residual influence from Sten. Maybe both she thought before replying out loud, "If just we two could talk in private? Without the Council? Without Lang?"

Aren pinched the bridge of her nose, her stomach rumbling. An urgent matter first thing this morning had required her attention forcing her to skip breakfast. Now, when all she desired was to eat her midday meal outside soaking up the warming spring sun, it appeared she would yet again be missing mealtime.

"Very well," she said, gesturing Kyreen to an empty chair as she lowered herself into the one she had recently vacated. "Talk to me."

Chapter 36

When Viggo entered a few minutes later, plates in hand, worried about his mate's hunger, he had not been surprised to see Kyreen. He had noticed Lang loitering nearby evidently waiting for someone, and looking agitated. Pausing in the doorway, Viggo wondered briefly about Lang's absence from the discussion Viggo's mate was conducting with her cousin.

When the two women looked over to him, he fully entered the tent saying, "Hail, Kyreen. I worried Aren would be missing another meal. No, do not get up. I will leave both plates."

He set a plate before each woman. Then leaning down to kiss his wife's cheek he looked to Kyreen adding, "Would you like me to take Lang to sup with me and the children?"

"That would be much appreciated," Kyreen replied.

Once Viggo had departed and the women, both famished, had begun eating, Aren said, "I appreciate your discretion on this matter with Sten. His antics would merely be a distraction for the Council. It sounds as though you and Brigit have things well in hand."

"Brigit does," Kyreen replied without hostility. "I am merely there. She does the work."

"I am additionally pleased that you will be working with her to hone your magic skills. Brigit is one of our most talented mages. Had she the interest, she could easily be the head practitioner."

"She will need her talents," Kyreen murmured quietly, taking another bite of food.

"In other news, but similarly related," Aren commented, pushing away her empty plate, "I sent for Vidar, to work with you on your Connate ability. He arrived late yesterday afternoon. Perhaps you could split your time between working with him and Brigit."

Kyreen nodded. "If that is where you want me."

"What I want is for this entire damn mess to be concluded," Aren replied. "But what I will settle for is having you well prepared for the upcoming fight to retake our homeland."

When council members began wandering into the tent, Kyreen took the opportunity to gather their dirty dishes and excuse herself. As she made her way back to the center of camp, she thought about what to tell Lang.

Depositing the dishes for cleaning she noted Viggo across the way finishing up his midday meal with his two younger children. Lang, curiously, was not to be seen. That Kyreen had not run into him on her walk from the Council Tent had her wondering if Lang was avoiding her. Absently her hand moved to the bandage on her neck.

"Do not fuss with it, woman," Brigit slapped at Kyreen's hand, her voice holding no sting. "I looked for you at the Council Tent. Aren told me you headed this way, and that she endorses our working together." She paused to peer at Kyreen. "Are you up to it today?"

Kyreen nodded. "Maybe it will help with the pain or at the very least give me something else to concentrate on."

Brigit lifted the pack in her hand saying, "I have everything I need here. What say you we head into the forest, find someplace away from here. Maybe that will help your concentration."

With Kyreen's nod, the two women walked out into the trees. Kyreen let Brigit take the lead. As predicted Kyreen's headache lessened the farther from camp they travelled. The forest here grew thick and, with such tall pines, the sunlight barely made it through the dense branches. Needles carpeted the ground below their boots. Inhaling the sharp pine scent, Kyreen felt more relaxed than she had since returning from the Great Valley. That thought caused her to worry again about Lang, about Sten, about magic.

"This looks as good as any place," Brigit announced, setting down her pack.

Kyreen glanced around. The small clearing, if it could be called that, consisted of three large pine trees clustered in a triangle. No bushes grew within their center grouping. The lowest branches canopied overhead high enough up that Kyreen would have to jump to reach the lowest branches should she desire to climb the trees.

Brigit sat down cross legged, gesturing Kyreen to sit opposite her. The older woman began pulling items out of her pack and setting them down on a small piece of cloth.

"Tell me your history with magic," Brigit said, hands resting lightly on her knees. "I need to find out why you are so closed off to it."

"Up until a few days ago, magic was the stuff of stories and superstition," Kyreen replied, yet again feeling the fool. "My mother taught me my family history, my morning ritual, all about healing herbs. Why did she never mention magic?"

"Because our people did not use magic until after the Battle," Brigit explained. "There were a few who dabbled, but for the most part we in Calan fell in line with the realm's banning of magic. There are ancient tomes chronicling about our magical history but most are written in an ancient language that only a very few can decipher. Suffice to say magic is what helped our people survive in those first few chaotic months. The few practitioners that survived cast protections around the camps and people so as to not be discovered. For all the gratitude the Council showed once the new council members were chosen."

Something in Brigit's voice, the bitter anger, made Kyreen ask, "What do you mean?"

"I mean there is not one mage on the Council. Not one! Aren has never sought counsel with the practitioners. We have no representation, no presence, no influence. We get treated like criminals or, worse, vermin. Everything is fine as long as the minor magics like illumination and wards are working. But when illness strikes or accidents occur everyone wants to know why we cannot do healing spells. It is because we are not permitted to dedicate time to practice casting or to research new spells. No, we have to limit our time with magic after we complete our 'real' jobs," Brigit paused to catch her breath, regain control of her temper before adding, "because working magic is not considered a worthy endeavor. Practitioners who practice openly are listed on a registry. Most of those on the Council are afraid that if we mages get too powerful then the practitioners will take over."

Kyreen thought back to Sten and his recent activities. Only by balling her hands into fists in her lap did she keep from touching the bandage on her neck. Her thoughts must have been reflected in her face for Brigit continued. "Sten was, is a radical. You have to believe me, Kyreen. None of us knew what he had been doing. When his sister died last summer, he took her death hard. He even disappeared for a while. When he returned, he had changed."

Brigit leaned back on her arms, gazing over Kyreen's head. "Sten had always been a better than average mage and he made a wonderful bard, with his charisma, his good looks, and beautiful voice. When he returned he still had all that, but with an edge, like all his attributes had been sharpened and, oh, could he be cruel! Several of the younger mages, especially the girls, found themselves the target of his cruelty. Around winter solstice, Sten stopped coming to the practitioner meetings. I believe he knew we were preparing to ban him or at least confront him."

Kyreen wrapped her arms around her body. The admiration in Brigit's voice made Kyreen edgy. She glanced around the shaded clearing, attempting to quell her panic, telling herself Sten could not be here. It did not work.

"Can we change the subject?" Kyreen asked, her voice a bit too sharp.

Brigit looked apologetic, and sat up. "Right. So, magic is completely new to you. What are your feelings towards it?"

"Feelings? I have no feelings," Kyreen replied crossly, pushing a curl from her face.

"Liar," Brigit said cheerily. "You are angry and defensive right now. Where does that come from? Sten? Or is it older?"

"I have frustrations from Lang attempting to teach me the illumination spell, but..." Kyreen thought back to the lessons in the cave. "Every time I attempt to cast I hear the voice of my foster mother. Like most Hanorians, she had many superstitions about sorcery. The cottage had no reflected surfaces, bowls or cups with water were not allowed to sit out, certain phrases were prohibited, dried herbs were sprinkled across the entryway for protection. A whole list of rituals."

"Superstitions have their roots in truth," Brigit commented. "You hear her voice?"

"Not really her voice. Not like she is a ghost," Kyreen responded. "More like I am about to do something of which she would not approve."

"Now we are getting there," Brigit nodded. "What if we meditate for a few minutes, clear our minds, then I will ask you to attempt to illuminate this sphere in my hand."

Kyreen complied. She reached inside, remembering the meditation Lang had used to guide her for the tracking exercises.

After a few moments, Brigit told Kyreen the words and hand motions for the spell, adding, "Let me know if your foster mother's voice shows up. If it does, we will meditate again."

By the time the two left the clearing to return to camp, Kyreen had managed to illuminate the sphere once, out of dozens of times. She felt exhausted but also accomplished. Once Ildri's voice had been dealt with Kyreen had discovered another issue. The smell of magic had triggered a panic attack. With Brigit's patient guidance in meditation, however, Kyreen worked through the anxiety to illuminate the sphere that one time. Her excitement had bubbled over into a laugh of delight which Kyreen quickly extinguished with a hand over her mouth.

"No worries," Brigit had said. "We are within a circle of silence. I cast it when we arrived."

Arriving back at the camp, Kyreen's headache returned but only a very slight throb, nothing like it had been before. When she mentioned it to Brigit, the mage had nodded.

"I am not surprised. The work we did this afternoon has helped your energies to flow much smoother. Another few sessions should help even more."

"That will be nice," Kyreen commented pausing at the edge of the camp center. Her eyes scanned the food line and people already eating, but she did not see Lang.

"If you will excuse me," Brigit said, clapping a hand to Kyreen's shoulder, "I have slept alone too many nights and I missed out sampling that gorgeous dark man."

Kyreen chuckled, waving farewell to Brigit. After watching the mage join a group of people waiting in the food line, Kyreen cast another glance around the area for Lang. Not seeing him and feeling self-consciously alone, she headed towards the tree line where the sleeping quarters lay. As she entered the forest, she felt the magic protections which only caused a small shudder of anxiety. Soon she found the spot where her and Lang's gear lay. Rubbing fingers to both her temples, Kyreen sat down upon the bedroll. Reaching into Lang's knapsack she found one of his light spheres. Drawing her legs up crisscross she began meditating and practicing the illumination spell. By the time night had fallen and her brain ached not from the Connate headache but from soreness of use, Kyreen had reached the point she could manage a dim illumination every fourth or fifth attempt.

Kyreen had just stood up when she sensed Lang's approach. When he saw her standing in the shadows, he stopped. For a few long moments, they stared at each other through the twilight shadows.

"I worried something had happened to you," he finally said. "I had trouble locating you."

Kyreen hesitated, trying to form a response that would not be a lie. "I did not see you at supper. I have been practicing casting the illumination spell."

"Council meeting ran late," he replied.

Silence, thick and uncomfortable, grew in the space between them. Each in their own minds trying to figure out how to proceed, how to close the space between them. Kyreen knew all she had to do was take one step or hold out her hand, but she could not do it. She feared her reaction to the feel of his skin on her skin, feared that Sten had spelled her to repel another man's touch, but more fearful he had not and that she simply may be broken beyond repair. Lang felt frozen by indecision, a completely new experience for him. Now he second guessed his instincts, afraid to see the pain in her eyes and know he had been the cause.

"I am not good with words," he finally said, realizing he needed to be the one to break the silence. "If I tell you I miss you, then you will feel guilty, but that is not what I want. If I say I want to help you, then you will accuse me of pitying you, making you feel weak, but that is not my intent. All that I desire is to be what you need, your friend, your lover, your steward. If you cannot tell me what you need, then there will be missteps on my part. I need you to remember my priority has always been, and always will, be your wellbeing."

"Those were good words," Kyreen said after a few heartbeats, the smile on her face almost reaching her eyes. "You should know that I cannot tell you what I want or need. Someone, no…Sten had me do things, had me feel things. At the time it was happening, I felt that I wanted to do those things, that I wanted to feel those emotions. Now I know it was the spell, but at the time it all felt so incredibly real. I have flashes in my mind, memories of it all and afterwards I am sad because I lost those feelings, that I lost him…and I know—*I know*—in my head, it was all a lie. It was him spelling me, that it was not real. Then I feel guilty because I let it happen, because I felt so happy, because I did not fight."

The tears had started flowing and Kyreen felt her control begin to slip away. There was so much more she wanted to say but she feared letting any more out might finally push him away, might finally cause him to walk away, might finally make him realize that she did not deserve him after her betrayal.

"Betrayal?" Lang asked and Kyreen realized that she had not stopped talking, that she had continued speaking aloud, that she had just confessed her most secret fears.

"Kyreen?" he said softly, holding out his hands, palms up.

Tentatively she took a small step towards him, extending one hand. After a moment, she moved forward one more step so that her fingertips brushed softly against the fingertips of his hands. Carefully she extended her other hand. For several more moments they stood like this, Kyreen's eyes fixed on his hands, Lang's gaze on her face. Then she moved forward so that her palms rested on top of his palms. Her hands were so cold and his were so warm. Eventually she raised her gaze to his face.

"Would you put your arms around me?" she asked in a timid voice that told him she believed he would refuse.

Without speaking he closed the gap between their bodies, leaving his arms extended until she slipped her arms around his waist. Not until she rested her cheek against his chest did he carefully close his arms around her. When she leaned into his body, he slowly exhaled his pent-up breath.

As they stood in the darkened woods, Lang thought back to earlier that day, outside the Council Tent, when Viggo had practically ordered Lang to follow him to midday meal. Since it had become apparent Kyreen would not be returning, Lang had complied. The two men had collected their food in silence before sitting down with Viggo's two youngest children.

While eating Lang had reviewed his conversations with Kyreen, slowly getting more agitated. Why had she hesitated when he had mentioned finding her an alternate place to sleep? He had thrown that out in jest. But then to watch her contemplate it?

"I thought we had already resolved your attitude," Viggo growled, glancing over at Lang. "You never struck me as stupid."

From his peripheral vision, Viggo noted Gunda and her brother exchange startled looks, probably due more to his tone than the actual words. He decided they both were old enough to hear his conversation with this man.

"You do not know…" Lang had started to say.

"No!" Viggo had interrupted, his voice still low enough so as not to alert their dining neighbors but his tone even sharper driving his children to exchange glances again. "You do not know, Lang! Have you even given a thought to Kyreen since her return? Do you know why she is back early? Do you know why she carries her sword? Do you know why she is paler? Why the circles under her eyes are darker? Do you know why she meets in private with Aren, instead of with the Council, or you for that matter? I only saw the girl for a moment and I have those questions."

Viggo ran a hand over his face, taking a deep calming breath. "You and Kyreen have something special with your bonding, something that has become a rare and precious thing amongst our people. Do not squander it for pride."

The four sat in silence for several long moments, Viggo lost in his thoughts about bonding; Lang seething in anger at Viggo's lecture; Reidar and Gunda caught in the middle, not sure what to do. Finally, Viggo set aside his empty plate, stretching his legs in front of him, settling back, his tone contemplative.

"Aren was not raised to take the throne. As the daughter of the king's brother, she was far down in line to be our queen. After the king was killed and our new queen delivering the twins soon after her coronation, the likelihood of Aren's taking the throne diminished even more. Was she pampered and spoiled? Most likely. I never met her before the Battle but I did see her once, a sennight before our world ended. I had been walking with my friends to supper, to school, to goof off, I cannot remember the reason. All I do remember is hearing this beautiful voice singing a song my mother had sung to me often as a child. I felt driven to find the person belonging to this voice, so I abandoned my pals and followed the sound to the castle gardens. When I saw her – Aren – I hid behind a bush so she would not see me. She had no audience; she sang just for the pure joy of the song; I could hear it in her voice. With her back to me I could not see her face, but I fell in love with her voice and right there felt the first tug of our bond. When I left the gardens, I vowed to find her during the Festival."

Viggo paused, losing himself in his memory a moment before continuing, "The next time I saw Aren, felt our bond pull, she was helping with the evacuations. She was a tired, scared teenager, but she was also the only royal family member left in Calan. Was it fair that everyone kept looking to her for guidance? No, but to her credit, she shouldered it and organized the Council. I watched her over those first months grow into a competent, confident leader. I also watched her become harsh and bitter, her heart hardening, the joy leaving her eyes."

"In the middle of all that chaos, I made the decision to pursue Aren, to complete our bond. It was not easy or smooth. It probably was not wise but I felt driven. She did not want me, did not want our bond. She saw me as another nuisance, another person clamoring for attention, wanting to use her. One day, after the umpteenth time she had yelled and screamed at me to leave her alone, I realized I had to make a decision. I could continue pursuing Aren straight on, working hard to convince her that she belonged with me, or I could let her go."

"I chose to let her go, but I did not choose to abandon her. Every day, when I woke up, my first thought was how could I make Aren's life better? How could I help her, not our people, not myself, just Aren? At first it was merely being the first to volunteer for any project she requested help on, digging latrines, overnight patrols. Then I noticed how she always held back in the food lines, always ate last, sometimes forgoing food all together, especially when food was so scarce. So, I began taking food to her, always with a question about whatever the problem of the day was so she would feel compelled to speak with me over the meal. By the time she realized she loved me, we had settled into a relationship based on mutual respect and support."

Viggo glanced over at his two children, listening with rapt attention. "Do not share my words with your mother. She would be hurt that I spoke so freely of something so intimate. Though she jokes all the time about me pursuing her, she does not like to remember those days and would shelter you from these memories."

He looked back to Lang. "For all her experience and strength, underneath Aren is still that same scared teenager, but she is committed to serving her people to the best of her ability. And I still wake up every day with my first thought being 'How can I make Aren's life better?' For that is my commitment. I do not deny that I would rejoice if Kyreen did take the throne. Then me and mine would be free to live our lives in peace. I also admit I worry over the goddess' choice in you as Kyreen's bonded mate. Even if she does not ascend to wear the crown, Kyreen has been thrust into the politics of our people. I do not believe Sten works alone. I believe he has help out there somewhere, and, mark my words, Sten is not done with Kyreen. She needs someone who will not abandon her, someone whose main priority is her, someone who can support her when she is most vulnerable. Quite frankly, Lang, I have my doubts as to whether you are that man."

At the time, listening to Viggo speak, Lang had simmered, silently fuming. When the older man had finished speaking, Lang had simply stood up and walked away. For most of the afternoon he had stewed, barely listening to the discussions during his meetings. But by the time Aren had called for the evening recess, his temper had calmed and he had realized Viggo spoke the truth. Lang had not been focusing on Kyreen. Exiting the Council Tent, Lang had felt an urgency to find Kyreen, hoping he could repair the damage he had caused.

By the time Lang had reached the camp center most everyone had already been through the line. Scanning the faces, he did not see Kyreen, so he approached Viggo and Aren. Neither of them had seen Kyreen but Aren mentioned she had been working with Brigit.

Before turning away, Lang had looked at Viggo and said, "Thank you for earlier."

The Hunter had merely shrugged, replying, "I did not do it for you. Or even for Kyreen."

Now, standing in the dark, having tracked Kyreen down, carefully wrapping his arms around her, Lang concentrated on her. Though he felt moved to stroke her hair, move his hands about her body, tilt her face to his for a kiss, she seemed content to lean against him, her head upon his chest, her arms wrapped around his waist, though her body remained stiff. So, he waited, patiently. Eventually as the night deepened around them, Kyreen relaxed into him until finally she lifted her head to gaze up at him.

"Hey," she said softly, grinning.

Resisting the impulse to kiss her upturned lips, he smiled back. "Hey."

With a soft sigh, sounding more like contentment than frustration, she rested her head back against his chest, snuggling into his embrace.

"Tell me about your day?" he asked quietly.

"If we can sit down?" she asked. Again, her tone led Lang to think she believed he would deny her this request.

"Anything you desire," he responded.

Once they had settled on top of their bedroll, Lang had opened his arms allowing her to snuggle against him, with her head resting on his shoulder, he repeated, "Tell me about your day? About your trip? About anything?"

Kyreen knew he was treating her with caution. She knew he was holding back. She felt his edginess. But that he did not act upon it warmed her heart. She knew when he had teased her, propositioned her, touched her earlier that he had not done it to hurt her or to trigger her memories. She appreciated the restraint he exhibited now. She simply was not ready to talk more. She felt content just being quiet, enjoying his embrace.

She realized he waited for her to speak. Reluctantly, worried about his reaction she said, "May we sit here like this in silence?"

He heard the tentativeness, could envision her worried expression, her wide eyes, her nibbling at her bottom lip. Instinctively he pressed a kiss to her hair and repeated, "Anything you desire."

Immediately he was rewarded by her relaxing fully against him. He could felt her relief in more than just her body. Softly he stroked her hair as they sat together in the dark.

Chapter 37

In the early morning dawn, Kyreen opened her eyes. Sometime in the night they had lain down and Lang had drawn a blanket up over them. She inhaled quietly, enjoying the warmth of his embrace. After a deep sleep free of dreams, she felt refreshed. Ready to face the day.

Picking up her head to look at him Kyreen found Lang gazing down at her. She smiled, scooting up to press a quick kiss to his lips.

"Good morning," she whispered, nuzzling at his neck.

"Yes, it is," he said, keeping his hands still as she placed a soft kiss upon his neck.

"Thank you," she murmured, kissing his lips one final time before sitting up, ruffling a hand through her loose curls, not remembering releasing her braid.

Lang sat up, unable to stop himself from placing a soft kiss on her shoulder before rolling to his feet. Gazing down at her with her wild hair, her still drowsy eyes, that smile she cast up at him, he extended a hand, a silent invitation to stand, when all he wanted to do was lie down with her and stay sequestered here for the rest of the day instead of attending council meetings.

As they made their way towards the camp center, Kyreen pulled Lang's arm around her shoulders so that they walked hip to hip. He enjoyed their contact, again regretting his day full of meetings.

"What plans have you for today?" he asked as they queued for food.

"Aren has asked me to meet with Vidar," Kyreen answered, glancing around the area. "I thought I would do that this morn, then work with Brigit in the afternoon if she is available. I do not see either of them. What about you?"

"Council," he responded. "Will you wait for me this evening, even if we are late to adjourn?"

"Of course," she smiled, giving him a quick hug before slipping from his embrace to fix her food, her stomach rumbling in anticipation of the meal.

As she finished eating, Kyreen spied Vidar across the way, just sitting down to his meal. He appeared to be alone so she gently nudged Lang with her elbow, nodding towards the blind man, saying, "I should go speak with him."

Lang nodded, taking her empty plate. "Go. Geir has requested the farmers meet during midday break. See you at supper?"

"I cannot wait," she said, kissing his cheek before standing up, knowing he could sense the truth in her words.

Approaching Vidar, Kyreen slowed down, unsure if she should interrupt the old man's meal. A few paces away she stopped completely.

Vidar turned his sightless eyes in her direction, saying, "Come ahead, my dear. I am always happy to speak with a young lady."

"Hail, Vidar," Kyreen replied, moving closer to stand before the seated man.

"Ah, Kyreen! Hail and well met," he responded, extending a gnarled hand in her direction. "Please sit with me. Have you eaten?"

Kyreen took his hand and settled beside him, saying, "Yes, I have. I was unsure if you would want to meet with me as you only arrived late yesterday."

"Any opportunity to spend time with you, my dear," he responded warmly.

For a few minutes, they sat in silence while Vidar returned to his meal. Kyreen glanced back at Lang. He appeared to be having an animated conversation with his friend Geir, who must have walked up directly after Kyreen left. She realized she had never had a conversation with Geir, unless him denigrating her in council meetings could be considered a conversation. Lang never mentioned Geir to her, so she reckoned her assumption about them being friends could be inaccurate, especially if Lang's current expression reflected his feelings towards the husky man gesticulating wildly with his hands.

"You are quiet, my dear," Vidar commented. "Is your talent causing you issues?"

"Not so much today," Kyreen replied. "I worked with Brigit yesterday and the meditations she did helped my energy flow, or at least that is what she tells me."

Vidar chuckled. "I thought I detected the stink of magic upon you."

"Is that how you knew it was I who approached?" Kyreen asked, her curiosity overriding good manners.

"No," Vidar replied with a shake of his grizzled white head. "Until you spoke I could not be certain. When you approached, I recognized the step to be that of a young woman and as you are who I am here to visit, it was an easy deduction."

Vidar picked up his walking stick. "I have finished. Shall we find some place less populated?"

"I will take those," Svein said, taking the man's empty dishes.

Kyreen blinked, rising quickly to her feet, surprised by the youth's sudden appearance. While Synnove's youngest sibling still sported closely shorn hair, the tunic she wore fitted her better than the one she had been wearing at their previous meeting. Kyreen's face flushed as she recalled their last meeting, their only meeting after Kyreen had knocked Sten unconscious during the Festival.

Rising to his feet more smoothly than one would expect for someone as old as he, Vidar placed a hand on Kyreen's forearm. "Are you alright, dear? I sense a rising heartrate."

"Just startled," Kyreen replied, smiling at the youngster. "Hail, Svein! I apologize I did not see you there."

The youth flashed a smile. "That was my intent."

"So, you know my assistant already? That is good," Vidar said, sliding his arm through Kyreen's. "Svein, dear, would you take us to that spot you were telling me about earlier?"

Assisting Vidar, Kyreen followed Svein out of the camp. The direction the youth led them went up a hill, then descended into a small hollow. Kyreen felt the camp's inhabitants but barely. Though they had not travelled far, the hollow seemed isolated. Vidar requested Svein put up a silence shield then lowered himself on one of the mid-sized boulder situated around the hollow.

"Now then," Vidar said. "Aren sent for me but I am not sure of what help I can be."

"From what I understand, your aunt and sister were Connates," Kyreen explained. "Aren hopes you may know of some trick for me to control all the emotions that I receive."

Vidar shook his head. "I am so sorry, my dear," he murmured. "That is a talent no one should have to endure."

The old man sighed. "My aunt, my mother's little sister, had been a surprise child to her parents, in more ways than one. My grandmother became pregnant when my own mother was already a teen. Then MorMor gave birth to a healthy baby boy, just as the Parturient had predicted. Katinka surprised everyone when she popped out a short time later. Her life force had been so weak and Boden's so strong, the Parturient had not sensed her at all. Uncle Boden and Aunt Katinka were only a few years older than my twin sister and me."

"You are a twin?" Kyreen asked, unable to hide her surprise or curb her curiosity.

"Yes," Vida nodded. "Connates and Aegis are always twins. I do not know if they are always girls and boys, though."

"They are," Svein commented quietly. At Kyreen's questioning glance, she added, "Mama was researching Connates and I may have taken a peek."

"Does that mean Quillan is an Aegis?" Kyreen asked.

"Most likely," Svein replied.

"What exactly is an Aegis?" Kyreen inquired, feeling a fool since she probably should know, but neither of her companions commented.

"A shield," Vidar replied. "The Connate absorbs the emotions of the people surrounding her, while the Aegis can shield her if the emotions become too much. An Aegis protects the Connate from danger."

"Is that why I feel so much better in your presence?" Kyreen asked.

"I am not an expert," Vidar shrugged, "but I believe that would make sense."

"Vidar is not as effective a shield for you as your twin, but you do gain some protections from his presence," Svein offered tentatively with a shy smile at Kyreen."

"Unfortunately for my aunt, her twin, Uncle Boden, died from illness when they were in their teens," Vidar commented, the sorrow thick in his voice. "Kelda and I were only children at the time. Our talents had not yet manifested, so Aunt Katinka did not have anyone to shield her from all the emotions. She held on for a few years, using herbs and meditations to manage the sensations, but in the end the emotions that filled her overflowed until she could take no more."

"That is unfortunate," Kyreen said, placing her hand over Vidar's.

"Without an Aegis, most Connates will end their life," Svein commented in her bland, even tone. "Even with an Aegis, they still have a high rate of suicide."

Kyreen flashed Svein a look of exasperation for discussing the subject so directly without tact, but the girl shrugged. "It was in Mama's book."

"My Kelda killed herself when I was away. I had been detained far longer than I had expected," Vidar murmured. "I never should have left her, but Rolf requested my assistance on a delicate matter. Even before he ascended the throne I could never deny my friend anything he asked."

For several minutes, the trio sat in silent contemplation. Just as Kyreen had decided to head back to camp, Vidar squeezed her hand with a smile.

"Enough dark tales for today, my dear," he said. "How about I share a tale about your grandfather?"

"I would enjoy that," Kyreen replied with a smile.

Chapter 38

When the sun reached its axis, the trio headed back to camp for midday meal. Svein had spent the rest of the time quietly observing and listening. Something about the girl spooked Kyreen. More than once Kyreen had wondered if Svein had truly broken Sten's enthrallment or could he have slipped back into his sister's mind.

When Kyreen shuddered at the thought of Sten, Vidar patted her hand reassuringly, "Twill be fine my dear."

The love exuded by Vidar, so pure, without any reservation warmed Kyreen's heart. Vidar's emotions reminded her of Ildri's unconditional love. It had been so long since Kyreen had felt such pure emotion. Unexpectedly her eyes watered.

Clearing her throat and wishing to distract herself, Kyreen leaned in to whisper, "Svein as your assistant? Is this new?"

"Yes, I travelled here alone with the courier. You may remember meeting my former assistant, my grandniece Britt. She delivered her baby, a big strapping boy, during the Festival. I felt Britt had enough on her plate with the new baby, and Aren thought Svein would be a good fit as my assistant. The poor dear is having some family issues and needed a warden."

Kyreen watched the young woman walking before them. Family trouble? That was putting it mildly. Kyreen knew she should say something to Svein but could not figure out what.

As they joined the queue, Kyreen spotted Brigit already eating amongst a group of people off to the side, separated a bit from the others. Everyone – about six of them including Brigit – appeared to be having a serious conversation.

Kyreen turned to Vidar, saying, "Thank you for this morning. May we do it again tomorrow?"

"I am not sure I am being of any assistance," Vidar replied. "But I will always agree to spend time with you."

Kyreen again felt a rush of happiness from both Vidar's words and his emotions. She realized his presence had soothed her ragged nerves. That alone would be enough to have her wanting to meet him again. The simple fact was she enjoyed the old man's company and his stories.

"Until the morning then," she said, giving his arm a soft squeeze and placing a kiss on his cheek.

With a wave farewell to Svein, Kyreen left the food line to walk across to Brigit. The group immediately quieted upon Kyreen's approach making her feel more than a little self-conscious.

"I apologize for interrupting," Kyreen said, turning to leave even as she spoke. "I can come back later."

"No need," Brigit said, scooting over and patting the log beside her. "This lot is simply speechless to have the Princess amongst us peasants."

"I told you not to call me that," Kyreen grumbled, her stomach clenching anxiously. After she sat down Brigit introduced the group – Munin, Idun, Dahl, Eivor, and Nils – although Kyreen knew she had no chance of remembering all their names, let alone match the right face to the right name. Her feelings must have reflected on her face for Brigit laughed.

"Relax! You will not be quizzed," the older woman said, her eyes twinkling.

Kyreen felt the blush seep into her cheeks. Then the moment passed and the others picked back up their conversation. After a few minutes, Brigit gathered up her empty dishes and, gesturing for Kyreen to follow her, stood up.

"I suppose you are wanting to practice magic again?" Brigit asked as she deposited her dirty dishes.

"If you have time," Kyreen responded.

"It just so happens I do," the mage commented, as they walked towards the outskirts of camp. "Miracle of miracles, my name has yet to appear on any duty rosters even though we returned yesterday before today's posting went up."

"Is that unusual?" Kyreen felt a rush of anxiety. She had not even thought about checking the daily chores list.

Brigit peered at Kyreen, her eyes narrowed. "I cannot determine whether you are addled-brained or simply naïve. Yes, it is very unusual. Common folk have to contribute, doing whatever menial tasks get assigned from those on high. In this camp, those are the members from the Council Tent. Mages and those associating with mages, get, in my experience the trash jobs, the messy, ugly tasks that no one wants. I am betting you do not usually get an assignment?"

"At training I did," Kyreen shrugged feeling self-conscious. "At Council Camp, not usually."

Brigit arched an eyebrow without speaking.

"Fine," Kyreen admitted. "Never!"

Brigit snorted. "So I thought. You may not want to be called Princess, Princess, but your title is giving you benefits."

Kyreen felt a flair of anger, wanting to defend herself. Last summer she had been a guest, granted temporary asylum with the Calanians. Then she had gone to deal with the Faldorian mercenary. When she returned Aren had assigned Kyreen the task of trade negotiations with Rhun's guild. When those were complete Kyreen had gone to the cliffs for training. Any time she had spent in the Council Camp had been limited, just the short visits.

Kyreen's expression amused Brigit and the mage burst into laughter. "Do not be so serious, woman! I am just joking with you. Everyone knows you are Aren's chosen emissary. Your official position exempts you from duty roster. I suppose now I am your official magic tutor which gets me out of digging latrines and peeling vegetables so I thank you, m'lady!"

Brigit gave a low courtly bow before gesturing for Kyreen to take a seat. They had entered the same shady clearing they had used the day before. Kyreen settled down to the ground crisscrossing her legs. Taking a deep breath, she began to clear her mind as Brigit set up the wards to soundproof the area.

Today's lesson, in Kyreen's opinion, went much better than the previous day's. By the time the sun had begun dipping behind the forest, Kyreen succeeded at illuminating the sphere more often than she failed. She also noticed her head did not ache nearly as much as it had yesterday. As they prepared for the walk back to camp, Kyreen looked forward to her evening chat with Lang, to be able to show him her progress.

Lang. Kyreen had not given much thought to him all day. She had been busy, her mind more occupied than she had been in a long time. It felt good, almost normal. Almost.

"Are you coming?" Brigit's question broke through Kyreen's distraction.

"Yes," Kyreen hurried to catch up with the mage. "Brigit, may I ask you a question?"

"Considering you just did, I suppose another one will not hurt."

Kyreen grinned and forced out the question before she lost her nerve. "Do you know where…I mean…is there some way I can get some rue?"

"Rue?" Brigit cast a sideways look at Kyreen, who blushed under the mage's scrutiny. "Why did you not say anything earlier? I could have shown you the contraceptive spell."

"Really?" Kyreen asked amazed. "There is a spell for that?"

Brigit held her face straight for a short minute before dissolving into laughter. "No, of course not! Could you imagine though. Oh, Princess, you should have seen your face! Priceless!"

Kyreen's cheeks blushed deep red, but she joined in Brigit's laughter. The mage held no animosity, no spite behind her joke. She had not been trying to hurt Kyreen. No, she had merely taken advantage of the younger woman's lack of knowledge for a harmless joke.

"My question still stands," Kyreen reminded Brigit once their laughter had died down.

"What? Rue? Sure, we always have a big pot brewing both morning and evening. Stop by the practitioner's area after supper and I can get you a cup," Brigit offered as they approached the meal line. She gestured in the direction opposite to the sleeping area, near the hollow Kyreen had spent the morning in with Vidar and Svein. "We are over that way."

Brigit waved farewell, leaving Kyreen by herself. Feeling more than a little self-conscious Kyreen stepped back out of the way where she could observe everyone. A wave of relief swept over her when she saw Viggo and realized he was headed her way.

"Hail, Kyreen," Aren's mate greeted her, holding both of his hands out to her.

Kyreen smiled, placing her hands in his. Viggo, like Vidar, exuded a refreshing purity of emotion with no undertones. She had always felt she could relax in his presence.

Their greeting complete, Viggo released her hands, turning so they stood side-by-side watching the people gather for their evening meal.

"I never had a chance to express how very grateful I am to you for tracking me and Sten," Kyreen said quietly. "I do not remember much but I do remember you, your essence. I felt it and it helped ground me."

"No gratitude needed or required," Viggo replied, gruffly, brushing off the woman's appreciations. "I am happy you are back safe with us."

Silence fell between them, not uncomfortable, yet not easy, and both were relieved when Aren and Lang appeared. Exchanging congenial smiles, they walked toward their corresponding partners.

Kyreen greeted Lang with a tight hug, holding him close for several heartbeats. She wanted to tell him she had missed him but she was not sure that would be truthful. As she did not wish to hurt him, she instead whispered, "I am happy to see you."

"As am I," he whispered back, sliding his arm about her, returning the hug.

When they parted Kyreen leaned up to place a soft kiss upon his lips. Though it was chaste without any passion, that she had initiated the gesture spoke its own promise, one of healing.

Queuing for food, Kyreen commented, "After supper I have a quick errand to run over in the practitioner's area."

Aren, overhearing, turned to give Kyreen a concerned look. "Should I be worried about you fraternizing with the magickers?" she asked, her tone only partially joking.

Kyreen's face pinkened slightly, as she thought of her reason for seeking out the mages, but she did not wish to make her errand public, as she still worried about resuming her physical relationship with Lang.

Fortunately, Aren reached the front of the line and turned away to fix her plate. The aroma of the food filled Kyreen's nose causing her stomach to rumble, reminding her that she had skipped the midday meal.

Twilight found Kyreen tentatively approaching the practitioner's area. Very similar to the place Svein had taken her and Vidar earlier that day, this clearing was close to camp but down in a little hollow so the camp could not be seen. As she entered, Kyreen felt the magic which surrounded the clearing. A tiny little flare of anxiety fluttered in her stomach then dissipated quickly. With a soft sigh, Kyreen stepped further into the clearing, scanning for Brigit.

"Hail, Princess," one of the mages said, breaking away from a group of people conversing. Kyreen recognized him to be one of the people she had met earlier in the day though she could not recall his name.

"Please," she said, "do not call me that. My name is Kyreen."

"Very well, Kyreen. I am Munin," he reintroduced himself. "Are you looking for Brigit? She is around here somewhere... Probably with Nils though I doubt they have retired yet... Still pretty early.... Oh hey! There she is."

Munin pointed to a clutch of people standing in the far side of the clearing. Having sent her in the right direction, he gave Kyreen a wave and went back to his own group. Kyreen gazing about the clearing began walking towards Brigit. Of the three dozen or so people scattered about the clearing most were in small groups of three or four people, some merely chatted, a few studied scrolls, and others appeared to be practicing spells. From those last groups, Kyreen could sense the magic. With deep breaths, she managed to quell the small sparks of panic.

"Hail, Princess!" Brigit greeted Kyreen when she noticed the younger woman's approach. "You remember Nils from this afternoon."

She did not but Kyreen still nodded at the young man with a smile. Brigit playfully wrapped an arm around Nil's should, saying, "No flirting. This one is mine. You have two lovely men already."

Kyreen shook her head, unable to stop the color from flooding her cheeks. She still could not figure out Brigit. The mage's intents had no malice. Maybe she just enjoyed keeping Kyreen off balance. If so, she did a good job.

Brigit released Nils, who gave the older woman's backside a playful slap before excusing himself. Brigit put an arm around Kyreen's shoulders to guide her to a cauldron sitting upon a small fire. Scooping up some tea into a mug, Brigit held it out to Kyreen.

"There you go," she said. "If you would rather not enter this den of depravity for your dose, you can get rue tea from the healer's area as well. If you really do not mind announcing your intent, there is always a batch brewed for morning and evening meal. The cooks keep it off to the side and require you to ask for it by name."

Kyreen took the mug, giving it a taste. "Thank you. I appreciate the information,"

"No thank yous," Brigit admonished, waving Kyreen away. "Go be with your man. Have fun. We will talk tomorrow."

The mischievous glint in the mage's eyes made Kyreen wonder what exactly they would be discussing on the morrow. She was still chuckling when she returned to center camp. Pausing on the edges of the area, she sipped down the last of the tea, her eyes scanning for Lang. He stood in a group of men, Geir included, listening more than talking. His eyes caught hers almost as soon as she had spotted him. The smile he gave her radiated heat throughout Kyreen's body. She felt such an immense relief at her reaction to him that she barely held herself back from running to him. Instead she stood still while he excused himself from his friends and strolled towards her.

In Kyreen's mind, his walk towards her took an interminably long time. By the time he stood before her, her entire body was vibrating. Without giving any thought to her actions, she flung her arms around his neck, pulling his head down so she could hungrily kiss his lips. The moan that escaped him made her pause, her body tensing.

Taking a deep breath, she wrapped her arms around him, embracing him tightly as she stretched on tiptoe to whisper in his ear, "I want you, but I cannot promise I will not pull away, will not get panicked."

"We can take it slow," Lang whispered back. "Whatever you desire."

"I desire you," she answered, pulling him to her for another steamy kiss. This time he slid his arms around her, gently pulling her body to his. Whenever she would stiffen he would pause, never pulling away, until she again relaxed.

After a few minutes, she broke away to whisper breathlessly into his ear, "I desire you. Now."

Chapter 39

The next morning Kyreen awoke encased in Lang's embrace. The sky above was still dark, but the birds in the trees energetically announced dawn's impending arrival. She knew without looking that Lang was awake. Snuggling against him she stretched sleepily, grateful for the previous evening, for the creation of new memories, for the reprieve from her nightmares. Impulsively, she rolled over so she lay on the top of Lang. He grunted softly in surprise, his hands moving to rest softly upon her hips.

Raising his head to gaze down at her, he murmured, "Good morn."

Kyreen lifted up slightly to smile up at him, then resumed the trail of kisses she had been pressing along his chest, working down his abdomen. Lang set his head back down, content without speaking for a while.

The next time Kyreen opened her eyes, the sky overhead shone pink as the sun rose slowly behind the trees. This time she lay on her side, Lang spooning against her back. With a soft sigh, she squeezed his arms tight around her before reluctantly sitting up. Beside her Lang groaned softly in protest, his fingers gently stroking her back.

When his touch stilled and she felt his concern flood back, Kyreen's stomach sank. Self-consciously she reached for her clothes, the hot tears in her eyes causing her to fumble. Before she could draw the tunic over her head, his hand on her arm stopped the motion.

"Please," he whispered, "do not pull away."

Swallowing the lump in her throat, she asked without turning to look at him, "How bad are they still?"

When he did not answer, she steeled herself, then turned so that she sat cross legged facing him. In the early dawn light, she watched his eyes drop to gaze over her bare torso. Though his expression did not waver, Kyreen felt his shock, his anger, then finally his pity wash over her, making her eyes water again.

She glanced down at the splotches of bruises adorning her shoulders, breasts, abdomen, hips, legs. The dark smudges, now faded to yellows and greens, were startling against her pale skin but nowhere near as spectacular as they had been days earlier at their dark purple peak.

"I forgot there for a bit," she commented, sorrow lacing her bitter tone.

"Kyreen, I..."

She held up a hand, shaking her head. "Please do not say anything. This is why I had hoped to keep them hidden. I do not want your pity. My body will heal, is healing. It is up here," she tapped at her temple, "that is not. Last night and this morning were good starts but he is still in here. It is going to take time and work to push him out. Work I cannot do if you look at me like that, like I might break or blow away."

"Am I supposed to ignore what he did to you? Pretend nothing happened?" Lang asked, unable to keep the anger from seeping into his voice.

"No," Kyreen responded, "but you cannot give it to me. I am not strong enough to carry both my distress and your outrage. Not right now."

He stared at her for a long moment then sat up to wrap his arms around her. She stiffened for a heartbeat then relaxed into the embrace. Softly he stroked her hair then said, "I understand. You may have to remind me from time to time but I promise to work harder. I want you to trust me, to feel like you can lean on me no matter what."

Pulling back, she gazed at him for a moment, then gently kissed his lips. "I want that, too," she replied.

He laid back down, opening his arms in silent invitation. Once she had snuggled against his side, he wrapped his arms around her.

The days that followed settled into a comforting routine for Kyreen. Mornings she spent in the hollow listening to the stories from Vidar about his family, soaking up his positive energies, gleaning bits of information buried in the tales such as the spearmint tincture his sister had used to combat the migraines. The afternoon lessons with Brigit progressed with Kyreen mastering the simple illumination spell and starting to learn how to manipulate the energies within her body to control and direct the flows. Brigit turned out to be not only a talented mage and patient teacher but also an entertaining companion. From her Kyreen also learned about camp politics from a very different perspective. When the council meetings ran late, which occurred more and more often, Kyreen found herself wandering into the practitioners' area. In addition to the magic, she found a plethora of discussions on all topics. Most often she would listen, absorbing and enjoying the conversations. Then, at night she and Lang would retire together to their bedroll, cautiously exploring and relearning each other. By the time all of the bruises disappeared from her body, Kyreen felt almost whole.

The Training Camp contingency also arrived about that time, just a few days before the planned attack on the castle and, with the Training Camp, came Kyreen's friends. Kyreen had worried what to tell Synnove about Sten, but enough time had passed Kyreen felt it unnecessary to broach the subject. Then Aren had once again requested Kyreen keep the incident quiet until after the castle attack. Evidently the bond between Kyreen and Lang had healed enough that Synnove did not make comment. Kyreen reckoned that also could be because Synnove had a bit of a distraction in her promised mate-to-be Eilert, with whom Synnove spent the majority of her free time.

The first night the trainees were in camp, Kyreen had supper with her friends. Lang, per usual now, had been delayed. In addition to Synnove, Yngve, and Ebbe, they were joined by Karine and Eilert. Though she never said anything outright, Karine still gave Kyreen dour looks during the meal. As uncomfortable as Karine's hostilities were, Kyreen had more issues with Synnove, specifically her treatment of Eilert. Synnove spoke about him as if he were not present. When she needed a refill of her tea, she did not ask, merely looked at him. None of the others present seemed put off by Synnove's behavior, so Kyreen withheld comment until she and Lang were talking later that night.

"I cannot exactly pinpoint why it bothered me," she commented having relayed the evening to Lang.

"I cannot say I am surprised," Lang responded. He lay on his back, hands behind his head, gazing up at the stars twinkling between the shadowed tree limbs overhead. "Synnove's family were upper echelon before the Battle. Many council members and advisors in her family tree. Eilert's family not so much."

"Really?" Kyreen asked, her head resting on his shoulder. "Funny she never mentioned it before."

"They fell out of favor when it came to light her uncle, on her da's side I think, had been the traitor working with Dolan since well before the Battle," Lang explained. "Since then they have kept low, staying out of politics, not causing any turmoil. At least until Sten."

Kyreen's stomach tightened at the mention of Synnove's brother's name. Overall her anxiety and panic attacks had diminished, but every once in a while, a word, a smell, a sound would send her back. Lang had become adept at recognizing the signs and many times he could soothe her terrors to avoid an incident altogether. When he could not, he simply waited with her, remaining available and neutral, until the brunt of the attack passed.

"Kyreen?" Lang asked as her silence drew on.

"I am fine," she murmured, nuzzling against his neck. "But I do not wish to waste any more time thinking or talking about him."

"Maybe I can distract you," Lang responded, pulling her body up on top of his.

With her hands on either side of his head, Kyreen gazed down at Lang. Everything about him - his eyes, his smile, his voice, his laugh – everything filled her with delight. She felt she could spend all day, every day with him and never tire of his company. So much had changed in so short of time. If everything went according to plan, much more would change in the next fortnight. She had slowly allowed herself to begin looking towards the future, towards the life they would build together, and the prospect thrilled her.

Leaning down Kyreen gave Lang a playful quick kiss, then pulled back with a grin. "You said something about distracting me?" she quipped.

He laughed pulling her head down so as to kiss her deeply and thoroughly. Within moments both were sufficiently distracted so no more discussions were had for quite a while.

One evening, just two days before the Calanian forces were scheduled to move on the castle, when Lang had been delayed yet again with a late council meeting and Eilert had been assigned an evening patrol, Kyreen and Synnove had opportunity to dine together, just the two of them. Lingering over conversation after the meal, it felt like their time as tentmates at the cliffs, until the conversation turned to the impending castle strike, or more specifically, to the aftermath.

"It is a shame your bond has linked you to Lang," Synnove commented casually.

"What do you mean?" Kyreen had asked, frowning at the implication.

"Do not get me wrong. He is a fine individual, exceptionally handsome even with his beard. For the most part Lang is a more than sufficient partner," Synnove had remarked just as nonchalantly as if she were discussing the weather on a sunny spring afternoon. "It is just that, given your position, it is a shame he has no ambition. From what I gather all he cares to do is get back to farming."

Synnove had emphasized this last word with a wrinkling of her nose then continued. "Take Eilert for example. He is working to join the castle guard, but he is not stopping there. No, he has plans to work up to an officer rank, maybe Guard Commander. He could eventually move onto the Council as Security Advisor."

"Lang is on the Council now," Kyreen said, hating that she felt the need to defend him to Synnove.

"Just because the old truth seer died or something," Synnove responded with a wave of her hand. "If not for that, you would not see him here. He would be back in the Great Valley. He would not even have been our instructor were it not for your bond, true?"

Kyreen knew her friend spoke the truth, but did not say so aloud. This conversation made Kyreen uncomfortable. She did not like the direction it appeared to be heading.

"You know I just realized who would have been a good bond match for you," Synnove said, with a sly grin.

"Who?" Kyreen asked when it became apparent Synnove waited for the question. Her stomach rolled nervously, threatening to heave her recent meal.

'Please do not say it, please do not say it,' Kyreen wished silently.

"Sten, of course!" Synnove exclaimed. "I know he can be frustrating, especially since Signe died, but I do think you are the one who could handle him. Besides, then we would be sisters!"

"About that, Synnove," Kyreen said shakily, her hand reflexively drifting to the now healed bite mark on her neck, staring down at her other hand, fisted in her lap.

"I know, you are bonded with Lang. It was just a thought," Synnove said, patting Kyreen's arm. "No harm in fantasizing, right?"

Kyreen nodded, rubbing the bridge of her nose. Synnove's expression immediately turned to one of concern.

"Head hurting? Is it your talent? I imagine emotions are running high here lately," Synnove consoled, glancing across the square as Kyreen shook her head. "Oh, here are the council members now. I should take my leave. Until morning, my friend."

"G'night," Kyreen replied with a wave. As Synnove walked away, Kyreen remained seated, waiting for Lang to finish his business. Once he concluded his final conversations, he drifted over to her. Seeing Kyreen holding her head in her hands, he frowned.

"Troubles with your head?" he asked, having finally learned not to ask her generically how she was feeling.

"Synnove," Kyreen replied, rising to her feet. Slipping her arms around his body, she leaned into him, instantly feeling better in his embrace. "I need to tell her."

"We have discussed this before," Lang murmured. "Aren has asked for discretion on this until after the upcoming castle assault. You cannot imagine the petty disputes and distractions that already bog down the council meetings."

"Sten's offense was more than a petty dispute," Kyreen objected, her temper flaring.

"You know that is not what I meant," he responded quietly.

Kyreen sighed. "I know. I am on edge. Maybe it is the camp emotions."

Lang kissed the top of her head, then with his arm around her shoulders settled them down on the log she and Synnove had been recently sharing. Before he could ask Kyreen about her day, a young man passed by giving a wave and calling out, "Hail, Kyreen! You coming by tonight? I have a question to pose to Eivor about her theory on city-state republics. She has to change her mind this time."

"Not tonight, Munin," Kyreen answered with a chuckle. "You can tell me about it tomorrow."

Munin gave a wave, disappearing into the night. Lang chuckled softly.

"You appear to be making friends," he murmured into her ear. "There are rumors about the wild goings on at the practitioners' area. Should I be worried?"

"Of Munin? Most definitely not," Kyreen replied. "Of none of them, in fact. I enjoy going over there because I do not stick out. Nobody makes me feel wrong if I do not talk. It is comfortable."

"They probably see your presence as you agreeing to take their side in the fight for the throne," Lang commented, his voice only half joking.

"At least they call me Kyreen now," she said. "And I am very clear about my position on the throne. They are not a bad group. I enjoy the time I spend with them."

"They are misfits and malcontents," Lang declared.

"Misfits because they perform the magic that keeps us all safe?" she responded sharply. "As for malcontent, can you blame them? How many agronomists sit on the Council, four, five?"

Lang held up five fingers while holding his tongue.

"How many mages?" Kyreen created an 'O' with her finger and thumb. "How is that fair?"

"I do not wish to quarrel," Lang replied quietly, brushing his lips gently across her temple. "Just do not let Aren hear you defend the magickers so vehemently. She has enough worries right now."

Kyreen sighed. "I look forward to moving on the castle. I am tired of waiting."

Lang did not answer. Instead he drew Kyreen's head to his shoulder, content to hold her close as the stars in the sky overhead continued their rotation. Last summer he had felt as she did now – eager and impatient for action. Now, sitting here with Kyreen in his arms, he wished for time to slow down so he could save these precious moments with her. The Battle would arrive in its time. Lang did not care to hurry it.

Chapter 40

The morning of the departure to the castle dawned bright and clear. Overnight a storm system had moved through drenching everything and creating muddy trails. Kyreen thought about her foster parents and how the weather would have been an omen from one of the Ten Lords of Hayrik. The Calanians, however, did not place a judgement of good or bad. It simply was. Looking around the quiet clearing with everyone gathered for morning meal, Kyreen thought the world looked fresh and clear. The flutters in her stomach came from her anxiety for action, while the dull pain at the base of her skull alerted her to the anxiety of her people, the five hundred assembling for battle and double that of their loved ones remaining behind.

As the soldiers gathered after breakfast, packs loaded, waiting for the council members to appear from their final early morning meeting, those remaining behind lingered, saying a final farewell. Kyreen stood with Ebbe and his father Atle, watching on, as Viggo spoke with his two youngest children who would not accompany their parents and older brother. Yngve and Karine stood by her. Kyreen wondered if leaving would be harder if she left family behind.

Then she noticed Vidar heading towards her. Svein walked beside him, guiding the old man through the crowd. Kyreen moved over to meet them.

"Hail, my dear," Vidar greeted her, taking both of Kyreen's hands into his gnarled grasp. "I hoped I would not be too late to say farewell."

Kyreen swallowed the lump in her throat before answering, "We are waiting for the Council to adjourn."

"I never thought to give thanks for long meetings," Vidar chuckled.

They stood together in silence, holding hands, until Aren and the rest of the council members appeared. Kyreen had the feeling the old blacksmith had something to say but if he did he never spoke. She was content being in his presence. Unlike Kasja whose talent suppressed the negative emotions, something about Vidar's presence smoothed out the anxieties of the people's emotions seeping into Kyreen's consciousness. With great reluctance, Kyreen kissed his leathery cheek.

"Farewell, Vidar," she murmured. "Thank you for spending time with me."

"As I always say, my dear, it is my pleasure," Vidar responded. "Safe journeys, and be safe."

Kyreen glanced at Svein, who had not spoken once this morning. Most days, the girl never uttered a word the whole morning. While she was always attentive to Vidar's needs, she remined unobtrusively in the background. Kyreen had seen the young girl at the practitioners' area on several different occasions. Much like Kyreen, Svein was content to hang back and observe. Once or twice, when their paths had crossed, Svein had given Kyreen a startled look as though she feared the older woman might say something or make her leave the area. Instead of engaging Svein, Kyreen had given her a greeting in passing, moving on quickly so the girl could resume her silent observations.

Now, as the soldiers prepared to head out, Kyreen decided to address Svein about what had been on her mind since the incident with Sten.

"Svein," Kyreen said, "I understand I owe you a great deal for your actions last fortnight. Thank you for contacting Lang so quickly. If not for you, I fear I may have been lost for much longer, maybe even forever."

The girl's gaze dropped to the ground, her bony arms wrapping around her body, clearly uncomfortable, with Kyreen's thanks. Then without warning the girl darted forward to fling her arms around Kyreen's waist, her head pressing against the tall woman's shoulder. With only a slight hesitation Kyreen wrapped her arms around the girl's slight frame. After a few short moments Svein pulled back, self-consciously running a hand over her short hair, which looked to be recently shorn. From across the clearing, Kyreen noticed Synnove watching them with a curious expression.

Kyreen bade Svein and Vidar farewell one last time before weaving through to the front of the crowd. Movement of the troops had been planned in five stages. As she had to be first in the tunnels Kyreen had been assigned to the first group. She had also been assigned three protectors - Viggo, Brigit and Ebbe – who had been instructed to accompany Kyreen to the tunnels, shadowing her until the battle concluded. Kyreen had resisted the assignment, arguing with Aren in private until the older woman agreed to take Kyreen's concerns to the Council.

From the look Aren gave her Kyreen intuited the order for her security had not been changed in this final planning meeting.

"You know this is ridiculous," Kyreen complained anew to Aren. "I am trained. I can take care of myself."

Viggo, who had taken point, glanced over his shoulder, first at his mate then Kyreen.

"Time for talk is done," he said firmly. "Concentrate on the trail."

Kyreen glared at Viggo, then Aren, before falling back a few paces so as not to be walking near the two. Brigit sidled up to Kyreen, bumping her with a shoulder.

"Watch it, Princess," she said blithely, her hands moving up to clutch at her chest. "Your attitude burns me to my core. I may begin to think you do not like me. Do not break my heart before we head into battle."

Her words had the desired effect. Kyreen chuckled and rolled her eyes at the mage. An added benefit was seeing the stiffening of Aren's back. Lately, Brigit usually reserved the 'Princess' talk to when she was within hearing distance of Aren. Kyreen recognized the mage's rebellious gesture to be more of a goading of Aren than anything else. Kyreen suspected the two women had a past history and waited for the right time to ask one of them the tale.

As Lang moved to walk beside Kyreen, he took her hand. Since he had always been in favor of Kyreen's security detail, however, Lang did not escape Kyreen's wrath. Lacking anyone else to blame, Kyreen glared at him, which only made him chuckle.

"It is for the best," he murmured, giving her hand a soft kiss before letting it go. With a gesture, Lang indicated Kyreen should walk ahead of him as they entered the forest single file.

The hike through the forest gave everyone time to think on the upcoming fight. It also provided Kyreen hours of sulking. The rains that started back up mid-afternoon did nothing to benefit her disposition. The one good point of that day's trek was the group did not encounter a single Galorian patrol, which meant they arrived to the meeting point earlier than scheduled. This close to the castle, everyone felt the pressure to remain quiet. No fire would be set. The plan being that a few hours before dawn, the first group would head out for the final push into the castle. If all went according to plan, the Calanians could have control of the castle by midday tomorrow.

As she settled on the wet ground to wait for sunset and arrival of the other groups, Kyreen tried to focus on that item – control of the castle. Unfortunately, as much as she relished the thought that she may be spending tomorrow night in the one place she had ever truly felt at home, she could not shake the anger, the discontent, the fear that snaked through her veins.

Lang cast a worried glance at her as he sat down beside her, but wisely held his tongue. Rummaging through his pack, he pulled out two small bruised apples, handing one to her.

"That is about the last of the fresh fruit," he commented taking a bite of his apple. "Still tasty."

Kyreen took the fruit from him without comment. Rolling the sphere in her hand, she frowned at it as if to blame the inanimate object for her emotional state.

"Hey, Princess!" Brigit remarked, squatting down before Kyreen, the opal necklace dangling from her fingers. "I need you to wear this again. I added some extra spells when I recast the wards."

"What is it?" Lang asked, eyeing the amulet warily.

"Do not worry, handsome," Brigit commented, flashing Lang her impish grin. "I am not swooping in to woo your woman away with pretty baubles. It is a protection amulet. Unless of course you are interested in the three…"

"Brigit!" Kyreen snapped crossly, grabbing the charmed necklace from the mage and slipping the rawhide thong over her head. Almost immediately she began feeling better as the opal settled against her bare skin.

"Fine. No need to snap off my head, Princess," Brigit said, holding up her hands. "I was just saying if your man here wanted…"

"I think we all know what you were saying," Kyreen interrupted, smiling, her voice less tense, a blush creeping into her cheeks. "What did you do to this amulet?"

"Like it?" Brigit responded. "I imbued the stone with some extra protection magic to block your empath talent."

She paused, glancing around, the smile slipping from her face. "There are strong emotions emanating around here right now. It will only get worse as the other groups join us."

"Thank you. It is helping greatly," Kyreen replied, impulsively reaching out to squeeze Brigit's hand.

The mage looked down at Kyreen's hand on hers, then glanced up at Lang. Her eyebrows waggled, the roguish smile slipping back in place.

Kyreen chuckled, retrieving her hand so as to wave Brigit away. "Enough of that! Shoo!" she said with a smile.

"A fine thank you that is," Brigit responded standing up. She brushed her hands together looking down at Kyreen with a fond smile. "Rest well, Princess."

With a parting nod to Lang, Brigit walked away, but not far. She had left her pack nearby with Ebbe. Watching the mage, Kyreen took a bite from her apple and leaned against Lang.

"You and Brigit seem to have connected," he commented, sliding an arm around Kyreen's shoulder.

"Yes. Strange, isn't it?" Kyreen replied. "When I first met Brigit, I thought she was serious and dull. That is just how she presents to people she does not know."

"Or trust," Lang offered.

"True," Kyreen nodded. "But she is quite a talented mage. I have learned so much from her just in these few days, and she was quite helpful in Gladys. I am fortunate to have her assigned to my protection."

She glanced up at his face, continuing before he could speak. "I am not happy that I have been assigned not just one nurse maid but three. But I also acknowledge that the team assigned to me is such talent that I should be honored."

Lang leaned down to kiss her lips, murmuring, "I am pleased. With your protectors in place, I will not be so concerned for your safety."

Kyreen rested her head on his shoulder, her eyes drifting to where Brigit and Ebbe sat quietly conversing. It bothered Kyreen that her friends had been tasked with her protection, that anyone had been. Kyreen knew the reasoning had nothing to do with her as Kyreen but her as the former princess. For she was the only one who had a connection with the gargoyle protecting the tunnels. As Aren had pointed out when she told Kyreen about the planned protections, no one knew how the gargoyle would react if Kyreen were incapacitated or worse killed while the Calanian troops were in the tunnels. Just because she knew the sound logic of the protection detail, did not mean she had to like it.

Slowly the sun set and the rains moved on. As night arrived so too did the last of the troops. The mood of the entire army seeped into Kyreen but only a fraction of what she had felt prior to donning Brigit's amulet. Kyreen's gratitude for the mage's foresight in the protection wards grew with each passing hour. At one point Lang rolled out a pallet for them to lie down upon. In the summertime warmth, they had no need for blankets, just each other's arms. With the dour mood of the camp, the lack of privacy did not matter. Kyreen merely wanted to be near Lang. As she rested in his embrace, her head upon his chest listening to his strong heartbeat, her mind wandered restlessly to the impending battle which could no longer be ignored. Slowly the tiny spark of fear resting in her belly like an apple seed sprouted, quickly gaining strength as she envisioned the tunnels full of Calanians, surging up through the passage ways, into the castle interior, the clang of clashing weapons ringing off stone walls.

"No, not tonight," Lang whispered, gently shaking Kyreen back to the moment. "Tonight is about hope and positivity. There will be time for tears and sorrow after, if at all. Do not mourn the loss that may never be."

He tipped her face up to his, kissing her tenderly. When they parted, he placed a soft kiss on the tip of her nose with a smile. "Now rest. Sleep if you can."

Kyreen settled back against him, grateful for his presence. Though her mind still swirled with random thoughts, she felt her eyes drifting shut. Soon she slumbered while Lang held her close, his gaze fixed on the twinkling stars overhead.

Chapter 41

The cacophony of the fight rung loud in Kyreen's ears. Instinct alone drew her weapon. The tricolor hilted sword slipping smoothly from its sheath, the clang of metal on metal as her blade met that of the wide eyed Galorian soldier bearing down on her. Staggering back, Kyreen adjusted her grip readying for the next blow. Then the gargoyle leapt, its strong jaws finding the delicate flesh below the soldier's helmeted head and above the plate spaulders protecting his shoulders. The soldier's body fell, his eyes still open in surprise from the sudden appearance of Kyreen and the gargoyle. Placing a hand on the creature's back, Kyreen ducked down, making herself a smaller target while she assessed her situation.

The irony of her arrival here was not lost on the woman. She had after all wanted to be in the middle of the fracas. Now that the gargoyle had transported her and she had been literally plopped into the fray, Kyreen cast about for what to do next. Behind her the first wave of Calanians fought the first wave of Galorians in the tunnels leading to the main entrance. The Galorian soldier Kyreen encountered had been a straggler descending the ramp behind his comrades. Kyreen glanced up the ramp leading into the main courtyard, just one of a dozen doorways between the castle and the tunnels, the only one wide enough for wagons and other large items to move through. Kyreen knew this entrance had been chosen for just that reason, but she would have preferred reentering the castle the same way she had exited all those years ago, via the War Room.

As soon as the thought crossed her mind, Kyreen once more experienced the stomach wrenching vertigo of transportation. When she again opened her eyes to complete darkness, the sounds of the battle had faded to a deafening silence. The air she breathed felt heavy and smelt stale. Returning the sword to the scabbard strapped to her back, Kyreen withdrew a small sphere from her pouch, the one Brigit had given her to practice illumination spells on. Softly reciting the words Kyreen lit the sphere. Her other hand she kept firmly planted on the gargoyle's back. Clearly touch was how the gargoyle had been able to transport Kyreen from the lower entrance where she had been watching the Calanians pour into the tunnels, to the battlefront, and now here which appeared to be the foot of a wooden staircase leading up to a closed door. Kyreen stared up at the door, fairly certain what she would find on the other side of that door, but also concerned about what condition she would find the War Room in. The Galorians had been in possession of her childhood home for a very long time.

With a sigh, Kyreen turned away from the stairs and the closed door. Looking down at the creature she said, "I suppose I need to go back to the lower entrance if you could take me there, Vaktare."

The next time Kyreen opened her eyes, she saw Viggo and Brigit standing almost nose to nose, apparently in a heated discussion. Ebbe stood off to the side idly waving Calanians into the tunnels. Sounds of the battle could be heard faintly in the distance. The joke on Kyreen's lips died when she saw her friends' expressions. The three of them descended upon her, all talking at the same time.

"Where have you been?" growled Viggo.

"Thank the goddess!" Ebbe exclaimed.

"Will you look at that? Welcome back, Princess," Brigit said, her twinkling gaze fixed on the gargoyle with new interest.

As Viggo grabbed Kyreen's arm, the gargoyle tensed. Its yellow glowing eyes stared at the man, a menacing growl rumbling deep in its throat. Viggo glared down at the creature tightening his grip on Kyreen's arm as if daring the creature to act.

"Hey!" Kyreen exclaimed, resting a hand on Viggo's chest. "Calm down!"

She stowed the illuminated sphere in her bag to free up both hands. Resting a hand on the gargoyle's head, keeping her other hand on Viggo's chest she said, "Be right back."

Brigit blinked as the creature, Kyreen, and Viggo disappeared. She glanced at Ebbe, who looked slightly awestruck, saying, "I get to go next."

"Not a problem," Ebbe responded.

Eventually Kyreen had the gargoyle transport Brigit to the War Room entrance while Ebbe stayed behind at the exterior entrance. Getting Ebbe to agree to remain in their assigned location had taken some convincing from Kyreen. Finally, the young man had agreed when Kyreen argued that someone needed to stay to let the others know what had happened. If Ebbe had been a little disgruntled about the change in plans, Viggo was simply enraged. That Kyreen had asked the gargoyle to transport him then she had left without consulting him had only made him angrier. When Kyreen and

Brigit appeared at the bottom of the steps leading up to the War Room they found Viggo pacing back and forth like a caged animal. He had his crossbow out, bolt knocked in place, looking more than ready for a fight. The sphere Kyreen had thrust into his hand before disappearing now cast shadows across the Hunter's angry visage.

"Do not ever do that to me again," he growled, glaring at the gargoyle, then at Kyreen.

"Me?" Brigit said a bit giddily. "You can do that to me anytime."

"I am sorry, Viggo," Kyreen apologized releasing Brigit's arm but keeping the gargoyle under her touch. "I had no idea Vaktare could do that. Then I thought if I..." her voice trailed off and she looked at him imploring.

"You thought if you asked permission I would deny you," Viggo completed her thought.

Kyreen nodded, her face sheepish.

"I suppose you are just as safe here as back at the exit," he admitted with a sigh, glancing around. "Just keep that thing here with you."

Kyreen glanced up the stairs at the closed door then back at Viggo, who shook his head.

"No," he said firmly. "We wait here or back at the entrance."

"Just a peek?" Kyreen asked. "It will harm nothing. Everyone is occupied with the battle."

"Do you know that? What good could come of going up there? What happens to this thing, to our people in the tunnels, if you leave the tunnel?" Viggo snapped back, gesturing to the gargoyle. He ran a hand over his face taking a deep breath. When he next spoke, his voice was less harsh. "Kyreen, I know how hard it is to stand by while others go into battle, especially a loved one. Do you think I enjoy my assignment with Aren and Yngve in the front wave? What about Ebbe? He lost his mother last summer and now when he is old enough to join the fight, he watched his remaining parent go without him."

Brigit stepped in between the two, glaring up at Viggo. "Ease up there," she said. "She got caught up in the moment. No need to heap guilt on top of her. She did not ask for you, or Ebbe, or me for that matter, to be her guard. It was your mate who made the decision to assign us, who made the decision to give Kyreen a protection detail, who has been making all these decisions of who and when and where to fight."

"It is fine, Brigit," Kyreen said, putting a hand on the mage's arm. "Viggo meant me no harm. He is correct."

She glanced up at the door, beckoning her, taunting her, saying, "A part of me has this irrational thought that maybe if I go back through that very door I will be three years old again, looking forward to riding my horse in the Festival parade and tormenting my twin brother because he cannot make his eyes go crossways."

Kyreen looked down one darkened tunnel from where the sounds of the continued battle could barely be heard. "There are people dying down there. I can feel it," she said quietly. "And for what? Why did the Galorians want this castle then? Why do they defend it now?"

Viggo sighed, running a hand over his face again. "I know I will regret this," he said. "We can explore…down here."

Though Kyreen knew he only agreed to it so to distract her, she did not let it stop her. But where to go? Kyreen tried to remember the map. Keeping a hand on the gargoyle's back, she silently reminded it to stay with her. Though it did not speak in words to Kyreen she could make out general feelings and sensed intelligence in the beast.

"Can you talk with it?" Brigit asked, seeing Kyreen watching the gargoyle.

"Not so much," Kyreen shook her head.

"If we knew how it received its power and connection to you," Brigit suggested, "then maybe you could communicate?"

"There has to be a way," Viggo commented. "The castle guards patrolled down here without any royals present."

"If Kyreen is correct and this is the War Room entrance," Brigit said pointing down a darkened tunnel, "then may I suggest we head that way?"

"Why that way?" Viggo questioned.

"According to the map there is a document vault down that corridor," Brigit said looking recalcitrant. "I would guess any archived records would be there, most likely undisturbed thanks to this friendly fellow here."

Kyreen nodded. "I remember seeing it, by the spring."

"But how do you know that?" Viggo asked, his eyes narrowing at Brigit.

"I am not simply a pretty face," the mage quipped.

"There is one map," he commented, still looking at Brigit with suspicion, "and it is locked in the Council Tent."

"So everyone believes," Brigit responded cryptically walking down the corridor she had pointed at. From within her pack the mage produced a sphere about the size of her fist. After illuminating it she recited another incantation so the sphere levitated just above her left shoulder illuminating the way before her but without shining in her eyes.

"Now you are just showing off," Kyreen said, following the mage, the gargoyle padding silently beside her. After a moment's hesitation, Viggo followed.

The farther down the corridor they walked, the less Kyreen felt from the battle. Even with Brigit's amulet filtering out the majority of the sensations, enough had been hitting Kyreen to affect her mood. With the face of the Galorian soldier that the gargoyle had killed still fresh in her mind, she felt off balance.

"There it is!" Brigit exclaimed, hastening her pace.

By the time Kyreen reached the doorway Brigit had begun scanning the various scrolls littering a large table occupying the middle of the room.

"This all is maintenance documentation, blueprints and specifications," the mage grumbled, standing upright to glance at the shelves lining the walls, full of scrolls and books. As Brigit turned around and saw Kyreen standing in the doorway something in the young woman's expression made the mage pause.

"Kyreen?" Brigit asked cautiously.

"Do you not smell it?" Kyreen asked so quietly Brigit barely heard the words.

Viggo, walking up from behind, had witnessed the stiffening of Kyreen's body. He stepped up with caution, staying well back. "What is wrong?" he asked, his eyes finding Brigit inside the room.

"I do not..." Brigit started to say.

"He has been here," Kyreen's whisper interrupted. She took a step back from the doorway, turning to press her back against the wall, her eyes finding Viggo.

"He has been here," she repeated, pulling the sword out of the scabbard strapped to her back. She placed a hand on the gargoyle's head and they blinked out of sight.

Brigit, in the doorway, looked over to Viggo and shrugged. "She said she smelled something."

"Oh, by the goddess," Viggo ran a hand across his hair. Then he started back down the tunnel towards the War Room door, calling back, "You stay there, continue looking through the scrolls. If Kyreen returns, keep her here!"

When Kyreen opened her eyes, she found herself in total darkness once more. The faint noises of battle came from her right side. With no other source of lighting to use, she shut her eyes again, visualizing the passageway, and slowly began shuffling in the direction of the staircase. Just as the toe of her boot hit the bottom step she heard running footsteps. She spun in that direction, holding the sword in both hands. The gargoyle pressed against her side, growling quietly. When Viggo appeared from the darkness, Kyreen's little glowing sphere in his hand, she gave a sigh, lowering the sword.

"I am not going back there," she said firmly by way of greeting.

"Fine by me," Viggo said. "But you cannot keep disappearing."

"I did not do it consciously," Kyreen glanced down at the gargoyle, still pressed against her leg keeping a wary eye on the Calanian man. "I smelled…magic has been performed in that room…recently. When I pulled my sword, I had the thought that I needed to get somewhere safe."

She glanced around the passageway. "I suppose Vaktare feels this is the safest place for me."

"At least it did not take you to the battle," Viggo commented.

"True. That was an unpleasant experience," she replied, sheathing her sword.

"Pardon?" Viggo arched his eyebrows.

A light in the tunnel saved Kyreen from having to answer. Brigit rounded the corner a moment later to Viggo with his crossbow at the ready and Kyreen with her sword redrawn. The mage stopped as soon as she spied them, waving two scrolls.

"Ease down, friends," Brigit said. "Right after you two bolted I found what I believe we need."

She unfurled one of the scrolls. "It looks like a fairly straight forward incantation to link the guards to the royal family. That is you, Princess, like it or not."

Brigit looked between Kyreen and Viggo. "Shall we try it?" she asked with childlike enthusiasm.

Kyreen looked at Viggo who nodded. "Very well," she said. "What do you need?"

"Your sword," Brigit replied. "And your blood. Yours and Viggo's."

"Seriously?" Kyreen frowned.

"Aw, you are getting wise, Princess," Brigit grinned. "No, the sword is all. Even then I think it may just be a prop for the ritual. The words are the important piece."

"Before I go reciting spells, I would like to take a look at that," Kyreen said, reaching for the scroll.

Brigit handed it over carefully saying, "Take care. That parchment is old and brittle."

Kyreen gingerly opened up the scroll her eyes quickly scanning the words. "This seems too simple," she commented. "Just a few words and Viggo is a protectorate of the royal family?"

"That is not correct," Viggo added. "My father used to complain all the time how guards could not be assigned to the tunnels because this creature would not accept them."

"Do not blame the spell," Brigit retorted. "Blame the caster. By the time the Battle happened magic had been in decline for decades. My bet is that nobody was able to perform the ritual as it had been designed thus the bondings did not work well."

She glanced at Kyreen, holding up the other scroll. "Fortunately, your tattoo has been applied and apparently correctly spelled, for it seems your bond with Vaktare here comes from the mark on your shoulder. Unfortunately, you were not yet spelled to communicate with it."

"Do you have that spell?" Kyreen asked hopefully.

Brigit shook her head. "I found these in a scroll case marked Royal Protection. There was enough room inside for more scrolls. It could be the spell was out at the time of the Battle or …"

"Or Sten has it," Kyreen finished for her.

Brigit shook her head. "I do not see how he could have gained access to the tunnels."

"When I came here last winter, someone was down here," Kyreen replied. "And someone performed magic in that room recently enough that I can still smell it. And it smelled like…like Sten's magic."

"Let us worry about one thing at a time," Viggo suggested. "How about we try the bonding spell?"

Brigit arched her eyebrows at Viggo. "Do you trust met to cast on you, Aren's mate?"

"No," Viggo replied. "I trust Kyreen."

"I am not sure about that," Kyreen shook her head. "I do not believe I am strong enough."

In the end, Brigit stood by Kyreen, hands on the young woman's forearms giving her magical energies with Viggo holding the scroll for Kyreen to read. With one hand on the gargoyle, the other holding her sword, Kyreen readied herself.

"Remember," Brigit said, "intent is the majority of the spell. Keep focused on your intent, channel your energies to that end."

Kyreen nodded and began the incantation. She felt the tingling of energies and focused on the words she recited. Placing the flat of the blade on one of Viggo's shoulders then lifting the sword high, she tapped it lightly to his other shoulder. The tingling sensations grew until Kyreen felt it like a great sphere surrounding them. As she finished with "By the ancestors' will may it be" the energies collapsed into Viggo and Vaktare.

Sheathing the sword, Kyreen asked, "How do we know if it worked?"

Brigit shrugged. "Do you feel any different?"

"Not that I notice," Viggo said. "Although I think that thing is not looking at me with as much malice."

Kyreen chuckled, then stopped to look down the passageway towards the battle. She took a few steps that way until Viggo reached out to stop her. She looked between him and Brigit.

"I think it is over," she whispered.

Chapter 42

Viggo led them down the auxiliary tunnel, refusing to allow the gargoyle to transport him again. With each step, Kyreen felt the dichotomy of emotions – joy and sorrow, cheer and remorse. When she thought the anxiety would overwhelm her, they rounded a corner to the chamber with the ramp out into the castle's upper bailey. Numerous Calanian soldiers milled around, some going outside, some coming inside. Viggo clamped a hand around one of Kyreen's arms so as not to get separated as they pushed through the crowd. At the mouth of the tunnel, he paused, scanning the crowd outside, but the entrance was too low for him to see anything clearly.

"Go," Kyreen said softly. "I will stay here."

Viggo shook his head. "No, I stay with you. I had hoped to catch a glimpse."

"My bond with Lang is nowhere near as strong as what you have with Aren and I know he is fine," she commented.

"It is not Aren," Viggo murmured reminding Kyreen that the Hunter had a child in the fray. "Our bond is not quite as strong especially now that he himself is covenanted."

Kyreen noticed the conversations around her had ceased. Glancing about she saw that the gargoyle, standing still with her hand resting on its back had attracted attention. Everyone had stepped away giving their little group a wide berth.

"Maybe I should go back inside a bit," she said. "We seem to be a distraction."

Viggo glanced around once more before turning his attention down the tunnel and agreed. "I suppose so."

As they made their way down away from the bailey entrance, Kyreen felt Lang approaching. A moment later he appeared from the tunnel the Calanians had used for their main attack. When she saw him Kyreen forgot about everything – the gargoyle, the anxiety, the battle, the magic. Without speaking she pulled away from Viggo sprinting to close the distance so she could throw her arms around Lang. He pulled her tight, whispering in her ear, "As soon as they surrendered, I went back for you. Ebbe said you had disappeared with that creature."

Kyreen had not allowed herself to think about how worried she had been until he was in her arms. Now she blinked back her tears giving silent thanks to the deities that watched over this world, whether that be the Hanorians Lords or the Calanian goddess, she did not care at this moment.

"Is this it?" she asked. "Is it over?"

He nodded. "Aren has some people rounding up the Galorians. She wants me there when she speaks with their commanding officer. But I had to find you and do this," he said, taking her face in his hands and kissing her hungrily.

After a moment Viggo coughed softly. He waited another few heartbeats then coughed again, a little louder. Brigit, watching on in amusement, finally reached over to tug on Kyreen's arm, earning her a growl from both Lang and the gargoyle.

"Sorry," Kyreen murmured, her cheeks reddening.

"I am not," Lang responded. His joy intoxicated Kyreen as much, if not more, than their kiss had.

"Enough time for that later," Viggo said. "Let Aren know we may have a solution for the tunnels. We are going back to the outer entrance. She should send over anyone she wants to work as tunnel guards."

Lang pressed a final kiss to Kyreen's lips then headed back into the sunshine. Kyreen watched him disappear before turning to resume the walk with Viggo and Brigit. Once fully inside the smile left her lips as they walked pass a line of bodies, the Calanian soldiers who had died. Two of the deceased Kyreen had known from the Training Camp. She clenched her jaw as tears welled up once more in her eyes. Viggo took her arm again, this time more to guide her and comfort her.

"So many less than last year," he murmured. "No less tragic though."

When they reached the outer entrance, Ebbe waited alone. He gave an audible sigh of relief when he spotted them walking towards him. After giving him an update on the battle, the apparent victory, and the gargoyle spell, Kyreen performed the spell on her friend.

Then she and Brigit sat down to look over the other scroll. As they reviewed it, Ebbe worked with the gargoyle. Though no communication seemed to be happening, the gargoyle appeared to be more relaxed, even lying down near Kyreen, its glowing yellow eyes ever watchful. So, the rest of the day passed. About a dozen soldiers, Eilert amongst them, showed up midafternoon to be spelled. Afterwards Kyreen felt lightheaded and unable to concentrate on her discussions with Brigit. The second time Kyreen nodded off Viggo hoisted her to her feet.

"The final load from last night's camp can go through the front gates," he told the soldiers, now tunnel guards, standing around waiting their orders. "You two, go outside and wait for them, take them through the front."

Once the pair had exited Viggo had the others close and lock the gates, commenting, "We will need to get those fortified as quickly as possible."

He turned to Kyreen, "Does this creature have a way to monitor the tunnel system? Does it track all movement in and out?"

"It must," Kyreen answered.

"We need to figure that out so we can devise a security plan," Viggo commented more to himself than the others.

"We are going to walk to the bailey entrance so these guards can leave, then we can go through the War Room door," he then explained to Kyreen, who could not refrain from hugging him.

Thus, as the sun began to set over the castle, Kyreen stood on the top step of the staircase with Viggo right behind her. Though he wanted to make sure the room was clear, he understood her desire to open the door. At the bottom of the steps, Brigit and Ebbe looked on with Vaktare the gargoyle. As Kyreen stepped through the door the entire room shimmered through the unshed tears in her eyes. The late afternoon sun shone in through dusty windows on a room void of furniture. A pile of gray ashes filled the stone fireplace. Remnants of furniture lay scattered across the floor. A glance above the hearth showed the wall void of her grandparents' portrait. Kyreen did not know whether to be saddened or grateful.

As she walked slowly around the outer edge of the room, Kyreen remembered how the room had looked before on that night so long ago. She stopped in front of the fireplace, eyes on the bare wall. In her mind, she saw the great canvas painting– Queen Ursula with ebony curls and emerald green eyes standing beside King Rolf with sapphire eyes and flowing brunette locks, in his hand the tri-color hilted sword now secured in the scabbard upon his granddaughter's back.

Swallowing the lump in her throat Kyreen glanced over at her friends standing by the tunnel doorway, then around the room. "It is not as large as I remember," she half-joked. Moving her gaze to Viggo she asked, "Is it alright to go into the rest of the castle?"

Viggo shrugged. "I suppose so. We may… hey, wait!"

Kyreen had taken off as soon as Viggo started speaking, out the door before any of the others could react. When he called out for her to wait, she merely thought about pausing, never lessening her speed. In the hall, she turned right, following the corridor to a massive foyer dominated by an expansive staircase. As Viggo, Brigit and Ebbe reached the foot of the stairs Kyreen disappeared around the corner on the second floor.

"By the goddess," Viggo mumbled as he began taking the stairs two at a time. "I was going to say we might want to clear all the rooms as we go."

"Oh, but the Princess's way is much more interesting," Brigit commented, right on his heels.

Viggo flashed an irritated look at the mage. She chuckled, wondering which of her words upset the Hunter the most.

The second floor had not been in use much, debris and dust littered the floor. Still only by his tracking ability was Viggo able to discern Kyreen's path took her up the next set of stairs not down one of the shadowy hallways. On the third floor, where very little of the dying day's sunlight penetrated, all three easily discerned where the young woman had gone, for only one door stood open allowing dim illumination.

Kyreen stood at the narrow window gazing down at the courtyard below. Years of dirt coated the paned glass distorting the images of her fellow Calanians milling below. In the back of her head, Kyreen thought with a flash of guilt that her time might be better spent down there being useful.

Then she rested her cheek on the cool stone wall, allowing her eyes to drift shut.

A soft breeze fluttered through the open window. A crescent moon cast silver light across the bedroom floor. Soft luxurious linens embracing her under a down comforter. The cotton nightgown chafing her right shoulder blade. Quillan with his golden locks asleep. The glint of steel reflecting in moonlight.

With a start, Kyreen pulled back from the window, her eyes snapping open. Running a hand over her braid, she glanced around the room. Void of furniture like the War Room downstairs, this space held only dust and broken remnants of what Kyreen could only guess were her and Quillan's beds. The thought made her heart ache. She had only spent one night in her big girl bed but how she had loved it and the childish notion that she was almost grown up. Hot tears pricked at her eyes once more.

"Kyreen," Viggo said quietly from across the darkening room, "I would feel more comfortable if we saved the explorations for in the morrow's daylight."

Kyreen nodded, crossing over to the door. Instead of turning to head back down the hall towards the stairs, however, she turned left.

"Kyreen," Viggo called, no anger in his voice, only resignation.

"I want to see Mama's room," Kyreen replied over her shoulder opening the next door down the hall, "then we can…"

Seeing Kyreen stop in the doorway and sensing something amiss, Brigit pushed by Viggo.

"Kyreen?" she said quietly, placing a hand on the younger woman's shoulder. Kyreen's body trembled slightly beneath the mage's touch.

"He has been here," Kyreen whispered.

Brigit did not need to ask for clarification. She slid past Kyreen and entered the bedroom, Queen Tyra's bedroom according to the young woman standing frozen in the doorway. The mage could sense the residue of magic. The final bits of daylight shone through the grimy windows as the sun dipped below the western mountains, leaving the room in purple twilight. Brigit pulled out her sphere to illuminate the space. Similar to the other rooms they had seen, this one was dusty with rubbish strewn across the floor. Unlike the other rooms, however, this one did have furniture but only one piece, a free-standing mirror placed squarely in the middle of the room. The reflecting surface and surrounding wood frame gleamed in the mage light, completely free of dust.

Brigit let loose a stream of obscenities before turning to look at Viggo who stood in the hallway behind Kyreen. "How many rooms do you reckon this place has? Not just the palace here, but everything?"

"I have no idea. Hundreds probably," Viggo answered, shaking head. "Why?"

"We are about to find out," Brigit replied, looking back at the mirror. "Better go tell your mate that we are in for a long night ahead of us."

Bogged down with post battle logistics such as debriefing the captured Galorians, lodging and feeding the troops, and preparing for resettlement Aren could not spare any energy for the type of operation Brigit proposed – a systematic sweep of the entire compound for any potential portals into the castle. Pinching the bridge of her nose she stood behind the large desk in the garrison commander's former office and looked at the two standing before her. That Viggo brought the mage directly to Aren without first speaking to her privately spoke to the urgency he felt. When Aren asked about Kyreen, Viggo explained he had sent her and Ebbe to get food.

"She is dead on her feet," he concluded. "But insists she can help with searching the tunnels."

"She spelled a dozen or more of your soldiers in an absurdly short span of time," Brigit added her voice containing a sharp edge, having seen the disparaging expression flit across Aren's face. "She is not tired. She is depleted. Between casting wards and receiving all the emotions from today's battle, I am surprised she is still conscious."

Aren raised a hand in surrender. "No need to get testy, Brigit. We are all tired."

"No, Aren, there is a need," Brigit retorted. "You simply do not get it. You have no idea how magic works. Energy exhaustion is not like being physically tired. But how could you know that? Right? If you had at least one mage counselor you would have been aware of the...Oh, you know what? I do not care!"

The mage spun around, stalking to the door, but before she got there Aren's voice stopped Brigit in her tracks.

"You are right," Aren said without emotion.

"My apologies," Brigit said, turning around slowly. "I was leaving in such a snit, I believe I may have misheard you."

Aren sighed, a ghost of a smile flitting momentarily across her face. "I said you are right. Are you happy?"

"There is nothing to be happy about," Brigit responded, drifting back to where she had been standing beside Viggo. "Not yet."

"I simply cannot oversee one more thing," Aren stated. "Would you, with Viggo's help, coordinate the sweep?"

Brigit pointed at her chest. "Me? You want me to be in charge? You must be tired."

This time Aren did chuckle softly. "I am, but I also do not want to lose this castle after all we have accomplished because of my pride and our ancient quarrels."

The smile left Aren's face as she continued. "I want this search to be as quiet as possible. Make it a mundane, routine sweep for possible hideaways and anything useful. What do you propose doing with the mirror in Tyra's room, and any other items you find?"

"My first instinct was to smash it and burn it," Brigit answered without any humor.

"I can agree with that," Viggo muttered.

Aren nodded her eyes drifting to the pile of papers on the table before her. "Very well. I leave it to your discretion, whatever you two decide. In addition to the tunnel guards, take as many more of soldiers you may need, but quietly."

As they headed out of the garrison, Viggo commented, "I would think we need to round up any magickers on site."

"What do you mean?" Brigit asked, eyeing Viggo suspiciously.

"I mean our task might be more quickly dispatched if we had the assistance of any magic users," Viggo replied.

"You know none of the practitioners were permitted to join the campaign," Brigit responded, her voice uncharacteristically level and cautious. "I am only here because of the…Kyreen."

"I know none of the registered magic users were permitted to volunteer, yes," Viggo responded. He stopped walking, motioning Brigit to follow him into an unoccupied room. After shutting the door, he turned to face her, and continued speaking, "I also know that your practitioner's area is always full of people playing at magic. Furthermore, I realize registering as a magicker is political suicide, so most avoid admitting publicly any association with your lot."

"My lot?" Brigit responded, two bright angry spots appearing on her cheeks. "You make magic sound like some illicit drug or worse, a disease. After all these years of abuse, followed by your lovely speech, you expect me to willingly point out to you any casters so after all this is over you can add their names to the Council's registry?"

Viggo ran a hand over his face with a tired sigh. "What if I do not know who the magickers in the group are?"

Brigit shook her head. "I will not risk exposing my people without guarantees in place ensuring they will not suffer for their assistance."

"While you delay with your petty demands, the entire compound is vulnerable to attack," Viggo stated.

"If not for Kyreen insisting on visiting her mother's quarters, we all would be blissfully unaware of the dangers. Dare I say, you would be in there with Aren right now, having delivered her food, without a care in the world. Me, I would be finding a warm body and a dark corner in which to pass the night away. Trust me, old man, I would much prefer that to the evening that is ahead of me," Brigit retorted. "This search can take as long as it needs to. No way I am giving up my casters."

Viggo stared at Brigit for a long moment before nodding. "I can respect that."

In addition to the fourteen tunnel guards, Viggo rounded up another thirty soldiers to search the structures inside the castle walls. Leaving those soldiers under the watchful eye of Atle, Brigit and Viggo took to the tunnels with Kyreen, Ebbe, and the tunnel guard contingency.

As they waited outside the document vault room for Brigit and Viggo to refer to the tunnel maintenance maps, Kyreen and Ebbe sat apart from the others, the gargoyle lying between them. Kyreen found comfort in contact with the creature as it seemed to be transferring energy to her.

Just as Kyreen's eyes began to flutter shut and she felt herself nodding off, Ebbe's quiet voice woke her up. "The person we search for, is he the one who hurt you?"

Kyreen suddenly felt chilled. "What do you mean?"

"You are different," Ebbe stated. "Since the Festival when you left with Lang, but I cannot believe he is the one who hurt you, not the way he gazes upon you and you upon him."

Kyreen stared at her fists balled up in her lap, trying to decide how much to tell her friend. Finally, she said softly, "No it was not Lang, and yes he is the one we hope to stop from coming through the portals."

"I always thought the rules about reflecting surfaces to be old superstitions, not anything real," Ebbe remarked.

"Superstitions have their beginnings in truth so no harm in keeping them." Kyreen commented. "My foster mother used to say that."

The pair sat in silence for a few minutes, then Kyreen spoke. Her voice quiet enough the sound barely reached Ebbe's ears.

"Please do not tell Synnove," Kyreen said, the tremor in her voice just registerable. "It was Sten. He... he enthralled me... among other things."

Ebbe held still without speaking so long Kyreen thought maybe he had not heard her. Then he replied, his own voice just as quiet as Kyreen's had been. "I am not surprised. He used to torment me as a child. Somehow, he knew I was not interested in girls long before I knew what being interested meant, and my preferences annoyed him to no end. He would taunt me with vulgarities, asking me if I wanted to kiss him and sometimes he grabbed me between my legs."

Listening to Ebbe's story, Kyreen felt his angst so she reached out to take his hand in hers.

"Of course, he always did this when we were alone," Ebbe continued quietly. "He was sly that way. I could not say anything. Who would believe me? Sten with the perfect manners, always volunteering to take me fishing or to gather firewood. Fortunately, his attention span was short. After a few days he would drift away, probably to some other victim. But then, just as I thought I was safe, he would turn back up."

"I am sorry," Kyreen murmured.

Ebbe squeezed Kyreen's hand, returning her sad smile. Then his eyes moved to the archive room's doorway. "I think they are ready."

Ebbe rose to his feet, extending a hand to assist Kyreen up. Together, with the gargoyle, they joined the rest of the group.

Down in the tunnels Kyreen had a tough time figuring out the passage of time. She only knew she felt bone tired as she and Ebbe with the gargoyle worked through their assigned area. By the time they had finished, without discovering anyone or anything of interest, she was having trouble staying on her feet.

"How about you have a seat while I report in?" Ebbe suggested, gesturing for Kyreen to sit back down in the tunnel where they had waited earlier.

Resting her head on the wall, Kyreen's eyes looked at the spring, still and dark, her mind wandering. As her eyes drifted shut, she had a thought, something to ask Brigit. Then Ebbe was shaking her.

"C'mon," he said. "Everyone is done. Time to head out."

Kyreen stifled a yawn, taking his proffered hand to rise to her feet. A few steps away Viggo and Brigit stood waiting for them. Seeing the mage triggered Kyreen's brain. She frowned, remembering there was something she had wanted to ask.

"What is the matter?" Viggo asked seeing Kyreen's expression when she and Ebbe walked up.

"I cannot remember," Kyreen shrugged off the nagging thought. "How did the search go?"

"Nothing down here," Brigit grumbled. "A waste of time."

"No," Viggo asserted. "Instead of uncertainties we have facts. Nobody will be transpiring down here."

Kyreen concentrated on the simple task of putting one foot in front of the other as her friends discussed the search. The walk back to the bailey entrance seemed to her, so very far. At the mouth of the tunnel she leaned down to hug Vaktare, mentally communicating with the gargoyle that she would return in the morning.

"It is not a pet," Viggo muttered. "I do not even know if it is a living being or just a magical construct."

Her defenses low from exhaustion, tears pricked at Kyreen's eyes. Shielding her face from the others, she did not comment but simply strode out of the tunnel. At the top of the ramp she halted, not knowing where she should go. The entire courtyard had shadows of sleeping soldiers. A lone light shone out of the barracks where Aren must still be working. A small fire burned across the yard where a few figures stood in conversation.

"Come on," Viggo said, quietly coming up behind Kyreen to place an arm around her shoulders. "Let us find Lang."

Brigit patted Kyreen on the back. "Find me in the morning so I can respell that amulet. I am sure the protections are almost gone."

The last things Kyreen remembered clearly from that night, after Ebbe and Brigit bid them good night, was Viggo leading her towards the barracks. She had a vague recollection of Lang setting out their bedroll in a corner of the bailey which had a few unoccupied spots. Even as they settled down, Lang's arms tightly holding her, Kyreen had fallen almost immediately into a deep dreamless sleep.

Chapter 43

Despite her weariness from the previous evening, Kyreen awoke before dawn. She opened her eyes with a momentary disorientation from the lack of bird sounds and the strangely shaped shadows on the castle walls. Then she woke more fully and remembered the previous day's events. With Lang spooned up to her, his arms tight around her, she lay still, allowing the realization to seep in that she had come home. It all seemed surreal right now in the gray predawn.

After seeing the pile of papers on Aren's desk, Kyreen imagined there would be plenty of time for the reality to sink in. As her mind turned to her day ahead, Kyreen wondered what role she had now that the battle had concluded, and the tunnel guard had access to the tunnels. She did not belong on the Council nor had she been assigned to any of the units. Would she be working with Brigit to decipher some way to communicate with Vaktare? Then there was the issue of Sten. He clearly worked with the Galorians, had been here in the castle recently.

"No, it is too early," Lang murmured softly brushing away her hair to place a kiss at the nape of her neck. He pressed his body more firmly against hers. "Let me distract you?"

Kyreen's entire body tingled, and she shivered as much from his words as his touch. Twisting around in his arms, she pressed her lips to his gently. "Do not tease. What would all these people think?"

Lang lifted his head to gaze at the shadowy lumps of their sleeping comrades. "These people? They are all sleeping." Sensing her rising anxiety, he dropped a chaste kiss to her lips. "Relax. I jest…sort of. I did distract you from the worries that have you nibbling that absolutely delectable bottom lip," he kissed her once more, but stilled his hands upon her body. While their physical relationship had returned, sometimes Kyreen's eyes would get just a bit too wide or her body would stiffen so he had begun to watch for signs that his actions might trigger a panic attack.

"I missed you yesterday," she whispered, conscious of the sleeping people surrounding them. "After the battle, all I wanted was to be with you."

"Believe me, I would have much rather been with you in the tunnels," Lang responded with a grimace. "Anywhere but those interrogations."

"What happened?" Kyreen asked, unused to hearing such angst in Lang's voice.

"Nothing happened. It is just...the stories from these Galorians are disturbing, hard to believe," Lang replied. "But the worst part is that to a man they tell the truth, or believe they speak the truth."

"Disturbing how?"

Lang shook his head, softly kissing her lips. "Not the sort of discussion for here. Are you certain you wish to deny me the pleasures of your body?"

He waggled his eyebrows in such a comical fashion Kyreen had to laugh. He chuckled, kissed her forehead and rolled to a sitting position. After handing Kyreen her boots, he began pulling on his own.

Once they had stood up, Lang packed the bedroll, commenting, "We should have a room assignment later today."

As they wove their way through the sleeping forms, Kyreen again thought about the extensive amount of work still ahead. She had a hard time wrapping her head around it all. Now all the long council meetings did not seem so senseless.

She slipped her hand into Lang's, giving it a soft squeeze. "I do not believe I ever fully appreciated what all you have to do on the Council," she murmured as they entered the barracks building.

After Lang stowed their gear in the room the Council had commandeered for their meetings, the couple wandered up to the parapet where they could watch the sunrise. The day dawned bright and warm, full of promise for the Calanians first full day back in their castle. Much too soon for Kyreen's liking, they went back down to the courtyard for morning meal and to begin their day's work.

The day progressed without issue for Kyreen until right before supper. After breakfast Lang had headed to his council meeting and Kyreen had met up with Brigit. Once Brigit had respelled the amulet, the two of them had stayed in the tunnels to look through the expansive library that the documents vault held. Then they had moved outside where Brigit had, at Kyreen's request, begun teaching her a silence spell. When the young man, still barely a boy Kyreen had thought despite the peach fuzz on his upper lip, approached them, Kyreen had been surprised to notice the long afternoon shadows. She and Brigit had found an out of the way corner of yard enclosed by overgrown hedges in the shadow of the palace. Kyreen thought it might be the gardens but any flowers that might have once grown here looked to have died away years ago.

"Spit it out, boy," Brigit commanded, not unkindly.

"You are requested in council chambers," the boy said timidly.

Brigit shrugged at Kyreen. "You go on then. We were about done here," she said rising to her feet. "If you want, we can take it up again tomorrow."

"Excuse me," the boy's voice barely audible as his face pinkened. "Both of you have been requested."

"Who has been requested?" Brigit asked.

"My orders were to fetch the Princess Kyreen and Brigit the Mage," the boy replied, his voice a little firmer. "I was told you would be together."

"Oh really?" Brigit flashed a playful grin at Kyreen. "We are a couple now, Princess. That tall handsome man of yours might get jealous, although I have already told you both…"

"Enough, Brigit!" Kyreen laughed, rolling to her feet. To the messenger she said, "My thanks. Please run ahead and let them know we are on our way."

As the boy scampered away, Brigit cocked her head at Kyreen. "I do not recall agreeing to run to the Council anytime they beckon."

"Oh, come on. We both know how this goes," Kyreen said, her tone friendly and teasing. "You rail about the offenses that the magic community has suffered, then I placate you and you realize the best way to change the system is to be visible and what better way to be a thorn in the Council's side than to get them into your debt, so you eventually agree to go to the meeting and save us all from our ignorance about magic."

She paused, looking at Brigit. "Does that about sum it up?"

"Yes," Brigit shrugged offhandedly.

"Since it is just you and me, can we simply skip to the part where you agree to go?" Kyreen asked.

"You take all the fun out of things," Brigit grumbled with a grin. She slipped an arm through Kyreen's. "But in the interest of time, shall we go?"

Kyreen felt the magical wards anytime she passed into a spelled area. Now the panic barely fluttered but she could not stay the shudder that coursed through her body as she and Brigit entered the council chambers. While Brigit did not comment, she did give Kyreen's arm a reassuring squeeze. Inside the room two large tables had been pushed together and a mishmash of chairs sat round the tables. To Kyreen's surprise the entire

Council was not present. In fact, only Aren, Lang and another man, a rugged bearded fellow with piercing blue eyes, sat at the table. The stranger's face looked vaguely familiar to Kyreen though she could not quite place him. She thought maybe his name might be Ole, Ola, Olaf?

Aren gestured the two women to sit down, saying, "Viggo should be back shortly with Atle. I also sent Reijo to fetch us supper."

Kyreen drifted over to sit in a vacant chair by Lang. She watched Brigit pointedly ignore the strange man, taking a seat as far away from him as possible. The mage's uncharacteristic silence triggered Kyreen's memory. She had seen the man in the practitioners' area once or twice, though she personally had not ever had the occasion to speak with him.

"Hey," Lang said quietly, reaching over to gently squeeze her hand.

"Hey, yourself," she replied with a smile.

Aren glanced around the table. "Does everyone know each other?"

Kyreen shook her head but before she could speak the man looked at her saying, "I presume this is Kyreen, and that is her mage Brigit?"

"Correct," Kyreen nodded, restraining a grin as Brigit bristled at the man's words.

"I am Olavi," he stated, his voice rumbled a deep bass.

"Well met," Kyreen responded.

Then Viggo and Atle entered, followed shortly by the young messenger boy Reijo with their meals. Aren waited until the food had been distributed and Reijo had exited, shutting the door behind him. For several minutes the only sound in the room was the clank of utensils. Kyreen ate slowly, her stomach rolling nervously as her mind flitted about trying to figure out what this meeting could be about.

"After yesterday's interrogations, I asked Olavi to go on a quick reconnoiter," Aren began. She looked at Lang, who Kyreen had felt tense up. "Given the recent developments, I did this without alerting the Council."

Aren moved her gaze to Kyreen, who felt her stomach drop as her cousin spoke, "I felt I had to speak with both Atle and Olavi about Sten and his recent activities. I apologize for this breach to your privacy, but I trust both of these men immensely. No one else outside this room has been told."

"Ebbe," Kyreen responded, earning her a glance from both Lang and Atle. "He knows. We talked."

"Fair enough. I felt it was time to get us all together," Aren continued. "Goddess knows, there is so much work to do and we do not need this distraction, but that is the way of life."

She leaned back, eyes drifting between Lang and Olavi. "Which of you prefers to go first?"

The two men exchanged looks. Lang gestured for the other man to proceed.

Olavi pushed away his empty plate and leaned both elbows on the table, his gaze resting on his tented fingers. "Per Aren's request, I set out yesterday afternoon with the bay as my destination. I have been monitoring the castle for the last fortnight so I knew the last activity on that road had been several days earlier, thus I was unsurprised to find the docks there practically deserted, five Galorians total.

"The interesting bits are," he raised a single finger, "first, a large two-mast ship sits in the bay. She rides high in the water so must have arrived empty, and," he raised another digit, "second, while I watched the Galorians sent a messenger bird which flew in the direction of Galor."

His tale complete, Olavi leaned back in his chair. Aren turned her gaze to Lang saying, "Would you give us a summation of yesterday's interrogations?"

Kyreen turned in her chair so as to be able to look at Lang as he spoke. Much like Olavi had, he leaned forward in his chair, only he rested his forearms on the table, and moved his gaze around the room as he spoke. Lang still never looked at Kyreen when addressing the Council, or right now this group. Kyreen now knew it was his way of avoiding the distraction Lang felt when he gazed at her, so she did not take offense.

"The commanding officer's attitude in our interviews puzzled us," Lang started. "He felt anguish, almost despair. At first, we thought it was because he had sounded the retreat so quickly in the battle, that he had surrendered without much of a fight. Then he began to talk about how we ruined everything, how it was almost complete. 'Just one more, just one more', he kept saying over and over."

Lang paused, shaking his head. "We heard the same thing from nearly every man we spoke with. By the tenth or twelfth man we began asking new questions. The short version is there has been a coordinated evacuation of the Galorian people happening right under not only our noses but the Galorian emperor."

"What?" Brigit and Olavi spoke simultaneously.

Kyreen's brow furrowed as she thought of the implications of Lang's last sentence. The way he worded it had been interesting. Why would the people be leaving in secret? She focused back on his words.

"The Galorian soldiers believe their emperor to be possessed. No, that is not right, they believe their emperor to be under the control of a demon," Lang was saying. "Sometime over the winter, Dolan began acting irregular. He sequestered himself in the throne room, only allowing certain advisors access, even limiting which servants could enter. Those asking questions began disappearing."

Lang paused again, taking a sip of his cooled tea. "Now these soldiers we spoke with, they are all very low ranking, even the commanding officer. I suppose he was sent here in retribution for some infraction. Everything we have heard has been diluted down and is measures past second hand. Many of the details do not correspond. The one thing that remained the same from each man is that their Emperor is no longer his own man, there is a shadow controlling him, a dark malevolent specter that cares not for the Galorian people."

As Lang spoke about the Galorian Emperor, Kyreen recalled something she had learned last summer from Aren but had never spent much time dwelling upon. This Emperor, this Dolan, this man controlled by an outside source, he was her uncle. Most times Kyreen avoided thinking about her father and her ties to the invaders, but today the notion tugged at her mind, buzzing about like a pesky insect. With a small shake of her head, Kyreen refocused her attention on Aren who had started to speak.

"...conclude another shipment will be making its way through the pass to the ship in the bay. The question is how do we stop it? The pass is risky but the road would take more soldiers."

"What about the bay? Or the docks?" Atle suggested.

Aren shook her head, "I do not want to risk getting outsiders involved."

"Wait," Kyreen looked around the table. She appeared to be the only one confused. "Why do we care? Why are we planning on stopping this...shipment? That is not even a good term for it."

"Of course, we are going to stop it," Lang replied.

"What else would we do?" Aren asked. "We control the road, the castle and by tonight, the bay."

"It is people, not cargo," Kyreen said. "Are you going to send them back to a man they are running from or are you going to hold them prisoner or…"

Kyreen's voice trailed as her brain registered the third possibility. She shook her head, staring at Aren. "You cannot be…you would not…"

"Execute them?" Aren asked with barely restrained anger. "Why not? It is nothing they have not been doing to our people for almost two decades."

As Kyreen opened her mouth to reply, Aren stood up, her chair slamming into the floor behind her. She leaned forward her palms pressed flat on the table surface, her eyes glittering with angry unshed tears. "Do not defend them to me, Kyreen! Do not tell me they are innocent. Do not explain that they had no say in what is happening. Did they think about the hundreds of children slaughtered during the Battle? Did they care about the thousands left homeless, starving, and freezing that first winter? Did they spare any Calanian man, woman or child they caught over these last two decades? No, Kyreen, they did not! Do not look to me to grant any of them mercy!"

For a long moment after Aren finished speaking, the room was silent. No one moved, or spoke, or even breathed. Then Aren stooped over, righted her chair, and sat back down. Kyreen pushed away her plate, steeling herself to speak. When Lang tried to take her hand, Kyreen slid it away from him, fixing her gaze on Aren.

"Do you remember last summer on the road from Myrddin?" she asked her cousin, her voice quiet and still. "When I did the Ritual of Knowing?"

Aren nodded.

Kyreen looked around the table. "My mother taught me those words and made me vow to recite them twice daily until I returned home to recite them to my people. How was she to know what had happened? I certainly did not. When I finished speaking Aren's reaction took me completely by surprise."

"I slapped you," Aren murmured. "I told you that we were in a space of safety then I struck you."

"Yes, you did," Kyreen replied. "But that is not my point. Do you remember what Viggo told you? Because I do. He said 'We are not barbarians. Do not permit them to make us such.' I remember because to me it represented what I thought Calan was, a people of tradition, a people of honor, a people of integrity."

"So, you would have us forgive the atrocities committed by our enemies?" Aren asked, her voice reflecting her exhaustion, the anger having drained from her.

"No," Kyreen shook her head. "As you said there is much work to do. We should focus our energies where we have the most to gain. As I see it we gain nothing by detaining that…shipment, but we could lose so much."

Aren regarded Kyreen for several moments, her features carefully guarded. Then she looked to Lang. "What is your feeling on the matter?"

"Kyreen has a point," Lang replied. "In addition to the work here in the castle, we need to deal with whatever is happening over in Galor. If we stop this shipment, word is bound to get out amongst the general populace."

Aren nodded once, then turned her gaze to Atle. "And you?"

"It shames me that I gave no thought to what we were planning," Atle responded. "Olina would never have sat by idly without speaking up while we discussed executing children. I suppose that is why she served on the Council instead of this old soldier."

"Yes, I miss her wisdom every day," Aren replied smiling fondly in remembering Atle's mate. She sighed turning her gaze to her own mate. "Any words, Viggo?"

"Considering Kyreen used my words as her argument? Not really," Viggo said, running a hand over his hair.

Aren glanced at Brigit, uncharacteristically quiet, then over at Olavi and back to Brigit, who shook her head.

"Just an observer," the mage said.

"Same," Olavi added. Though they never looked at each other, Kyreen had the distinct feeling Brigit and Olavi were communicating.

"So, the shipment is off the table," Aren announced. "That means the bay can wait. Next steps?"

"What plans have you for the Galorian soldiers in the holding cells?" Kyreen asked, surprising herself with the question.

"The Council has not decided," Aren answered.

"We need to know what is happening in Galor before a decision can be made," Viggo said.

"Preferably without alerting the Council," Lang added.

"I will go to Galor," Kyreen said. Once the words left her mouth, she realized she needed to go, to get out of this castle, to go across the pass, to see the place of her father's birth.

This knowing must have shown on Kyreen's face, for Aren said, "You would go without my blessing anyway, would you not?"

"How will you go?" Lang asked. Kyreen could feel his anger at her. "You cannot simply walk into Galor, to the castle, and up to the emperor."

"Why not?" Kyreen replied. With her decision made she felt calm. "It sounds as if their soldiers feel something is amiss."

"The soldiers here do," Lang stated. "They are the ones banished to this post. You know not what the environs may be in Galor."

"Then I shall speak with the Galorians before I go," Kyreen said.

"Kyreen is right," Viggo interjected. "She should go and we should enlist the Galorians here for information."

He looked at Aren, adding, "If we can eliminate this man, this demon, whatever it must be, maybe we can end this conflict for good."

"I suppose you will need a mage," Brigit boke her silence with a grin, "considering your abysmal casting abilities."

"And a guide," Olavi added. "I have been monitoring the pass for more years than I care to admit."

By the time the sliver of new moon had risen in the night sky, all present save Aren had volunteered for the expedition into Galor. Kyreen had fought for Lang to remain, but her argument that his absence could alert the Council had not swayed even Aren. Judging from the grim line Aren's mouth made when Viggo stepped up, she too had reservations about her own mate joining the group. Unlike Kyreen, however, Aren kept her opinion quiet.

"In the morn, you will be granted access to the Galorian prisoners," Aren told Kyreen. "I will leave that to you to pursue. Do not trust too easily, my cousin."

Kyreen nodded. "I shall not."

With that the meeting ended. Kyreen stood, watching Brigit and Olavi from the corner of her eye, feeling there was something there but unable to pinpoint. As Aren, Viggo, and Atle stood speaking quietly, Lang took Kyreen's hand, drawing her attention away from the mage and the scout.

"Shall we find our room?" Lang murmured.

"Room?" Kyreen asked.

He nodded. "Assignments went out this afternoon. Thanks to last night's search, the Council had a good list of accommodations."

"At least something good came from the searches," Brigit commented, having walked up behind Kyreen and Lang.

"Several potential portals were turned in," Lang commented over his shoulder.

"Which reminds me," Kyreen said as they exited the building. "I was so tired last night I could not think straight. Looking at the spring down in the tunnels, could Sten use it as a portal?"

Brigit stopped walking. "He could."

"But how would he have access?" Lang pointed out.

"Someone has been going into those tunnels," Kyreen insisted.

"Maybe it would be good to have a guard or two posted there," Brigit commented. "I will go speak with Viggo. He appears to be in charge of the tunnel guard."

After bidding Brigit good night, Kyreen and Lang resumed their walking. Kyreen noted Olavi waiting in the shadow of the barracks building, though she did not acknowledge him. Instead she slipped Lang's arm around her and rested her head upon his shoulder. When she realized their path headed towards the keep she slowed.

"Problems?" Lang glanced down at her.

"Are we…" Kyreen cleared the lump from her throat. "Are we assigned a room in there?"

"Second floor quarters for council members," Lang responded.

Entering the palace Kyreen marveled silently at the transformation from the previous day. Lang chuckled at her expression. "A large troop of idle soldiers is not good so they have been assigned to getting the palace in working order. When the camps begin arriving, we need to have spaces to accommodate everyone."

They walked in silence up the grand staircase. Kyreen knew not the hour, but it felt late and they met no one on the stairs or in the hall. Lang stopped before a closed door, his hand upon the latch.

"A room," Kyreen commented softly.

"A room," he repeated, pushing open the door to reveal a small square chamber void of furniture. Both their packs had been placed on the cold stone floor in one corner. Despite the room's sparseness, as the door closed behind them and Lang took her in his arms, Kyreen thought she had never seen anything so luxurious.

Chapter 44

"Do you think if you asked Aren would allow me to accompany you?" Synnove asked the next morning.

"Accompany me?" Kyreen responded with confusion. "Where?"

She and Synnove sat together in the upper bailey eating breakfast together and Kyreen had not been paying much attention to Synnove's conversation. Kyreen's mind had been thinking about the upcoming conversations with the Galorians. Much to Kyreen's relief, Lang had indicated he would be there to assist. She worried what questions she should ask, so having him there to gauge the truthfulness of the prisoners' answers could be beneficial.

This morning, waking up in their room, Kyreen had once again marveled at the experience. The luxury of privacy had been something she did not realize meant so much to her. When she had remarked on it to Lang, he had simply kissed her then proceeded to once again remind her the benefits of privacy.

She smiled now at the memory as Synnove answered. "To Myrddin, of course? By my calculations, you have another trip coming soon. Why? Are you going somewhere else before then?"

"No, I simply forgot about Myrddin," Kyreen answered, covering the lie with a sip of her tea.

"If you could ask, I would be very grateful," Synnove said. "Anything to get off this cleaning detail. I cannot believe I spent all day yesterday washing windows and I believe that is my duty again today. Then I did not even get a room to myself."

"You and Eilert are still sleeping outside?" Kyreen asked. With her breakfast eaten, Kyreen desired to be out of Synnove's presence, because she worried her friend might be able to discern Kyreen had not been forthcoming about her activities of recent.

"Eilert is," Synnove shook her head. "I am in the barracks, but you are correct. Maybe if I put in for a couple's quarters we would get a spot in the palace."

Synnove paused, her eyes narrowing at Kyreen. "Is that why you are acting unusual? Are you concerned that you have private quarters at the palace? Do not fret. Of course, you would have such an assignment. You are still the Princess after all, and you are Aren's cousin."

"No," Kyreen responded, again annoyed with herself for feeling the need to defend Lang. "I did not get assigned these quarters. Lang did because he is on the Council."

"You can believe that if you wish," Synnove commented waving her hand. "I would wager you will receive one of the third-floor apartments once they are cleaned up which should be tomorrow thanks to me and my fellow laborers. What are you working on today?"

Kyreen, her mind still on the subject of housing, floundered for an answer to Synnove's question.

"Hey, Princess, if you are done with your meal, we should get back to the tunnels," Brigit spoke up from behind Kyreen, who turned to see the mage standing up, her empty breakfast plate in hand. Olavi sat next to her, still eating.

Synnove and Kyreen watched Brigit saunter away. Then Synnove sighed collecting her dishes. "I suppose it is time to report in. At least I am not stuck in some dark tunnel."

Kyreen walked with Synnove to drop off their dishes before the younger woman waved farewell and disappeared in the direction of the palace. Kyreen continued towards the tunnel entrance, worried Synnove might see her if Kyreen attempted to double back for the barracks where she was scheduled to meet Lang after his early morning meeting with the farmers.

"Geir is driving me crazy," Lang had complained this morning as they had been getting dressed. "Things are still bedlam here and the other camps are due to arrive soon, yet he wants to rally the Council into settling the land deals."

"Land deals?" Kyreen had asked.

"Yes, the farmers had an agreement that each one of us would be deeded a parcel of land, a large parcel of land in exchange for the horticultural work done all these years. Now there are worries that the Council will get bogged down in resettlement and not address the land deals. Then there are those that have no desire to return, but instead prefer to set up a proper village in the Great Valley and parcel out that land into homesteads."

"Sounds messy and complicated," Kyreen had commented and thought without saying, 'and boring.'

Lang sensing her disinterest had chuckled and given her a long goodbye kiss that left her wondering if they might stay sequestered in their room the rest of the day.

Now as Kyreen descended into the shadows of the bailey, she spied the golden glowing eyes of the gargoyle. The sight warmed her heart and brought back a flood of memories.

"Hallo there, Vaktare," she murmured, placing her hand on the creature's massive head. His furless skin felt cool under her hand.

"It is not a pet," Viggo commented from behind her.

"I know," Kyreen replied, turning to face the Hunter as he entered the tunnel.

"Have you given any thought as to how we can communicate with it?" he asked.

"Since we last saw each other last night?" Kyreen asked, barely attempting to mask her irritation.

"I will be looking through the records today," Brigit called from the top of the tunnel ramp. "Since I have not been authorized, however, one of your guards will need to escort me."

"Come on down," Kyreen said, wondering if Brigit had been following her.

"By the way, Synnove has gone into the castle. You are clear to go back up to the barracks," Brigit commented coming to stand before Kyreen.

"How did you know…?"

"You need to work on hiding your emotions, Princess," Brigit teased. "Else your friend will figure out you lied to her before we leave."

She turned her attention to the gargoyle, saying, "What a handsome boy you are, Vaktare."

Viggo frowned at the mage. "Come on. I will escort you to the documents room," he said, then glanced at Kyreen. "We will see you at supper. Good luck with the interviews."

Kyreen bade them both farewell before heading back across the bailey. In the shadows of the barracks building she waited for Lang, watching the bustling activity around the castle grounds. Everyone appeared to have a job, moving with purpose and no idle chatter except for those still eating breakfast. When she felt Lang's approach Kyreen purposefully did not turn right away, just so she could experience him slipping up behind her to slide his arms about her waist. Softly he nuzzled at her neck, his whiskers tickling her skin.

"Are you ready for this?" he murmured against her ear.

She chuckled at the ambiguity of his words. Holding his arms tight around her, she leaned back against him, relishing the feeling. After too short of a moment, she sighed. "I suppose we should get on with it. I have no idea really what to say or ask."

Lang pressed a soft kiss to the side of her head before releasing his hold. "Trust your instincts."

Kyreen did not know what she expected from the Galorian commander but he surprised her still. The man had been brought in before Kyreen and Lang arrived. Sitting he appeared of average height, solid, not fat, not yet, fully muscular that just hinted at going soft about the middle. His straight hair had at one time been a honey blond but had faded to a colorless straw. Kyreen knew this because his bushy eyebrows had not faded. The two-day stubble covering the lower part of his face would probably grow out to that same honey gold shade if not shaved. But it was his eyes which most caught Kyreen's attention. His eyes were not the dark sapphire blue of the Calanian people, but a piercing, bright blue.

Once when Kyreen and her mother had been fleeing from the Faldorian mercenary, before Kyreen had sliced his face, but after the horse had been sold, the two had hidden in the barn of a homestead. It had been late in the Harvest but before the first snows had arrived. Tyra had snuck them into the barn in the middle of the night, Kyreen, so tired it took her several tries to make it up the ladder to the hay loft, had gratefully settled into the hay where for once she had felt cozy and safe. In the morning as they snuck out in the early morning dawn, there had been a bird in the middle of the yard. The creature had stood as tall as the Calanian child with a long train of feathers dragging on the ground behind it. The feathers shone in the early morning sunlight all greens and blues, so bright, so vivid, so vibrant. When the bird had spied Tyra and Kyreen sneaking out of the barn it had made a loud screeching sound that startled Tyra so much she had grabbed Kyreen up into her arms and bolted for the bushes. Just as the bird went out of sight, Kyreen, watching from over her mother's shoulder, had thought the blue feathers on the body of the magnificent bird were the exact color of her twin's blue eyes.

This man sitting at the table across from Kyreen and Lang had eyes that same vibrant blue. As she settled in her chair Kyreen wondered if she and this man could be related. He looked to be about Aren's age, maybe older, close to the age Kyreen's mother would be had she still been alive. She wondered if this man had known her father. Kyreen rejected her thought of asking him, instead she decided to tackle the shipment.

Lang had told Kyreen the man's name was Cargan. As she appraised him she sensed his conflicting emotions – concern, vexation, agony. She glanced at Lang, his advice ringing in her ears.

Before Kyreen could speak, Cargan looked at Lang. His skin shone ashy in the dim light, the lines in his face looked new not ingrained.

"I said everything yesterday," the Galorian commander stated. "I have nothing else to offer."

Kyreen noticed his gaze never shifted to her, as though she were not in the room. Inwardly she groaned. Leaning over to Lang, she whispered very quietly in his ear, "Were there any women among the soldiers?"

Lang shook his head negative, confirming Kyreen's suspicion.

"Do you have a family?" Kyreen asked, leaning back in her chair.

Cargan's eyes flicked towards Kyreen then back to Lang. "What does that have to do with anything?"

"Simply answer," Lang said.

"Yes." This to Lang.

"A wife?"

"Yes." Still looking at Lang.

"Children?"

"Yes."

"Sons, daughters, both?"

"A son and baby girl."

"Are they waiting for you in Galor?"

Cargan's eyes drifted to Kyreen, then back to Lang. After a moment of silence, he again glanced at Kyreen.

Kyreen leaned forward in her chair, catching his gaze in hers. Pushing back thoughts of her twin, she said, "Look I know you have no wish to be here, to answer questions. I have no wish to be here. Well, in this room, asking you questions. So, in the interest of time, I would like to skip all the skirting around questions and get to the big ones. Is that agreeable with you?"

The Galorian, having realized Lang would not be conducting the interview, regarded Kyreen for several long silent moments. Though his face remained neutral, his emotions ran high. Kyreen thought this man would be formidable in a game of cards. Maybe that was the reason he had been banished to Calan, to the castle where nothing ever happened, to the place careers came to languish.

"So you can kill me or worse, spell me?" Cargan asked, finally addressing Kyreen directly. "Why would I want to hasten my fate?"

"Why indeed?" Kyreen's mind raced for her next steps as she leaned back in her chair. "Which would you prefer?"

"Pardon?" Cargan blinked.

"Death or bewitchment?" Kyreen felt Lang's question though his face remained impassive.

"I do not care what you do to me," Cargan replied. "Just be done with it. I am tired of waiting."

"My apologies," Kyreen said. She knew Lang could feel the nervousness of her bluff, but she also knew her face revealed nothing. Over the years, she had become practiced in shielding from those without the Calanians' empathic ability, and she drew on that now as she asked, "I referred to your family. Death or bewitchment?"

Cargan looked between Lang and Kyreen. Finally, he settled his gaze on the bearded Calanian. "You never mentioned my family yesterday."

"That was yesterday," Kyreen replied. "Before we intercepted a group heading towards the bay in the dark of the night. It seems news of yesterday's battle had not reached Galor."

Cargan swiveled his gaze to Kyreen. She suppressed a smile that she finally had his attention.

"Your family was in this group, correct?" she continued without waiting for an answer. "I am sure I could suss them out quick enough."

Cargan's face transformed, crumpling before them. "Why now?" he mumbled more to himself.

"I agree. The timing is less than opportune," Kyreen replied. "How long will the boat wait?"

"Four days. Then it sails."

"Then we have time."

Cargan's features closed. He looked sharply at Kyreen, who felt he finally saw her for the first time.

"Time?" he asked.

"To get your family and all the other families to the boat," Kyreen explained her tone insinuating that Cargan should have already known that.

"What do you want?" the man looked resigned. Having to choose between his loved ones and his country tugged at him, but his family could still be saved. His country, though, Cargan felt could not.

Kyreen's natural curiosity wanted to ask about the evacuation, where the Galorians headed, how they made arrangements but she did not. Instead she asked about the Emperor, the ruler of Galor who had ordered the extermination of her people. She asked about her uncle.

"Tell me what changed with the Emperor," she said.

Chapter 45

Hours later over supper with the same group who had dined together the previous evening, Kyreen gave her report, only this evening's meeting took place in the recently restored War Room. Everything Cargan told her had mostly matched the information Lang had collected in the first interrogations.

"The timing of last winter corresponds with Sten's behavior," Aren observed. "That was when he first enthralled Gisli and Svante."

"Svein," Kyreen commented almost without thought. Ignoring Aren's look of displeasure, Kyreen added, "The one gem we did manage to mine today is that support for the Emperor has disappeared. With this last batch of citizens removed, the entire province must be fairly empty. The men here in the castle had all planned on deserting with this last ship."

"Though we here all believe their emperor to be under the bewitchment of a mage," Lang commented, "Cargan again said 'demon possessed' today."

Aren pinched the bridge of her nose, sighing softly. "What I would like to do is take some of that explosive powder of Vidar's and blow the pass so no Galorian can ever come through. But I know that will not contain a transpiring mage."

"It is still a good option," Viggo commented. "For after."

Kyreen's eyes drifted to the map newly affixed to the wall. A landlocked country, Galor had two main access points available in and out. The first was the pass between Calan and Galor, a relatively easy thoroughfare. The other, however, was a steep windy trail over the northwestern mountains to a tiny fishing village. Though the bay upon which this village lay could harbor big ships, its location meant an additional two days' journey by sea from the Calanian Bay. Not to mention the water and weather became less hospitable the farther north one sailed.

Shutting off the Calanian pass would severely limit travel to and from Galor. With all her people having fled this should not be as much an issue as it would have been a fortnight prior. Kyreen wondered though if the people wished to return someday. Still she reckoned it might be wise to let this question pass for now and turned her attention back to Aren, who was discussing the arrival of the herd.

"We expect the horses from our camp to arrive tomorrow. Most will be stabled outside the castle walls until the castle stables can be repaired. The Galorians only housed a dozen or so horses…"

"Mangy animals," Atle muttered under his breath.

"…which I had thought we could use for this trip into Galor," Aren finished without acknowledging Atle's interruption. "Which means you could leave at first light tomorrow. How long do you estimate you will be gone?"

When no one spoke Olavi cleared his throat. "It will take most of the day to clear the pass. This time of year we should not encounter any bad weather. Figure two days at most for travel."

Aren looked to Kyreen. "How long do you expect to be in Galor?"

Kyreen bit back the snide comment which came to mind about how would she know, opting instead for a non-committal shrug. "A few hours? It all depends on what, who we find there."

"All of the camps, except those in the Great Valley, should have arrived by tomorrow evening," Aren said. "Then I and the families of our fallen must leave for Silver Lake to send their souls to the Great Hall. We leave in three days' time. It would be good for you to be back by then."

"What about the soldiers?" Kyreen asked again.

"The Council is still considering what to do," Aren replied, her tone indicating she wanted no more questions about the Galorians.

Aren stood up. "I believe we should call it a night. I would appreciate it if you all could slip away before camp wakes."

"Atle and I will get the horses," Viggo said then indicated to a bundle of cloth in the corner. "I will also bring the Galorian uniforms."

The rest of the assembly rose and exited without speaking. In the foyer, someone had left the exterior door propped open. Through it Kyreen could hear singing from the quad, a lively merry sound. She glanced at Lang, who had his gaze fixed on her.

"Do you want to go out and join in the celebration?" she asked.

"Not particularly," he answered with the twinkle in his eyes that she had come to love. He slid his arms around her waist, pulling her close to whisper in her ear, "We could go upstairs and have our own private celebration."

Much later that evening Kyreen lay awake, unable to sleep, her back spooned against Lang. Her mind raced thinking about the last two days, the upcoming excursion into Galor, and even after that. For so long she had been focused on getting through each day, each next task, that she had not spent much time pondering the future.

Lang tightened his embrace, murmuring quietly, "Having trouble sleeping?"

"Yes," she whispered, keeping her voice low out of habit. "I apologize if I woke you."

"At least you are not talking in your sleep again," Lang teased, nuzzling her neck.

"I do not talk in my sleep," Kyreen retorted, rolling over to face him.

"Oh, yes you do, but I like that you are awake so I can do this," he responded, kissing her thoroughly.

Kyreen pulled back. "What do I say?"

"Not much. Just a name," Lang murmured, nuzzling at her neck.

"A name?" Kyreen inquired, her stomach clenching. "Who's name? Not Sten?"

"No," Lang shook his head, pulling back to peer at her in the shadows. "You talked in your sleep long before he came along."

"Then who?" Kyreen's mind raced over the possibilities. Quietly, she whispered, "Please not Collin."

Lang chuckled. "I did think it was him at first, but no, you say your brother's name."

"Quillan?" she asked, her body relaxing.

"Not all the time. Only occasionally," Lang reassured her. Then he lowered his lips to her again, driving any further questions away.

"Now, what was on your mind, keeping you awake?" he asked when they finally parted, shifting onto his back so Kyreen could snuggle against him. She nuzzled at his neck, thinking about her answer.

"So much," she finally replied. "Recent events, tomorrow...after tomorrow."

"After tomorrow? You sound hesitant," Lang said, running a hand lightly up and down her bare arm.

Kyreen nibbled at her bottom lip. "Sometimes I wonder where my place is here. What my role is."

Lang thought on this a moment before saying, "Resettlement is going to take several months. Things may settle down by next Spring Festival. No need to worry until then."

"Will you want to go back to the Great Valley after that?"

Lang stilled his hand. "What are you talking about?"

"Once everything has calmed down, will you not return to the Great Valley, go back to farming?" Kyreen inquired.

Lang pushed up to a sitting position. "Calan is my home. Why would I return to the Valley? This is what I, what we have been working towards."

Kyreen sat up also, bending her knees to sit cross-legged facing him, his features shrouded in shadows from the very little light tricking in through the tiny slit in the brick wall up by the ceiling. "You seemed so happy there, so relaxed, so comfortable. I thought you would want to stay there, especially with Kasja and the children there."

"I do love the Great Valley. I had a wonderful childhood there. I know I was fortunate to have family who took me in. What you saw at the farm was me being with family," Lang explained. "But I was born here in this castle. I lived here for the first six years of my life. Though I love my aunt, and my uncle, and my cousins, and I appreciate everything they did, they are not my parents or my siblings. I owe it to them who died to do everything I can to bring our people back here and to whatever normalcy we can find. As for Kasja and the children, she has always planned on coming here as well."

He paused, taking her hands in his. "You were worried all this time that I would want to go back to the Valley?"

Kyreen shrugged. "I thought on it a few times. There has been lots happening lately."

"True," Lang chuckled, pressing a kiss to her hands. "Rest assured I am not going back there, except for a visit."

"Yes, you do owe me a pile of berries," Kyreen laughed.

"That I do," he chuckled, pulling her back to lean against him. "So now that we have solved where we will live, what else is on your mind?"

"I do not want to be crowned," Kyreen replied, snuggling against his warmth. The darkness created an intimacy which helped her speak her mind more freely than had she been able to see his face.

"Oh that," Lang commented thoughtfully. "That has been discussed in council meetings."

"Relax," he continued when Kyreen tensed up. "Nobody will force you to ascend. We have been discussing the procedure to have you abdicate. But there is an issue."

Kyreen lifted her head, peering up at him in the darkness. "An issue?"

Lang nodded, absently stroking her hair, running his fingers through her curls. When he spoke, his words came slow and measured as though he proceeded with caution. "Even if you abdicate, Aren is not next in line for the crown. She could not claim it unless..."

"Unless what?" Kyreen prompted.

"Unless your brother is dead or abdicates himself."

"Quillan?" she murmured quietly. As far as she knew nothing had been heard from her twin since he and Arvis had ridden toward the Elf Lands so many years ago. Her heart grieved at the memory, the loss of their bond still strong.

"I am sorry," Lang whispered, pressing a kiss to her hair. "I did not mean to upset you. I thought you should know the Council wants to send someone to find Quillan."

Kyreen could not imagine how it would feel to be reconnected with her brother. For so long his absence had been an ache upon her soul. She could not imagine what had kept him from returning. Her mind easily conjured up many negative scenarios. Still she refused to believe that her twin was dead. Despite the years and distance that had separated them, she held firmly to the belief that had Quillan died she would have known.

"Having him here would complete me," Kyreen commented softly.

"You so rarely speak of him," Lang responded. "When you do, I feel your sorrow. Sometimes even when you do not speak, I can feel it."

"When we rode out that morning from the castle, I did not feel a loss," Kyreen stated. "Not even waving at Vaktare. It felt as though we headed out for a picnic, just a ride through the woods."

She paused in her memories for a few moments before continuing. "I did not have a chance to bid him good bye. Arvis took him, then Mama and I headed in a different direction. I did not know we had truly been separated until our bond weakened. It stretched so far, for so long. Then when it broke I felt as though my heart had been ripped from my chest. He was my first loss in this journey."

She pulled Lang's arm tighter around her snuggling into his warm embrace. "I barely dare now to think about reuniting with him. It would be...magnificent."

They sat in silence for a few minutes. Lang sensing Kyreen's mood calming, nuzzled at her ear. "Anything else on your mind?"

"Well, since you asked…" Kyreen responded, her tone playful. She wiggled in his embrace.

Lang chuckled softly, and without thought shifted his weight, flipping both of their bodies over in one smooth movement so that Kyreen rested on her back with him hovering over top of her. As soon as he realized what he had done Lang froze, waiting for her reaction.

"I am fine," Kyreen whispered, reaching up to stroke his beard before pulling his face down to hers. That he considered her reactions no longer made her feel self-conscious. His patience and understanding had healed so much, had eased the hurt inside her, had deepened their connection. When their lips parted and he began nibbling along her jaw line down to her neck, she murmured, "I love you."

When he paused and she realized what she had said, Kyreen tensed. This broke whatever held Lang in place. He cupped her face in one hand, gently kissing her lips. She then felt his feelings, an intense wave of love cascading through her, like he had been holding back, waiting for her.

"Oh," she whispered breathlessly.

He pulled back to gaze down at her through the shadows, his voice thick. "I told you I did not wish my feelings to sway you."

Unable to speak for the lump in her throat Kyreen nodded mutely.

Then, as he lowered his lips to hers, he whispered, "I love you, too."

Before dawn they rose, dressing in silence, then made their way into the gray misty courtyard. Fewer bodies slept in the bailey but still a fair number. Lang released Kyreen's hand so they could maneuver through the sleeping forms. At the postern gate, they found Brigit and Olavi already waiting, standing close together, conversing quietly. When Kyreen and Lang approached, Brigit stepped back.

"Viggo and Atle already headed out with the horses," Olavi reported in his deep gravelly voice.

As they passed through to the outside Kyreen hung back, allowing the men to walk ahead so she could move next to Brigit. Leaning into the mage's ear, Kyreen whispered, "Olavi?"

"What?" Brigit whispered back, then chuckled. "Oh, him. It is not what it appears."

"Oh, really?" Kyreen teased, barely containing her laughter.

"Are you jealous?" Brigit responded, then held up a hand. "Do not tell me. You will break my heart yet, Princess."

Kyreen shook her head, turning her attention to their walking. Barely visible in the dark stood Viggo and Atle with the Galorian horses.

Taking a set of reins from Atle, Brigit turned to whisper into Kyreen's ear before swinging up into the saddle. "Olavi is my baby brother."

Kyreen shook her head again. Brigit's brother? She had not thought about Brigit having family. As she mounted the bay mare, Kyreen realized Brigit never discussed anything personal. She was full of sexual innuendos and cheeky banter. Kyreen knew virtually nothing about the mage who had become her friend. Urging her mount into a jog after her companions, Kyreen pondered how to rectify this upon their return from Galor.

The trip took less time than Olavi had predicted, possibly because the group were able to travel on the road without worrying about stealth. Clearing the pass just a couple of hours after midday, the group had to decide whether to ride into the small village surrounding the massive gray stone citadel. From their hidden position in the woods staring down at the deserted scene, the area appeared completely devoid of life.

Lang glanced at Kyreen, a frown creasing his forehead. "You have been overly tense since we began our descent from the pass."

Kyreen shrugged, running a hand across her braided hair. "I feel...I want..." she paused, visibly collecting herself. "I am drawn towards this place. It gets stronger the closer we get."

"Then you stay here," Lang insisted. "We have enough in our group. You need not go."

Kyreen's temper flared but before she could respond Viggo intervened, his voice firm. "Enough! We do not have time for this discussion. Our time is limited if we desire to be done by nightfall. We stick to the original plan. Olavi remains here with the horses. Lang and Atle, don the Galorian uniforms."

Without speaking Lang grabbed a bundle of clothing from Viggo, retreating to get changed. Atle similarly took a uniform and set apart to don the Galorian uniform, although without the anger.

"I, for one, am in favor of finishing as quickly as possible," Brigit commented. "This place feels haunted."

Viggo gave the mage a sharp look. "Do not start, magicker."

"I was just making a comment," Brigit replied, holding her hands up in surrender. "But it sure seems to have you on edge. Crankier than usual you are."

Chapter 46

In the end, the masquerade of the Galorian soldiers proved unnecessary. As the five Calanians – Viggo, Kyreen and Brigit with Lang and Atle in disguise - walked into the village, no one appeared in the streets to witness their arrival. Their footsteps echoed eerily off the cobblestones beneath their boots. At one time, the village had been a bustling center of activity for the small isolated province. Over the years, since the invasion and capture of the Calanian castle, the entire province had sunk into a general state of disarray. With their emperor obsessed with the obliteration of their neighboring country and allowing their country's day-to-day operations to fall into management of high ranking officials with selfish intents and no oversight to limit their power, the citizens of Galor had found their quality of life declining dramatically with each passing season. This last winter with nary enough food to sustain their dwindling population – a population diminished by disease and hunger, not to mention the handful of smart souls who escaped in the early years – a few brave Galorians had begun planning a way out. Soon all the citizens had agreed to relocating. Earlier generations had stripped all the natural resources of the land leaving very little for this generation, who took the unusually practical approach that the unknown dangers of resettlement were more acceptable than the dangers here at home.

"Did all the people leave?" Brigit commented, glancing into the open doorway of a bakery. "I thought some ornery soul would be left behind."

"They are in the keep," Kyreen replied, pointing towards the Citadel. "I feel a few people."

"You know, if you had honed in on this talent earlier, you would have easily rivaled Yngve and Synnove during tracking," Atle commented quietly.

"Have you not realized Kyreen prefers to do things the hard way?" Brigit wisecracked.

Kyreen chuckled at the mage, before glancing at Lang. He gave her a small smile, conveying his continued concern for her, for her presence here. Tentatively she reached a hand out to him, grateful when he took it with a soft squeeze before releasing it.

Feeling better for the contact, Kyreen inhaled deeply, focusing her gaze on the unattended entrance to the large square fortress. Unlike the Calanian castle, this structure had been erected, not as a defense against invaders, but a statement of opulence. The smooth polished stone rose overhead several stories and the cobblestone street underfoot gave way to a smooth walkway. A faded banner, bearing the same blue and yellow crest that adorned the uniforms Atle and Lang wore, flapped lazily in the afternoon breeze.

Kyreen and Brigit both felt the magic wards surrounding the building at the same time. Kyreen glanced at the mage, who shrugged.

"Fortunately, not trap magic," Brigit commented. "But I believe our presence is not a secret."

Without speaking, all five drew their weapon of choice. For Kyreen, Lang and Atle, that would be their swords. Viggo notched a bolt into place on his crossbow. Brigit pulled two orbs from her pouch, one a smoky blue color, the other a dusky red.

At Kyreen's questioning glance, the mage grinned. "I found a plethora of yummy spells in that archive."

Kyreen allowed her feet to follow the pulling sensation, through the foyer to a side hallway. Briefly as she turned a corner and the outside light faded, she felt a jolt of claustrophobia. Then her eyes adjusted to the dimness and the panic receded. The third turn had them enter a massive throne room. Five soldiers lounged about the steps to the throne. From this distance Kyreen could not tell if they slept or were passed out from drink or even if they breathed. As she and her companions continued forward cautiously on the once plush, once bright blue runner, she allowed her eyes to lift to the motionless figure sitting upon the black granite throne. This person too appeared asleep or unconscious. He listed in the seat, the tarnished crown upon his head tilting precariously close to falling off. Though the body of the emperor outweighed all present by double, bloated and swollen, Kyreen could not help thinking he also looked shrunken, diminished. That could be from his vastly wrinkled visage peeking out from a wild tangled mess of gray beard and the untamed gray hair floating about his head.

When the group reached the halfway point to the steps leading up to the throne, the Emperor's eyes snapped open, halting the group's progress and prompting all to renew their defensive stances.

The dull black orbs of the Galorian Emperor Dolan observed the Calanians for several long, silent moments. Then the emperor began to laugh, a harsh cackling sound that echoed off of the stone walls of the empty chamber designed to hold a hundred or more citizens. Kyreen forced her gaze away from the laughing man to scan the area. A balcony above surrounded three walls of the chamber. Perfect for an ambush she thought then pushed the thought away. In addition to these five soldiers, she sensed another five in a nearby room. The emperor, disturbingly, did not register at all so she focused her attention on him as the laughter died down.

"I disbelieved him that you would come," the emperor said, his voice unnaturally reedy and thin. Kyreen took a step forward and he nodded, the crown on his head wobbling with the motion. "Yes, you."

The emperor stood, shakily, his hands resting on the arms of the throne to steady him. Standing the man's size could not be ignored. The cape about his shoulders, worn and faded as it was, had been tailored for a much thinner man than the one it currently adorned. Kyreen doubted two people could clasp hands about the bulk of the Galorian's girth. The fingers extending from the distended hands at the end of his sleeved arms were swollen a size painful to witness. One of those hands now reached to the side of the throne to produce a sturdy ebony cane. Using the device, the emperor slowly laboriously made his way down the steps.

As Kyreen watched the emperor, who was also her uncle, she kept an eye on the slumbering soldiers, who showed no sign of stirring. Still she kept her sword at the ready, her body in a defensive stance.

When at last he reached the bottom step, Dolan paused to catch his breath. How he had arrived at this state he could not recall. So much of his past eluded him on the occasion he thought about it. Take for example the woman standing before him. She looked achingly familiar, like someone he should remember. Then his eyes fell upon the sword in her hands and knowledge bubbled forth.

"So, it has come to finish the prophecy after all these years," the last emperor of Galor murmured.

Kyreen glanced down at her sword, then to Dolan. "What does that mean?"

"That means the old crone has the last laugh," Dolan responded, leaning heavily on the cane, as he lifted his gaze to Kyreen. "I begged your mother to leave it here. To allow me to melt it down. But she refused me. Then she seduced my brother and stole him away, turned brother against brother."

Seeing Kyreen's blank look, the emperor laughed again, this time his outburst ended in a coughing fit that doubled him over for several moments.

"Did she not tell you of the great curse lain upon the house of your father?" he wheezed once the coughing receded. "It was my grandfather who condemned us all. An old woman came to the keep requesting an audience with the emperor. Cathal the First had recently ascended the throne. Newly crowned, he was young and smug and arrogant. When he saw her in the foyer, he laughed, saying such an ugly old woman could not have anything of worth for him the Emperor of Galor and he had his soldiers escort her out."

Dolan paused glancing around for a seat. Finding none, he laboriously lowered his bulk down onto a step with a series of grunts and groans.

"Where was I?" he wondered aloud.

"Old lady escorted away," Kyreen answered unable to stop listening.

"Ah, yes. Evidently Cathal's soldiers did not treat the old crone nicely, roughing her up a bit on the way outside. Once dumped into the streets, she had risen to her feet to scream at the keep. It took a bit before the people realized the strange old woman was threatening the Emperor."

When Dolan paused, Viggo leaned forward, placing a hand on Kyreen's arm to whisper, "We are not here for story time. We should leave now. Let him and his be."

Kyreen stepped forward, slipping away from Viggo's grasp.

Dolan's eyes moved to the sword as he continued his tale as if he had not paused. "So Cathal the First in his wisdom had the old woman thrown into the dungeons below us. Then he forgot about her, as young men tend to do."

The rhythm of the words made Kyreen believe the Galorian emperor merely repeated the words of this tale he had probably grown up with. Like with most stories, she desired to hear the end but she felt the restlessness of her companions. The entire scene with the empty chamber, the ancient looking emperor, the slumbering, or rather passed out by the smell of them, guards, it all felt artificial. Reluctantly she straightened up, made to turn around.

"Wait!" Dolan cried out, extending a swollen hand causing all five Calanians to resume a defensive pose. "You cannot leave before it is done."

He continued in a strange sing song voice.

> *"Beware the three-ore blade*
> *Of your neighbor's hand was made;*
> *For by its rune edge fine*

It shall ever end your line."

Then Dolan threw back his head and resumed his wild cackling. His gaping mouth revealed blackened teeth, his tongue purple and swollen. Kyreen took a step back as the sound of the emperor's laughter bounced anew off the stone walls.

Viggo put a firm hand on Kyreen's arm, his voice more insistent. "We should leave…now."

Kyreen nodded, her eyes fixed on the man sitting on the step. As she made to turn, however, he stopped laughing, his eyes drawn to the motion of her leaving. Without warning, with a speed defying his bulk, Dolan sprang forward, catapulting himself towards the young woman. Reflexively, Kyreen turned back towards the charging man, bringing her sword up. Dolan's momentum brought his bulk onto the blade, impaling his abdomen. Kyreen staggered back from the man's weight. Had Viggo not been directly behind her to brace her body, she surely would have fallen to the floor.

"Oh, niece of mine," Dolan sighed, his meaty hands gripping her shoulders, his thick fingers digging into her flesh, pulling her towards him or him towards her, she could not tell, so that they appeared to be in an intimate embrace. "Thank you," Dolan whispered into her ear, then his body collapsed.

Viggo pulled Kyreen back, the sword drawing out of the fallen emperor's body with a bloody squelch. As the five Calanians watched, the body began to morph, to transform, shrinking down. As the body changed so, too, did the deceased emperor's face and hair. The wrinkles smoothed away. The scraggly hair and beard thickened, the gray fading into honey gold, his open sightless eyes changed from obsidian black to bright blue. In the blink of an eye, Dolan's body looked as he should have for a middle-aged man, not the ancient relic he had appeared to be in life.

"Now," Viggo commanded, tugging Kyreen who had instinctively leaned down to wipe clean the blade.

"Past time to leave," agreed Brigit.

Kyreen cast a final look upon the face of her uncle before turning away. The five of them hurried out of the throne room, through the corridor and finally out of the keep into the late afternoon sunshine.

"What was that?" Atle asked.

"Magic," Brigit answered. "That man was dead long before we stepped foot in…Kyreen?"

The group paused in their retreat, the four turning almost as one to seen Kyreen facing the building. She took a step forward, feeling drawn back. A faint buzzing sounded somewhere in her head.

"Kyreen," Viggo said, taking a step towards her.

Kyreen waved without looking back. "No, do not come closer. I need to go back in there."

Lang started towards her, but Brigit grabbed his arm. At his glance, she nodded towards the parapet over the entrance from which they had just exited. In the shadows stood a figure looking down over their little band.

As the buzzing in her head grew stronger, Kyreen tilted her head, eyes closing. She kept seeing flashes of visions of herself standing in the street, Viggo directly behind her, with Lang, Atle and Brigit in a row behind him. Then her vision zoomed in focusing on Viggo, showing the man falling to the ground. A flash and she saw Brigit crumple. Next Lang's body went limp, dropping into a pile.

"No!" Kyreen screamed. Wrenching her eyes open, she spun around to stare at her friends and Lang all standing behind her. The visions had been false. The sorcerer in the parapet had been playing with Kyreen's mind.

Pulse pounding in her ears, Kyreen turned back towards the keep. Slowly her eyes lifted, finding the figure standing cloaked in shadows.

Then a piercing pain blossomed in Kyreen's chest. Looking down Kyreen thought she would see an arrow protruding from her torso, but her tunic remained intact with no visible wound. Then Kyreen's knees went weak as a new pain, an unimaginable hurt, worse than anything she had ever experienced, wrenched Kyreen to her very core, unravelling her entire being, severing the bond that had so recently made her whole.

"No," Kyreen whispered, hearing the rustling of action behind her even as Viggo released a bolt up into the keep parapet and Brigit sent up the blue orb. Kyreen struggled to turn around, tears springing up to blind her, as she stumbled forward to the body stretched out in the middle of the street.

Falling to her knees, unable to breath, Kyreen placed her hand on Lang's still warm cheek. He had no mark upon his body, but he reeked of the black magic that she remembered so well. He looked so peaceful. Except for his eyes staring up sightlessly into the sky, he could have been asleep. Kyreen raised a fist to her mouth biting down to keep from screaming. For if she started, she would never stop.

Viggo and Brigit, standing unnoticed behind Kyreen, turned around as Atle ran back from the keep. He shook his head to indicate he had not found the mysterious figure. He had, however, recovered Viggo's bolt, its tip bloodied.

"So, it is flesh, not an apparition," Viggo growled, taking the bolt from his friend's hand. Glancing down at Kyreen still kneeling by Lang's body, he said, "Atle, run ahead. You and Olavi get the horses ready. Brigit, try to get her moving. I will see to Lang."

Somehow, Kyreen did not know how, she found herself back at the castle. She sat in a room full of people she knew but had trouble recognizing. She remembered being in Galor, of the emperor impaling himself on her sword, and a rhyme, a riddle, a prophecy. Then they were outside the Galorian keep. Something happened there. She wrapped her arms around her body. She felt cold. She tried to remember what happened but she could not. She recalled Brigit making her stand up. Then she climbed onto the back of the bay mare. The sun went down and a loud explosion had startled the horses.

She blinked, looking around the room, still unable to focus. A cup of tea found its way into her hands. She clung to the warmth that did not chase away her chills until the pottery had cooled. Finally, someone pried the cup from her hands.

From the doorway Aren watched Brigit pull the cup from Kyreen's hands and walk towards her. The mage shook her head as she slid by.

"Just keep trying," Aren said, then place a hand on the other woman's arm. "Thank you."

Brigit inclined her head and exited. Aren leaned against the door jamb, her eyes on her cousin's daughter, yet her mind on the dozens of logistical items still facing her with the Council. Viggo walked up behind her, placing his hands lightly on her shoulders leaning in for a chaste kiss to her cheek.

"His body is with the rest of the fallen," he whispered. "As long as no one lifts the tunic, it will appear he died from a chest wound."

Aren nodded, her voice cracking slightly with her reply. "I do not know how I could function if something happened to you. I cannot even begin to imagine her pain."

For several moments, the couple watched Kyreen, each lost in their own thoughts. Then Aren shook her head, pushing off the door frame.

"I need to get back to the council chambers," she commented. "Do you think Gunda could sit with her for tonight?"

Viggo nodded. "I will make the arrangements."

Aren put her arms around her spouse and hugged him close. With great reluctance, she released him and exited. Scratching the stubble on his cheek Viggo stared at Kyreen a few more moments then headed out to find his youngest child.

The late afternoon sun glinted off the slow-moving current as Kyreen exited the woods, her boots crunching the gravel along the lake's shore. Lang – no she corrected herself – Lang's body had been lain upon a funeral pyre, the last body in the row of fifteen. In the far reaches of her memory she recalled the interminably long line of bodies in the wake of last year's battle. She knew it selfish but truly the only body which concerned her lay right here before her.

She knelt down beside Lang's body. She remembered how his eyes had looked before, after. She did not know which was worse, his beautiful green eyes dulled and open staring sightless at the sky or closed how they were now so that he appeared to be sleeping. She wished she could lay down beside him, feel his arms around her again, just drift off to sleep with her head upon his chest, his steady heartbeat beneath her cheek, and never wake up again in a world where Lang was not alive.

She did not know how long she had been there when she felt the calm settling over her. Looking up she watched Kasja, a sleeping Esben in her arms, with Jetta holding her free hand walk towards her. Kyreen was surprised to see the other funeral pyres no longer lined along the beach. Glancing over her shoulder she saw only two flaming pyres remained on the lake. All the others had already disappeared.

"Thank you for waiting," Kasja said as she and Jetta came to a stop opposite Kyreen. "The trip took longer than I expected."

The little girl stared down at the only father she had ever known. In her hands, she carried a handful of wild flowers. Kasja awkwardly leaned down to help her daughter place the bouquet in Lang's hands.

Though Kasja's calm washed over Kyreen, she did not need calm. No, she was more than calm, she was numb. Detached Kyreen watched the little girl kiss her father's bearded cheek. Then Kasja leaned down pressing a kiss to the same cheek. Then the two stood back, looking at Kyreen expectantly.

After several long moments Kasja asked, "Are you going to light the pyre? It is your right as Lang's mate."

Kyreen stared down at the body, Lang's body. How could she be expected to burn him when he looks so peaceful, so beautiful, so not dead?

As the twilight crept over the lake, Aren appeared beside Kyreen. With gentle hands, she helped the mourning woman strike the spark to ignite the pyre which, along with the body, had been doused with oil. Viggo then pushed the pyre into the murky waters. For a long time, it sat still, the flames slowly growing brighter. Then the current found the pyre and it began its long, slow journey across the lake, down the river, to the bay, and into the Great Sea.

Kyreen stood at the edge of the water watching the flames grow higher as the pyre receded until finally the glow disappeared around the bend. If it had been daylight she could have followed the smoke as the pyre journeyed. But as night had fallen she simply stared into the dark, unaware of Kasja and the children turning to walk back to the temporary camp with Aren and Viggo, unaware of the moon rising over the forest, unaware of the night continuing on as it had for millennium before this moment and as it would for millennium after. At some point Kyreen sat down, the gravel digging into her hips. She pulled up her legs to rest her chin upon her knees and continued to wait. What she waited for Kyreen did not know. After all, once your world has come to an end, what else is there?

Chapter 47

The horses pausing their grazing had been the first warning that someone approached. Gunda continued stirring the rabbit stew she prepared for this evening's meal, using the leftover meat from last night's supper. Not that it mattered. When she ate, Kyreen did not seem to notice what crossed her lips.

Secretly Gunda was pleased someone had come out to check on them. Though the young girl could maintain a camp in the wilderness for any length of time, much longer than the fortnight they had been here, she harbored concerns for her charge. Most days Kyreen refused to eat. When she slept, it was not for long. Gunda looked forward to having someone else to make the decisions for a while.

When the leggy bay gelding trotted into view, Gunda stood. With her passion for horses, the girl's eyes first looked to the gelding, appraising its merits and faults, as always comparing it to the Calanian horses she cared for. Per usual, the horse of an outsider did not measure up. Then she moved her gaze to the big man astride the bay. Even from this distance, he could not be mistaken for a Calanian and not just because of the ebony skin glistening in the summer sun. His seat in the saddle gave him away as a proficient rider, but not a natural. His size, even on a horse as big as the bay, could not be disguised.

Though she had been to Myrddin and seen the vast diversity of people, Gunda had only ever really interacted with the Hanorian outsiders Kyreen brought to Calan last summer. She did not count the fruit vendor who accused her of theft nor the city guard who arrested her in Myrddin as interactions. There still remained a chance this stranger, now pulling his horse to a halt and dismounting, could be a random wandering stranger, but Gunda doubted that greatly. Calan, being so far north and not on the way to anywhere, did not receive random wandering strangers. So, even though she remained alert and ready to respond to any threat, Gunda did not feel alarmed as the stranger stepped forward, stopping just outside the camp circle.

"Greetings," the stranger said, his voice a deep bass. "You must be Gunda. I am Kyreen's friend, Rhun. Your mother sent me."

"If that be true, then you know the protocol," Gunda responded. Though the youth did not believe the man to be lying, she knew if she did not properly assay him that her father somehow would discover it and would be livid about her carelessness. So, she remained at the ready and waited for the correct response.

Rhun suppressed a smile as he watched the girl, a young woman really. She favored her mother, thus also Kyreen, looking as Rhun imagined Kyreen had in her early teens. She also possessed that same edge of alertness he had recognized in Kyreen the very first time they had met in Myrddin, in Collin's house, which seemed so very long ago right now.

Realizing the girl waited for his response, Rhun said, "Moonlight."

Immediately Gunda dropped her defensiveness, the tension draining. She closed the distance between them, her arm extended, as her father had taught her to do when greeting outsiders.

"Well met, Rhun," she said, attempting to remain collected as the big man's dark hand grasped her forearm. Up close he had even more of a presence. Though tall for her age Gunda felt tiny next to this outsider and she could not help but feel a little flustered by his exotic good looks.

"Where is she?" Rhun asked now that the greetings and niceties had been concluded.

"By the lake shore," Gunda replied nodding towards the woods behind her. "She stays there. Sometimes pacing. Sometimes skipping stones. But mostly sitting."

"Does she eat?" Rhun inquired, his eyes drifting to the rabbit stew simmering on the open fire.

"Rarely."

"Does she talk?"

Gunda shook her head. "She has never said anything to me. Sometimes I sit beside her and talk. Papa always says I could chat up a stone wall, but evidently not in this case."

Rhun stood still, thinking, his eyes on the woods to the lake. His thoughts drifted back to his journey to Calan. He himself had only ever travelled as far north as Gladys thus the journey had been a new experience. So too had been his encounter with the Calanian guards at the pass leading into this extraordinarily isolated province. Fortunately, Rhun had possessed the appropriate password which garnered him an escort directly to the castle, where his mount had been taken to the stables while he had walked behind his escort into the castle. Though none stopped to openly stare, he had seen the many furtive glances his way as he made his way into the keep. His escort had paused before a closed door upon which she had knocked. At the muffled response, the woman had opened the door and gestured Rhun to go inside the office, closing the door behind him after he had.

Aren stood up behind her desk, extending her hand. "Rhun, I presume," she said. "Well met."

Once the greetings had been completed and both seated, Aren behind her desk, Rhun in one of the two guest chairs, he had begun the conversation, a smile playing about his lips.

"Imagine my surprise a few days ago when word reached me in my guildhall that a collection of Galorian soldiers waited at the city gates to speak with me, asserting that I would grant them sponsorship and pay their entrance tax."

"Yes that," Aren commented, allowing a sheepish expression to fall into place upon her face. "It seemed the best way to tackle two problems at once. You are here so I presume you received the message."

"You presume correctly," Rhun nodded. "And those soldiers should have departed from Myrddin to join the rest of their people at their settlement in the New Territories."

"Thank you," Aren said. "Please make sure to deduct any expenses from our accounts."

Rhun leaned forward, his elbows resting on his knees, the smile slipping from his face. "Kyreen."

Aren pinched the bridge of her nose, sighing. "Kyreen. Yes. I do not know how much you know of recent events…"

"I know everything up to when she and the mage departed Gladys almost ten weeks gone," Rhun interrupted, adding with emphasis, "Everything."

Rhun did not miss the flicker of surprise that the Calanian leader quickly hid. Aren recovered almost instantly and proceeded to catch him up on the most recent events. When she reached the part about the Internment Ceremony, Aren had leaned back concluding, "Kyreen came back to the castle with us but the next morning Gunda, my daughter, reported Kyreen's gelding missing from the herd. Viggo did not have trouble tracking Kyreen to the lake. He brought her back to the castle but two days later she left again. That time I sent Brigit to fetch her. Then again two days later Kyreen went back to the lake. I sent Gunda to keep an eye on Kyreen and, at Brigit's suggestion, decided to send you a message."

"And the Galorians?"

"That was Viggo's idea," Aren grinned. "It seemed much more efficient solution than finding a ship to come here."

Now standing here, with Aren's daughter's eyes upon him, Rhun's brain raced to find a solution. In his bags Rhun had brought books and sweets, even a bottle of mead, all of Kyreen's favorites. But he knew those trivialities were not what she wanted or needed. He could not give Kyreen what she wanted. No one could. As for what she needed, he had not yet figured that out. Not enough time had passed for him to reassure her that the pain would recede, though never completely disappear, but that someday it would eventually fade enough to allow light back into her life. Still too early for him to tell her that someday she might again laugh and be happy without feeling like a traitor to her love. That someday she may find another reason for living and continuing. She may even love again. Rhun drew a hand across his face, chasing away his memories to focus his attention on the present.

Kyreen heard the heavy footsteps behind her, felt his presence approaching, thus was not surprised when Rhun sat down beside her. For a very long time they sat still and silent as the afternoon shadows slowly lengthened.

"I will not stay," she finally said, her voice hoarse from the rawness of her throat. "I cannot bear to feel them, all those people, going about their lives as though…as though everything…"

Her voice trailed off as the tears began to flow for the first time since she experienced Lang's death. Rhun sat still beside her as Kyreen trembled, the deep wracking sobs tearing through her body. With her legs pulled up, she hugged her knees, slowly rocking. Every once in a while, she would inhale, a hoarse ragged breath, the sound echoing across the lake. When at last the final tears and sobs had drained from her, they again sat in silence.

"I am to blame," she whispered as the sun began to dip behind the mountains. "Viggo urged me to leave but I wanted to hear the story. Me and my curiosity. If I had heeded Viggo, if I had turned away sooner, we could have left. He still would have seen us, but he would not have stopped us."

This time the tears staining her cheeks ran fast, and hot, and silent. With barely a sniffle, she cried once more until she had no more tears. At the end, she released another single jagged sob before leaning her head against Rhun's shoulder.

Five evenings later two riders pulled their horses to a stop at a fork in the road. To the south a wide road stretched, not nearly as well travelled as it had been in past years, while to the east a smaller, much less used trail pointed toward the desert badlands. Kyreen noticed but did not comment how much this lone oak had grown over the last two decades.

"Are you certain you wish to continue solo?" Rhun asked, leaving unspoken his offer to accompany her. They had already discussed this topic both at the castle and on the road here.

"Yes," Kyreen asserted one final time. "My vows to Aren are fulfilled, and for her to take the throne Quillan must be found. This journey may help, and I cannot bear to be around people right now."

"I understand," Rhun replied, not wanting to say farewell, desiring to keep her close a little while longer, but without any valid reason to do so.

After Kyreen had completed her cry and leaned her head on his shoulder, they had watched the night creep into the forest, heading back to the camp after the moon had risen high in the starry skies. Gunda had kept the stew simmering on the fire and, at Rhun's request, had dished up a bowl for each of them. Kyreen had eaten without speaking, woodenly spooning every bite until her bowl was empty. Then Rhun had taken the mead from his saddlebags, pouring Kyreen a healthy portion which she swallowed silently. At Gunda's questioning gaze, Rhun had poured the youth a small dollop, swearing her to secrecy. When offered the white pastry box, Kyreen had shaken her head, handing it to Gunda. Then Rhun had prepared a bedroll for Kyreen to settle down upon. For the rest of the evening Rhun had sat vigil over Kyreen, silently reading his book as she slept, comforting her when she woke.

When the trio had reached the castle the following afternoon, Rhun again noticed the people never openly gawked as he escorted Kyreen to the keep, though they did cast furtive glances their way. Aren had directed Rhun take Kyreen up to a third-floor apartment, but on the second floor Kyreen had turned down the hall, pausing before a closed door.

Placing her palm against the wood, she had rested her head against the door. A few tears had leaked from between her closed eyelids. After a moment, she had taken a deep breath and turned to face Rhun. She had nodded and he had led her upstairs, to an apartment which thankfully had not been hers nor her mother's. There Kyreen had moved lethargically into the bedroom and lain on top of the bed, fully clothed, not even removing her boots, falling into a deep slumber.

Brigit had arrived a short while later to spell the room. Rhun liked the mage and knew she liked him, but neither felt inclined to continue their flirting from Gladys, nor had their association with each other yet progressed enough to be called friendship. So, with just a tentative acquaintanceship between them, Rhun had merely nodded his greeting to Brigit when he opened the door and she explained her errand. He had followed her into the room where Kyreen slept so deeply that the only reaction she made when the mage removed the amulet from around her neck was a soft groan. Brigit worked quickly to re-spell the opal amulet. The sleeping woman gave a soft sigh, relaxing as Brigit settled the stone around Kyreen's neck once more. The spelling of the room took only a few additional minutes.

Rhun had followed Brigit out to the sitting room, leaving the door behind him slightly ajar.

"He was a good man, especially with her," Brigit had said softly, her customary humor absent in both her face and her voice. "She already lost so much. I had hoped…"

Angrily the mage had turned away, brushing impatiently at her eyes. "I am not sentimental. I lost that a very long time ago."

Rhun had leaned against the wall beside the bedroom door, waiting as the woman composed herself. When Brigit turned back, all sympathy and sadness had been erased from her features, but the twinkle had not returned to her blue eyes.

"I apologize I cannot remain to keep you company," she said, after clearing her throat to speak. "I must return to the tunnels. Sten attempted to transpire down there last night."

Rhun had straightened up, his brow furrowing, but she waved a hand at him. "He did not have the opportunity to do anything, thanks to Kyreen. She had asked if the spring could be used as a portal so Aren stationed guards to the area as a precaution. Vaktare, that is the gargoyle, appeared just before Sten materialized so the guards were ready, but not quick enough to nab him before he disappeared again. Now I am looking for a way to sever the permissions Sten has to the tunnels. With luck, there will be a scroll down there somewhere."

Brigit then closed the space between them to look up at Rhun with a remorseful smile. "You know, handsome. Another time, under different circumstances…"

Rhun had nodded, allowing his smile to reach his dark eyes. "Yes, mage. I know."

She had stretched up on tip toes to press a chaste kiss to his lips, then exited.

Hours later, Aren had knocked softly on the hall door. When Rhun answered and she asked about the trip he had given her the report, even knowing she had most likely received a report from her daughter which meant Aren had another reason for visiting. After he had finished speaking Rhun had gone to the doorway between the sitting room and bedroom, peering into the semidarkness to make sure Kyreen still slumbered and that their voices had not awakened her. Asleep she looked even more vulnerable than she had at the lake. She had lost weight since he had last seen her in Gladys, weight she did not have to lose after her initial ordeal with that bard mage. Knowing Kyreen would not appreciate him watching her with the sadness in his eyes, he worked to push away that emotion.

"She requested the door remain open," Rhun said, glancing back at Aren, unsurprised to find the woman had followed him to the doorway.

For a few moments, they gazed at the sleeping woman before Aren softly cleared her throat. "How long have you been in love with my cousin?"

Rhun remained silent so long Aren thought he may not answer, though she felt the depths of his emotions.

"When do you fall in love with a song? Amid those first initial sweet notes? Through the melodies? Or with its final fading descant?" Rhun said quietly. "At what point does the sunset take away your breath? When does a book enchant you to the point you cannot put it down? I neither sought nor expected to love again. It simply happened."

He looked at Aren. "If I have my way, she will never know how deep my feelings run for her. All I want, all I have ever wanted is Kyreen's happiness. I can never be that for her."

Now as he watched Kyreen gather up her reins to ride away from him once again, Rhun delayed with a question that had been floating in his head since the lake.

"Kyreen," he said, "if I may ask a question, tell me if you do not wish to answer."

"Alright," Kyreen nodded.

"You said if you had left earlier, if you had turned away he would not have…"

"Would not have killed Lang?" Kyreen finished, her heart tightening as she spoke his name. "That is correct. He told me so."

"Who? Sten?"

"I cannot be sure," Kyreen answered, cautiously. "The voice in my head did not sound like a voice. It just spoke. He said since I had taken one of his, then he had to take one of mine."

Her eyes filled with tears again and her throat closed so she could not speak any more. Rhun reached over to pat her hand.

"Would you like to camp here? Start fresh in the morning?" Rhun offered, hoping yet knowing the answer before she shook her head.

"No," Kyreen replied, pausing to clear her throat. "I would rather get started sooner than later."

"Fair enough," Rhun responded, pulling his horse's reins to back away from her and her gelding. "Then I wish you safe journeys."

"Farewell, Rhun," she said, with a smile that only partially reached her emerald eyes.

This time she did not linger, did not look back, but urged the gelding into a lope, heading west towards the desert. Rhun, however, waited, watching until long after she had disappeared into the night.

Acknowledgements

To Rebecca and Renee: Thank you for your continued support and enthusiasm for Kyreen's story. You inspire me to keep writing!

To Nancy: Thank you for your hard work transcribing my hand-written words which are sometimes less than legible and a jumbled mess. Thank you also for your input, your advice, and ongoing encouragement.

To Ryann and Kyle: Thank you both for your obvious delight as I follow my dream. Being your mother has been my greatest joy and I relish watching you both as you follow your dreams.

To Clark: As always, my undying gratitude for being my partner in everything and for always being there for me.

Look for the third *Chronicles of Calan* novel coming in
<u>Spring 2018!</u>